STARSWEPT

Mary Fan

Snowy Wings
PUBLISHING

Starswept

For the violists

Act One

a performing arts school
in a remote region of Earth

THEY TELL US NOT EVERYONE DESERVES TO MATTER. DREAMS have to be earned, and every day, I grow more afraid that I'll never be among the worthy.

My footsteps against the pavement seem terribly loud. I walk so quickly, I'm practically running. Yet I can't escape the hailstorm in my head. What if my ranking never rises? What if I age out of the Papilio School before I find a patron? What if I'm never good enough?

Everyone else is asleep. I envy them. Though it's past curfew, I couldn't stand tossing and turning any longer. The minders shouldn't care too much as long as I stay on campus, and I'm not planning on going anywhere. All that lies beyond the school's walls are wild forests and the small, austere town of Dogwood. Papilio's founders chose this isolated location so we'd have nothing to distract us from our studies. I'm usually too busy to care, but right now, I wish I could escape for just a moment.

I crane my neck, wondering if my mother, who's somewhere on Adrye, suffered the same anxieties when she attended the Papilio School. Red and blue satellites—force field generators the government set up to block Adryil telepathy—blink among the white stars. They seem denser than before. Milo told me that the government's growing mistrustful of our alien allies. I think he has a point. For an Adryil to use telepathy on a human would violate the interstellar peace treaties, but the satellites tell me that our government doesn't entirely believe the Adryil will honor that agreement.

The Wall of Glory glows in the middle of the quad. Intricate sculptures of instruments, dance shoes, masks, and other symbols of Papilio's six Arts adorn the back and edges of the twenty-foot-high structure. Across the front, the illuminated blue names of alumni drift against a black background. Some names shine so bold and bright, your eyes don't want to leave them. Others appear so tiny and pale, you can barely see them.

As always, the Wall makes me feel very small. Not just physically—at barely five-foot-two, I'm used to being the little one—but in every sense of the word. These are the names of Papilio's best, the ones who turned their talents into careers and now live on a resplendent world across the stars. While positions for Artists exist on Earth, they're so rare that only the few born to the rich fill them. The elites of our time remind me of the royalty depicted in operas and ballets—small in number, but great in power. Owning so much while leaving so little for everyone else. I find it all unfair, but at the same time, the Adryil can only hire from specialized schools like Papilio as stipulated by our agreement. I'm luckier than most, since I at least have a chance at a better life.

I scan the names for my mother's, but can't find it in the crowded text. I'm not surprised. She wasn't extraordinary—a section player hired two weeks before she would have aged out. Maybe there's hope for me yet. Then again, she was ranked in the top 500 at fifteen, and I've yet to break 1,000. Considering there are only about 1,500 ranked performers at Papilio, that's beyond pathetic.

I press my hand against the Wall's smooth surface and whisper, "Theia Lei." The sound of my voice, the lone disturbance in the silence other than a soft electric humming, makes me uncomfortable.

4

A section of the Wall glows white under my palm. The light plays with the shadows, making my hand look like some kind of five-legged insect—small but freakishly flexible with long, skinny fingers. Not very pretty, but good for playing viola. I have Mom to thank for that. Actually, I have her to thank for every part of me except my face. It's not obvious who I resemble more, since Mom and Dad were both of East Asian descent, but from all the time I've spent peering at their images, I'm sure my large, round eyes and snub nose come from Dad.

A red line circles Mom's name, which drifts along the Wall's bottom edge in tiny, dim letters. Her holographic portrait flickers into existence, and I retract my hand. The image was taken shortly before she left for Adrye. I wonder what she looks like now. Probably still as beautiful as she was at twenty. I've thought about cutting my hair short like hers, but every time I consider my long, straight locks, I know I'd miss them.

The scroll of her red violin leans against her smooth, golden cheek, and her fingers rest against the instrument's gentle curve. The powerful, eagle-like aura surrounding her makes her look mature, but she was only five years older than I am now.

Five years. That's how much time I have left to prove myself. There's only space for so many students, and each week, the school's scouts find more talented children who deserve admission. If no one hires me before I turn twenty-one, Papilio will kick me out. I'll have had my chance; I guess it's only fair to make room for new blood. If I'm lucky, they might place me in a job with one of their partner schools—as a coach or maybe a minder. Or hire me themselves if someone retires. But more likely, I'll end up in a factory. That's what happened to Dad. According to the school's records, he was sent to a textile plant in California, but they offered no further details.

Refusing the assignment isn't really an option, since you won't find work any other way. Thanks to machines, there aren't a lot of jobs left, though sometimes humans are still cheaper than bots.

My gaze turns to the text beneath my mother's portrait: "Sponsored by the Kandar Family, 2255." That means she's still with the patrons who hired her thirteen years ago. Yet in all

this time, she's never once sent me a message from Adrye. I try to understand; interstellar communications are highly regulated and, with the costs of technology and permits, very expensive. Most of what she earns funnels back to Papilio to pay her debt to the school. I like to think that she's also sending money to my father. Most alums support their families on Earth with whatever remains after their debt to Papilio is paid.

Dad's saddled with the same debt, only he has to pay it off with a laborer's menial wages. He couldn't afford to send a message either, even though he's in the same country as me, just on a different coast.

Still, their silence hurts. I'd reach out to them if I could, but the school's computers aren't connected to the outside world. Again, Papilio doesn't allow any distractions for its pupils. All I have of my parents are the loving messages they left on my Linx profile, which is set up for every student the moment they arrive at the school. Even if that happened to be the same moment they were born, which is how it was with me. Most students endure a grueling audition process to get in, but those born on campus are granted automatic admission. I prefer to think that my parents chose to have me, even knowing they'd have to leave before I could talk, because they wanted to know the joys of raising a child before being locked into employment contracts that forbid Artists from having families. But more likely, I'm one of the five percent of cases in which the birth control pill doesn't do its job.

If that's so, then it's the only time I've been in the ninety-fifth percentile of anything.

Knowing I started with an advantage and fell behind only makes my mediocrity more embarrassing. In her portrait, Mom's sharp gaze seems to accuse me.

"I'm sorry, Mom," I murmur. "I'll work harder. Maybe someday, I'll join you on Adrye."

My dream is that the Kandar Family will hire me for their orchestra too. Maybe together, Mom and I can earn enough to bring Dad to Adrye. Be a family again, in a new world I can hardly imagine.

My eyes well, and I reach my fingers toward Mom's

shimmering portrait. How is it possible to miss her so much when I barely remember her? I don't remember Dad at all. Since he aged out, his name's not even on the Wall. At least I can still watch Mom's student performances.

I withdraw my hand and whisper, "Play archive."

A hologram of a stage appears. Mom stands in the center, sparkling in a flowing, silver dress. She strikes her violin strings, and the strong, open chords ring hollow in my ears. Though she plays passionately, there's something missing: subtlety. Her notes slash through the air like the coarse strokes of a paintbrush pressed too hard against a canvas, lacking the nuance it takes to create true beauty.

Strangely, that encourages me. Her playing may be flawed, but she still found patronage. And she never gave up. I shouldn't either.

Her performance ends. Smiling, I applaud with the audience in the recording. Maybe on Adrye, she's smiling and thinking of me too.

"End." Mom's portrait dissolves. I gaze at the names swimming across the Wall. "Inna Havener" shines at the top, lording over the rest in her splendor. She's who we all want to become. Born to impoverished laborers, she's now one of the greatest sopranos in Papilian history. Patrons fought over her, each offering her more money than the next. She eventually earned enough to move her family out of Dogwood and bring her sister along to Adrye.

I find it fascinating that the Adryil value our Arts so much. We have Katarin Kaminski to thank for that. She was the first Earthling they truly admired, a brilliant aerialist who lived decades ago and captured their imaginations in a way no one on their world could. A silver statue of her, beautifully contorted with limbs wrapped in frozen silks, tops the Wall.

I check my watch. The white numbers "12:56" blink against the slender black band; it's later than I thought. I leave the quad and enter an alley between two concrete buildings, heading to my dorm in the Orchestra's sector.

A shrill mechanical wail rips through the silence.

Alarm lights flash, turning the world red. I freeze. *What's happening?*

A shadow approaches, running toward me. I can tell it's a boy from the shape of his silhouette, and no one here stays long enough to be called a man. Only students are housed on campus; coaches and other staff either live in Dogwood or remote in from other parts of the world.

The boy throws a glance over his shoulder. Who is he? What's he running from?

"Halt immediately," a deep voice blares over the school's speakers. A line of silver security bots stream out of an alley on their large black wheels, chasing the boy.

Why are they after him? Would they come after me, too, if they saw me here? I should run, or hide, or *something*. Not knowing what to do, I turn back the way I came. My heart beats so rapidly, I fear I'll collapse.

Blinding white lights flood the quad, and tall security bots emerge from the alley. The red signals on their metal heads flash as they repeat in unison, "Halt immediately."

They must be talking to me—they're coming right at me. I stop inches from the Wall, trembling. I don't want to find out what they'd do if I disobeyed.

Someone behind me grabs my shoulders, and I nearly jump out of my skin. Before I can do anything else, he spins me to face him.

I gasp. The boy stares down at me, his thick black hair gleaming under the lights. The intensity of his gaze takes my breath away. His azure eyes glow with otherworldly luminescence beneath his straight black brows, mesmerizing against his amber skin. He's not human—he's Adryil. I blink, stunned by his presence, and find that I can't take my eyes off his hypnotic gaze. I've never seen a face like his, a face so beautiful and fierce it frightens me. Its planes slope with statue-like perfection, and his skin is smooth with youth.

How did he get in? Papilio has strict rules about who can enter; even the families of students are barred except during visiting hours. What does he want?

For a moment, we stand there in silence. His stare bores into mine, like he's trying to read my mind. No—he *can* read my mind. Earth's telepathy-blocking satellites only work when you're at least a few feet away from an Adryil; this close, he could see my every thought if he wanted to. Is he in my head? My heart trembles. I shrink, knowing I should run but too paralyzed to move.

He breaks his gaze, and his eyes dart around wildly. Expressions flicker across his face—fear, anger, panic, then strangely, something akin to triumph. When he turns back to me, something about him pleads.

"Take this." The crisp accent of the Adryil colors his voice. He grabs my hand and presses what feels like an oval-shaped stone into my palm. "Don't let them take it from you."

I wrap my fingers around the small object, barely aware of what I'm doing.

"Freeze." A security bot's mechanical voice rings in my ears.

The Adryil boy leaps away from me and runs, but he barely makes it a few steps before a flash of white engulfs him. A stun blast—white means nonlethal shots. He collapses onto the ground, and half a dozen security bots approach him, weapons raised.

Terrified, I back away. Dull points stab my back; I've walked into the Wall's carved edge.

My eyes fix on the Adryil boy. Unconscious and surrounded, he suddenly looks vulnerable. He can't be much older than me. For some reason, I want to protect him. I don't know him, yet I can't bear the idea of those heartless machines taking him away.

Don't be stupid, Iris. If Security's after him, he must be dangerous.

And he's a telepath. I've never encountered an Adryil before and have no idea what telepathy feels like. For all I know, he planted that thought in me. But to what end? If he read my mind, surely he'd have realized that I'm not the one to pin his hopes on. I'm barely brave enough to argue with my coach, let alone defy Security.

A bot wheels toward me. It's at least five times my size, and the black weapons at the ends of each arm point straight at me. I haven't done anything wrong, but does it know that? I try to

9

back away further, and the Wall's sculptures carve painfully into my back.

I suddenly realize I'm still clutching the item the Adryil boy gave me. Security must want anything he brought with him. Fresh fear chills my bones, and my whole body shakes as the bot draws closer. I should turn in the forbidden object while I have the chance. If I don't, the school could expel me, destroying all the dreams I've worked so hard for.

But this item, whatever it is, meant enough to the boy that he spent time he could have used to escape entrusting it to me. I peer at his face. Even with his eyes closed, something about him still strikes me to the core. For the first time, I notice how he's dressed. Simple black pants and a black T-shirt—like the kind Milo wears. He's… just a boy. He may be called an alien, but from here, he seems like one of us.

What if he read my mind to see if he could trust me? Did he see something that made him believe in me? Who is he, and why did he come?

Questions swirl through my head. A powerful voice inside me says I shouldn't risk myself for a stranger, but the need for answers overcomes it. The school would never tell me—they don't like to encourage interest in anything outside our studies. The item is my only chance.

The Adryil boy can't be in my head now—he's unconscious. These thoughts are mine, and they're saying that handing the object over to Security would mean destroying any chance I have at learning the truth—and it would mean betraying him.

I can't do that.

The bot stops in front of me. It's now or never. I move my hand behind me, feeling along the Wall's elaborate edge. My fingers brush against a crevice, and I shove the object inside, tucking it as far back as I can.

Even though it has no eyes, the bot seems to stare at me. "State your name."

"I–Iris Lei." I clench my empty fist behind my back. Heat rises from every inch of my skin, and yet my face feels cold. *Did it see what I did?*

Yellow light shoots out of the bot's black torso, surrounding me in a holographic haze. "Come with me, Iris Lei. You are needed for questioning." It wheels forward.

I follow. If I leave the bounds of the hologram, alarms will peal. Since the bot didn't search me, Security must not have seen me hide the object. I'm safe—at least, for now.

I glance back at the Adryil boy. Metal ropes, extending from two bots on either side of him, coil around his slender yet broad-shouldered body. They wind around his long legs and pin his arms to his sides. The sight of him bound like that fills me with horror. The bots draw closer and use the ropes to lift him, then wheel away. The other machines follow, blocking him from my view.

I can't help feeling as if I should have saved him somehow.

 11 

Chapter Two

I TWIST MY HANDS UNDER THE STEEL TABLE. THE CHAIR ACROSS from me remains empty, and I wonder if the official that Security contacted will show up in person. The name on the door read "Mistress Medina," but I have no idea who that is. This is the first time I've been sent to the office for disciplinary reasons.

What was I thinking? The minders are always watching, though I've seen enough people get away with breaking the rules to know that they aren't always paying the closest attention. I pray that I was in their blind spot tonight.

A light flickers above the chair, and a moment later, the seated hologram of a brown-haired woman glows across from me. "Hello, Iris. I know it's late, so I'll keep this quick. It's my duty to ensure the safety of Papilio's student population, and I take all security breaches very seriously. What were you doing in the quad after curfew?"

"I couldn't sleep, so I visited my mother's profile on the Wall of Glory." Though I'm telling the truth, a nervous quiver tints my voice. "She inspires me."

"That's lovely." Mistress Medina's lips twitch, but her expression can hardly be called a smile. "What did the intruder want with you?"

"I don't know."

Mistress Medina narrows her eyes. "You're not in trouble, Iris, but I want to remind you that we have very strict rules here." Her voice isn't loud, yet there's something intimidating about its low sternness. "Noncompliance may result in your expulsion. Since the boy's crime occurred on school grounds, we're handling it ourselves, but we will bring in the authorities if need be."

I swallow hard. "What did he do?"

"He trespassed on Earthling property. While this may not sound dangerous to you, relations between our two worlds are delicate. If he'd committed any further crimes—stolen something or, Creator forbid, hurt someone—he would have sparked an interstellar incident. That's why it's important for us to understand what he was doing. Security saw him speak to you. What did he want?"

"I wish I knew." I widen my eyes, using the truth to shield myself from her prying gaze. "They captured him before he could tell me anything."

"What *exactly* did he say to you?"

My lungs tighten, making my breaths shallow. If I'm expelled, I'll never play my viola again. Why should I risk everything for an alien stranger?

I squeeze my eyes, pretending to search my memory when really, I just need a respite from Mistress Medina's unforgiving glare. The Adryil boy's otherworldly face appears, glowing against the darkness of my mind. The slant of his cheekbones, the angles of his chin, the lines of his mouth—and most of all, those fierce eyes. None of the holovids about the Adryil could have prepared me for what I saw tonight.

Who is he? That I'll probably never find out frustrates me in a way I've never felt before. Questions gape like a great hole in my mind, a hole only he can fill. I only have one chance at finding the answers I seek: the alien item tucked into the side of

14

the Wall. I made my choice back in the quad, and I'm standing by it.

"He spoke Adryil." I open my eyes with renewed resolve. "All I caught was—"

"We don't expect you to know their language." Mistress Medina cuts me off. "That will be all, then. Thank you for your cooperation."

I blink, startled by her abrupt reversal. But I'm not about to question it. And I'm glad I won't have to make up alien syllables and hope she doesn't realize I'm pulling them out of thin air.

Mistress Medina stands. "The school is currently on lockdown, but I'll send a security bot to escort you back to your dorm. If you think of anything else, let me know immediately."

"Yes, ma'am."

The hologram flickers out, and I release a long breath.

A haze hangs over the campus. In the early light, the pavement appears a dull shade of bluish-gray. The plain dress I tossed on is the same color, and I feel like I'm fading into the background.

I rush into the quad, telling myself that the object must be where I left it. If someone discovered it, Security would have come for me already. They lifted the lockdown an hour ago, but I feared heading out too quickly might seem suspicious.

Black carvings cast dark shadows upon the Wall's edge. I survey the quad to make sure no one's around. Of course, the minders could still be watching, so I must be careful.

I turn warily, trying to recreate the exact position I was in when I hid the item. Reaching behind me, I feel the crevices until my fingers brush something round, and my throat tightens with excitement. I turn back around to find my hand in the bell of a stone tuba. Tightening my thumb and forefinger, I wiggle the object until it comes loose.

Staying in the shadow of the Wall, I examine it. A smooth, oval-shaped stone, about an inch wide and two inches long, sits in my palm. Etched lines snake across its black surface. They

must mean something to the Adryil, but they look random to me.

"Iris?"

Recognizing Estelle's deceptively girlish voice, I close my fingers over my palm as I turn to face her. "Good morning!" I notice that she's straightened her usual red curls and, hoping to distract her, say, "I, uh, love what you did with your hair."

She looks down at me with narrowed green eyes. I keep my hand behind my back, shrinking under her glare despite myself. Her broad face, with its prominent cheekbones and bold features, gives her an authoritative air. "You need to stop being so fake."

"Excuse me?"

"You think playing nice will fool me?" Her voice lowers to a growl. "I know you're after my position, and I'm watching you."

I gape in surprise. Estelle's the Principal—*every* violist wants her position. Why would she single me out? "I—"

"You don't deserve to be here." Estelle glowers. "How's it fair that you inherited your spot when the rest of us had to claw our way in? Do you know how much my parents had to sacrifice for me to be here?"

If I were cruel, I could point out that had she been a better child musician, her parents wouldn't have had to sacrifice anything. Papilio offers a free year of beginner education to all three-year-olds born in Dogwood, assigning each to the Art that best suits their abilities. Those who do well enough are granted a second year, and then a third, and so on until Papilio deems them ready for admission—or until another school's scout offers them a place. The families of children who don't qualify can pay for continued training, though from what I've heard, it's not cheap. Estelle could have spared her parents the expense by being a prodigy instead of a late bloomer.

But I have no desire to hurt Estelle, even though she seems to be doing her best to hurt me. And I don't want to fight with her, especially with the secret I'm clutching.

I brush past her silently, then quicken to a run. After a few moments, I glance back and realize she's not following. I stop to catch my breath, wondering what's gotten into her. My left hand, still clenched around the Adryil item, feels cramped, and I

 *16* 

loosen it. Imprints from the object's snaking lines streak across my palm.

I suddenly don't care about Estelle or rankings or anything else Papilian. The Adryil boy's face seems as etched in my mind as these incomprehensible markings are in the stone-like object. *Whoever you are, I did as you asked. Now, what do you want from me?*

I run my finger across the black oval, feeling the narrow grooves. Wondering if the object is a device that can be activated, I press its center.

The etchings glow green. I gasp, then stare anxiously, waiting for something to happen.

Nothing. I turn the object in my hand. The lines continue to glow, but that's all.

It occurs to me that I'm out in the open. I clench my fist closed around the object and speed toward my dorm, wondering how I'm going to unlock its secrets.

As I pass the Circus's rehearsal hall—a stone rotunda with a violet roof—I wonder… if I were to peel back the walls, would the holoprojectors and computers behind them look anything like the device in my hand? Most of the school's technology was built from Adryil designs. Thanks to our alien allies, Earth now holds several gleaming, high-tech enclaves with not a crack in the pavement nor a weed in the gardens. Such as this school, and half a dozen others like it within the United States. Each was given a name that evokes the Arts; Papilio, also the Latin word for *butterfly*, was named after a song Katarin Kaminski performed to called "Butterfly's Lament."

Outside of these institutions, however, few can afford to live in such places. Advanced cities like Charlotte, our state's wealthiest metropolis, are too expensive for even the professional class—the coaches, the doctors, the administrators. According to the history books, it didn't used to be that way. But as the elites wove more and more Adryil tech into the city's infrastructure, prices rose until only they remained. They even replaced those who worked for them with bots and computers.

When you think about it, there really is no middle. Only the rich and those who are different shades of poor.

I've heard it's different on Adrye. Even their lowest class

lives like our elite. What must they have thought of us when they first made contact? Did they find us as fascinating as I find them? Or do they look down on us the way Greek gods look down on mortals in the operas depicting those legends? I wish I could speak with the Adryil boy and ask all these questions—and so many more.

A cool wind rustles my hair, carrying the crisp smell of autumn leaves from the forest outside. Looking at that feral land, you'd never guess that two centuries ago, people feared there were too many of us on Earth. But our numbers shrank as fewer people chose to have children; most simply didn't have enough to support large families. Yet technological progress marched on, so that by the time an Adryil exploration ship entered the Solar system in 2157, our telescopes were powerful enough to spot it right away, and our computers sophisticated enough to answer the aliens' communications.

Our ancestors had long looked to the stars, wondering whether life lay beyond our world. Scientists and artists alike speculated about what we might find if we encountered beings from another life-supporting planet. Of course, the limits of the imagination meant that many pictured beings that resembled us. Those people were derided; life forms evolving countless lightyears away would surely be inconceivably different. I can imagine the shock people must have experienced when the Adryil turned out to be not all that different from humans. Looks like those with narrow vision had the last laugh.

From what I've read, many on Earth would have preferred that the aliens stay away from our planet. But those eager to learn from a more advanced civilization won the battle. Earth's nations had united under one central planetary government by then, and those at the top brokered the peace and trade agreements that stand to this day.

As I make my way toward the Orchestra's sector, I pass a line of novices—all around eight or nine—carrying miniature instrument cases. A middle-aged teacher leads them into the rehearsal hall. They still have a few years in the junior ensembles before they're ranked as active performers, but most

have already faced the kind of competition that's been stealing my sleep. I wonder if any of them were born here like me.

One girl glances at me with an expression of awe, and I give her an encouraging smile. When I was her age, I used to look up at the Artists too, thinking they were so mature. Though I'm now old enough to get married, I don't feel grown-up. But I don't feel young, either.

The child's gaze shifts toward my closed left hand, and I hurry away. She probably didn't see anything, but as long as I'm holding this alien thing, I feel like there's a spotlight leveled on me, and not the kind I would welcome. I wish I could stuff it in my pocket, but I doubt my skirt's light fabric would hide its green glow.

Looking for a distraction, I flip the switch on the edge of my watch to disable the "hold" function. Also, my clenched fist might look less suspicious this way. I swipe my right index finger across the device's face. The white numbers fade to gray, and a holographic menu appears above them.

I press the red "L" icon for *Linx*. The menu vanishes, replaced by my Linx profile. "Iris Lei, Violist" splashes across the top in blue letters, to the right of my miniscule portrait.

Although I came to check my messages, not my ranking, I can't stop my eyes from wandering over to the small red numbers beneath my name: "1,034." I tell myself it's only because no one's really seen what I can do yet, but I don't know if I believe it.

I try to ignore the shout-out column, but nonetheless notice that the only notes there are from Milo and a few younger violists. Unable to help myself, I press his name to see how he's doing. A green 132, which means he's not only ranked in the low hundreds, but he's on the rise. Not bad for a sixteen-year-old. His ranking skyrocketed after his solo dance in the last Spectacle. Maybe mine will do the same if I can secure a solo— or even qualify to play on stage instead of in the orchestra pit.

I shouldn't check anyone else's rankings, since it'll only make my heart sink further, but my curiosity gets the better of me. I press the search icon in the corner, and a holographic

keyboard appears to the side. Each letter I press glows green under my fingertips as I type "Estelle Carver."

Her profile appears, a green *33* glowing under her name. Cold hunger gnaws at my insides. I'll never possess a number that high. Estelle may be older than me, but I doubt I'll be as exceptional a violist as her when I'm nineteen.

I press an icon to return to my profile. The number has changed: "1,035." Someone must have left a shout-out on another Papilian's profile. Or maybe an outside reviewer endorsed them. As the day goes on, my ranking will probably sink further.

Not wanting to see those mocking red numbers anymore, I press "M" for *Messages*. A handful of reminders greet me, as well as a note from Milo asking if I want to join him in the Ballet's sector for lunch. I press "R" for *Reply* and type:

Sure! Do you mind if we grab and go? I have something to show you.

I swipe my watch's face. The holograms disappear, and the numbers "8:12" brighten against the black band.

I enter the wide street lined with the angular glass-and-steel buildings that make up the Orchestra's sector. Through the windows, I glimpse an assortment of instrumentalists—flautists, pianists, cellists, and more—practicing in their rooms.

Pausing, I take a moment to admire the image. Usually, the Orchestra performs as one unit, blending individual voices into a collective mellifluence. Right now, I'm able to catch a glimpse of the unique styles of the others in my Art. In a third story window, flautist Kiki Fiore blows across her silver instrument with a grace usually seen only in the Ballet. In the next room over, Alex Mbanefo plays the same instrument, but with bold, vivid movements.

I've mostly become accustomed to Papilio's charms, but every so often I realize just how magnificent a place this is. It's more than a school—it's a nebula. Where stars form from undisciplined dust, where talented children transform into performers the Adryil fly across the universe to see.

My eyes wander from Kiki's porcelain delicacy to Alex's

striking African features, then down to the baby-faced prettiness of Felicity Liang, a clarinetist on the floor below.

But as much as I admire the Papilians, they all seem plain next to the face of one who etched himself into my memory. If only I knew his name. "Adryil boy" sounds so generic, almost condescending. But what else am I supposed to call him? "Adryil man," maybe? No, that doesn't seem right. He may be more than a boy, but he wasn't quite a man. Not only because he looked about my age, Estelle's at most. It takes a certain kind of youthful bravado to break interstellar laws. Either that, or pure insanity.

Maybe that was it: he was just a crazed, thrill-seeking alien boy looking to enter someplace forbidden. My heart cries out in protest at the thought. He had a purpose; I felt it in his eyes, in his voice. That fierceness—it *meant* something.

Either way, my only chance of finding out what he wanted is to solve the puzzle behind the strange machine he gave me.

Chapter Three

I SHOULD HAVE TAKEN A CAFFEINE SHOT INSTEAD OF HOPING coffee would do the trick. I thought being a little slow would be preferable to fidgeting, but from the stern look Vera's giving me, I would have been better off as a twitchy jitterbug.

The lines between Vera's arched, black eyebrows deepen. With her narrow black eyes, high nose, and wild black hair, she always reminds me of a holographic harpy. Especially with the frown crinkling her thin lips.

"Play it again, and *concentrate*." She looks ready to knock my skull with her marbled purple cane if I don't get this run right. If she weren't remoting into Papilio from her home in Indiana, she probably would. I'm glad the school didn't assign me a local, in-the-flesh coach.

My right hand tightens around the smooth wood of my bow, and the polished stick digs into my forefinger. This isn't the first time I've been nervous at a coaching, but I've never felt so tense before. Vera stands about two feet from where I hid the Adryil device. I really should have chosen someplace safer than my sock drawer, which is probably the *first* place the security bots are programmed to look.

Thud. Vera slams her cane on the floor.

Taking the cue, I start playing, my fingers flying to the run's fast melody, and the sweet smell of rosin flies up from the strings. But my mind keeps whirling. I should have tucked the object into my viola case. No one would look for it there, right? Or maybe I should carry it in my pocket instead of leaving—

Thud. Vera's cane interrupts my thoughts. "Iris! Where's your mind today?"

"I-I'm…" My throat clenches.

Vera reaches toward my left elbow. An alarm beeps as her holographic hand surrounds my skin. I hastily move out of her glow. She pushes up, and the beeping continues as I raise my gleaming, umber instrument. When I reach the height she wants, she draws back, and the sound finally cuts out.

Vera shakes her head. "I've seen better posture from beginners."

Clenching my teeth, I straighten my spine.

"Again!"

If I'm to play this passage well, I have to relax. I close my eyes to picture something that calms me. Milo's face appears in my mind, with his playful gray eyes and boyish blond curls. The silly smirk on his lips, telling me that he doesn't take life too seriously, and I shouldn't either. He may be older and taller than me, but out of the two of us, I'm definitely closer to adult. If he were in my place, he wouldn't care that Vera was here. She has no way of knowing what I hid. She's halfway across the country, walking around an empty room and yelling at a holographic student. A trick of light and sound in my dorm, physically unable to open a drawer.

"Iris! I said *again!*"

At the sound of Vera's voice, I strike the lowest string and begin my run. The melody flutters through my head like a fledgling bird, each note an instant in its flight. The bird rises, trying to reach the sky, but falls under weariness. It sulks near the ground, then regains its fervor and rises again. Then, triumphant, it ascends.

After finishing the last note, I lower my instrument.

Vera beams. "Now that's the Iris I know. What happened earlier?"

"I… was up late last night. Sorry."

I might have been all right today if I'd been able to sleep after returning to my dorm, but it's not every day you run into an alien.

Alien? The word rings false. *Alien* means something foreign and unnatural—something that doesn't belong with you. The Adryil boy may be from another world, but he doesn't seem… alien. There was something familiar about him. I've read about how the Adryil and the Earthlings are essentially versions of each other, like how roses and lilies are both flowers. If that's the case, then the Adryil boy isn't really all that alien, is he?

Other than the telepathy—and the glowing eyes, of course—there are no obvious physical differences between his kind and mine other than that the Adryil possess sharper senses, stronger bodies, and longer lifespans. Some speculate that, in the far future, we may evolve into them, since though Adrye is about half a billion years older than Earth, its environment was once similar to how ours was during a comparable era. If that's true, if they were once just like us, then the Adryil and their thriving, advanced civilization are an encouraging glimpse at the future of humankind. At the same time, something must have been lost through the generations, because before they came to Earth, the Adryil had never seen a ballerina's sublime movements, nor heard a pianist's transcendent harmonies.

Without the Adryil, we'd have no starships or holograms, but without us, they'd have no music or dance. They brought us the future, and, in exchange, we brought them true beauty.

Thud. Vera crinkles her brow, and I realize I've let my mind wander off again. "Sorry," I repeat.

She sighs. "Let's move on. Have you chosen an audition piece?"

The tension surges back, but for a different reason. The audition, which was only announced yesterday, could be my ticket out of obscurity. Master Raucci, the Orchestra Director, decided to include a viola solo in the next Spectacle. One person,

alone on stage, reminding everyone that violas are more than just filler for string sections. I know he means to give it to Estelle, but he did specify that *all* violists are eligible. I mentally list the viola solos I know, but nothing seems adequate.

Except one: the song no one dares play. "'Butterfly's Lament' by J.W. Colt." The words slip from my mouth. I bite my lip—I hadn't meant to say the piece's name out loud.

Vera raises her thick eyebrows. "My, that's bold."

It's more than bold—it's sacrilegious. "Butterfly's Lament" was one of five pieces Katarin Kaminski performed to in the first Earthling-Adryil Spectacle, a gala for interstellar peace showcasing the best of both cultures. I can't count how many times I've gone into the archives to watch Katarin's slender body, intertwined in gleaming red silks, unfold from the theater's ceiling to the dissonant yet fervent chords of Colt's masterpiece, played by the renowned Jianguo Shan. The perfect partnership between the violist and the aerialist moved even the Adryil to tears. We hadn't known before then that they could even cry.

And I, a mediocre musician at best, dare emulate that? I drop my gaze. "I'm sorry. That's—That's not appropriate, I know."

A *beep*. I look up to see Vera's hand, pressing up slowly beneath my chin. I lift my head. Although she's hundreds of miles away, I can still sense her touch.

Her eyes warm. "It's brave, Iris. I approve."

"Really?"

"You have nothing to lose by auditioning with 'Butterfly's Lament,' and you'll put yourself on Raucci's radar. Estelle won't be here much longer. She'll probably find a patron after the next Spectacle, leaving Raucci in need of a new Principal Violist. If you impress him, he could pick you. That's worth taking a chance for, don't you think?"

I brighten, glad that Vera believes in me so much. "I have the song memorized already."

"Very good. Show me."

I lift my viola and picture Katarin's flawless performance and the low, immaculate instrumental voice that accompanied it. I can't compare with Jianguo Shan's brilliance, but I can imbue

the piece with my own kind of sparkle—something he never had.

How has it been just half a day since I ran into the Adryil boy? I feel like I've been awake forever. His mysterious device sits deep in the pocket of my black pants. It's the only pair I own thick enough to shield the object's telltale glow. Enough time has passed for me to conclude that Security isn't looking for the device, or doesn't suspect that I have it. Still, its presence makes me nervous.

I wish rehearsal would end so I could examine it again. This morning has dragged on for much too long. If only the Circus didn't view us, their accompanying orchestra, as a human compuplayer they can rewind at will. I want to stand on my chair and yell, "We're not a recording! We're Artists like you, and you're wasting our time!"

But if I did that, Mistress Asif would promptly expel me from the Pit, and I can't risk that. Since I haven't made it into the Orchestra's main ensemble yet, the Pit is the only way I can participate in Spectacles at all.

Behind her narrow-boned figure at the conductor's podium, the giant screen imitating an audience turns black, then resets to an image of a shuffling crowd easing into their seats.

Master Malkin, the bald, barrel-chested Circus Director, claps his hands. "Back to starting positions!"

The acrobats and contortionists, in their colorful bodysuits, retreat into the rehearsal stage's wings. From my angle, I can see the aerialists perched on the catwalks above, waiting.

Apparently having received Master Malkin's signal, Mistress Asif cues the soft clarinet introduction. I turn my eyes to the stage. A blue-and-gold-clad aerialist descends from the catwalk in an elegant fall, with only the skillfully wrapped silks around her body supporting her. As she winds her graceful leg around the red cloth, I hear the three-bar cue for the string entrance.

I come in with the other violas without having to look at the sheet music. My knack for memorization comes in handy for moments like these. The other Orchestra members don't care much about the other Arts, but I want to see it all. I don't want to miss the aerialists' twisting glory between the silks, the acrobats' lively stunts as they tumble across the stage, or the contortionists' fluidity as they bend themselves into unnatural yet alluring shapes.

A loud *rip* tears through the music. The aerialist plummets through the air and lands on the stage with a grotesque *thud*. I gasp in shock. One of her silks flutters down on top of her, forming a pool of red around her limp body.

My viola drops from under my chin, and the music peters out.

The aerialist groans. Her peers shout in panic, and the other Pit members mutter nervously. Master Malkin waves, his expression frantic. Seconds later, a pair of security bots wheels onto the stage with two multi-limbed med bots close behind.

I look up at the frayed end of the torn silk, wondering how this could have happened. A girl with a long, dark braid stands on the catwalk, looking down. Her calmness amid her shouting peers chills me. Then, I notice something even more disturbing: an unmistakable smirk curling her lips. Was she behind this?

"She looks happy." Zuriel, the violist who sits in front of me, sounds unperturbed. "She must be the understudy."

I glance at him, and his round-featured ebony face is as calm as his tone suggested. Before I can reply, Mistress Asif's voice cuts through the chaos.

"Orchestra! We're done for today. Pack up and return to your sector."

I look up again, aiming to get a better look at the girl on the catwalk, but she's gone. *If she did sabotage the aerialist, Security will find out*, I tell myself.

I press the red X in the corner of the electronic music stand. The music disappears, leaving only a blank screen on a silver pole. A black, velvet curtain, rapidly closing, blocks the stage.

I tuck my viola under my arm and follow the others. The

crowd grows tighter as we enter the staircase leading to the area under the stage, where we stored our cases.

Something bumps my shoulder, nearly knocking me over. Then a hand grabs my arm, steadying me. I look up and see a pair of hazel eyes adorning a strikingly handsome face.

Brent, the Pit's concertmaster, gives me an apologetic smile. "Sorry, Mouse."

I'm not clear on what just happened. All I know is that Brent Lachen is looking down at me.

"Mouse?" His brown eyebrows furrow with concern. "You okay?"

I try to steady my breath. This is stupid—he's engaged to Kiki Fiore. But his charm coupled with the immensity of his talent has held a kind of power over me for as long as I can remember. It's idiotic, but at least I know I'm not alone. Everyone from Estelle to twelve-year-old novices has gazed at him with longing eyes.

"I'm fine," I manage.

"Glad to hear it." He rushes down the stairs toward Kiki, who's waiting at the bottom with a glowing smile. They're so lucky to have found each other. The look in Kiki's eyes as she gazes at him—I'd give anything to share that with someone.

I meander down the stairs toward my case, mentally listing all the reasons I can never be with Brent. Not only is he engaged to Kiki, but he's the Orchestra's local Prince Charming. And I'm the local… mouse. Besides, I barely interact with him, even though I've known him my whole life. Like me, he was born here, though Estelle's never thrown that in his face like she did to me. At least I'm smart enough to know that the pull he exerts over me is a meaningless infatuation brought on by striking looks and talent.

I used to think Brent's was the most beautiful face I'd ever see, but last night, a boy from another world proved me wrong. I recall his shining eyes, the intensity and unearthly beauty behind them. His mouth, an incongruence of hard expression and soft lips. His smooth, tan complexion, too flawless to be human. I remind myself that I'll never see him again, but I don't

want to believe it. The story can't end with the inexplicable device in my pocket.

I reach the bottom of the stairs and start toward my case, then freeze at the sight of Estelle waving at me.

"Iris!"

Oh, no. I glance around, searching for a way to avoid her.

"Hey!" She runs up to me, quashing any chance of escape.

I tighten my grip on my viola, and the metal strings dig into my fingers. "Yes?"

"Sorry about earlier." She drops her mouth into a sheepish expression. "I was in a bit of a bitchy mood."

That's an understatement. "It's okay," I reply automatically.

"I mean it." She sighs. "It's this solo audition… it's been eating at me. Everyone keeps saying 'Oh, Estelle will get it,' so it'll be humiliating if I don't. Also… I'm old." She bites her lip. "If I don't impress a patron soon, I might never get the chance."

I suddenly feel awful for her. At nineteen, she's coming close to aging out. No wonder she's so sensitive about it.

She inhales. "Anyway, I'm not trying to make excuses. Just want you to know I'm sorry."

"It's all right," I say. "I understand."

"You guys talking about the audition?" A low voice rings in my ears, and I turn to see Zuriel towering over me. "I think it's driving us all a little crazy. Have you chosen your pieces yet?"

Estelle shrugs. "I'm going to play safe and go with Amsel's 'Adagio.' If Master Raucci meant for me to have the solo like everyone says, he'll give it to me anyway. If not, well, I'm too worn out to keep panicking over it."

"I know what you mean." Zuriel drums his fingers against his viola. "I'm playing it safe too, with 'Forest Anthem.'"

"Can't go wrong with that." Estelle looks at me. "What about you? What are you playing?"

I stall. Vera warned me not to tell the other violists that I'll be attempting "Butterfly's Lament" in case they decide to play the same piece in order to one-up me, but I didn't have the foresight to think of a lie in case someone asked. I hadn't expected Estelle, of all people, to engage me in this kind of conversation—or talk to me at all.

Estelle rolls her eyes. "If you're worried about someone copying you, you can stop, because everyone's already picked out their pieces. No one else is keeping it secret." She raises one eyebrow at me. "But I guess you think you're better than us."

"Of course I don't!" I exclaim.

"Then why so secretive?"

"I…" I can't come up with any response that won't affirm her belief, so I trail off.

She crosses her arms. "Fine. Be sly about it, then."

Zuriel shakes his head of tightly cropped black hair, shooting me an expression of disgust, then walks off with Estelle. I stare, my mouth hanging open with indignation. I almost want to run after them and confess that I'm attempting "Butterfly's Lament," but every performer instinct I've cultivated screams at me not to.

I turn with a huff and continue on my way. My case, with its black exterior and dark red lining, sits open along the edge of the wall. I kneel beside it.

"Iris!" A boy's voice rings in my head.

I whirl. Was that Zuriel? Brent, maybe? Several people surround me, but no one pays me any attention.

"Iris, can you hear me?"

I can't tell where the voice is coming from, but in case it's someone I can't see through the crowd, I straighten. "Who is it?"

A handful of Pit members give me strange looks. I wait, hoping whoever that voice belonged to will approach. After a full minute, I turn back to my case.

That voice—it sounded like the Adryil boy's. But it couldn't be… I *saw* them take him away. Besides, I think I'd notice an alien with glowing eyes among my Pit peers. The stress must have me hearing things.

I shut my case, then place my palm on top to indicate that I want it to stay closed. The edges glow green, telling me it's safe to pick it up.

Meanwhile, I know that, even though no one else can see it, the Adryil device glows green as well in the depths of my pocket.

 *31* 

SLIP INTO THE EMPTY ORCHESTRA PIT BELOW THE BALLET'S practice stage. Minali, the rehearsal pianist, glances briefly at me, then turns back to her music.

On the stage, Mistress Duval, in holographic form, watches the dancers twirl and leap to the bright piano notes. Thanks to technology, Papilio was able to secure her as the new Ballet Director even though she lives in Paris.

I spot Milo among the boys, each of whom wears a form-fitting white t-shirt, black leggings, and dance shoes. The girls pirouette in unison, the short black skirts of their leotards rippling above their pale pink tights.

The music speeds up. Milo breaks away from the crowd, kicks up a leg, and spins on one foot. His blond curls whip through the air as he repeats the move at a dizzying speed.

He finishes his turns with a flourish before joining the line of dancers across the back of the stage. I want to clap, but resist. Mistress Duval would banish me in a moment if I disrupted her rehearsal.

Although Milo performs the same movements as the

rest of the boys on stage, the strength with which he sweeps his arms and the passion in his expression set him apart from the rest. Mistress Duval gives him an approving beam, and that sends a spark of excitement through me. I'm glad I'm not the only one who sees his talent.

"Wake up!" she shouts. "You are soldiers returning from war, not puppets dangling from strings! I want vigor! Triumph! Like what Milo's doing!"

A satisfied smirk creeps onto Milo's mouth. One of the other boys shoots him a look of hatred. Catching his eye, Milo mouths two words that look suspiciously like, "Suck it!" I cover my mouth to suppress a giggle.

"Milo!" Mistress Duval glares.

He widens his eyes innocently as he continues the dance routine. His gaze lands on me, and he gives a slight grin in greeting before firming his expression and returning to his character.

No matter how many times I watch Milo perform, I'm always surprised by the contrast between the serious, single-minded dancer on stage and the mischievous boy I know. To me, he'll always be the hyperactive eight-year-old who still pulls my hair when things get dull.

Minali concludes the piece with a loud, rolled arpeggio, and the dancers strike their final, proud poses, forming a victorious tableau.

Mistress Duval shakes her head. "Sloppy, sloppy. Tomorrow, I want to see improvement." She glances at her watch. "Let's do the ballroom scene once before we go. Sabina! Nikolai!"

A long-legged girl with a gleaming golden bun lopes onto the stage, followed closely by a red-haired boy. They take their places in the center. Their solemnity makes them both seem much older than their seventeen years.

Milo and the other background dancers form a semi-circle around them, and then Mistress Duval signals Minali. A light, joyous melody floats up from the piano.

Nikolai takes Sabina's hands, holding one at chest level and raising the other. Their arms form an arc above their heads, and they dance together across the stage. Sabina lifts her leg and

leaps behind Nikolai, almost seeming to fly around him before landing lightly. She rises onto her toe and curves her figure into sinuous, elegant shapes, keeping her gaze fixed on his. Their bodies entwine and interlock, portraying unyielding ardor with their fervent movements. If I didn't know any better, I'd think Sabina and Nikolai were deeply in love.

Yet, I know that all the emotion I'm seeing is feigned. Sabina's hatred toward Nikolai is well known, and she's declared many times that she'll never marry or even date. According to Milo, she thinks herself superior to all the boys at Papilio, although that doesn't stop him from pining after her. Nikolai, meanwhile, has no interest in girls at all, preferring the company of a Troupe dancer named Benjamin Cox.

But on stage, they're no longer Nikolai and Sabina. They're a prince and princess who love each other so wholly, their bodies move as one. Their characters possess a wondrous connection we all dream of, a fantasy impossible for us earthbound mortals to attain. I've seen plenty of couples at Papilio, but none seem to share the kind of transcendent love they bring to life with their Arts.

Or maybe I'm just so used to seeing exaggerated passions on stage, real life seems pale and dull in comparison.

The sight of Nikolai and Sabina's duet fills me with longing. I want to fall in love someday, but I don't think I ever will. If my hope of finding a patron comes to pass, I'll have to sign away my heart. The standard contract stipulates that an Artist must not engage in romantic relationships, as these are considered distractions. Marriage is forbidden. This means our years in school are the only ones we have to forge that kind of connection until after we retire.

Even if I age out, I doubt I'll find someone. I don't connect with other people the way everyone else seems to. I wish I knew why. Sometimes, I feel as if life is a giant ballroom, where everyone else's invitation informed them of what to wear and what the orchestra would be playing, but I was told only to show up and arrived in whatever I happened to be dressed in. So while the rest of the world dances to a familiar beat, I smile and try to keep up, never knowing if I'm right or if I'm just making

a fool of myself. Milo's my only true friend, and sometimes, I wonder if our closeness grew only from the certainty of each other's company. I guess we're like siblings that way.

Nikolai puts his hands around Sabina's waist and lifts her. She spreads her arms like a swan stretching its wings. Her character's so in love, she's flying. What wouldn't I give to be like that? Not literally, of course—in spirit. But who would be the prince making me soar? Each time I've tried to picture him, only an empty shadow greets me.

"Stop!" Mistress Duval's sharp voice startles me out of my reverie. Nikolai sets Sabina down—none too gently—as Mistress Duval's glowering hologram strides toward him. "Are you asleep, Nikolai?" She rattles off all the things he did wrong.

I tilt my head, puzzled. The duet looked perfect to me— beautiful enough, anyway, to send me into a wistful trance.

Nikolai protests Mistress Duval's statements, but she cuts him off.

"Excuses! You've been getting complacent, but being ranked in the top ten doesn't make you irreplaceable." She lifts her chin. "Milo!"

Milo straightens. "Yes, ma'am?"

"Dance the ballroom duet with Sabina."

He blinks. "Yes—yes, ma'am!" He scampers center stage.

I cover my grin with my fingers. Milo's filled my ears countless times with his daydreams about replacing Nikolai at Sabina's side, and now he finally has his chance.

Mistress Duval points at his empty spot in the line of dancers. "Nikolai, take Milo's place among the nobles."

Nikolai storms toward the back, glowering. Milo claps a hand on his shoulder as he passes. "Sorry, man."

"Don't touch me." Nikolai sweeps Milo's hand off.

Sabina gives Milo a doubtful look. "If you drop me, I'll kill you."

"Don't worry." He throws her a confident smirk. "After we're done, you'll never want to dance with Nikolai again." When she looks away, he flashes an incredulous look in my direction, as if to ask, "Is this really happening?"

I beam and pump my fist at him.

Mistress Duval's hologram flickers out, then reappears at the front edge of the stage. "From the top!"

The music begins, and Milo takes Sabina's hand. His eyes fill with wonder as they begin the dance. His every gesture betrays the true desire that was absent in Nikolai's performance. I don't know if it's because Milo's a more expressive dancer, or because his real life yearning translates well on stage.

Mistress Duval nods approvingly. "Good, Milo! Good, Sabina! Perhaps there's hope after all."

Sabina raises her arms, and Milo lifts her, spinning across the stage with her aloft. She seems weightless, and I marvel at how he can carry another person so effortlessly. The stage lighting highlights his toned arms. Often, I forget that he's no longer the spindly boy I played with when we both were little.

Milo sets Sabina down, and she lands with weightless grace. She poses with one leg in front of the other, stretching her arms like an angel unfurling her wings. He leaps away from her as the music speeds up, then stands with one hand on his hip as the music enters its final sequence. She spins toward him, a whirling image of joy. Milo catches her around the waist, and Sabina falls back with her arms flung above her head, striking the dance's final pose.

I jump up and start clapping with abandon, then freeze when I realize I'm the only one.

Mistress Duval raises her eyebrows at me. "I see we've impressed the audience." Her expression warms as she turns to the dancers. "Sabina, Milo, well done." She glances at her watch. "Everyone except Nikolai is dismissed. Nikolai, meet me in the office." Her hologram flickers out unceremoniously.

"Sabina!" Milo chases Sabina as she starts to leave.

She turns toward him with a bored expression. "Yeah?"

Milo quickly steps so that he's beside her and holds up his left arm. "Smile!" He gives his watch two quick taps with his right hand. A second later, a white flash emits from the tiny screen.

Sabina rolls her eyes and continues on her way. Milo walks offstage in the opposite direction. Figuring he's probably heading to change into regular clothes, I activate the holographic menu

on my watch and check my Linx profile to see if my ranking has risen, even by one or two points.

1,043. My chest tightens. Though I tell myself that everything will change after the audition, part of me whispers, *No one wants to sponsor a mediocre player. I'll never make it.*

I press a circular icon at the bottom of my profile, and my Linx feed appears. Milo's already posted the picture of him and Sabina with the caption: "Danced with a princess today." To my surprise, Sabina looks happy in the holopic, pressing her cheek against his with a wide smile.

"We look good together, don't you think?"

I hear Milo's voice and look up, at the same time swiping my watch to set it back on its clock setting. "I thought you went to change."

"Wanted to say hi first." He collapses into the chair next to mine; even that movement is effortlessly graceful. "Can you believe what just happened? Mistress Duval's been talking about making Nikolai sit out the next Spectacle all week. If she actually lets me replace him…I'll lose my mind. In a good way." His gray eyes glaze over in a dreamy expression.

Unable to resist the chance to tease him, I say, "So, now that you've danced with Sabina, I'm guessing a proposal's around the corner?" Milo shoots me an irritated glare, and I giggle. "It's not like your crush is a secret."

He sighs. "What's wrong with us, Iris? Me and Sabina, you and Brent—we're like Echo, doomed to waste away while pining for people in love with themselves."

"I do *not* pine for Brent!"

"Sure, you don't." He flops back in his chair and stares at the ceiling, blowing at a wisp of hair that settled over his eye. "Maybe we should just marry each other and hope that solves our problems."

I turn away, heat creeping into my cheeks. Though I know Milo's being sarcastic, I can't say I haven't considered the possibility of marrying him. The *actual* possibility—not a faraway daydream like with Brent. But Milo told me that he's holding out for Sabina, hoping she'll decide she wants to know love after all. I'd like to know, too. True love, like the kind

depicted in the duet, even though I'm not sure such a thing's possible.

I want to believe in fate and destiny and a whole constellation of other grand ideas, but the fact is, there aren't very many of us at Papilio. I've met everyone at least once, so if there were a Prince Charming for me, logic dictates that I would have run into him already. Milo's probably the closest thing I'll find to someone I love. In a way, I *do* love him. I'm just not *in* love. So I shove the thought of marrying for convenience out of my head, but the emptiness it leaves behind is almost worse.

Silence ripples around us as we both stare into space, together in our misery.

Milo sits up. "By the way, I got a message from my family today."

I brighten. Though Milo's family lives in Dogwood, he barely sees them. His parents always have work during the school's visiting hours, and his baby sister's too young to travel alone. Sometimes, he leaves campus to see them, but finding time is always a challenge. They can only afford to send him a few messages a month. At Papilio, it's easy to take technology for granted, but for most, it's not so accessible. Still, I envy him. I'd love to receive even one message from my parents.

"What did they say?" I ask.

"Nothing good." Milo's jaw clenches. "Alice didn't qualify for a third year of free beginner ed, and my parents are still paying off what they borrowed to get me here. They can't afford to keep her in the program so… she's done."

My heart aches for him. I know how much he was hoping that Alice would get into Papilio too, both so she could escape a hard life as a laborer and so that someday, they could both support their parents. He was under enough pressure before and now, it's doubled. "So sorry to hear that."

"It's all on me now. If I don't find a patron, my whole family's screwed."

I give his arm a squeeze. "You're brilliant, Milo. Mistress Duval will make you a principal for sure, and after the next Spectacle, the richest patrons on Adrye will be clamoring to have you."

His lips quirk. "Thanks. Anyway, I should get changed. Meet you by the Ballet's cafeteria?"

"Sure."

He leaves, disappearing through a narrow door. Now that it's just me, the rehearsal hall is chillingly quiet. Everyone else has already left. I pick up my viola case and stand.

Something lands on the ground with a *thunk*. I look down and see the Adryil device glowing green below me—it must've fallen out of my pocket.

I scoop it up, and my pulse hammers. Was there a minder watching? I shove it in my pocket, keeping my fist closed around it, and try to calm myself. Surely the school wouldn't expel me just for hiding something. I'm not hurting anyone.

A white light catches my eye. I whirl. It flickers a few feet in front of me, giving off a wraithlike glow. Is it Mistress Duval's hologram glitching? But why would she appear in the orchestra pit when everyone's gone?

"Iris…" A distant voice floats through my head. It's the same one I heard back at the Circus, the one that sounded like the Adryil boy's.

The light stops flickering. I gasp. The Adryil's translucent image stands before me, barely visible.

He vanishes. I keep staring at the place where he stood, his tall, broad-shouldered form dressed all in white, his black hair swept across his forehead, and his piercing gaze fixed on me. He couldn't have been a hologram—his voice came from *inside* my head. And he couldn't have been contacting me telepathically. Earth's satellites block his abilities.

Did I imagine him? Am I crazy?

I can't help wondering: was he a ghost?

Chapter Five

Y NAME SCROLLS ACROSS THE FOOD DISTRIBUTOR'S screen, and I take my hand off the scanner. Machinery hums behind the wall the distributor is attached too. Half a minute later, a small door slides open, and a plate of pasta covered in creamy red sauce appears.

I slide it onto my tray and step aside. As I wait for Milo to receive his lunch, I notice a table full of dancers giving me disdainful looks. I'd like to think it's because I can eat whatever I want while they're assigned meals designed to maintain their slim figures, rather than because I'm not one of them. I'll never understand why people in different Arts don't like mingling.

Milo makes a face at the fish fillet and steamed vegetables the distributor issued him. There's a lot more food piled on his plate than on mine, but it looks miserably plain.

He approaches me. "So, where to?"

I consider which place in the Ballet's sector would be the most isolated. "How about the stairs by the stage?"

"Sure."

We exit the cafeteria and make our way to the rehearsal stage. A few Ballet girls pass us, and each gives me a slantwise look, as if asking why I'm trespassing. I wonder what it must be like living in a place where everyone has the same build as you. I must admit—I find their appearance a little unsettling. They're beautiful on stage, but up close, their birdlike limbs, dainty heads, and lack of body fat make them seem not quite human. I've seen an *actual* alien, and he seemed less strange.

"So, how was your day?" Milo asks.

The memory of the fallen aerialist at the Circus flashes through my mind, and I recount the episode.

When I finish, Milo shakes his head. "Damn. That poor girl."

"I don't understand how it happened." I picture the Circus's stage, trying to recall if I spotted anything unusual. "She didn't fall until we were almost done with rehearsal, and she was on the same silks all afternoon."

"Whoever did it must've cut partway across the silk so it'd hold up when they did the safety tests, then gradually tear during the routine. I've seen the same thing happen to the ribbons on the girls' pointe shoes. They'll seem fine when you're tying them on, but tear in the middle of a dance. That's how Abigail broke her ankle. She'll never dance again."

"That's terrible." I'm suddenly aware of how fragile my hands are; they look especially delicate compared to the sturdy tray they're holding. If someone broke my fingers and I couldn't play anymore… That would kill me. My music is as much a piece of me as my beating heart, and taking it away would shatter my soul.

"Don't feel too bad for her. The school hired her as a coach for the beginner classes. Last time I saw her, she told me she was kind of glad about how things turned out. Much less pressure now." He gives me a slight smile. "I'm sure the aerialist will be fine too."

"I think I saw who did it, but I don't want to accuse the wrong person." I look up at Milo. "Should I report what I know?"

"Don't bother," Milo scoffs. "Everyone *knows* Eva D'Antonio cut Abigail's ribbons, but she's still a soloist."

"They didn't expel her?"

Milo lets out a cynical laugh. "Without Abigail, they needed her. So they confined her to her room, but gave her so many exceptions for rehearsals and such, it hardly mattered. Basically, Eva got what she wanted, and her only punishment is that she has to eat in her room instead of the cafeteria."

I knit my eyebrows, outraged. "That's terrible!"

"That's life at Papilio." Milo shrugs. "Abigail should've paid more attention. Every dancer knows to check their equipment. I found broken glass in my shoes twice in the last month."

"That's awful." I guess I shouldn't have been surprised at Estelle's paranoia this morning. I make a mental note to keep an eye on *her*. I'm not planning to sabotage her, but she might take a preemptive strike against me. Does thinking that make me paranoid, too?

This stress is enough to make a person lose her mind. No wonder I'm hallucinating about an Adryil.

Milo and I reach the deserted stage and enter the staircase leading from the orchestra pit. He closes the door behind us. I sit on the bottom step and set my viola case down.

Milo takes a seat beside me and looks disappointedly at his meal. "You'd think with Papilio's advanced tech, they would've found a way to make 'nutritionally optimized' food taste good by now."

"Want some of mine?" I take the cover off my tray.

He considers my offer, then shakes his head. "Nah, it's okay." He picks up his fork and stabs the listless fish fillet. "Anyway, what's the big secret?"

"I ran into an Adryil last night. Actually ran into." The words I've kept bottled up for half a day tumble out of my mouth. I glance around to double-check that we're alone, and then I tell him everything that happened, except the part where I'm seeing ghosts. He keeps eating while I talk, but his eyes express his disbelief. "I just wish there were some way to find out what he was doing," I conclude. My stomach growls, and I take a large bite of pasta. A savory burst of bright, pungent flavor fills my mouth.

Milo remains quiet for a moment, absorbing the information. "You lied to a school official?" He bumps my shoulder. "Nice! Never took you for a rule breaker."

"Trust me, neither did I."

"What was that thing he gave you?"

I take another bite, glance around again, and then take the object out of my pocket, cupping my hands to shield it from any minders who might be watching.

Milo stares at it. "Whoa. Did the Adryil say anything about it?"

"Just 'take this' and 'don't let them take it from you.'"

"Seems important. Unless..." His eyes glint. "If this were a ballet, he'd be a prince, you'd be the fairy princess he fell for from afar, and this object is the token of his affections he risked life and limb to present to you in order to prove his undying love."

I elbow him. "Milo!"

Milo grins. "Sorry." He regards the device. "I wonder what those etchings mean. I remember seeing a holovid about something with green lines like that once... I think it was some kind of weapon."

"A weapon?" It never occurred to me that the Adryil boy might wish me harm. "Do you think that's what this is?"

"No clue." He hands the device back to me.

The glowing lines suddenly seem menacing. What if it's some kind of alien time bomb?

A calm feeling sweeps over me, one that conveys, *Don't be afraid.* I relax, and the memory of the Adryil boy's face floods my mind. Absent from it are any traces of the fierceness I saw in him. His expression is gentle, almost as though he was the one saying those words, telling me that he'd never hurt me. I don't know why, but I believe him, even though I know he's just a memory.

As I put the object back in my pocket, an idea occurs to me. "What about the library?"

"Yeah, right," Milo scoffs. "Have you ever looked up something *not* related to the Arts?"

I try to remember an occasion where I went to the library for something other than a composer or performer bio, but draw

46

a blank. "I guess not."

"Believe me, there's next to nothing. The administration thinks there's no point in keeping the library stocked with information that won't help us advance our Arts." His eyes light up. "But I know a guy in Dogwood who might know more."

"Really?" I've ventured into Dogwood a handful of times, but never stayed for long. Seeing where I'll end up if I don't find a patron stresses me more than I care to think about.

"It's a long shot," Milo says. "Still, it's better than nothing. We could go this evening, if you want."

"We'll be back before curfew, right?"

"Of course."

Though I have little desire to visit Dogwood again, going there is my best chance at learning the truth. I have to take it; I owe it to the Adryil boy—and myself. "It's worth a try."

Despite what Milo said, leaving out a library search feels wrong. Besides, rehearsals are done for the day, and I have nothing else to do between now and meeting him.

The library lies along the northern edge of the campus. Outside the line of oval-shaped windows, scraggly gray trees tower over a leaf-strewn ground. Shadows from the setting sun mute the reds and yellows of autumn, and branches sway under a strong wind.

I turn away from the window and sit down at one of the computer consoles. Apart from me, the library is empty.

A face flashes across the screen. I jump, startled, then blink rapidly, my heart pounding. It was the Adryil boy—again. His expression, one of intense concentration, was strained. *Am I really losing my mind? Should I go to the med center?*

But if I do that, they'll drill me questions, like "what were you doing when the hallucination occurred?" I'm not sure I could keep from confessing about the Adryil device this time, and then they'll know I lied to Mistress Medina.

A chill runs up my spine, and a feeling overwhelms me—the feeling that he's here in this room, standing beside me.

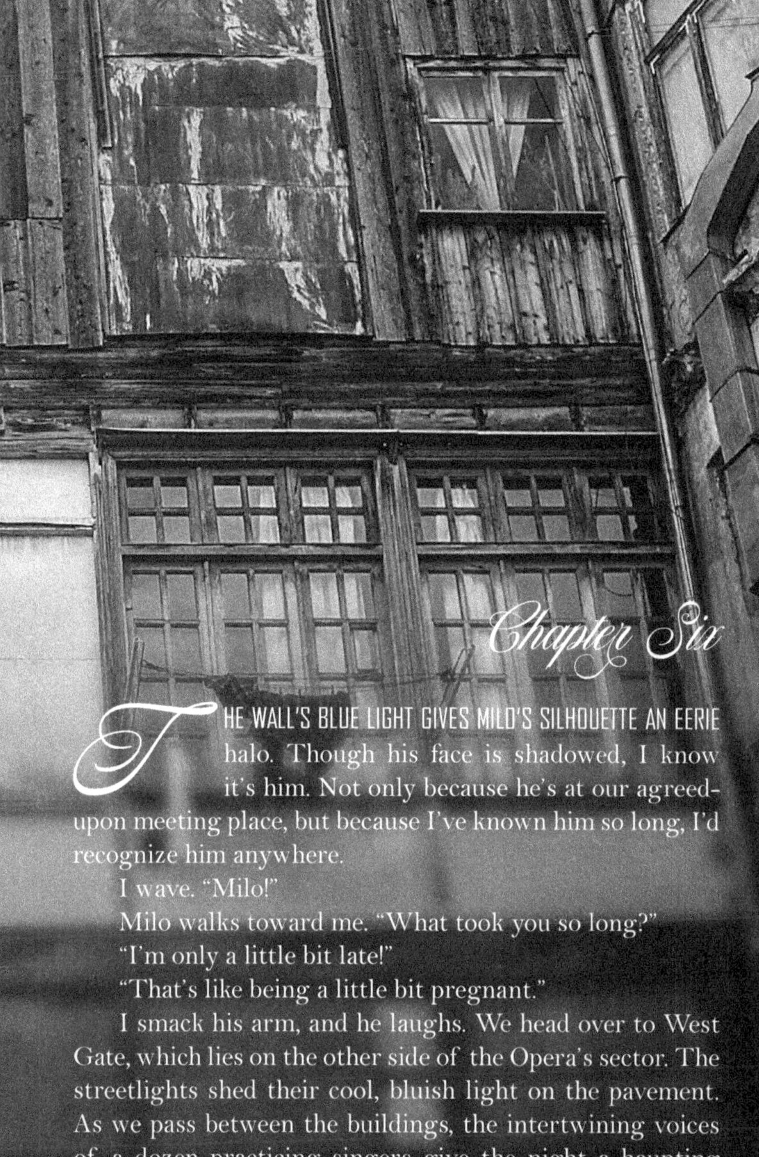

Chapter Six

THE WALL'S BLUE LIGHT GIVES MILO'S SILHOUETTE AN EERIE halo. Though his face is shadowed, I know it's him. Not only because he's at our agreed-upon meeting place, but because I've known him so long, I'd recognize him anywhere.

I wave. "Milo!"

Milo walks toward me. "What took you so long?"

"I'm only a little bit late!"

"That's like being a little bit pregnant."

I smack his arm, and he laughs. We head over to West Gate, which lies on the other side of the Opera's sector. The streetlights shed their cool, bluish light on the pavement. As we pass between the buildings, the intertwining voices of a dozen practicing singers give the night a haunting soundtrack. Soaring sopranos and commanding basses, lilting melodies and spinning arpeggios.

The memory of how little I found in the library gnaws at me. I spent two hours in there, scouring the archives for anything about Adryil technology, but turned up nothing more than I already knew.

I glance at Milo. "You were right."

"Of course I was." He throws me a teasing smile. "About what this time?"

"The library. I went just in case, but didn't find anything."

"Figures. Even if Papilio didn't think non-Arts-related knowledge was a waste of time, the government's pretty guarded about Adryil tech."

I glance at the Opera's rehearsal hall, an angular white building with arched windows. Though it looks simple, it contains all kinds of complex machinery from cleaner bots to holoprojectors. "But Papilio was built from Adryil designs."

"That's true." Milo shrugs. "Well, even within the school, there's a hierarchy. Maybe those at the top know what the rest of us aren't allowed to." He tilts his head. "Do you ever find it wrong that the people who do the least gain the most?"

"What do you mean?"

"This school is run by officials who live so far, they don't even visit us in person. The Adryil buy tickets to see our shows, then pay Papilio a finder's fee for each Artist they hire. Meanwhile, most of our earnings go to paying back tuition and everything else, whether we land a patron or not." His expression darkens. "We work our asses off, but it's the bosses who profit. Doesn't seem fair."

Recalling what he told me earlier about his family, I lay a sympathetic hand on his arm. "They're the reason we have a chance at all. If it weren't for them, Inna Havener—"

"Yeah, yeah, Inna Havener." He jerks his arm free. "Most of us won't be her. Most of us won't be *anyone*."

His words land like a punch. He's right. Only a quarter of Papilians find patrons while everyone else ends up back where they started. Worse off, actually, since they still have to pay back their debt. Part of the contract your parents sign when you enroll states that the loan applies to your entire family, which means if you age out, the school can seize their property and earnings as well as make you hand over most of your wages. For that reason, virtually every family of aged-out Papilians disowns their children to avoid ruin. That means they're not

allowed to contact them anymore, even if they live in the same town.

If Milo doesn't get hired, he won't just lose his prospects. He'll lose his family.

Violating the no-contact law means prison, and while it's possible to meet surreptitiously, most find the risks too great. Some aged-out Papilians even request jobs in other states to avoid the possibility of running into their families, and for the most part, the school is able to accommodate them. I used to wonder if that was the reason why my father ended up in California. I've tried asking around Dogwood to see if anyone knew him or my mother—or their relatives—but I never found anything. In addition, student files are confidential, so the school wouldn't let me look at my parents'. I wish I knew where they came from. If I have aunts or uncles or cousins, I've never heard of them. At least I don't have to worry about anyone depending on me.

Milo rakes one hand through his short curls. "Sorry, I didn't mean to snap at you. Guess I'm a bit on edge."

"I understand." I give him an encouraging smile. "But like I said earlier, you have nothing to worry about. You'll find a patron for sure."

"I wish I could believe you."

The towering metal doors of the West Gate, flanked by two imposing security bots, open as Milo and I approach.

"Please remember that curfew is eleven p.m.," one says in its mechanical voice. "The doors will not open past that time."

A wide street stretches before me, lined with slender streetlamps and tight rows of concrete buildings speckled with dim windows. The colors are so dull, I feel like I'm gazing at a grayscale hologram. I spot Mistress Asif walking down one of the sidewalks and wonder where she's heading. Home, perhaps? Does she have a family waiting for her? I know nothing about her life outside of Papilio. The same is true for every member of the school's staff I've ever encountered, even Vera. Though she's been my coach since I was seven, we've almost never spoken of anything other than music. I've tried asking her about her life,

but each time, she sternly reminds me that she's my coach, not my friend, and that the school's policies require that we keep our relationship strictly professional. Though she did let it slip once that she's a mother.

Mistress Asif's gaze lands on me, and I wave hello. She frowns with disapproval, as if asking why I'm not on campus practicing or studying. I shrink a little and look away.

"Mind if we make a detour?" Milo strides forward at a brisk pace. "Won't take long."

"No problem." As we approach an intersection, a rumbling sound rolls toward me. Glancing to the right, I spot a truck heading down the far street. It's a rusted metal thing with large, dirty tires and a long flatbed in the back. Dim yellow headlights barely illuminate the ground ten feet in front of it. Several people sit in the flatbed, leaning back against the low walls. They must be laborers returning from work. I'd hate to have to ride like that for the hour or so it takes to reach the local manufacturing plant that employs most of Dogwood's residents. Yet that's probably what I'll end up doing. Other than the retired Artists, most of whom now work on the school's staff, every person in this town failed at the Arts at some point in their lives. Either they aged out of Papilio or a similar school or, like Milo's sister, didn't get in at all. The thought depresses me, and I try to banish it.

I wonder what it must be like to live in a place where success and failure doesn't revolve around the Arts. Out there, in other parts of the world, people go about their lives without obsessing over a chance at glory like we do. Yet that's because unless they're born wealthy, they don't *have* a chance. They're trapped in an eternal cycle of labor and debt, trying to make ends meet. So are we, but at least we have the possibility of breaking out, as Inna Havener did.

Milo and I cross a wide street. Though the pale tenements before us are shaped similarly to the buildings we just passed, they appear beaten and world-weary. Weeds spring from cracks in the pavement, and ragged brown vines snake up the walls and strangle the lampposts. The forest is reclaiming this land, and it appears no one in this part of Dogwood cares enough to fight

back. Only a few flickering lights illuminate the sidewalks, and the presence of so many dark corners makes me nervous.

"Awful, right?" Milo appears to have taken my anxiety for disgust. He turns toward one of the buildings. "I promised my parents I'd get them out first chance I have. I guess now I have to get Alice out too." Bitterness clings to his tone as he approaches a row of small, metal mailboxes. "I don't understand why she didn't qualify. She's a beautiful dancer… better than I was at that age. Don't they realize what they're wasting?" He slams the mailboxes, and the clanging noise splits the air. "Maybe if I were better, I'd have found a patron already and could pay for her to keep learning."

My usual encouragements feel limp even in my head, so I just put my arm around him. Sometimes, there's just nothing to say.

He retrieves a key from his pocket, then opens one of the mailbox doors. *That must be his family's.*

He takes off his watch and places it inside, and I give him a puzzled look. "What are you doing?"

"My dad can pawn that for a few coins." Milo locks the mailbox. "It's barely anything, but maybe it'll help."

"But that's school property."

He waves dismissively. "I do this kind of thing all the time when I need quick cash. Whatever I sell or trade, Papilio just issues me a new one and adds the cost to my debt. It's already a mountain. A few extra boulders won't make a difference. Anyway, let's go."

I gesture at the building's door. "Don't you want to say hi?"

"Not tonight." He walks away so quickly, I have to jog to keep up.

I follow him down a few more dark streets, wondering where he's taking me. Ahead, the doors to a rust-stained building lie open, leading to an entryway glowing under a dim yellow light. Austere as the other tenements were, they looked like palaces compared to the chipped walls and cracked windows of the one we're heading toward.

"What is this place?" I ask.

Milo strides up to the door. "Our future if we don't make it."

This must be one of the government housing projects the school sends its aged-out students to. It's meant to be temporary, but from what I've heard, many ex-Papilians never earn enough to move elsewhere. This glimpse at the world I'll face if I can't get my ranking up makes my gut twist.

As we step through the doorway, a stench wafts toward me—a mix of sweat and decay wrapped in smoke. I resist the urge to wrinkle my nose. Many of the doors to the individual units lie open with the sounds of voices drifting out. Multiple bunk beds cram each small room. Almost every person I spot has either an opaque cup or a cigarette in their hand; some have both. Their eyes are glazed over, and their movements limp. I guess when you've lost everything, it's easier to just forget. Some look old and worn, but many appear only a few years older than me. I have a hard time believing that these lost-looking people were once dedicated Artists like me.

How can Papilio make us work so hard, only to throw us away when they're done? I wish I could change things, but I guess the school doesn't owe us anything. No one's forced to enroll.

A boy with long, brown hair and stubble covering his jaw emerges from a room. He must have aged out pretty recently, since he still looks like a teenager. Milo quickens his step.

"Phers!" He waves.

The boy must not have heard him, because he turns back toward the doorway, laughing at someone inside.

I give Milo a funny look. "His name is Fierce?"

"MacPherson Gill—Phers for short." Milo's lips quirk. "Though he sometimes pretends it *is* Fierce. He's one of your kind: Orchestra guy born at Papilio."

MacPherson? As in "MacPherson's Farewell"? I wouldn't put it past a Papilian couple to name their son after an ancient fiddle tune. Though, on second thought, that song was supposedly played by a legendary bandit on the gallows, right before he smashed the instrument and was hanged, so maybe not.

After Milo calls the boy's name again, Phers spins around on his heel. In his hand, he holds a slim white cigarette. The bittersweet scent of its pale gray smoke curls toward me,

overwhelming my senses. Whatever is wrapped inside that paper, it's not tobacco.

"Oh, hey, Milo!" Phers's brown eyes shift toward me. "Who's that lovely lady you've got with you?"

"Iris," I say.

"Welcome to my domain." Phers leans forward in a deep, exaggerated bow. "And what's your Art?"

"Orchestra."

"Orchestra!" Phers sweeps his arms to the side. "I was in the Orchestra too! Trombone! Got pretty good, until I figured out the school's full of shit. I was never going to make it anyway, so I figured I might as well leave on my own terms."

"You dropped out?" I don't recognize him, so he must have left before I moved up from the junior string ensemble. Also, he doesn't have the reddish marks around his mouth most brass players do; they must have faded. "But… why?"

"Saw no point in killing myself over something I could never have." He shrugs. "Besides, that's three years' worth of debt I won't have to pay back."

I almost understand. Still, even in my most desperate hour, I could never bring myself to walk away from my instrument. Especially since dropouts are always placed in menial jobs, never good ones as coaches or anything.

"Hey, Milo, check out my latest. They call it lotus." Phers hands Milo his cigarette—or whatever you call "lotus" wrapped in paper.

Milo puts it to his lips and inhales. My surprise must show on my face, because he throws me a smirk. "Oh, loosen up." Smoke drifts from his lips. He hands the cigarette back to Phers. "Tastes fine, but I guess it'll take a moment to kick in."

Phers puts the cigarette between two fingers and offers it me. "How about you?"

"No, thanks." The smoky atmosphere is already making my head spin, and I don't feel like getting any dizzier.

Milo jerks his thumb at Phers. "Phers knows more about Adryil stuff than anyone I've ever met. He might know what that thing is."

Phers rubs the back of his shaggy head. "What thing?"

After glancing around to make sure no one's spying on us, I pull the Adryil device out of my pocket. Phers plucks the small machine from my fingers. "Where'd you get this?"

"Found it." I pull my lips in, hoping he won't ask for details.

He peers at it, examining its etchings. Lines of green light appear on his pale face from the winding patterns. "Never seen anything like it." He points at an etching in the center, which is shaped like a swirl with angular edges. "This symbol means 'activate,' but that's all I know."

Disappointed, I take the device back. "Thanks anyway."

Milo angles his mouth. "Sorry, Iris. Guess this whole adventure was for nothing."

"It was worth a shot." I drop the device back into my pocket. "Let's go."

"No need to run off." Phers peers at my watch. "You've got a few hours before curfew. Why not stay and hang out?"

"Thanks, but I have rehearsal in the morning." The words come out faster than I intended. They're true, but the real reason I'm eager to leave is because the unfamiliar smells are starting to make me nauseous.

"Oh, I get it." Phers raises his eyebrows. "You think you're too good for this place. Let me guess—you were born at Papilio?"

I blink. "I was, but—"

"I used to think like you." Phers cuts me off. "Then I realized how twisted that place is. You're squeezed for every ounce of skill you've got, ranked and measured to please a bunch of aliens who'll decide your fate. Papilio traps you for the entertainment of the rich, profiting off your sweat. And you're expected to be grateful for their crumbs while they gorge themselves on cake. At least I don't serve them anymore. I'm free." He puts his cigarette in his mouth and inhales. "As for you"—he blows a stream of smoke into my face, and I cover my mouth—"They own you."

"What the hell, man?" Milo steps between Phers and me. "Leave her alone."

I smile a little, glad that Milo's on my side.

Phers snickers. "You know I'm right."

Milo crosses his arms. "Maybe, but you don't have to be an ass about it."

I knit my eyebrows. What did he mean by "maybe"? He'd never actually agree with Phers, would he?

"Didn't mean to rile you." Phers raises his hands as if surrendering. He looks past Milo, meeting my gaze. "Life's about more than work. So how 'bout it? There's fun to be had."

Something about the way he talks says that he thinks himself better than me. What right does he have to act superior? He *quit.* I think about what Estelle said about her family's sacrifice, about the look on Milo's face when he told me about his sister. Yet here's someone who, like me, was born into the opportunity Estelle and Milo had to fight for. At least I'm doing my best to be worthy of it. "I don't need your kind of fun."

"You're delusional."

Fury simmers within me, churning up something deeper than what Phers is provoking. "No, you are. How is *this* freedom?" I gesture at the smoke-filled tenement around me. "You were born with a chance others would kill for, and you threw it away. So don't talk to me about what life's all about, because clearly you don't know. You're glib about your very existence, smothering it with external pleasures because you can't find *anything* inside. You're a manifestation of hopelessness. That doesn't make you freer than the rest of us."

"That's nice." Phers leans back against the wall. "Wouldn't expect anything different coming from a slave of their system."

Something about his slack expression adds a new spark to the flame. "I may be part of a system, but I'm doing what *I* want to do. You think I haven't gotten frustrated and wanted to quit?" My mind flashes back to the times I strove to my limits at an audition only to be rejected, the times Vera lectured me to tears, the times I attempted difficult pieces and found my feeble fingers unable to keep up.

I sense a presence near me, like someone's watching me in anticipation of what I'll say next. Not wanting to let that invisible audience down, I keep going. "It's easy not to care. If you don't believe anything, you can never be wrong. But that

doesn't make you right. As much as I want it, I'll probably never find a patron. In five years, I might be living across the hall from you, and you can laugh at me then. But until that happens, I choose to try anyway. I choose to believe."

"Believing isn't the same as knowing something's worthwhile." Milo's voice is quieter than usual.

I whirl toward him, surprised that he's the one who spoke those words and not Phers. "What do you mean?"

Milo's eyes are distant. "Phers has a point. We're trapped. Forced into the system because it's the only way out of something even worse."

I bite my lip, bothered by the bitterness in his voice. "But you love dancing, don't you?"

"Yeah, and that's why I let Papilio swallow me." Milo looks at the ground, his expression tight. "I just wish I had a damn choice."

"You *do*." Phers puts his hand on Milo's shoulder. "Walk away. Isn't this where it's all headed anyway?"

"Of course not!" I want to slap Phers. If he were saying these things to me, he might have a point, but Milo's *good.* "Milo, don't listen to him. He doesn't know what he's talking about."

"Don't I?" Phers drops his arm and glances at me. "*You're* the hopeless one. Hopelessly enslaved to Papilio."

I narrow my eyes. "I don't just play for Papilio. I play for the music. For me."

Phers puts his cigarette to his lips and inhales slowly, keeping his eyes on me. He's probably contemplating what else he can say to make me concede that he's right. Well, I won't, and I return his stare to let him know I'm not backing down.

He exhales, shaking his head, and his whole body loosens visibly. His stance becomes a slouch, and his expression loses its spark. Far from arguing back, he looks like he doesn't care enough to respond, like he's giving up. The sight is unnerving after the hostility he just showed, and I wonder if it's the effects of the lotus—whatever that is.

Phers turns back to Milo, tilting his head. "I don't get it, Milo. You come here looking for escape, but you keep going

back." He sticks out his hand, offering Milo the cigarette. "Why not stay?"

Milo's mouth becomes a thin line, and worry creeps into my mind. The idea of Milo dropping out is ridiculous, especially when he's flying high at the Ballet and has a family counting on him. But then I recall all the times he's confessed to me how anxious he was about a particular audition, or how upset he was by his coach's criticisms, or how scared he was of disappearing into mediocrity. Of not mattering. Of being forgotten, then tossed out. These are my demons too, but I'd never stop fighting them. Would he?

I peer into his face, trying to read his expression. "Milo?"

Milo glances at me, then gives Phers a dry smile. "I'm holding out, Phers. Still got a shot at Sabina, after all."

Phers barks out a laugh. "Fair enough."

A veil seems to have settled over his eyes, robbing them of the focus they'd held just moments ago. There's a strange mix of emptiness and euphoria in his expression—the way his lips curve, the way his eyelids droop, the way his brows tilt—as if someone smothered a piece of his soul, and he's glad they did. Unnerved, I turn and head down the hallway.

As Milo walks beside me, he gives me a sheepish grin. "Phers takes some getting used to. You know, he may be an ass, but that doesn't mean he's wrong."

I meet his gaze, worried. "Do you really agree with him?"

"Sometimes. Sometimes not." He lifts his mouth into something of a smile. "Don't fret, Iris. I don't plan on dropping out. Couldn't if I wanted to."

Despite his casual tone, I sense something dark behind his eyes. I don't know how to reply. After everything he's said since I met up with him in the quad, I'm beginning to realize that there's a whole other side to him that he's kept hidden from me.

I continue in silence. Perhaps I am complacent, following Papilio's system without question. None of us have a choice—Milo was right about that. We do what we do because we love our Arts, and those who run Papilio know it. Nevertheless, I won't rebel like Phers, just for the sake of rebelling. What kind

of life is that, existing without purpose? Even if I stood at the edge of the universe with only my viola and the abyss yawning before me, I'd play to oblivion.

A warm feeling glows within me, like someone's smiling at me. I look around, but see only the empty haze of the tenement.

Chapter Seven

ALE LIGHT STREAMS THROUGH MY WINDOW ONTO THE desk before me. The screen displaying tomorrow's rehearsal schedule glows yellow in my otherwise dark room. I should have been in bed hours ago, like everyone else. Instead, I lean forward in my chair, turning the Adryil device in my hand. A day ago, I wouldn't have dared to keep it out like this, fearing that a minder might be watching me, but now, the need to know what it is outweighs my instinct toward caution. Considering the number of times I've handled it without getting caught, I get the feeling that the minders aren't nearly as watchful as I thought they were.

Two whole days have passed since I went to Dogwood, and despite coaching, practice, and rehearsals, I haven't been able to shake the Adryil boy out of my mind. It seems my hallucinations have been replaced by his invisible presence—I *feel* like he's here, even though I can't see or hear him. But I don't mind. When I was practicing earlier, I sensed a rapt audience of one watching me, and I think it helped me play better, knowing someone thought I was brilliant.

I run my finger across one of the green etchings. The grooved surface, warm from my constant touch, presses into my skin. If the center symbol means "Activate," the other patterns must have meanings as well. Maybe if I play with them long enough, the machine will reveal its purpose.

Minutes roll by, and all my poking doesn't seem to do anything. I sigh, feeling defeated. Maybe I'll have better luck tomorrow. I get up, aiming to go to sleep.

Something's off. For a moment, I can't put my finger on what's changed, but then I notice that the monitor has gone blank. But I didn't switch it off—is it glitching?

The Adryil boy's presence sweeps over me, stronger than it ever was before. This is the first time it's happened in my room other than when I was practicing, and I'm glad I didn't change out of my blue dress. If he's here somehow, I wouldn't want him to see me in my pajamas.

That's ridiculous. He can't be here.

Suddenly, white letters type across my monitor, brilliant against the blackness:

Iris, don't be afraid. I mean you no harm.

I blink, stunned and confused. Despite what the words tell me, my breath quickens with fear. More letters appear on the screen:

I ran into you at the Wall of Glory. The Zexa device I gave you allows me to communicate with you telepathically, despite Earth's satellites. It keyed itself to your DNA when you touched it, so you're the only one who can hear me when I try. I can also communicate through nearby machines, which is how I'm typing this message.

So the device *is* connected to him. Still unable to believe what I'm seeing, I whisper, "Who are you?"

The letters vanish, and new ones appear in their place:

My name is Dámiul Verik.

"Dámiul." At last, I know his name. It sounds like the name of one of the angels from the ballet "Heaven's Fury"—Gabriel, Nathaniel, Barachiel. Dámiul. He's real, not a figment of my imagination. Excitement replaces my fear. Questions swirl in my mind, and I can't pick which one to ask first.

Dámiul must anticipate them, because he starts answering:

I tried communicating with you telepathically before, and then through Papilio's holoprojectors, but the Zexa device wasn't on the right settings. I'm also new to this, so I might have made a few errors in my attempts. I'm sorry if I scared you.

I glance at the stone-like object in my hand. A Zexa device. So that's what it's called. "Is it on the right settings now?"

More or less. However, before I say anything else, I must warn you that what I'm doing—sending unauthorized interstellar transmissions—is illegal on my world and yours. And by responding, you would be complicit in the crime.

Crime? How is talking to someone a crime? The logical part of my brain reminds me that interstellar communications are tightly controlled, and that the authorities could arrest me for bypassing their systems. But I must've already broken one law or another by hiding Adryil technology in the first place. That bridge is burned—I might as well see what's on the other side.

"I don't care." I glance up at the holoprojectors. "Can you appear holographically?"

Yes. I'm only using typed messages because I didn't want to show up suddenly and frighten you again. Do you mind if I appear?

I start to say yes, then remember something. "What if a minder's watching?"

I can alter the images they see. Even when I'm not here, the device emits a signal that interferes with any monitoring technology within a twelve-foot radius. To your minders, it looks like nothing more than a stone as

long as it's active. Don't worry, Iris. I took precautions to ensure that these transmissions would not be discovered.

No wonder they never spotted it. "In that case… um… please appear." My heart speeds up with anticipation.

The letters dissolve from the monitor. Something glows behind me, and I turn to see a shaft of white light in the middle of the room. The light shimmers, then takes the shape of a person's ghostly silhouette. Tall, with broad shoulders and an elegant figure. Colors fade in from the white—black hair, amber skin, black-and-silver outfit reminiscent of a military uniform.

The next thing I know, Dámiul is standing before me. If this were an opera, now would be the moment the hero appears, and the music would swell to epic heights. And I…I would be the awestruck maiden.

Those azure eyes, luminous even compared to the glowing hologram, are once again fixed on me. I long to know who lies behind them, but remind myself that this is *not* an opera. I'm not the giddy soubrette, and he's not the gallant tenor. He's a stranger who broke the law and dragged me into his trouble.

Dámiul lifts the corner of his mouth into a rakish half-smile. "Hello again." Even those simple words are melodic in his crisp accent, which sounds like a combination of Arabic and Italian accents spun together by threads of British.

I realize I'm staring like an idiot and force myself to say something, but all that comes out is, "Hello."

Dámiul's smile falls. "Do you want me to go?"

I realize he mistook my fascination for fear and shake my head. "No. I'm just… I never thought I'd see you again. What were you doing here the other night?"

Dámiul shifts his gaze, his eyes darkening. For several seconds, he doesn't say anything. Then, he looks up, and any trace of whatever bothered him vanishes, replaced by coolness. "I was visiting the city of Charlotte when I learned the Papilio School was nearby. This place is legendary among my kind: the original training ground of Artists, where Katarin Kaminski herself studied, and where Earthling performers spend their days doing things we, in all our advancement, never could. I had

to see it for myself, so I hired a transport to take me as close as possible then scaled the wall. As for the Zexa device—I gave it to you so I could return later, either telepathically or through the machines. After I was caught, they sent me back to Adrye." He pauses. "I'm forbidden from entering Earthling space again."

There's something he's not telling me—I can feel it in every word he says. It doesn't make sense to me that he would have come out of simple curiosity. His expression crackled with purpose that night.

My suspicion must show on my face, because Dámiul says, "I'm sure it's not as interesting a story as you were hoping to hear, but it's the truth."

Though I don't really believe him, I decide to turn my questions elsewhere. Maybe if he comes to trust me, he'll tell me what he really came for.

It hits me that, as a telepath, he should automatically trust me because he knows what I'm thinking. That must have been how he knew my name, maybe even how he anticipated my questions—and how he knew he could trust me with the Zexa device in the first place. Telepathy on humans may be forbidden, but the law clearly means nothing to him. Or to me, since I accepted his invitation to break it.

The presence I felt—that must have been him in my head. I suddenly feel as if everything I've done in the past two days has been in a glass box under his scrutiny, and I shudder. I don't like the idea of him invading my mind.

Dámiul's black eyebrows knit together. "Is something wrong?"

If he's in my head, he would know already, wouldn't he? "Can you see my thoughts?"

"I could if I wanted to, but I'm not looking right now. The one time I did was when I first encountered you, and it was only for an instant to see whether I could trust you with the Zexa device."

So I was right about that. I'm somewhat disturbed by the idea that he knew I'd disobey the school's authorities before I did. "What did you see?"

"I read enough from your personality to know how much

unanswered questions bother you, and I believed that would keep you from handing over the device. After that, I didn't pry further."

He read me right, then. But that doesn't mean I like it. "What about later? I felt your presence in my head."

"I was only trying to communicate," he says quickly. "You knew I was there, but you thought I was a ghost. It wasn't my intention to spy on you. My kind can share their thoughts as well as read those of others—if you don't believe me, let me show you mine and prove that it's true."

His hurried reassurance amuses me, and part of me believes I don't need to look into his head to know he's telling the truth. But I'm not sure I can trust that instinct, and I'm curious to see what it's like to have someone share his thoughts with me, so I say, "I'd like that."

Dámiul looks into my eyes, and I feel myself pulled into his bright gaze. A feeling floods my mind—the kind you get when you say something you know is true. It tells me that, yes, after our first encounter, he was only in my head to try to talk to me, and each time, I knew he was there. He tried to speak to me backstage, attempted to use the library's computers, and followed me to Dogwood, hoping that someone there would know how to put the Zexa device on its right settings. He never meant to spy on me; he just didn't know how to make his presence known. And he'd certainly never telepathically manipulate me. Using that ability for control rather than communication goes against everything he believes in, and I feel his fury spark in my own chest.

Then, I see something else: myself, through his eyes. Not the shy, awkward mouse I know myself to be, but a strange beauty from another world.

The feeling disappears, and he turns away sharply. "There you have it."

I blink, surprised by how I look to him. I realize that he might be as fascinated by me as I am by him. To him, *I'm* the alien, and Papilio is as foreign as Adrye. If I had the chance, would I break the law to see a faraway world I might otherwise

never reach? I think I would. Looking at it that way, his desire to simply see Papilio doesn't seem so far-fetched after all.

Dámiul's back is still to me. I don't see why he's so embarrassed—he was hovering in my mind while I was obsessing over our perceived connection.

I move to face him. "Is that how people talk on Adrye? Through their minds?"

"Sometimes." His expression relaxes. "Our language is much simpler than yours because we can share what we mean without words. It's the reason we never developed anything like your Arts—we don't need to find creative ways to express ourselves. We can simply let people *know* what we're feeling."

"Can you say something in your language?" I feel stupid asking, but I can't resist.

Dámiul presses his lips together, as though contemplating what he should say. His gaze meets mine. "*En selár Karovyil dira.*" His words sound almost sung. "It means, 'You're a beautiful Earthling.'" He gives me that half-smile again.

I drop my gaze. "Thank you, but compared to everyone else at Papilio, I'm actually quite plain." The words come automatically, and too late, I realize how awkward I must sound. It's true, though. Maybe I'd be considered attractive elsewhere, but at this school, I'm just a decent-looking swallow in a flock of elegant swans and vivacious cardinals. Looking for another subject, one that won't turn me into a blushing idiot, I ask, "Does everyone on Adrye speak the same language?"

"Yes. Our ancestors spoke in different tongues, but over time, their languages blended into one, which we simply know as *Cambr'endra Adryil,* or 'Common Language of Adrye.' For centuries, that was the only language anyone knew, until we encountered Earth. Now, we're all taught the most common Earthling languages."

"How many do you know?"

"Only six, I'm afraid."

"*Six?*" I have a hard enough time with the Italian musical terms in my scores. Just thinking of learning six whole languages—seven including Adryil—makes me dizzy.

"It's much easier to learn when one can interface with machines and absorb information. For example, shortly before arriving at the Charlotte spaceport, I read in a map of the city. It was like swallowing a bitter medicine—somewhat unpleasant, but simple enough."

The mention of Charlotte brings me back to the question of what he was doing in Papilio. Hoping to learn a little more, I ask, "Why were you visiting Charlotte?"

"My father is a businessman, and he has several contacts there. I volunteered to go on an assignment on his behalf. He wasn't happy when he learned what else I did." Dámiul looks away with a private smile. "But it was worth it."

"Really?" I tilt my head skeptically. "Even though you were knocked out and dragged away?"

"Even so. If nothing else, I defied my father." His eyes glint.

Maybe I was right about his motives being pure insanity. Maybe his coming here really was just a stunt. Yet I have a hard time reconciling what he's telling me with what I saw before. But I could have been wrong, reading into things that weren't there.

"Who is your father?" I ask.

"The business he conducts is unique to Adrye." Dámiul's tone becomes terse. "There's no equivalent on Earth. Do you have any other questions?"

His brusqueness makes it clear that he doesn't want to talk about his father's business. That annoys me, but I suppose if it's private, he has no reason to share it with a stranger. "I have too many questions to count. Where do you come from? What do you do on your world?"

"I live in Adrye's capital, Nathril." His words are stiff, as if he's picking them carefully. "My life is not particularly fascinating, especially compared to that of an Artist. All I do is attend classes and prepare for exams."

On the contrary, even if he considers himself ordinary among his kind, I find everything about him interesting. "So you're a student? What do you study?"

"I won't need to choose a concentration until I reach university. Right now, I'm simply educated in the standard

subjects—and taught to think the same way as everyone else. My people revere such conformity and order, unlike Earthlings, who value individuality." Dámiul's expression grows distant. "Sometimes, I think I don't belong here."

I glimpse the buildings outside my window. "Papilians are obsessed with standing out, and in their efforts to be unique, they blend into each other. I want the same things as they do, but… I often feel like I don't belong, either."

"Do you want to leave?" Dámiul's eyes regain their fierceness, and I wonder what angers him.

"No." Despite everything Milo—and Phers—said to me, a few bitter words aren't enough to turn me against my home. Maybe we are bound to Papilio by the threat of poverty, but I spend my days doing something I love. As long as I'm here, I'll enjoy what I can. "I wouldn't want to be anywhere else."

Dámiul's expression falls into something akin to sadness. He remains silent, and I wish he'd let me read his mind again. An idea strikes me. "Do you want me to show you around? It's after curfew—no one else will be out."

Dámiul's face brightens. "I would be honored."

Who talks like that? I smile and hold up the Zexa device. "All I have to do is carry this, and you can use the holoprojectors?"

"That's right."

I tuck the device into my skirt pocket. Dámiul's hologram follows me to the door. I still can't quite believe that he's here with me after days of haunting me through captivating visions I couldn't trust. In a way, that hasn't changed. Each question he answers opens a hundred more, and no matter how many I ask, I'll probably never understand him.

But I'd love to try.

 71 

From the top of the grand hall, Papilio's campus appears spectral, with icy light washing over silver-and-white buildings. An abstract, mirrored sculpture rises from the roof's center. From below, it always appeared pristine—a flawless gem crowning the school's oldest structure. But from this close, I can see how dusty and blemished it really is. Yet the stars reflected in the gleaming surface are no closer.

A metal fence runs around the roof's edge. I approach the side facing the quad, hoping I don't look too out-of-breath from the long climb up the stairs.

Dámiul walks beside me. If it weren't for the glow surrounding him, I would have forgotten that he's only here in holographic form. He carries a certain kind of presence. It reminds me of how Master Raucci can silence a room just by showing up, or how Sabina can light up a stage by walking onto it, or how Brent can awe an audience before he's played a single note. It's quiet, yet bold.

I point at the concrete building across the quad. "That's the supply center, where they issue us clothing and any equipment we need for our Arts. Behind it lies the children's sector, where I used to live before I became an active Artist." I point to my left. "See that giant stone building? That's the Circus's rehearsal hall. Everything past it is the Orchestra—we're the biggest Art by far." I turn toward Dámiul. "What do you call the Arts on Adrye?"

"*Ka'ris.*" Dámiul approaches the fence, surveying the campus below.

"Kah-*rees.*" I repeat the word slowly.

"Don't let your school officials hear you say that—or any other words in Adryil."

"Why not?"

"They wouldn't like it, and they'd ask where you learned the word."

The second part of his statement seems obvious, but the first… Why wouldn't the school want us learning the Adryil's language when our goal is to live among them? I suppose this question never occurred to me before because every holovid of the Adryil I've ever seen showed them speaking perfect English.

"Everyone on Adrye must speak Earthling languages," I muse aloud. "Or could learn them quickly through telepathy. Still… It seems strange that we wouldn't be taught the native tongue of the place we're supposed to live someday."

"I can't speak to your school's intentions. I'm unfamiliar with their particular policies." Dámiul's words sound a little too businesslike, and I wonder if he's using them to circumvent something.

"Maybe they don't teach us for the same reason they don't teach us science or history." I peer at the library—a barely visible mass of shadowy angles. "We're supposed to dedicate all our efforts to our Arts. There's no room for anything else." I turn back to Dámiul. "Tell me more about your language."

"*Ka'ris* is short for *Karovyil ris,* which means 'Earthling Arts.' Before we made contact with your world, *ris* referred to literal representations of reality."

"Kah-*roh*-vye-ill *rees.*" Sounding out those strange syllables gives me the thrill of speaking a secret code. I wonder what it must be like to live in a world where you can simply show people

how you feel. "It must be nice to have people always know what you want to say."

"It's good for cooperation. Perhaps too good." Dámiul leaves the words hanging, like he wants to say more, but doesn't continue.

I look down at the quad, where Estelle accused me of being after her. If I could have shown her my thoughts then, maybe she wouldn't have treated me as an enemy. "If we had your abilities, life would be a lot simpler."

"Even with understanding, people still disagree." Anger darkens Dámiul's tone. "Don't envy us, Iris. By taking the easy way, we've missed much. That's why the Arts fascinate us so—in your efforts to express what's within, the Earthlings gave rise to something sublime."

"And impossible." I stare at the Wall. "The Arts are all about endless reaching. When I play my viola, I feel the music, both within me and beyond me. It's a force of its own, possessing everything I am, carrying me toward a perfect world. But when I try to release it and show others what I hear, what comes out always seems so weak."

"I've seen you play, and I don't agree. I think you're brilliant." Dámiul's voice rings with sincerity.

I turn to him with a wry grin. "You must not have watched many violists play, then."

Dámiul returns my smile. "Contrary to what you may think, you're not the first *Ka'risil* I've seen."

"Kah-*ree*-sil?" I draw out the word, hoping I'm not mispronouncing it too badly.

"It's what we call the Artists. I've seen plenty of shows, and you… there's something genuine about your performance. It's more than technique and showmanship. You play like you have something true to say."

I feel a blush tiptoe into my cheeks. "Thank you."

Dámiul's gaze turns contemplative. "A famous memoirist from my world once said that the Earthlings aren't less advanced than the Adryil—they just advanced differently. I think he was right. You can do things we can't even imagine."

I lean back against the fence. "Building spaceships that can bridge the stars beats twirling on silks, I'd say."

"That's just it though—you look at a pair of silks and see an instrument of beauty. Until we came across the Earthlings, we'd look at a pair of silks and see only fabric. My kind might have brought you technology, but you… you brought us the transcendent. You can pick up a box of wood with metal wires strung across it and create sounds we couldn't imagine. It's magnificent."

His gaze is too magnetic to turn away from, and I find myself lost in its azure beauty. I've often dreamed of taking to the stage, catching the eye of a handsome young man in the audience, and going backstage to find him waiting with an expression not unlike the one bright on Dámiul's face.

I take a breath, cursing my mind for wandering into such ridiculous places. "It's not so difficult. The Adryil's lack of Arts is just cultural, isn't it?"

"I suppose," Dámiul replies. "Though they've had a great impact on our world since we encountered your kind."

I look up at the night sky. "Can we see your star from here?"

"Not yet." I catch a glow in the corner of my eye—Dámiul stands beside me. "Irinn is two trillion lightyears away, in another galaxy. Its light hasn't even reached Earth yet. But when it does, it will be in the constellation you call Gemini."

"Oh?" I scan the sky, searching for the celestial twins. Spotting the winking pattern, I point one finger at the center. "About there?"

The glow of Dámiul's hologram draws closer, and I glance over to see him eyeing the constellation. He stands so close, I could feel his breath against my cheek if he were really here. The still air suddenly feels hollow, deprived of the warmth and life that should have filled it. When he places his holographic hand on top of mine, I can't help wishing I could feel his touch instead of seeing an illusion. The usual beeping that occurs when one touches a hologram is absent; he must have disengaged it.

Still, I somehow sense the slight pressure against the back of my hand, and I move my outstretched arm to the left in response, allowing him to guide me.

"About there." He lowers his hand.

My finger points at a black void, and I imagine it's where the twins' hands would meet were the image more complete. I gaze at the space, beyond which lies a star I can't see, that I might never see. By the time its light reaches this spot, Earth will be long gone, along with the sun, the moon, and even Gemini. A pang fills my heart. That's enough space to make contact between our worlds utterly impossible if it weren't for the Adryil's ability to travel through hyperspace. They can fold space like origami paper to reach worlds across the universe, but unless I find a patron, I'll never leave Earth. I'll probably never even leave North Carolina. So much lies between the stars that I'll never know. And it'll be my own fault for failing. My eyes sting, and I blink rapidly.

Stop it, Iris. I turn further away from Dámiul, hoping the feeling will subside before the tears spill.

"Iris?" Dámiul sounds worried.

"I'm sorry." I try to keep my voice from trembling. "It just gets to me sometimes—all the pressure. I want nothing more than to go to your world someday, but… I don't think I will. And I can't stand the thought of them taking away my music when I age out."

Sympathy fills Dámiul's eyes, and he places his hand on my shoulder. Though I know he's just a projection, I can almost feel his warmth. Yet such a gulf lies between us, I can't even see his star. I never knew it'd be possible to experience both comfort and sadness at once.

"I'm sure you'll find a patron if that's what you really want." Dámiul's voice is quiet, like he's afraid anything louder will bring forth the rest of my tears.

I turn my gaze toward the sky, wondering what it would be like to travel through the glittering abyss. "What's Adrye like?"

"Most of the planet is covered in cities. Even though we have no Arts, we still have design. I think you'd find it appealing."

"I've seen the holovids." I try to smile. "It's so beautiful."

"On the outside, perhaps." There's a hard edge to his voice. But before I can ask more, a mix of worry and surprise flashes

across his expression, as if he abruptly remembered something. "I should go. I've already kept you too long."

I want to tell him that I'd stay up all night if it meant getting to learn more about him. But that would sound crazy, so instead I ask, "Will I see you again?"

"Only if you want to." A cloud seems to have descended over his expression.

I approach his holographic form. How can I say, "Come see me whenever you want" without sounding foolish or desperate? Realizing I can't, I let the words out and bite my lip, hoping he doesn't make fun of me for it.

Dámiul gives me a slight smile. "Are you sure? I might keep showing up."

"That's okay." I shrug, trying to seem casual. "You're the first Adryil I've ever met, and… I'd like to get to know you."

"All right." Dámiul's smile falls, and he looks behind him. "I'll return soon." Before I can say anything, his hologram dissolves.

I reach into the empty space where he just stood, suddenly feeling isolated.

I HEAD TOWARD THE ORCHESTRA'S REHEARSAL HALL, drowsiness fogging my mind even though I've been awake for hours. Staying up last night was worth the lecture from Vera. Thoughts of Dámiul cling to my mind, tugging at me in a way I wish they wouldn't.

As I walk down the street, I sternly remind myself that I'm only fascinated by Dámiul because he's beautiful and from another world—the perfect recipe for ridiculous dreaming. I used to mock characters in operas and ballets for swooning over someone they just met, and here I am, swept into their ranks by an unwelcome riptide.

At least I know I'm certainly not in love with him—how could I be, after one night?—and I know better than to pin my hopes of a happily ever after on him. That's a step up from the Juliets and Cinderellas. My infatuation with him is no different from my old crush on Brent—and just as meaningless.

The door to a nearby dorm building opens. A pair of security bots emerges. Alfred Winters, Concertmaster of the Orchestra's main ensemble, walks between them, surrounded by a yellow hologram. I'm confused for a moment, then realize it must be his twenty-first birthday. He's too old to remain at Papilio.

He keeps his head held high, and the way the sun splashes across his mahogany features makes him look like a heroic statue. But his stony expression betrays him.

Shock and disbelief anchor my gaze to him. How is the *Concertmaster* aging out? His ranking's never been below 200.

Then again, he never made it much higher than 200 either. I've heard it said that it's better to start low and keep improving than to float consistently with a good-but-not-good-enough number. Especially if Papilio promotes you as a rising star, as they did with Alfred. Though he's a strong violinist, I always found his solos to be labored—technically correct, but lacking the natural charm of a performer like Brent.

If even the Concertmaster can age out, what chance is there for me?

"Al!" Caroline, Alfred's wife, rushes past me. She throws her arms around him and kisses him deeply, her dark locks spilling over her face.

A security bot places its metal appendage on her shoulder. "Miss, please do not interfere with protocol."

"Give me a moment, for Creator's sake!" She shakes herself free, then wraps her fingers around Alfred's.

Alfred places his other hand on her pregnant belly. "Just take care of our baby. I'll be fine."

Is this what happened to my parents fourteen years ago, when my father aged out? Did he hide his despair as well as Alfred's doing? Did my mother weep as Caroline's weeping now? I was a year old when Ronan Lei left… Did my mother hold me up for one last kiss? Did I cry for reasons I didn't understand?

I can't watch as a security bot grips Caroline's wrist and rips her hand out of his. She says over and over that she'll find a patron and take care of him from Adrye.

My parents. My family. This could have been us.

I swallow a lump in my throat. Hearing a giggle behind me, I whirl to see who would laugh at a time like this.

Kiki watches Alfred leave with visible glee. Beside her,

a smirk of satisfaction contorts Brent's handsome face into something hideous. Along with being the leader of the Pit, he's also the main ensemble's Assistant Concertmaster. That means he's about to inherit Alfred's position. Good for him, I suppose, but does he have to be so smug about it?

I turn away with disgust and continue toward the rehearsal hall, wondering how I ever found him attractive.

Vera slams her cane against the floor. "You're rushing again! Play from measure ninety-six."

I struggle not to scowl. I thought the slight *accelerando* I added to the end of the phrase emphasized Butterfly's emotions spiraling out of control, but if Vera disagrees, then it probably sounds out of rhythm. I position my viola, count out a beat, and try the run again.

Instead of letting my fingers fly, I hold back and pay attention to every single note. When I finish, I look to Vera for a reaction.

Vera nods. "Better. But listening to you, I can tell you have no idea what 'Butterfly's Lament' is about. Before tomorrow, I want you to go to the library and look up the song's history and the story that inspired it."

I grit my teeth. "Yes, ma'am."

Vera frowns. "What's the matter?"

"It's just that I know what 'Butterfly's Lament' means."

"Oh?"

"Yes!" Too frustrated to hold back, I say, "I *was* being expressive, but then you told me I was rushing, so I held back. Now you're telling me I'm too precise! What do you want from me?"

Vera crinkles her forehead. "You have to be both in time *and* expressive. Jianguo Shan didn't rush that passage."

"Maybe, but he definitely sped up the reprise."

"Yes, it's acceptable to speed up there."

"Why? Because *he* did?" My frustration threatens to spill out into a long string of complaints, and I do my best to restrain

myself. Vera was once an Artist herself—she should understand what it's like to take a piece and make it your own. Yet she's insisting that I imitate someone else's performance. "Why can't you let me play like me?"

Vera gives me a stern look. "That's enough. Shan's performance was a definitive moment for the viola as a solo instrument, and a fifteen-year-old student has no right to challenge his legacy. You have ten days to make this piece worthy of Master Raucci's ears. I suggest you make the most of them."

Her hologram flickers out, leaving me with no way to argue. Annoyed, I go to stow my viola away.

As I kneel beside my case, I feel a presence enter my room.

"Iris? May I come in?"

The sound of Dámiul's voice brings an excited smile to my lips. Two whole days passed without any sign of him, and I was beginning to wonder if he'd decided he'd seen enough of Papilio—and of me. "Yes, of course."

Dámiul's hologram appears. "I wanted to return earlier, but…I couldn't."

"Where were you?"

"Occupied."

What does that mean? From the shortness of his words, I can tell he doesn't want to elaborate. If I pry, he'd probably just think me rude. I slide my bow into its place and close the lid of my case. The frustration Vera stirred continues churning in my chest.

"Is something the matter?" Dámiul asks.

"Just a bad coaching session."

"What happened?"

"My coach wants me to be something I'm not. I know she's supposed to know best, but I wish she'd listen to me once in a while. Everything here is so controlled, and I thought my one freedom lay in my instrument. But it looks like even *that's* supposed to bow down to someone else's will." Frustrations upon frustrations bubble up, and words spill out of my mouth seemingly of their own accord. "Performers can't judge their own performances. We're playing for the audience, not ourselves, and they're the ones who decide if we're any good or not. That

makes us slaves to their will, and they don't care that I'm pouring all my time and effort into entertaining them."

It hits me that I've just confessed to someone who's practically a stranger, and heat fills my cheeks. I'm glad my hair's fallen over my face, blocking Dámiul from my view.

I catch a holographic glow and realize he's right beside me. My embarrassment deepens. "I'm sorry."

"You have every right to be angry." Dámiul's voice is low. "They do make you slaves—to your Arts, and ultimately, to them."

His words ignite a defensive flame within me. That's what Phers said, but at least Phers knows what it's like to be one of us. What right does Dámiul have to speak like that?

I look over at him. "No matter how hard things get, I'm grateful to be here."

Dámiul kneels beside me, fierceness sparking behind his eyes. "Doesn't it bother you how little control you have over your own life?"

"Sometimes. But I'd rather be at Papilio than anywhere else. I've seen what it's like for those who don't have this opportunity, and I know how lucky I am."

"I'm glad you're happy." Dámiul's expression once again takes on that strange, melancholy tint I can't interpret.

What are you hiding? I wonder.

"I don't mean to be secretive." Dámiul seems to have read the question in my eyes. "But what I know would put you in danger."

"What does that mean?"

"I can't say. Please, just trust me."

It occurs to me that he's keeping his secrets for a very good reason: to keep me safe. If he revealed his knowledge to me, and those who run Papilio found out, they'd destroy me.

Abrupt fear grips my heart, and I shudder. "I believe you."

Dámiul's brows gather with a mix of puzzlement and surprise. Then, his jaw sets, and he looks away.

The fear fades from my mind. Without it, I realize how strange my thoughts and reaction were. I've feared being

expelled, but I've never been *scared* of the school—not the way I was just now.

Dámiul turns back to me. "Remember when I showed you what I was thinking?"

"Of course."

"Many Adryil simply take over Earthling minds and bend them to their will." His eyes flash. "I don't want that to happen to you."

I give him a puzzled look. "But that's a crime."

"Some people think they're above the law," he says dryly. "You mustn't speak of this to anyone here. If Papilio found out you were making the *Ka'risil* doubt their future patrons, they'd send you away. But I want you to be prepared. The Adryil sometimes try to impose their thoughts on each other, so we're taught from an early age to control our minds, although…" He trails off. "The skills are the same for both our kinds. Will you let me teach you?"

I don't know whether to believe him. The Adryil wouldn't try to control our minds when doing so would violate interstellar treaties, would they? Then again, our government surrounded Earth with telepathy-blocking satellites because they didn't trust the Adryil to stay true to the agreements. Maybe I should take a cue from them. "All right."

Some of the tension leaves Dámiul's face. "I'm going to impose a thought on you to show you what it's like. Are you ready?"

"Sure."

I suddenly realize how horrifying the possibility of being brainwashed by the Adryil is. Why would I hesitate to accept Dámiul's offer? I must learn to block my mind now, because otherwise, the Adryil could erase everything I am, leaving only my skills and a few impersonal memories behind. I'd lose my free will.

The horror subsides. I look up at Dámiul, wondering what he's waiting for. "Are we beginning now? We should hurry."

"That was it," Dámiul says. "I just projected my fears into your mind."

Those were *his* thoughts? My face grows cold. I was so sure they came from my own mind. I… I *thought* them myself.

Dámiul leans toward me. "This is where the danger lies: Earthlings can almost never tell the difference between their own thoughts and an Adryil's. The more often an Adryil infiltrates an Earthling's mind, the harder it becomes for the Earthling to recognize the brainwashing."

"That's horrible." I'm still reeling from the fact that my *thoughts* were actually someone else's. I'd expected something more obvious, like when I felt Dámiul's presence.

"I've done it before." Dámiul sounds nervous. "When you thought the Zexa device might be a weapon. I used my telepathy to calm you."

I remember that day. At the time, I'd thought it was my own instinct. And my inclination to trust him, was that a false thought, too? I shake my head in disbelief.

"I wanted you to know I'd never hurt you." His voice is tense. "And… I did it again, just a few minutes ago, when I was telling you that what I know is dangerous."

"When you asked me to trust you?" I think back to the sudden, strange fear that gripped me and the unquestioning way I believed him. No wonder those thoughts felt strange—they weren't mine.

"It was an accident. I knew you had more questions that I couldn't answer, and I was looking for a way to dissuade you from pursuing them." His words rush. "Even when we don't mean to, the Adryil can use their telepathy to persuade others. To us, it's as natural as talking. Had you been trained as I have, you would have known right away that the thoughts were an invasion. That's why I'm telling you about all this now. I swear, Iris, I won't do it again."

I wish I could believe him, but what if he's planting this desire in me? I stand and back away, fear creeping into my heart. Even this thought, *this one*, could be because of him. I stare at him, trembling, still unable to believe what he's capable of.

Dámiul looks at the floor, gloom covering his face. For a full minute, neither of us speaks.

"If you want to deactivate the Zexa device, all you have to

do is press the center and hold it down for ten seconds." He stands but keeps his gaze on the ground. "I won't be able to return, and you'll be safe from me forever. I'll go now." His hologram flickers.

"Wait!" The cry bursts from my lips, and my hand instinctively reaches out to grab his, but my fingers go right through the light.

Dámiul's hologram steadies, and he gives me a questioning look. I withdraw my hand, feeling idiotic for trying to hold onto someone who isn't really here.

"I don't want you to leave." That's all I can come up with. I couldn't stand the thought of losing my connection to him before, and now that I've met him, the feeling is even stronger. He's my one link to the world beyond Papilio. Possibly the only link I'll ever have to Adrye. This thought must be mine, because it's how I felt even in his absence.

Dámiul tilts his eyebrows apologetically. "I didn't mean to frighten you."

"I know."

A pause. "*How* do you know?"

What does that mean? I bite my lip, searching for an answer. "I just do. It's something deeper than reason, something I can't really explain. It's…" I trail off, looking for another way to say what I mean. "It's like how I *feel* the music I play, on a level mere pitch and rhythm can't explain."

"Good. That's what's you need to focus on to separate your thoughts from mine. Are you ready to begin?"

I take a moment to gather my thoughts, reminding myself that I alone know who I am and what I'm thinking. No matter what external forces try to influence me, there's always that kernel of truth within a person, something that's always consistent, even if it's not obvious.

This time, I'll remember it's inside me.

Chapter Ten

Y MIND IS BLANK. COMPLETELY BLANK. IT'S JUST ME and the darkness—nothing else. I should go to my closet and wrap my red scarf around my head. It would look particularly nice if I stuck some feathers in it as well. Maybe I can pluck some from my yellow boa—what? I don't even own a red scarf, much less a feather boa! That thought isn't mine.

The urge to create an absurd headdress fades, and I grimace at the fact that I even considered it.

Dámiul lifts the corner of his mouth. "Well done. I think we're ready to move on to subtler suggestions."

"That wasn't so bad." I sink into my chair, and heaviness weighs down on my shoulders. "I never thought it'd be so exhausting, though."

"It gets easier with time."

I glance at the time on my monitor. It's well past the hour I said I'd give Dámiul. But we've come so far since yesterday, and I don't want him to leave just yet. "How long did it take you to learn?"

"I'm still learning," Dámiul closes his eyes, and a

holographic chair appears beside mine. He takes a seat. "It's one of those things you have to keep working at, or you'll lose what you have."

"I guess it's a bit like the Arts."

"Yes, except the Arts are about beauty, and this is about defending something you shouldn't have to defend." Darkness clings to both his voice and the look in his eyes.

"What's the matter?"

"Nothing."

I gaze at his face. In the short amount of time I've spent with him, I've seen so much rage and intent, determination and curiosity, and behind it all, a deep well of melancholy. I've never known anyone whose expressions and tones could hold so much while saying so little.

He glances at me, and his eyebrows come together with concern. "Is something wrong?"

"It's just… I don't know anything about you."

"There's not much to know."

I should drop my questions. There's nothing interesting about someone so ordinary, even if he's Adryil. The mind training is far more important, and I should concentrate on that.

No, those aren't my thoughts. I throw Dámiul an annoyed look. "Nice try."

He gives me a slight grin. "You're a fast learner." He pauses. "Someday, I'll tell you more about my life on Adrye, but right now, it's more important that we continue your training. I don't know how long we'll be able to keep communicating like this."

"What do you mean?"

"My government's sending me away. I don't know exactly when, but it won't be long. Before I go, I want to know that you're safe."

"What?" I feel as if the floor dropped beneath me, sending me tumbling down a rabbit hole of confusion. "Where are you going? When will you be back?"

"I don't know if I'll return." His jaw tightens. "And I'm afraid I can't say where I'm going."

I glance at his black jacket, the one so reminiscent of a

military uniform. "Are you in the army? Are they sending you to war?"

"Please, Iris, I can't talk about it." His voice is hard, but not with anger. It sounds more akin to fear, or maybe pain. "I don't want to lie to you, but I can't tell you any more. My government doesn't want certain information reaching Earthlings like you, and they're not kind to those who know things they shouldn't."

And they'd punish the person who spilled their secrets. I bite the inside of my cheek. My best guess is that Dámiul is part of some kind of classified government program, and that they're going to send him on a dangerous assignment. When people break the law on Earth, our government sends them to work in the most perilous parts of the world and do the jobs no one else wants. I wonder if that's what's happening to Dámiul, if he's being sent away because he trespassed on Earthling property. But that's hardly a crime worth a death sentence. Even the harshest government wouldn't do that, would they?

I tell myself I'm jumping to conclusions, making dire leaps of logic that barely make sense. Of course he's not talking about dying. Maybe he just means he's going to be assigned to a deep space exploration ship, like the kind that discovered Earth, and that the journey through the unknown reaches of the universe could take the rest of his life.

I feel like I'm plummeting through the endless questions, and my heart is heavy with disappointment. Though I barely dare think it, let alone speak it, it wasn't lost on me that if I make it to Adrye, I might see Dámiul in person someday.

Dámiul's firm expression makes it clear that I won't get any answers out of him, at least not today. And if telling me his secrets would get him in trouble, then I don't want to press him.

"All right." I sigh in resignation. "Then answer this: why me?"

"What do you mean?"

"Hundreds of Artists have been sent to Adrye over the years, and more go each day. What about everyone else? Why are you so worried about training *me* to guard my mind?"

Dámiul leans back in his holographic chair. "Because by giving you the Zexa device, I put you in danger."

I recall what he said about how just by talking to him, I'm breaking interstellar laws. If I'm right about what his government's doing to him for trespassing, then I hate to think about what could happen to me. Still, it's too late for regret. "You didn't endanger me. I did that myself."

"Even so, I see in you something too precious to be destroyed. If the worst should happen, I can't protect you, so I'm teaching you to protect yourself."

His eyes blaze, drawing me in. I don't need him to show me his thoughts to know he means what he says. My mind lingers on the word "precious," and I warn myself not to read anything into it. *Every* life is precious. And without free will, there is no life.

Dámiul breaks his gaze, glancing at the window. "As for the others… The more people know about me, the more likely it is that the authorities will discover my presence. They'd scour the population and punish all who knew I was here. And I could never return." He turns back to me. "I know I've said it before, but please, you can't tell *anyone* about me."

I nod. Before Dámiul left yesterday, he warned me to keep quiet about his visits. I wanted to make an exception for Milo, but Dámiul was adamant. That I have to hide something from my closest friend doesn't feel right, especially since it meant I had to lie and tell Milo that I'd given up on understanding the Adryil device. "I promised I wouldn't."

Dámiul leans forward. "Not even your friend Milo."

I give him an irritated look. "Not even him. Don't you trust me?"

"I'm sorry, I don't mean to doubt you." Dámiul tilts his head. "But he was the only one you specifically wanted to tell, and you don't seem happy about keeping this from him."

"I'm not. But I keep my promises." I brush a stray hair out of my face. "It's just that this is something he'd want to know, and I don't like lying to him."

Dámiul furrows his brow. "Is he your lover?"

A laugh bursts from my lips. "My lover—of course not! He's like my brother!"

Suspicion creeps into Dámiul's expression, which surprises and annoys me. Why would he think I'd lie about Milo? Unless… Could he possibly be jealous?

"I promise, we're just friends." For some reason, those words remind me that I'll probably never know what it's like to share a life with someone. A familiar ache presses against my heart, and I look away. "Though that's probably the closest thing to love I'll ever find. I'm nearly invisible around here."

"Then everyone here is a fool. I can see you perfectly well."

His smile, so full of sincerity, sends a pang through my heart, and I look away. It won't do me any good to dwell on these thoughts.

"Anyway." I turn back to him, looking to change the subject. "Let's continue the training."

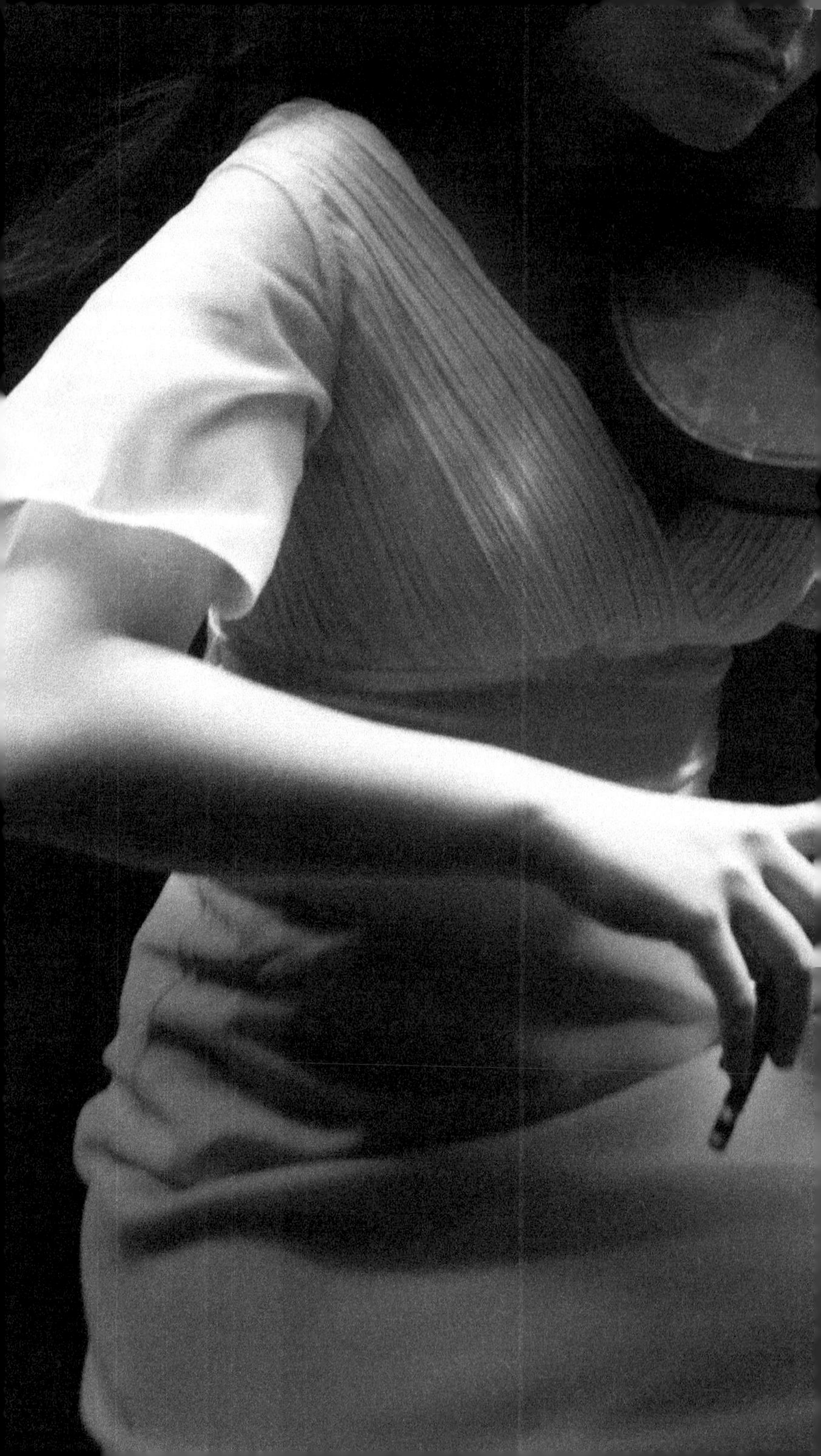

Chapter Eleven

LONE OF WHITE SHINES IN THE CENTER OF THE REHEARSAL stage. Master Raucci stands before it, his hands clasped behind his back. His dark ponytail and black outfit blend into the shadows, making him look like a stern, disembodied face.

I try not to jitter as I wait in the wings for my turn to audition. I tap my fingers against my fingerboard, moving them to the notes of the Lament's run and listening to the faint pitches the strings make. The song is so drilled into me, I do this every time I hold my viola. During rehearsals, while everyone else takes their seats. Backstage, while the others are tuning. And now, in the wings, while I wait my turn.

I know this piece. I know this piece. I know this piece. I might have a better time believing myself if I had, as I led Milo to believe, spent all my time practicing instead of mind training with Dámiul. Which was a *really* foolish thing to do, since each session left me too worn out to do anything but sleep afterward.

My entire future hinges on my ability to attract a

patron. This solo is my opportunity to be seen for once. How could I have let myself become so complacent about it?

I sense Dámiul's presence, and I turn to see his hologram standing behind me. Ever since the night we met, I carry the Zexa device around everywhere in case he appears. His schedule is so unpredictable, even he doesn't know when he'll be able to visit me, and I don't want to risk missing him.

He gives me an encouraging smile. "I just wanted to wish you good luck."

"Thanks." I check to make sure no one's nearby.

"Do you mind if I watch?"

"Of course not." Anxiety squeezes my insides, and I draw a long breath, trying to relax.

"Are you all right?"

"Just nervous. I wish I'd practiced more."

A look of guilt fills his expression. "I'm sorry if I monopolized your time."

"Don't worry about it." Choosing to spend time with Dámiul instead of practicing was my own fault. Each time he asked to appear, I was too curious to say no. After the fifth or sixth time, I should have known better than to think I could be disciplined enough to send him away after the time I allotted him. I'm usually so good about my schedule, but then again, I've never had a distraction from another world. I keep telling myself that I've played the Lament so many times, a few more repetitions wouldn't have made a difference. But with my audition moments away, my mind keeps fixating on the "what-if."

Dámiul puts his hand on my arm, and although I know he's just a projection of colored light, my skin tingles. "You play beautifully. I'm sure the master will love your performance."

"Thank you." It brings me some measure of comfort, knowing that he's here for me. At the same time, the sight of his hand on my arm sends a twinge through my heart. Instead of the warmth of another's touch, all I feel is empty air.

Master Raucci claps his hands, and I turn toward the stage. "Quiet in the wings!" His sharp Italian accent makes everything he says seem more commanding. "First up: Estelle Carver."

Footsteps approach, and I whirl. Fortunately, Dámiul's

hologram is no longer visible. Estelle brushes past me as she makes her way onto the stage, flashing a smile. Unease washes over me—there was malice behind that grin.

Master Raucci extends an arm toward her. "Whenever you're ready."

Estelle places her viola on her shoulder, raises her bow, and strikes the strings. A sorrowful melody floats from her instrument, filling the stage with rich, mournful notes.

My mouth falls open. There's no mistaking the opening of "Butterfly's Lament." *She said she was going to play the Adagio!* Did she know I was playing the same piece? Or is this an unlucky coincidence?

I try to force myself to relax. *It doesn't matter if we play the same song. Now, I'll get to show Master Raucci that I can do anything Estelle can.*

Estelle goes into a dissonant run, the one Vera never stopped scolding me about. My heart sinks. Estelle's fingers fly so effortlessly, portraying the mounting madness with perfection. *How can I compete with that?*

She plays a frenzied variation of the opening melody, high on the A-string, and finishes with a flourish. She keeps her final pose for a few moments to let the last reverberations fade, then relaxes and looks to Master Raucci.

Master Raucci beams. "Very good, Estelle."

"Thank you, sir." Estelle flounces off stage. As she passes me, she whispers, "Did you really think I wouldn't figure out your secret weapon?"

I glare after her, shaking with rage. How could she have known? I never told *anyone.*

"Iris Lei," Master Raucci calls.

I inhale deeply and walk to the spotlight. *I have nothing to lose, and I've played this piece a hundred times. I just have to do it once more.*

Master Raucci nods at me. "Go ahead."

I bring up my viola and lower my jaw onto the smooth curve of the chinrest. In my nervousness, even the familiar scents of varnish and rosin make my stomach turn. The spotlight is so bright, I can barely see Master Raucci anymore.

I glimpse a hologram from the wings. It's Dámiul, watching me with a subtle smile. Closing my eyes, I imagine that I'm playing for him, and him alone. For someone who's seen me play and thinks me brilliant. Someone I find infinitely fascinating, and who, for whatever reason, sees me the same way. Yet chances are I'll never really be with him, and that thought hurts more than I care to think about.

I begin the song, and the soft melody rises from the strings, a plaintive sigh that embodies everything I'm feeling. My fingers move to the melody, smooth and effortless.

So far, so good. I open my eyes as I move into the next section, which involves shifting up the A-string. A section of my highest string feels rougher than usual—frayed with tiny metal threads. The sound comes out choked—how did I not notice before?

I accelerate as I move into the fast section, which takes place primarily on the A-string. Each time my fingers press against the rough patch, I tense a little. The sound coming out of my viola is awful. My string sounded fine when I warmed up earlier. How did it wear out so quickly?

My fingers keep slipping slightly out of pitch. I tell myself to focus and at least finish strong. I start the run—

Snap!

My heart stops. I stare, frozen in disbelief, at my broken A-string, hanging pathetically off the edge of my fingerboard.

A snicker. I look into the wings and see Estelle standing there with a satisfied grin. Fury burns within me. She was behind this—I know it.

Master Raucci clears his throat. "Thank you, Iris. Next time, make sure to check your strings. Next up—"

"Wait!" Glaring at Estelle, I bring my bow toward my remaining strings. "I can finish it."

The notes I need can be achieved through high positions on lower strings and harmonics. Estelle may have lost me the solo, but I won't let her have the last laugh.

I start the run once more. This time, instead of moving onto the A-string, I shift up higher and higher on the D-string. As I near the upper limit, where the distance between the strings

and the fingerboard is greater, my fingers ache from the metal digging through my calluses. When I run out of pitches, I shift back down and place my fingers gently on the strings. Empty harmonics ring out in place of what should have been rich notes. They may be hollow, but at least I'm playing them.

I finish the piece with an angry flourish, then turn to Master Raucci. "Thank you, sir."

Knowing he'll upbraid me for wasting his time, I sweep off the stage without looking back.

Estelle blocks me, a simper spread across her pale face. "Nice playing."

I clench my teeth. "How did you know about my song?"

"Oh, please. It was obnoxiously easy. You were always plucking it during warmups."

My mind flashes back to all the times I let my fingers run up and down the strings while everyone else was tuning. I never played the melody aloud, but if Estelle was watching me...

How could I be so stupid? I push past Estelle and keep running until I reach my case. Kneeling beside it, I realize, to my dismay, that the lights aren't glowing, which means the lock's disengaged. I recall leaving my viola unattended for a few minutes to help Zuriel tune his instrument after he told me he was too anxious to do it himself. He must have been in on Estelle's scheme.

A flicker of light. Dámiul crouches beside me. "Well done, Iris."

"You don't have to say that." I open my case and shove my viola inside.

"I'm sure the master won't blame you for an accident."

"It wasn't an accident!" I slide my bow into its slot. "Estelle replaced my string with one she knew would break."

"What?"

"She practically told me so. I should've checked but... I didn't think I had to." I slam my case shut, my hands trembling. "I'm so stupid."

"You're not." He clenches his jaw in anger. "It's this place—how they rank you, pressure you, pit you against each other...

It's toxic. They use false promises to manipulate you, forcing you into a life of desperation. And for what? Just to entertain them."

That's how Phers talked. I can't stand hearing such words from someone who couldn't possibly understand how grateful I am to be here. "Papilio didn't sabotage me—*Estelle* did. There's nothing wrong with this place, only the people who don't know how to play fair."

"That's the problem." Dámiul's eyes flash. "*Nothing* about Papilio is fair. Your Earthling government knows the Arts are the only thing on your planet worth selling to Adrye, so they let Papilio use you to enrich themselves."

"Don't you think I know that?" Phers was wrong about a lot of things, but he had a point when he said that the school profits off our sweat. And they in turn pay the government in taxes. But leaving would mean bowing down to a miserable future. "What would you have me do? Quit? Where would I go?"

Dámiul is quiet for a moment. "You're right, of course. I apologize. I just believe you shouldn't have to live in a world where survival dictates your life."

"It's more than survival that drives me." I run my fingers across my case's smooth surface. Losing my instrument would break my heart. That would be the worst part about aging out— worse, even, than a life in the tenements. "Performing is what I love. I don't expect you to understand, but music… it's who I *am*, what I believe in. In a way, it's my faith, standing side-by-side with the Creator."

"You really love playing, don't you?"

"More than I could ever say."

Any trace of his previous fury has seeped from Dámiul's expression, leaving only that strange sorrow I wish he'd let me understand. He opens his mouth as though to say something, then shakes his head. "I'm afraid I must go. I'll see you soon." His hologram vanishes.

Without him, the backstage area suddenly seems lonely, with only a few distant viola notes from someone else's audition breaking the silence.

Chapter Twelve

Milo's room is by far the neatest I've ever seen. I should know better than to compare myself to a member of the famously disciplined Ballet, but I could try a little harder to keep my closet in order, rather than slamming the door shut to hide the mess each time Dámiul asks if he can visit.

"Hello, stranger." Milo gives me his familiar carefree smile, which seems incongruent with his strained posture. He sits on the floor with his right leg extended in front of him, positioned on top of a wooden device that seems designed for torture. His heel fits into a groove in the slab of wood, a rubber pouch covering the upper part of his foot. The device forces him to arch his foot into an almost complete C.

I cringe at the sight.

But if the device hurts him, Milo doesn't show it. He flattens his torso on top of his stretched leg. "So you've crawled out of the practice hole. How'd the audition go?"

"Horribly." I plop down in the chair by his desk and recount how Estelle stole my piece, then sabotaged my instrument. "How could she? I've never done anything to her! And now Master Raucci's telling everyone how brave she was for playing 'Butterfly's Lament.' He thinks *I* copied *her!*"

"What a bitch." Milo rises up onto his left knee, keeping his right leg in the device and holding it against his thigh. I can't tell whether the look on his face is in reaction to the strain from the foot stretcher or if he's as angry as I am.

"I was so careful, too." I lean back sullenly. "But she was watching me. Even enlisted Zuriel to distract me so she could replace my string with a faulty one. Why would she do that? I'm not even a threat!"

"Don't be so sure. Your ranking jumped past eight hundred overnight."

I bolt up. "What?" I haven't checked Linx since the audition yesterday, since the last thing I needed was to see Estelle's number take off while mine continued sinking.

Milo nods at my watch. "See for yourself."

I scramble to bring up my profile, and, to my shock, a green 709 sits beneath my name. I finally broke a thousand. Several shout-outs from various members of the Orchestra congratulate me for finishing a difficult piece with a broken string, including one from Brent welcoming me to main ensemble. Once, that might have made my heart flutter, but now, I do my best to ignore it. I still can't believe he was cruel enough to smirk when Alfred left.

It hits me that I'll finally perform on stage—not just in the pit—at the next Spectacle. That's a small consolation next to what Estelle cost me, but it's something. And I'm on my way up—a patron might actually notice me now.

"See?" Milo says. "It wasn't a total loss."

"I guess not." I return my watch to its clock setting, somewhat mollified. Spotting a wooden crescent under Milo's desk, I approach and pick it up. "What's this for?"

"To practice spins." Milo lies on his stomach, raises his right leg behind him, and grabs the end of the foot stretcher. "Put the curved side on the floor, stand on top, and... spin."

Curious, I place the wooden crescent on the ground. "So, what's new with you?"

"One moment." Milo sounds strained; the stretches must finally be getting to him.

I eye the wooden crescent on the floor, then kick off my shoes and put my right foot on it. The device rocks under my weight. I push against the floor with my left foot and twirl.

"Whoa!" My head rushes. Teetering, I put my foot on the ground to stop myself and stumble to a halt.

"Not bad." Milo lets go of the foot stretcher and sits up with a grin. "Next step: toe shoes."

I grimace. Milo's been trying to make me walk en pointe since I was eleven. It's his idea of revenge for the time I dared him to play my viola, then laughed at him for the screeching noises made by his attempts. "Never."

"You say that now, but just wait." His eyes twinkle. "I'll get you into ballet slippers one of these days." He winces as he pushes back the elastic covering his foot. "Floor burn."

He removes his foot from the device, and I, too, wince at the sight of several raw, red sores. "That looks awful."

"It was worth it." Milo stands, his gray eyes bright with happiness. "I did it. I'm replacing Nikolai as Sabina's partner."

"Milo, that's… that's amazing!" A grin spreads across my face.

"Thanks." Milo rubs the back of his neck. "I still can't believe it. I keep expecting Mistress Duval to show up and tell me this was a huge joke."

"I told you this would happen!" I can scarcely keep from jumping up and down. "You're the best in the Ballet."

"I wouldn't say that. I didn't exactly *surpass* Nikolai." Milo twists his mouth into a grimace. "After Mistress Duval called him out, he cleaned up his act, and he's actually been promoted. He'll be doing two featured solos and several duets with Valeria Volkova, who's currently ranked number one in all of Papilio."

"Well, you're still a principal now." I give him a playful smirk. "And you finally get your shot with Sabina!"

Milo gazes past me with a faraway look. "Yeah, I guess I do. Although now that she's so close… I don't want to screw things up."

"If she's got an ounce of sense in her, she'll realize how wonderful you are."

A *ding* emits from the monitor behind him, and words appear across the screen: "All Artists ages thirteen and up, please gather in the Grand Hall for an announcement."

Milo regards the message. "I wonder what it is."

I run through the list of things it could possibly be, then gasp in delight. Every winter and spring, Papilio throws a ball for the students, and the next one's just around the corner. "I'll bet they're announcing the theme for the Semiannual Ball."

"Great," Milo deadpans.

"Oh, stop. You know you want to hear it, too. Come on, let's go!" I slip on my shoes and rush out the door.

Milo groans as he follows. We exit his dorm building and cross the quad along with a number of other Papilians, most of whom chatter excitedly about what they think the announcement's about. From the animated twitters of the girls, everyone else has also realized that it's time for the next Ball.

We enter the Grand Hall. The white double staircases sweeping down into the main floor are already almost full of people. Milo and I grab seats on the bottom step, squeezing in next to a line of Orchestra members. The banister presses painfully into my shoulder, but I barely notice.

Even though I'm a perennial wallflower, I adore the balls. I loved them even when I was underage, performing instead of participating. The fashions, the décor, the dreams they create— the perfect combination of splendor and fantasy. It's enough to dress up like a princess and watch the others find their Prince Charmings while I dream about the day mine will come for me. Just being a part of the beauty makes my heart soar.

The Grand Hall finally fills, and an enormous holographic screen appears in the space above the double doors. But instead of displaying the usual school official, it features a face that makes the entire room gasp.

"Hello, Papilians!" Inna Havener spreads her crimson lips into a dazzling smile. She has a lush, resonant voice. Shimmering makeup accents her dark, regal face, and with the silver

headdress wrapped around her magnificent crown of black hair, she looks every bit as majestic as the queens and goddesses she's so famous for portraying. "Greetings from Adrye! It's so good to see the old school again!"

The hall erupts in cheers, and I happily join in. I can't believe the famous Inna Havener's actually speaking to us, or that Papilio arranged for her to send this message across the universe.

Inna waits for the din to die down. "The administration thought it would be a nice surprise if I announced the theme of the upcoming Semiannual Ball. So when they approached me, I couldn't say no. Before I do, I want you to know that I believe in each and every one of you. You all possess extraordinary talent, and if I could succeed, then so can you."

Another round of cheering erupts. I clap, but my excitement dims. *Most of us won't be her. Most of us won't be anyone.* I glance at Milo, wondering if his words are echoing through his head too. But the cynical Milo from two weeks ago is gone, and the bright-eyed boy I grew up with is back. His smile is every bit as wide as Inna's. Being promoted to principal seems to have renewed his hope, and I'm so glad.

"Thank you!" Inna waves. "Oh, I really am honored to see all of you. You're the future of the Arts—don't ever forget that. And now, for the announcement. On behalf of the Papilio School, I am pleased to announce the twenty-two-sixty-eight Semiannual Ball, which will be held on December nineteenth at eight p.m. right here in the Grand Hall. The theme will be Wintertime Masquerade, a sparkling world of ice and magic." A conspiratorial glint sparks in her brown eyes. "Perhaps this is the night you'll meet your fairytale prince or princess. Thank you for your attention, and have fun!"

The hologram bursts into a shimmer of white sparkles, which transform into snowflakes. Inna reappears to the side, this time at full length. Her white gown glitters as if someone stitched the stars together and draped them over her undulating figure. A celesta chimes an enchanted introduction of broken chords. When she sings out in French, her voice tumbles

through the air like emeralds spilling from a treasure chest. I can only imagine how magnificent she must sound in person, surrounded by the resonance of a concert hall.

An icy palace fades in beside her, its dazzling blue parapets sparkling under a holographic moon. The silhouette of a princess in a long gown appears. She looks around wistfully as Inna's voice rolls through the air. A rush of symphonic instruments rises, and the silhouette of a prince dashes onto the scene. The two lock gazes, then dance to Inna's haunting melody.

After a minute, the scene dissolves. I keep staring at the place the silhouetted prince and princess stood, imagining myself in the princess' place. Whose would be the face behind the shadowy prince? Whose do I dare imagine?

I glance at Milo. If I asked, would he go with me? Not as an actual date, of course, but just so neither of us would have to go alone?

Then, I realize where Milo's eyes are fixed. A familiar golden bun gleams under the lights—it's Sabina, laughing with one of her fellow ballerinas.

Right, he has someone to be in love with. It's only me who needs a friendly date, and it wouldn't be fair to hold him back. I grab his arm and stand, pulling him up. "Ask her." I nod at Sabina.

Milo shakes his head. "I don't know…"

"*Ask her.* You've got nothing to lose."

"Except my pride." He inhales. "But you're right—I have to try." He raises his arm and walks toward the ballerinas. "Sabina!"

Sabina straightens. "Yes?"

Milo stops in front of her, then hesitates. "It would be… it would be an honor if you would accompany me to the Wintertime Masquerade." He takes her hand in his, raises it to his lips, and gives it a gentle kiss.

Sabina narrows her eyes as she considers Milo's proposal. After a moment, she lifts her mouth into a small smile. "I accept."

"Really?" Milo's entire demeanor brightens.

I beam, but sorrow weighs down heavily upon my heart. While Milo's dream has come true, mine remains as impossible as ever. I lean back against the banister, annoyed at myself for

being so selfish. I should be rooting for him. But misery loves company, as they say. And now, I really am alone.

In the corner of my eye, I catch a glimpse of Brent standing at the top of the staircase with his arm around Kiki. Not far behind them, Nikolai pulls Benjamin toward him in a close embrace. I shift my gaze, and it immediately falls upon Estelle, laughing as Zuriel plants a kiss on her cheek. Even that schemer has someone who loves her. Everywhere I look, I see the light of young love falling upon happy pairs, leaving me in the shadows.

A pang runs through me, and I make my way toward the door, weaving my way through the crowd. There are hundreds of eligible young men here. Surely, one of them can take the place of the noble silhouette.

As I try to picture whose face might lie behind the shadow, only one comes to mind. One who haunted me for days when I thought him a hallucination and continued haunting me after I knew him to be real. Those azure eyes, which carry more mystery and depth than the most skillful of composers could portray. Otherworldly, yet present. Unreachable, yet magnetic.

Dámiul: my alien prince.

I almost laugh. The riptide is powerful indeed. Part of me wants to stop swimming away, even though that would mean drowning. But this is ludicrous. I barely know him. The laws of his people won't *let* me know him. And he's so far from me his home star isn't even visible in the night sky. Impossibility upon impossibility upon impossibility.

It's really just me, then. Me and my absurd, stupid, and utterly hopeless obsession with love.

 *111* 

Chapter Thirteen

THE MOURNFUL NOTES OF "BUTTERFLY'S LAMENT" FLOW through me. Even if I'll never perform it before an audience, I can still play it for myself. Here, in my room, where no one can judge me. I close my eyes and imagine I'm on stage in place of Estelle.

I try not to resent her, especially after seeing how her eyes filled with tears of happiness when she learned she'd won the solo. "This is it," she said. "Every patron on Adrye will want to hire me."

I wish I could be happy for her. She's a talented musician, and she deserves the spotlight. Also, with a family depending on her, she needs a job more than I do. But did she have to sabotage me?

A presence sweeps into my room. Knowing it's Dámiul, I smile but keep playing with my eyes shut. I let the music possess my arms, as the madness possessed the butterfly. She leaps up in a final burst of energy before falling into silence.

I open my eyes. Dámiul stands before me with an apologetic smile. "I hope I'm not interrupting."

"No, I'm done for the night." I go to my case and kneel beside it. Maybe I should play the Lament one more time. Or maybe run through a different piece, a new one Dámiul hasn't heard before—wait. I've already practiced for more than two hours, and I'm too tired to keep going. I look over my shoulder. "Do you really want me to play for you? Or was that another exercise?"

Dámiul kneels beside me. "You're getting good at this."

"It's not hard when you pester me about it every single day." I place my viola in the case, internally groaning at having to spend the next hour or so concentrating on my thoughts. I'm exhausted, and as much as I like Dámiul's company, I'm getting tired of his incessant instruction. "Is there a test I can take to pass this mind training?"

"Why?"

"It's just that we've been at it for two weeks, and it's all we ever do when you visit." I also find it unfair that I'm always answering his questions about my life while he remains vague about his.

"It's something you have to keep working at." Dámiul must sense my agitation, because his brow furrows. "Is something else troubling you?"

I should just say it. He may be psychic, but that doesn't mean he should have to read my mind when I can speak for myself. "Dámiul, I really appreciate that you're trying to help me, but after all this time, I still don't know anything about you. And I don't think that's fair."

"I told you, I can't say anything about where my government's sending me."

Irritated, I stand. "You never talk about anything else either. You're from a place that's so different from everything I know, and… I just want a glimpse."

Dámiul gets up slowly, eyes lowered in thought. After a few seconds, he brings his gaze back to me. "What do you want to know?"

Glancing at his black, uniform-like outfit, I chance a question that's been on my mind. "You said you're a student… Are you a military cadet?"

"No, of course not." He tilts his head, as if puzzled that I'd think that.

"Oh. I just thought, since you always wear the same thing, that it's some kind of uniform."

"It is a uniform, but not military." Anger flickers through his eyes. The darkness behind their luminosity makes them all the more mesmerizing. "Conformity is valued on Adrye, and they're not forgiving toward those who think differently."

I look at Dámiul in a new light. Because of his authoritative presence, I always assumed he was a leader among his kind, perhaps training to be an army officer. Now, I get the feeling that he might be an outcast. "That must be frustrating."

"Change will come." His expression hardens. "Whether they like it or not, things won't stay the way they are. Earth's had more influence over Adrye than many of the Adryil would like to admit."

"Oh?"

"Yes. For example…" He trails off and looks around my room. His gaze falls on my monitor, which I left on a display of the Wintertime Masquerade invitation—a static version with Inna's words printed beside her beaming portrait. He nods at it. "Ballroom events have become popular among the Adryil elite. It's the simplest way for us to take part in the Arts without having the skill and dedication of the *Ka'risil.*"

Though I knew about the balls on Adrye, the mention makes me smile. I can't help thinking about how dashing Dámiul would look in a ballroom, with his effortless charm. "Have you been to any?"

"I'm afraid not."

A thought occurs to me. "Do you want to come to this one? I can carry the Zexa device in my bag." As soon as I speak the words, a mixture of nervousness and embarrassment twists my stomach. Yet, I don't regret asking. It's a harmless question. Bringing him to the Wintertime Masquerade is just another way of showing him Papilio.

Dámiul gives me a skeptical look. "I think your peers would notice a hologram among them."

That's not a no. My heart insists that I pursue the notion,

crazy as it is. "We wouldn't have to stay on the main floor with everyone else. The Grand Hall is huge—there are always empty rooms, and you can hear the music from every part of the building."

"Won't the young man escorting you mind that you'd be running off?"

I shake my head. "I'm just going with some of the other girls."

Confusion crosses his expression, and I can only guess that he didn't realize people could go to balls alone. He lifts his mouth into his rakish half-smile. "In that case, I'd be a fool to pass up such an invitation."

A grin spreads across my face, and I break eye contact. Him showing up in holographic form resembles a remote tour more than a date of any kind, but I can't help thinking: *I won't be going alone after all.* As long as I know not to expect anything, there's no harm in daydreaming just a little, is there?

Looking for another topic to talk about before I say something embarrassing, I ask, "Can you tell me more about your world?"

His face brightens. "I can do better than tell you. Let me show you."

Wondering what he means by that, I wait for him to continue. He closes his eyes and knits his eyebrows in concentration.

The holographic image of a globe appears. Blue sea surrounds grand continents, similar to the pictures of Earth I've seen. But the shapes are different from the landmasses I'm accustomed to. And smaller—there's much more water on this world. Most of the planet twinkles with city lights, but some areas shine lush with greenery.

I recognize the image of Adrye. I suppose if I really wanted to learn about it, the library holds a decent amount of information. But I'd rather hear about it from him.

Dámiul gestures at the planet. "It looks a lot like Earth from here, doesn't it? The atmosphere, gravity, and day lengths are nearly identical to your world's."

I regard the globe, which slowly rotates on a slightly tilted

axis. "What about the landscape? I've seen a few images, but not many."

"Here's one that's probably not in your library." He closes his eyes again, and a new hologram appears in its place, occupying the entire space from floor to ceiling. I gasp at the sight. White trunks of magnificent trees stretch from the grassy ground to the cloud-filled sky. But the grass isn't green—it's blue and purple. Red leaves dance on a gentle breeze, crowding the branches so tightly, it's impossible to tell where one tree ends and another begins.

"How tall are they?" I ask.

Dámiul tilts his head, considering, then says, "If you and I were part of this image, we would be as tall as your thumb."

I stare in awe. "What place is this?"

"Rovann, an island near the equator." He closes his eyes again, and the image changes to one of a churning ocean. A wide, disc-shaped building with marigold walls stands on a sturdy column in the middle, surrounded by several smaller versions of the same design. "More of Adrye is covered in water than on Earth, so my kind learned to build in the sea. Those buildings are flat because their roofs serve as landing pads for flying transports. Much of the city lies underwater."

Envy flashes through me at all the wondrous places Dámiul must be able to visit. Even our wealthiest cities and grandest nature preserves look dull compared to his world. It's a small wonder that our government works so hard to maintain the trade agreements that bring pieces of Adrye to Earth.

"Is that near where you live?" I ask.

Dámiul shakes his head. "Nathril is inland." He shuts his eyes for a third time. The hologram of a magnificent city, with strangely shaped skyscrapers—some twisted like antelope horns, some bulbous like stacks of onions, some sharp and straight like blades, and everything in between—reaching toward the slate clouds, appears between us. "This is what it looks like."

I stare in wonder. I've seen holovids of the Adryil capital before, but images on a screen can hardly compare with what Dámiul's created through the holoprojectors.

He opens his eyes and puts his hands on a silver building,

which resembles crystals growing in a gleaming cluster. The building magnifies as he moves his hands apart, and I make out several windows. "My family lives in this building, right about… there." He points to a section near the top.

Considering the size of the windows, the building must be enormous. I'm pretty sure all of Papilio could fit within its walls. "What does it look like inside?"

The hologram morphs into a three-dimensional image of a room. A waterfall runs down one of the white walls, and a long, black table surrounded by silver chairs sits in front of it. The pristine silver floor gleams, and beautiful, abstract designs streak across it in white lines. A chandelier made of what look like tiny sapphires glimmers in the center of the high ceiling.

I gape. "You live *here?* Is your family royalty or something?"

"My father runs one of the biggest corporations on Adrye."

"He must be brilliant."

Dámiul lifts his mouth into a humorless smile. "You could say that."

Hoping he trusts me enough now to answer the question he refused to before, I ask, "What does your father's company do?"

"He sells things the Adryil find irresistible." His words are quick and somewhat sarcastic.

I can tell he doesn't approve of his father's business. "What kinds of things?"

"There's no equivalent for Earthlings."

Annoyance flashes within me. "Dámiul—"

"I'd rather not talk about it."

The sharpness of his tone surprises me. There's something tormented about the look on his face. The only thing I can think of that might cause such distress is that his father deals in something immoral—maybe something like Phers's lotus. My mind itches to know more, but pressing him to talk about something that pains him would be cruel. "Fine."

His eyes take on a regretful tilt. "I know there are a lot of things I can't talk about. I promise, Iris, I have my reasons."

"It's all right." I gesture at the hologram. "Can you show me more of your city?"

He brings back the view of Nathril. "I've lived here my

whole life, but I've barely seen a quarter of it." He points at a wide, pyramid-like structure not far from the silver building. "That's my school. Most of the building is underground."

"Are there many underground buildings?"

"Yes, but most of those structures are very old. They were built before we developed weather machines to tame the rain, and most have been forgotten." He points at a white spherical structure, and the dry smile returns. "This is what they call the Hall of Justice. It should be called the Hall of Sentencing, since most cases are settled within minutes. It's hard to hide the truth when the Justices can read your mind."

I gaze at the alien city before me, which must be full of wonders I can scarcely imagine. My corner of the universe seems pitifully small in comparison. "I'd love to see all this someday." But I try not to hope too hard. After all, hope, like a flame, can burn as easily as it illuminates.

Dámiul places his hand on my shoulder. While I know he's not really here, I sense his touch. "You will."

"You don't know that." I know he means well, but unless he can guarantee that someone he knows will hire me, his words are empty encouragement. Part of me wonders if he *could* help in that way, but asking feels wrong. If I make it to Adrye, I want it to be because I earned my position.

He draws back, and his expression falls. I guess he realized that he made a promise he can't keep, no matter how much he might want to.

Nevertheless, I appreciate that Dámiul cares enough to try comforting me. Not wanting to make him feel bad about it, I decide I might as well indulge a few what-ifs. "Maybe I'll find a patron in Nathril, and I can see you in person again."

"I'd travel across the planet to see you." He looks away. "But I won't be here by the time you arrive."

"It could be another five years before I'm hired. You might be back by then. Even if you aren't, I'll still be on Adrye." I manage a small smile. "Whenever you return, come find me."

"There's no returning from where they're sending me." His voice is quiet. "That's all I can say. If you knew any more, and they found out…" He trails off.

A chill runs through me. The fatalistic note in his voice—it sounds like he's expecting to die. I warn myself not to let my mind wander down that path again. It's a guess based on an assumption, and it's too awful to consider.

What secret could possibly have such dire consequences that he'd fear for me so much? "Found out what? Whatever it is, I swear, I'll never speak a word of it."

Dámiul looks me in the eye. "It's not that I don't trust you. But they're watching." He glances at the ceiling. "I can keep your minders from seeing me while I'm here, but when I'm gone... I don't want anything to happen to you."

"Are you in some kind of trouble?"

He avoids my gaze and doesn't answer, leaving me to once again guess at what could be going on behind his eyes. I wonder if his secrecy is to protect himself more than me, and if by prying, I'm selfishly asking him to put himself at risk. But if that's the case, why wouldn't he just say so?

A stiff silence hangs between us.

Finally, he turns to face me. "Do you want me to show you more of Adrye?" He nods at the holographic map.

The gleaming artificial peaks of Nathril twinkle. Realizing I won't learn anything more from him, I decide not to press further. So I say, "Sure."

Dámiul smiles, but sadness lingers in his eyes. He brings up another building, and I know he's using Nathril's sights to distract me from the fact that he's barely said a word about his own life. Despite what he said before about his life being ordinary, there must be so much more to him.

I wonder if I'll ever understand.

Chapter Fourteen

THE MAIN FLOOR OF THE GRAND HALL GLOWS UNDER A marbled pattern of blue, indigo, and violet lights. Strings of bright, illuminated crystals dangle from the high ceilings, glistening like enchanted snowflakes above us. Between them, lithe aerialists in gleaming silver costumes twirl, snow fairies on white silks. Gowns swirl on the dance floor to the music of the Junior Wind Ensemble, the offshoot of the Orchestra currently performing on the white stage between the two halves of the double staircase. Papilians laugh behind colorful masks, some of which are embellished with feathers and jewels, others of which are minimal and elegant.

Beka puts her cup down with a sigh. Of the six of us who came to this table as single girls, she and I are the only ones left without dance partners. Which she's been complaining about for the past ten minutes.

"I should have chosen a different dress." She looks gloomily at her skirt. "I thought red would help me stand out, but now I think it's scaring everyone off." Admittedly, her sparkling scarlet gown is a bit overwhelming to look at, especially with the large gold mask she paired it with.

Tired of her complaints, I say, "Why don't you just find a boy and ask?"

"Call me old-fashioned, but I'd prefer to be asked. Like in a ballet, you know?" She gazes into the distance with a dreamy expression. "I want to believe my Prince Charming is out there."

"I understand." Knowing that Beka clings to the same kinds of fantasies as I do brings me some comfort. I'm not the only one who wants to see the ideals we portray on stage come to life. All our lives, we're surrounded by the beauty of true love—or, at least, depictions of it. No matter how many times I tell myself to be realistic, my heart refuses to let go of the hopeless dream. I imagine Beka feels the same way.

My mask starts sliding down my nose. I push it up, then give the sides a light squeeze, hoping that'll keep it in place. I'm glad I chose a small, light mask, rather than an elaborate one like Beka's. I picked it because its intricate silver wires, embellished with a handful of white crystals, matched the sparkling belt of my navy blue dress. That it happened to be practical was a bonus.

I look down at the blue ribbon embroidery adorning my long skirt and admire the way the light reflects off the satin. My neck feels strangely exposed, partially because I opted for a strapless sweetheart neckline, and partially because I'm so used to my hair falling onto my shoulders. Now that it's pinned back in a stiff updo, I feel like it's missing.

Beka heaves yet another sigh, and I nudge her.

"Just ask someone already." I nod at a group of boys standing by the edge of the dance floor. "What about one of them?"

Beka hesitates, then stands with resolve. "You're right. Enough sitting around. Here goes..."

She walks over and taps a boy on the shoulder. I can't make out their words, but after a few moments, he gives Beka an admiring smile and takes her hand. Beka flashes me a grin as he leads her onto the dance floor.

I recline in my chair, taking a moment to appreciate the scene before me. All around me are familiar people, and yet each

seems to glow, as if a fairy godmother cast a spell to transform them all into princes and princesses. I don't see Milo, though. I haven't seen him all evening—he's probably in some private corner with Sabina. Looks like the storybook dream he held on to for three years came to life at last. I wonder when—if ever—it'll be my turn.

Beautiful young couples dip and swell with the music, each one wrapped in their own fairytale. Even under the dim lights, Beka's red dress commands attention. Almost as commanding is Estelle's glittering gold gown, which seems especially bright next to Zuriel's simple black suit. Not far from her, Brent and Kiki dance so closely, they almost look like one being.

And here I am, watching. Maybe I should take my own advice and ask someone to dance. But there's no one I'd want to dance with—no one here, anyway.

Brent lifts Kiki's purple, feathered mask and presses his lips to hers. *What must that be like?* All the songs make it sound like one kiss can electrify two people and seal the bond between them. I wonder if I'll ever find out for myself.

I glance at my sparkling silver clutch, into which I tucked the Zexa device. Dámiul said he'd be here, but I've yet to feel his presence. What's delaying him?

"Excuse me, miss, may I have this dance?"

I whirl. Those words weren't meant for me, were they? A boy in a slate-colored suit stands before me, bowed at the waist with his right hand extended invitingly. Though a plain black mask covers the top half of his face, from his forehead down to the tip of his nose, there's something familiar about those gray eyes…

"Milo?" I glance around. "Where's Sabina?"

"Powdering her nose with a gaggle of ballerinas. I'm sure she'll be back soon, but meanwhile"—he extends his hand again—"How about it?"

"You know I can't dance."

"Not a problem. I happen to be a dancer." He takes both my hands and pulls me up. "Come on, Iris. I hate seeing you moping all by yourself. Sabina won't mind—if she even notices."

From the way he tugs at my hands, I can tell he won't take

no for an answer. And it's *Milo*—he already knows what I'm like, so at least I don't have to worry about hiding my awkwardness. Maybe it would be fun to partake in the dancing for once, instead of always watching.

He leads me to an empty spot on the dance floor. The sweet mixture of perfumes swirls around me. The Wind Ensemble strikes up a lively tune, with flute accents that skitter through the ballroom. He puts one hand on my back and keeps his other around mine. I don't know what I'm doing, but I've been watching long enough to know that I'm supposed to put my left hand on his shoulder.

"Just follow my lead." Milo steps back and forth to the rhythm of the music, and I follow.

Easy enough. I do my best to keep up, hoping I won't trip over my heels.

Suddenly, Milo releases one hand and raises his arm. The next thing I know, I'm twirling under it. I gasp in surprise. He takes my other hand again and gives me a playful smirk, then leans forward. I yelp, falling back into an unexpected dip.

"Milo!" I giggle.

Milo grins. "Fun, isn't it?"

The music crescendos, and he spins me out. Imitating what I've seen the others do, I extend my arm, then let him reel me back in. As he leads me through some of his other ballroom tricks, I can't keep myself from laughing up at him.

The song comes to an end, and Milo finishes with one last dip. This time, I manage not to yelp.

I stay down as I wait for the Wind Ensemble to finish their last note, trusting that Milo won't let me fall.

He draws me back up with a smile. "Ready for another?"

"What about Sabina?" I glance around, wondering what's taking her so long.

The music starts up again—a slow song this time. Milo pulls me closer and starts swaying to its beat. "She'll find me when she's ready." He looks past me and shakes his head. "I spent so long dreaming about her, I think I started making things up. I always thought that something more lay behind the snooty ballerina she comes off as, but the more time I spend

with her, the more I realize that, wow, she really is just in love with herself." He meets my gaze. "I can't help wondering if, by carrying a torch for a distant princess… I might have missed the one right in front of me."

I drop my gaze, not knowing what to think. Could he really see me as more than just a friend? And if so… what then?

The song continues, slow and steady. I always imagined that dancing this closely with someone, especially someone as handsome and elegant as Milo, would ignite some kind of spark. Instead, all I feel is gentle affection. It's warm, yet hollow. Though I find comfort in the familiar safety of his presence, my heart is a million miles away.

Or a million lightyears.

"Milo?" Sabina approaches, looking more beautiful than ever in her pale pink gown. Her eyes betray a look of dismay while her lips hold a hopeful smile. "Sorry. I didn't mean to be gone so long."

I pull away from Milo. "Thanks for the dance." I speed back to my table, hoping Sabina didn't take our dance for anything more than what it was.

An invisible but familiar presence materializes beside me, and all thoughts of Milo vanish. "So you made it after all," I whisper. "Give me a minute—I'll let you know when it's safe to appear."

I grab my clutch and rush up the staircase. As expected, the second level is all but deserted, save for a few people going to and from the restrooms. I walk down a long corridor and enter a room at the end. Even after I close the door behind me, the Wind Ensemble's bright notes ring through the walls.

"All right," I say. "It's safe."

Dámiul's hologram unfolds from a stream of light. Instead of his usual black uniform, he wears a white, tunic-length jacket with a crisp silver belt. Lustrous gray lines run down the jacket's center and along the sides of his black pants. If I thought he looked like a prince before, I guess I hadn't seen the best of him yet.

He smiles. "You look lovely."

"Thank you. So do you." *Did I just call him lovely?* Blushing,

I glance around the dim, empty room, wishing I could take him downstairs and show him the gorgeous decorations. "I'm sorry we have to hide in here."

"The music's beautiful, but I guess it's not exactly a ballroom… yet." Dámiul closes his eyes. The room's yellowish lights fade to blackness. A blue-and-purple holographic haze fills the air, and crystal snowflakes float down from the ceiling. Bursts of white light make the world around me sparkle, and I feel like I'm standing in a frozen nebula, surrounded by newborn stars and falling snow.

Dámiul opens his eyes. "It's not quite what I saw downstairs, but I hope it'll do."

I look around in wonder. "That's amazing."

"I'm sorry I was so late. I had a previous engagement that wouldn't end."

I know better than to ask for details. "That's all right. I'm glad you could make it at all."

"I glad you asked me. I think this is the first time, outside of official Adryil-Earthling gatherings, that our kinds have attended a ball together."

Still enchanted by the holographic vision around me, I walk around the room. Dámiul walks beside me. I sense something different about him, though what, I can't pinpoint.

A question occurs to me. I always assumed that his experience with the holograms was the same as Vera's, but he controls the projectors with telepathy, not machines. "When you visit, do you see a hologram of me, like I see of you? Or is it all a vision in your head?"

"To me, both you and this room are a vision only I can see. Sometimes, I just close my eyes and act in my head, but most of the time, I move as if I'm here." He looks down with a slight, self-conscious laugh. "Right now, if anyone were to spot me, they'd see me roaming around an empty room. But in my mind, I'm here with you."

His luminous eyes warm as he gives me a fond smile, and I realize why he seems different. The traces of anger and sorrow I've grown accustomed to seeing in him are absent. For the first

time since I met him, he seems to be all here, not brooding over something he won't tell me about.

Despite all the questions he's answered in the past week, I still know so little about him. He's deft at distracting me with tales of Adryil history and culture. Come to think of it, I don't even know why he visits so often.

I stop. "Why do you keep returning? I'm glad you do, but… if it's Papilio you came for, well, you've already seen everything."

Dámiul continues walking, then stops with his back to me. "I come for you."

He must mean that he comes to continue teaching me to block telepathy. I approach him. "Why is it so important that I learn to block Adryil powers?"

"Because I can't stand the thought of someone erasing who you are and using you as a puppet." He turns to face me, an intense look in his eyes. "I care about you, Iris, more than I meant to, and probably more than I should."

My breath catches in my throat. "What?"

"Every time I see you, I remember why it was worthwhile to break into Papilio. I contacted you for the school of Artists, but now, each time I visit, I leave remembering just you." His expression grows pensive. "The moment you touched the Zexa device, it opened a telepathic bridge between us, and the more time I spent with you, the more I sensed it… there's something wondrous about you. I keep asking the Creator: 'Why her?' If you'd been anyone else, my world would have turned on as I meant it to. But there's something endlessly fascinating about you. I've never known anyone so passionate and untiring, even in the face of darkness and doubt. Though meeting you changed everything, I'm glad I did. I return, day after day, because you're my sanctuary from the insane world I live in."

My heart pounds so loudly, I'm sure he can hear it. No one's ever looked at me the way he's looking at me now, like I'm all he can see. Still, I can't help noticing his vagueness. "You mean the world you won't tell me about?"

"If there were a way to tell you without endangering you, I would confess everything." Dámiul looks away. "I've already confessed too much."

Yet I've never felt more clueless.

The Wind Ensemble's bright song comes to an end. For several seconds, there's only stillness. Then, a lonely clarinet melody rises, accompanied by a soft, steady beat.

Not knowing what else to do, I place my clutch on a nearby table, then offer my hand to Dámiul. "Will you dance with me?"

Dámiul knits his eyebrows. He places his holographic hand on mine, and I swear, I can feel the heat of his touch. "I'm afraid I don't know how to dance."

"Neither did I, until tonight." I attempt a playful smile. "But how hard can it be to step to a beat?"

I raise my left hand to his shoulder, and he places his hand on my back. Entire galaxies lie between us, and yet I feel so close to him. Perhaps it's because we're connected on a level higher than the physical world around us. He's seen my mind, seen me play, seen me at my worst. And yet, he says I'm his sanctuary.

Everything about him—his presence, his words, his eyes— calls to me, and I'm helpless to resist.

I don't want to resist.

I take a step, and he follows uncertainly. Usually so assured, for once he seems nervous. For the first time since I watched Security take him away, I see the vulnerability that lies within him. I'd forgotten that he's just a teenager like me, and that perhaps the same confusion torments us both.

We move slowly with the song, neither of us really leading. We couldn't if we wanted to, I guess, since in reality, we're both nothing but air.

Yet, he's so much more to me.

He was the one who taught me to look within myself for that kernel of truth that's always there. The often subtle but ultimately undeniable instinct that tells me what I know is true. It tells me that no, my feelings for him are not just the fantasies of a hopeless romantic.

Perhaps it's the music, or the stars surrounding us, or the words he spoke to me, but I'm finally able to listen. It wasn't only his face that captivated me the night he entered Papilio—it was what I sensed when he looked at me, and what I continue to see each time we meet. A heart that's both kind and passionate,

that's not afraid of anything. The more I learn about him, the more I want to know. Perhaps, if I dared think it, I could even love him.

I should stop hiding behind my fears and confess as he did. If he sees what I see, his response will tell me so. I draw closer to him and look into his hypnotic eyes. "I just realized I haven't told you—I care about you, too. Every time you leave, a part of me dies a little, because I never know when—or if—you'll come back. You're such a mystery to me, and yet I feel like I know you, and I can't stand the thought of you disappearing."

Dámiul places his hand on my face, his eyes never leaving mine. He leans in, and our foreheads almost touch. For a moment, I forget that he's not really here. "I wish I didn't have to leave you. If I could return…" His expression fills with sorrow, and he turns away. "I think we both dream of the impossible."

Despite the heaviness in my heart, a smile creeps onto my lips. No, I'm not imagining things. I can tell from his words and expressions that, in another life, he might come to love me as well. It shouldn't matter since, as he said, we both dream of the impossible. Ours is a tale that can only end in tragedy. He's forbidden from returning, and I'll probably never leave. Even if I make it to his world, he won't be there anymore. Circumstances and realities separate us, as much as the lightyears do.

But not tonight.

Just for tonight, my prince has come. When it's over, he'll disappear again, possibly forever. Which is what makes this moment all the more precious.

His body may be a trick of light, but his mind, his heart, his soul—those parts that really matter—are here with me.

"Just dance with me," I whisper.

And he does, without another word.

Chapter Fifteen

THE TRAIN STATION LOOKS BLUE UNDER THE FADING daylight. With my viola case strapped to my back and the garment bag containing my concert dress in my hand, I make my way into the low, flat building along with the other Papilians performing in the Spectacle.

I barely notice them. Ever since the Wintertime Masquerade, I haven't been able to take my mind off of Dámiul. No matter how many times I try to dismiss my useless longing, my heart won't stop fluttering each time I remember the way he looked at me.

I descend the staircase leading to the underground tracks, trying to bring my mind back to reality. It's useless to pine, for I can never be with Dámiul. First of all, he's on another planet, and I'll likely never leave mine. Secondly, he's Adryil, and I'm human. And thirdly… I can't actually think of a thirdly. But the first two should be enough to keep my wandering mind from creating any more fantasies.

Yet, the longing persists. The memory of his soft words makes my heart glow in a way I've never known before. I didn't think it was possible to feel both so wonderful and so miserable at once.

I stop at the bottom of the stairs. A crowd of Papilians waits on the wide platform by the tracks. Seeing Milo a few feet ahead of me, I approach him, laying a hand on his shoulder.

He glances at me. "Hey, Iris."

The silver bullet of a train shoots through the tunnel ahead, sending a cool gust howling through the station, and then draws to a halt. On each of the seven cars, a wide screen displays the name of an Art in vivid purple letters. The two Orchestra cars sit at the back, adjacent to the Ballet's. Milo and I head toward them.

Fresh excitement courses through me. I'm going to perform before thousands of Adryil and Earthling elites. Not just in the pit this time, but on a magnificent stage, where they can all see me. And this train is going to take me to that performance hall in Charlotte, a hundred miles east of here.

Milo glances at me. "Excited?"

"I can't wait." I adjust the viola case on my shoulder. "How about you?"

"Yeah, I guess." His eyebrows tilt with worry. "Just a little nervous."

"You'll do great."

"What if I don't?" He stops walking and faces me. "I've poured everything I've got into this performance, and if it's not good enough… I don't have it in me to do any better."

"Come on, Milo." I give him an encouraging smile. "I've seen you at rehearsals, and I think you're the best dancer at Papilio."

"You only say that because you're my friend." He continues down the platform. "I know I'm not as good as Nikolai. Ever since I took his old role, Mistress Duval keeps asking why I can't be more like him."

I rush to keep up with his brisk pace. "That's odd. Just a few weeks ago, she was asking *him* why he couldn't be more like *you.*"

Milo scowls. "That was only because he wasn't practicing. I, on the other hand, have worked until I wanted to drop dead, and I still get nothing but criticism. Sometimes, I wish I'd never

been promoted. Would have a better chance at being hired as a standout soloist than as a disappointing principal."

I recall how Alfred Winters aged out because he was merely good when he was supposed to be great, how he might have been better off remaining a section player. But I refuse to believe that could happen to Milo. "Directors are always hardest on their favorites. Mistress Duval wouldn't have picked you if she didn't believe in you. They're going to love you out there."

Milo attempts a smile. "I hope so."

"Milo!" Sabina waves from one of the train's doors. "Where are you going?"

Realizing we've walked past the Ballet's car, I stop. "How are things going with her?"

"All right, I guess. I'll see you backstage." Milo heads toward Sabina, his expression no more enthusiastic than his flat tone was.

My heart sinks. He seems so unhappy, and even finally winning Sabina over hasn't changed that.

Feeling helpless, I step into the first Orchestra car and enter the storage room. The rod for garment bags looks full. I shove the others aside to make room for mine and hang it up. After checking to make sure the edge with my name on it is facing out, I leave the storage room.

An unwelcome voice assaults my ears the minute I step out. "Can you believe it?" Estelle shows Beka the holographic program projected from her watch. "They even included a note saying that I'm the first Papilian to perform 'Butterfly's Lament.' Master Raucci says all the reviewers are excited to see me—I still can't believe he's letting me play it."

I grimace. If she hadn't known I'd chosen the Lament for my audition, she wouldn't have dared play it for Master Raucci. I've accepted that she stole my piece and sabotaged my instrument, but does she have to act so superior?

Estelle catches my eye and steps in front of me. "What're you looking at?"

In no mood for a confrontation, I simply say, "Excuse me."

"You're not still upset at me, are you?"

Of course I am, but what good would yelling at her do? The competition is over, and I lost. All I can do is be more careful next time. So I settle for throwing her an icy glare and try to maneuver around her.

She blocks me again, and her green gaze bores into mine, sparking with malice. "*I'm* the Principal Violist, and the solo was meant for *me.* You had no right to try to steal it with a stunt piece."

My mouth falls open. "*I'm* not the one who sabotaged someone's instrument." There are a thousand more things I could say to her, but I'm above that kind of arguing.

I push past Estelle without another word, but I feel her gaze following as I continue through the train.

If Milo's still nervous, he doesn't show it on the stage. Equally invisible is any hesitation he has toward his princess. His expression carries such longing as he kneels before Sabina, who stands en pointe before him with one leg raised behind her in an elegant arabesque, that he must still love her.

I recognize the two-measure cue before the violas come in and turn back to Mistress Asif in time for my entrance. As much as I want to keep watching Milo, we're coming up on the big finale. I follow the ebb and flow of Mistress Asif's baton as the music rolls toward its climax. Behind her, the colorful, glowing eyes of the Adryil who fill most of the seats accent the shadows in the audience.

Mistress Asif cues the cutoff. I turn back, eager to see Milo receive his applause. Since it's the end of the Ballet's segment, Nikolai runs on stage first. The audience cheers as he takes his bows. Then Sabina steps forward for hers, and the audience grows a little louder.

Milo walks up center stage. To my dismay, the clapping softens to a polite spattering. He smiles, but I can see the disappointment in his eyes. I grit my teeth, wanting to shake each member of the audience, demanding, "What's wrong with you?"

Valeria runs on stage, and roars of approval greet her. I've always thought she danced like a dull imitation of the great ballerinas who came before her, with no personality of her own. But audiences are fickle, and they're easily fooled by the kind of crowd-pleasing antics Valeria likes to pull. I don't know enough about dance to judge Milo's technique, but I found his performance far more captivating in its sincerity.

Mistress Asif motions for us to leave the pit, and I exit with everyone else. I enter the backstage area. Seeing Milo ahead, I run to him.

"Milo!"

He doesn't react, and I run faster.

"Milo, wait!" I grab him by the shoulder.

He shakes me off and keeps walking. "Leave me alone."

"You were fantastic. Really—"

"What do *you* know?" He stops and faces me. "Everything is all fairytales with happy endings to you. I see things for what they are, and the fact is, I'm no good. I just wish I realized it before I wasted all that effort."

Stunned by his anger, I watch him walk away. I want desperately to cheer him up, to tell him that this audience is blind and that he'll do better next time, but how can I talk to him when he seems determined to see the worst in everything?

"Iris?"

Hearing Dámiul's voice in my head, I tear my eyes away from Milo's retreating form. Maybe he'll listen after taking some time to recover from tonight's disappointment.

"Give me a minute." I go to the room where the instrument cases are stored. As I hoped, it's deserted. "All right, it's safe."

Dámiul's hologram flickers on before me, and lines of light distort his image. For several seconds, he struggles to appear. This is strange—he's never had trouble before. His hologram steadies, and my worry increases.

Something's terribly wrong. He looks haggard, pale, as if someone has drained the energy from him. His eyes have lost some of their luminosity, appearing a duller shade of blue.

"What's the matter?" I ask.

"Nothing. I'm afraid I must, once again, apologize for being late." Even his voice sounds weak.

Worried, I put my hand on his holographic arm, hoping the illusion of my touch will comfort him. "Are you okay?"

"I'm just tired."

Before I can respond, the door to the instrument room bursts open. Dámiul flickers out erratically.

Beka, who stands in the door, gapes at the spot where he just stood. "What was that?"

"What?" I pretend I don't know what she's talking about, but any confusion she sees on my face is real. Dámiul's always been quick to disappear before—what happened just now?

Beka shakes her head. "Never mind. Master Raucci wants to see you in Office B. *Now.*"

"Why?"

"Just come with me."

Still holding my viola, I follow her toward the offices at the back of the backstage area. *What's going on?*

The door to Office B opens slightly. Beka waves her hand at it, gesturing at me to enter. I slip in through the narrow opening, giving her a puzzled look, but she says nothing. The door slams shut.

"Good, you're here."

I hear Master Raucci's voice and whirl. "Yes, sir?"

A retching sound catches my attention. My eyes grow wide at the sight of Estelle curled up in the corner, shaking as she holds an opaque white bag to her mouth. Tears stream down her cheeks, and she struggles to breathe. *What's wrong with her?*

"Iris!" Master Raucci snaps his fingers in my face. "Do you still have 'Butterfly's Lament' memorized?"

"What?" I blink, not understanding.

"As you can see, Estelle is in no shape to perform." His voice is calm, but the way he taps his fingers against his arms betray his anxiety. "The audience was promised 'Butterfly's Lament.' Do you have it memorized?"

My eyes wander back to Estelle. She throws me a look of pure hatred, but can't seem to speak between her sobs.

He wants *me* to go on in her place. Alone in front of

thousands. Even though I can't believe what's happening, I find myself nodding.

"Good." Master Raucci relaxes visibly. "You have five minutes before the Octet finishes, and then it's time. Get ready."

"Y-Yes, sir." Still stunned, I turn toward the door.

"*She's behind this!*" Estelle's cry buzzes in my ears.

I spin toward her. She seems ready to melt the flesh off my face with her glare.

Master Raucci approaches her. "Now, now, Estelle. A panic attack—"

"*She did this to me!*" Estelle points at me.

"How dare you?" I clench my hand around my instrument, infuriated by the false accusation. "After everything you did, how *dare* you?"

"Iris!" Master Raucci claps his hands. "Go!"

I try to ignore Estelle's hysterics as I leave the office. The door shuts behind me, blocking out her retching and sobbing.

This is beyond insanity. Estelle, who's always been so haughty, fell to pieces five minutes before her moment of triumph. How can that be? I've heard of it happening to others in the past, but I never imagined she'd join their numbers. All this time, was her arrogance a mask, hiding a desperate, terrified performer? If so, then she's a spectacular actress. She must have fooled Master Raucci too, or he would have prepared an understudy. Instead, he turned to me—*me*—to take her place. I should be excited, but too much terror fills my heart. What if I ruin it? No one would hire the Artist who botched the most famous viola solo in the world.

I automatically return to the case storage area and begin tuning my instrument. My mind can't seem to focus on anything other than the familiar, mechanical motions of plucking my strings and twisting the pegs.

Colored light flickers beside me, and I know it's Dámiul's hologram. My mind is too blank to react. I just draw my bow across the C and G strings, making sure they harmonize.

"What was that about?" he asks.

"I'm playing the Lament." My two lower strings ring out in

a perfect fifth. I move on to the middle ones. "I… I'm replacing Estelle."

"That's fantastic." His face brightens.

"I-I don't know if I can do it." Another perfect fifth. I'm scarcely aware of what I'm doing as I move on to the last two strings.

"I've heard you play this song a dozen times. Believe me, you can."

He sounds sincere, but his words don't impact me. I continue tuning my instrument because it's the only thing I know how to do. A high-pitched *beep* sounds over the comm, indicating that it's time for the next act to take their places.

Which, in this case, means just me.

I approach the door, and it hits me: I'm about to walk on stage and play a legendary solo never before performed by a Papilian. Everyone's anticipating a shattering performance from the great Estelle, and instead, they're getting a section player who barely made it into the ensemble. My face goes cold, and I freeze, suddenly nauseous.

Dámiul reaches toward me. "Don't be afraid. I know you can do this. And I'll be there for you."

I sense his touch on my shoulder and nod. Inhaling deeply, I walk toward the wings. Scared as I am, I can't back out.

The audience is waiting.

I'm suddenly aware of the Zexa device in my skirt pocket, and I feel Dámiul's presence follow me even though I can't see him.

My breath shakes. If I'd come prepared, sparkling in a soloist's gown instead of shrinking in my simple black concert dress, I might feel slightly better. The audience claps for the Octet. There are so many people, staggeringly many, and I've never even played for them outside the Pit. How can I face them alone?

I'm not alone. Dámiul's with me, and I'm playing for him.

The Octet walks off, but I barely see them. This fear—I wonder if it's anything close to how Butterfly felt when she learned her prince was dying.

The audience quiets. A soft beep from behind me tells me it's time. I stride onto the stage, telling myself the story of Butterfly to distract myself from the thousands and thousands of eyes staring at me.

Once upon a time, there was a magic kingdom where people could transform into the animal closest to their souls. Butterfly was as beautiful and lively as her wings would suggest.

I stop center stage. The lights around me dim, and a watery spotlight surrounds me.

In a kingdom above the clouds, a prince looked down and was enchanted by the girl's loveliness. He broke the laws of his kind to descend to Earth.

Like how Dámiul violated interstellar laws to enter Papilio. As I bring up my instrument, I catch the glimmer of a faint hologram in the wings and know it's him.

They fell in love at once, but after three days, the prince's strength began to fade. An old prophet told Butterfly that the prince had to return to his kingdom—or he would die.

That's where the Lament begins. I think of Dámiul and how a part of me wants to cry each time he leaves, since I can never know for sure if he'll return. I play the opening melody, pouring my longing into the strings.

The prince's father sent his guards to bring his wayward son back. Butterfly watched, helpless, as they took her love away.

I recall how powerless I felt when Security dragged Dámiul out of the quad. Because of them, I'll never feel the warmth of his touch. My chest tightens, and I dig my bow into the strings.

Every day, Butterfly looked to the clouds. She could see her prince's face and knew he loved her still. But no matter how she cried, no matter how he fought the guards, he couldn't return to her.

No matter how I dream, no matter how fierce his spirit, Dámiul will never return to me. If I tried to tell someone how much that hurts, my words would surely fail. So I let the melody speak for me, and I mean every mournful, sighing note.

One day, unable to stand the heartache, Butterfly transformed into her namesake creature and flew toward the clouds, determined to be with her prince again.

My fingers flutter up and down the strings. Around and around she flies, losing pieces of herself as she reaches for the impossible. The aching in my heart deepens. I can reach for Dámiul all I want, but my hands will only grasp empty air. That doesn't mean I won't keep trying, won't keep acting like he's here.

But he's a ghost, and I'm playing make-believe. I almost want to laugh as I share in Butterfly's madness. Why, Creator? Why send me someone I can never have?

She kept flying until her heart gave out. With her dying breath, she flapped her wings, soaring up in one final burst of energy.

My finger leaps up to the Lament's final note on the highest string, and I hold it out as long as my bow will let me, letting its wail tell the world how I, too, reach in vain.

She fell to the ground, lifeless.

I lift my bow. Even the most valiant of efforts can't last forever. I wait for the reverberations to die down and realize that my cheeks are wet.

I did it. I relax and look to the audience for a reaction.

Silence.

Clapping hands—one person, alone but enthusiastic. More join in, and the thunder spreads through the auditorium. I can hardly make out the "Bravas" of the Earthlings through the Adryil's enthusiastic cries of *"Toká!"*

"Iris…you were amazing." Dámiul's breath of a voice feels warm in my head. I look to the wings, but he's no longer visible. In his place, Master Raucci grins and applauds with the audience. Vera, here in holographic form, stands beside him, her face glowing with pride. Master Raucci must have called her at the last minute.

I bow. As delighted as I am that the audience appreciates me, I can't erase the aching in my heart.

Enough, Iris. I've indulged my mythical tragedy, and it's time to return to the real world.

Master Raucci motions for me to approach, and I leave the stage. As soon as I reach the wings, he spreads his arms. "Brava, Iris! Not since Katarin has an audience made a noise like that!"

"Thank you, sir." My mind is still in a haze, dulling the joy I should feel.

Vera beams, almost sobbing with happiness. "That's my Iris!"

I walk backstage. Several Orchestra members congratulate me, and I nod, attempting to look appropriately thrilled even though I'm still reeling.

"*This* was her plan!" Estelle's shrill voice is audible even through the office's thick walls. "*She poisoned me!*"

I ignore her and continue on my way. A sudden emptiness hollows my heart; Dámiul's presence is gone. It's more than the usual absence—it's desolation. He wouldn't leave without saying goodbye unless it was urgent, especially now. Something on Adrye must be pulling him away from me.

Butterfly's lament may be over, but mine's just beginning. If Dámiul really disappears this time, I may find myself crying to the stars, as Butterfly cried to the clouds.

Chapter Sixteen

I STARE AT THE ZEXA DEVICE IN MY HAND, WONDERING IF something's wrong with it. Three days have passed since the Spectacle, and there's been no sign of Dámiul. Did I accidentally change the device's settings? Even if I had, and Dámiul tried to contact me, I would still feel his presence, wouldn't I?

I'm sure he'll be back as soon as he can. My own thoughts ring of false reassurance. I keep recalling how weak he appeared. Is he sick? What if he's dying on Adrye?

I fling the thought away. *I'm being ridiculous.* He's probably caught up in something. Or maybe he left for his mysterious government assignment. But if that were so, wouldn't he at least say goodbye?

I need to stop this. I've told myself time and time again that all this longing and dreaming can't lead to anything good. What's the sense in yearning when you know you can never have what you seek? Even if I were sent to Adrye tomorrow, I still couldn't be with him. Maybe, by some miracle, he could find me there, but he'd still be called away

I'd find myself right back here—alone and lost, like the sole survivor of a shipwreck at sea.

Why is it that even though I've just experienced the greatest triumph of my life, all I can do is think about a boy? I should be worrying about how I'm going to keep up the momentum from the Spectacle, not about where Dámiul is. But no matter how much I try to bring my head back to where it belongs, I can't take my mind off of him.

It won't do me any good to lie around pining. I sit up in my bed. The schedule on my monitor tells me I have the next hour free. I drop the Zexa device in my pocket and slide off my bed. It occurs to me that Dámiul's not the only one who disappeared after my performance; I haven't heard from Milo since the Spectacle either.

I've tried messaging him about a dozen times, but he hasn't responded. Not that I've had much time to worry about it— Master Raucci has been keeping me busy. I've rehearsed with more small ensembles—quartets, chamber orchestras, and such—in the past few days than in my entire life before that. Apparently, he wants to find more ways to showcase my skills. Could Mistress Duval be doing the same with Milo? Or has he been in a practice hole of his own, like I was in the days leading up to the audition?

Wondering if he responded to my messages yet, I bring up my Linx profile. The green number 13 beneath my name makes me grin. From over a thousand to the top 20—I can scarcely believe it. I've never heard of anyone's ranking rising so fast, and every patron in that audience now knows who I am. Typically, a patron will watch an Artist in at least three or four performances before deciding to hire. If I can keep my ranking at these stratospheric heights, I could be on Adrye by this time next year.

I glance over my inbox, which is full of congratulatory messages. Milo left a shout-out on my profile, but hasn't contacted me otherwise. Wondering if he posted anything, I go to his profile. To my dismay, a red 144 sits beneath his name. That's still decent, but a far cry from what he was hoping for.

And for a principal, having your ranking decline after a show can be disastrous. This must be killing him.

There's nothing on his profile since before the Spectacle. Maybe he knew his number would sink after the lukewarm reviews of his performance and has been avoiding Linx altogether. I check the time. It's getting close to noon. I might be able to catch him for lunch.

I leave my room and head to the Ballet's sector.

As I approach the Ballet's dormitory, I see Sabina ahead and wave, calling her name.

She turns to face me, eyebrows raising. "Yes?"

"Have you seen Milo?"

She purses her lips. "No. He's missed every rehearsal and coaching since the Spectacle. I've tried to get him to come, but he keeps ignoring me."

My spine tenses. The reviews must have affected him more than I thought. "I'd better go talk to him." I turn toward the dorm.

"You won't find him in his room. I saw him heading for Dogwood earlier."

"What?"

"That's where he's been spending his time, though at least he's been returning before curfew." Sabina sighs. "You're a good friend of his, right? Maybe you can convince him to return to his assignments before the school expels him. He won't listen to me."

"I'll do my best." I rush down the street, heading toward the West Gate. The Milo I know is too dedicated to skip anything, let alone miss three whole days. I don't blame him for needing a break after pouring so much effort into the last Spectacle, but what he's doing could destroy any chance he has.

By the time I make it to the West Gate, I'm breathing so hard, I barely hear the security bot's customary reminder about curfew. I speed through the town, retracing the steps Milo and I took last time.

The sun highlights every dying vine and dried-out blade of grass surrounding the stained tenement walls. With the winter-gray hands of nature seizing the buildings and the

wind-chilled silence in the streets, I feel like I'm entering a ghost town. Everyone must be at work in the manufacturing plant. I start toward the building where Milo's family lives, then freeze. He didn't want to speak with them before because he was too stressed. I doubt he'd go to them now, when he's neglecting the school they worked so hard to get him into.

The only other place I can think of to check is the housing project where I met Phers. I hope Milo's not there. As I enter the building, I tell myself I'm going in to make sure he *isn't*, not because I think he is.

"Milo?" I make my way forward. Most of the doors stand open, and every room I peer into is empty. I wonder if they leave their doors open because they have nothing worth stealing.

The chatter of voices drifts toward me from the end of the hallway. Recognizing Phers's voice among them, I break into a run. When I reach the open door of the cramped room, I find Phers sitting on the floor, along with several young men and women, each with either an opaque cup or a cigarette in his or her hand.

"Hey, you're back!" Phers raises his eyebrows at me.

Spotting a head of blond curls, I feel my face fall with dismay. "Milo!"

Milo turns toward me. His eyes are glazed over, and his slouch is so unlike him, I briefly wonder if I've got the wrong person. "Oh, hey Iris." He holds his cigarette out toward me. "Want some?"

"What are you doing here?" I step over someone's legs to approach him. "It's the middle of the day!"

He puts the cigarette to his lips. "So it is."

I feel a hand on my shoulder and turn to see Phers leering at me. "C'mon, pretty lady. Make yourself comfortable." He presses down on my shoulder, trying to force me to sit.

"Get your hands off her!" Milo jumps up and shoves Phers.

Phers holds up his hands. "Cool it, man."

Milo's eyes snap with fury. "Touch her again, and I'll beat the shit out of you."

"I'm all right," I say, startled by Milo's sudden and unwarranted violence. I've never seen him like this before.

He grabs my arm and pulls me toward the door. "You shouldn't be here."

"Neither should you!" I let him lead me out of the room, then shake him off as soon as we're in the corridor. Someone shoves Phers's door, which swings shut with an unceremonious *click*. "What's going on?"

Milo shrugs. "I'm finished. Thought I'd give it a few days just in case, but my mind's made up. I've already started filling out the resignation docs."

"You're *quitting?*"

"Yeah." He leans back against the wall. "I'll never make it anyway. Whether tomorrow or in four years, I'm going to end up here. Might as well spare myself the extra debt."

"What about your family? They're counting on you!"

"Sucks for them." He gives a limp shrug. "My parents hate me for blowing my big break. Sent me a message telling me how disappointed they are. They sacrificed my sister's chances by spending all their money on getting me into Papilio first, so they can't forgive me for failing them. They're ready to disown me anyway. Well, now they can pull the trigger."

Sorrow pricks my heart. How could his parents say that? "But… But you're a wonderful dancer."

Milo examines the cigarette in his hand, avoiding my gaze. "Have you seen the reviews? 'Decent,' they said. And that's all. I gave them *everything* and got a collective shrug in response. Do you know what it's like when your best isn't good enough?" He angles his mouth in a humorless smile. "No, of course you don't. You're gifted. I'm not, and… I accept that."

"I'm not gifted. I—"

"You don't even realize how talented you are, do you?" Milo gives me an incredulous look. "Estelle had good reason to be afraid of you. Your playing *speaks* to people. We all saw it on stage. I, on the other hand, have nothing but technique. Maybe a little flair. But no matter what I do, something's just missing."

"That's not true! Mistress Duval—"

"Mistress Duval picked me because I'm better than the other guys in the Ballet, but that doesn't make me worthy of a patron." He drops his cigarette and stomps on it.

</p>

"Come on, Milo." I want to shake him. "You'll do better next time."

He stares at the ground, a look of pain distorting his face. "I can't do this anymore. That school… it's driving me insane. I used to come here because it was the only way I could escape. Each time, part of me wanted to stay. But I had no choice—I had to go back or lose everything. Now that I know it's going to be lost anyway, I can finally let go."

I bite my lip. I knew he had his anxieties, but I never realized how deep they ran. "Why didn't you tell me?"

"I knew how you'd respond. 'Oh, just keep trying. Everything will turn out okay.'" He lets out a humorless laugh. "Isn't that right?"

My eyes sting. Who's this bitter young man before me, and where's the friend I knew so well?

Milo softens his expression. "I'm sorry. I know you're just trying to help, but there's nothing to help anymore."

I blink to keep the tears from spilling. "I thought you loved dancing. Forget patrons and debts and rankings… Isn't the stage enough?"

"If we were anywhere else…" Milo's expression hardens. "It doesn't matter if I love my Art. Numbers and reputations are all that count. It's time to cut my losses. You're not going to change my mind, so you should just go."

Does he realize what he's saying? If Milo drops out, I'll barely see him anymore. "What about me? What about Sabina? How can you leave us?"

"Sabina will get a new partner soon enough. As for you…" Milo turns away, angling himself so I can't see his face. "I can't be the person you want me to be. I'm pretty damn worthless."

"Don't talk like that. You're family to me, and I love you." I reach toward him, but he steps back.

"Come see me now and then. I won't be hard to find." He turns toward Phers's door. His face has become an inscrutable mask, and I'm at a loss as to how to answer.

I should say something. There must be a way to convince him to come back. He said it himself—he loves ballet. It's Papilio's system that's getting to him. I should have seen it. If

I had, maybe I could have been there when he needed me. How could I have been so blind?

Milo enters Phers's room, shutting the door behind him. I stare in silence. I should go after him—drag him out of this place and shove him back where he belongs. But if he won't listen to me, then all my pushing won't do any good.

Still, Sabina said he's been returning before curfew. That means part of him still wants to stay at Papilio. It's possible that between now and this evening, whatever kept him from burning his bridges before will bring him back again. I'll return tonight, armed with actual arguments. Right now, my brain seems too paralyzed to come up with anything convincing. Maybe if I bring Sabina, the two of us can convince him.

But what if the pressure's really too much? I recall Estelle's panic attack; she looked like someone had snapped her mind in half. Maybe Milo's afraid something like that will happen to him. Or maybe it already did, and he didn't tell me.

Dried weeds crunch beneath my boots as I walk down the street, which seems haunted by the ghosts of fallen dreams. Surely, this can't be where he was meant to end up—or anyone, for that matter. Yet for most Papilians, this is their future.

A flame ignites within me, and I clench my fists. Milo was right—we're all trapped. They give us two choices: do as they say or rot in the tenements. There's no space for anything else in this bleak world.

Dámiul said they drive us to desperation so they'll get better performances. Now, I understand why that made him so angry. If this place weren't so relentless, maybe Milo wouldn't be so miserable.

How would I change things if I could? Is it even possible? Or are we all cursed by the very things that motivate us? Take away patrons and rankings and Spectacles, and I would still cling to my viola, searching for a way to show the world what I can do. The music commands me, and I'm helpless to resist.

I reenter Papilio, stopping briefly to let a security bot confirm my identity, then head back to my dorm.

When I reach my hallway, I find the door to my room open. Surprised, I dash forward and catch the doorframe, swinging inside. Two security bots wheel around, rummaging through my drawers. A minder's hologram stands between them, watching them with a severe expression.

I approach tentatively. "What's going on, sir?"

The minder turns toward me. "Estelle Carver filed a formal complaint against you, stating that you poisoned her prior to the last Spectacle."

My jaw drops. "She's lying!"

"That may be, but all complaints must be investigated." The minder's eyes relax. "Look, if you didn't do anything, you have nothing to worry about. We're not here to entrap you."

I nod. They can turn my room inside out—they won't find any poisons here.

One of the security bots flashes a hologram that says: "Clear. No contraband found."

"Good," the minder says. "Search her person."

My heart jumps. The Zexa device is in my pocket. I turn to run, hoping I can get away long enough to hide the device.

A metal rope wraps around me, pinning my arms to my sides. I scream and stumble to the ground. The rope coils, forcing me to turn around, then pulls me to my feet.

I struggle to escape. "Let me go!"

"It's not going to hurt you." The minder sounds exasperated.

Lines of green light shoot out of the rope binding me. I keep twisting, trying to find a way to free myself.

"Object detected in subject's pocket," the bot says in a mechanical monotone. A small claw extends from its side.

I can't stop it—its grasp is too tight. I squeeze my eyes as the claw reaches into my pocket.

"What's that?" the minder asks.

"Unknown Adryil technology." The bot keeps its rope coiled around me.

I open my eyes, clenching my jaw to keep my voice from quivering. "I can explain—"

"Don't." The minder's sharp voice stops my words. "You are in illegal possession of alien technology. The school is obligated to turn you over to the local authorities." He turns to the machine holding me. "Bot A-Fifty-Three, bring the subject

inside and keep her confined to her room. Bot A–Fifty-Four, take the contraband to the Security Center."

Both machines beep with acknowledgement. The second bot takes the Zexa device—my one connection to Dámiul— from the first.

"You can't!" I writhe within the first bot's rope. "I—"

"Save your breath." The minder's hologram disappears.

The rope around me pulls forward. The bot drags me into my room. The second bot retracts its claw, and the Zexa device disappears into its metal body.

Without that machine, I'll never see Dámiul again. Any chance, any hope of even a goodbye is gone. I'll surely be expelled for having it. I'll probably be jailed too—maybe for the rest of my life. A painful mix of dread and misery strangles my lungs, suffocating me. I've lost Dámiul, I've lost my music, and I've lost my future.

I've lost everything.

Chapter Seventeen

ESS THAN AN HOUR HAS PASSED SINCE THE LAST TIME I was in Dogwood, and yet here I am again, but this time in the severe interrogation room of the police station. When Mistress Medina first appeared in my room and told me I was to be sent here for questioning, I thought I'd be dragged out as Dámiul was. Thankfully, they let me walk, escorted by two security bots. I felt all the eyes in Dogwood watching me as they marched me to the station.

I expected to be intimidated by the officer they sent to question me, but instead, I find myself facing a kind-eyed woman with a loose bun that looks like spun sugar.

"Hello, Iris." She leans her elbows on the metal table between us. "I'm Officer Klassen. Do you know why you're here?"

I nod tensely, expecting that any moment, she'll tear away her sheep's mask, revealing the wolf beneath.

"Where did you get the alien device?" Her voice remains silky. "Did you find it on campus after the Adryil intruder broke in?"

I don't want to tell her that I spoke with Dámiul because if word got back to his planet, that could get him in trouble. But I don't have to lie completely either. "Yes, ma'am. It was wedged into one of the sculptures on the Wall of Glory. I… was curious. I'm sorry. I know I should have turned it in."

"Did you know what it was for?"

"No, ma'am. I couldn't read the Adryil symbols."

"Understandable. Did you do anything with it while it was in your possession?"

"All I did was carry it around."

Officer Klassen smiles. "Like a talisman?"

"Something like that."

"And it never activated? Never made any sounds or displayed any lights?"

"Never." I twist my fingers under the table, but the lie is calm on my tongue.

"Good." Her lips remain curved, and there's a trace of satisfaction on them. But not the malicious kind Estelle displayed after the audition. A contented kind, as if I'm giving exactly the answers Officer Klassen wanted.

That confuses me, especially considering how sternly Mistress Medina spoke the night Dámiul was captured. I thought an officer of the law would be harsher.

I expect her to ask further questions, but instead, she stands and says, "Wait here." She leaves, closing the door behind her.

Time ticks by, though I have no way of telling how much. As I wait, my mind fills with thoughts of Dámiul. He's the reason I'm here. This must be what he feared would happen, why he kept insisting that I keep his presence a secret.

I should resent him for putting me in this position, but I don't. Neither do I regret encountering him. I can't believe I'll never see him again, never look into his luminous eyes and marvel at all the secrets they hold. If only I'd had a chance to say goodbye. If only I knew he was all right. No matter how many times I tell myself to stop worrying, I can't dismiss the strange weakness that weighed down on him the last time we met. Or forget that he might have been sent on a secret, possibly dangerous assignment, and I'll never know what became of

him. I'll spend the rest of my life with a part of myself missing, with no way to ever get the answers that could fill the chasm Dámiul left behind.

A wave of grief rolls over me. What if he hasn't left yet and tries to contact me, only to receive silence in response? Would he think I abandoned him?

A light appears and flickers into the holographic form of Mistress Medina. She stands on the other side of the table with her hands clasped behind her. "I'm disappointed, Iris. I told you to come to me if you found anything related to the Adryil intruder, and yet you concealed what you discovered."

"I'm sorry." Anxiety snakes through me, and I brace myself for the inevitable. She's going to tell me I'm expelled, and it will take all my self-control not to break down in tears.

"Fortunately, aside from this incident, you've been a model student." Mistress Medina's tone is matter-of-fact. "While you are guilty of illegal possession of Adryil technology, the fact that you did nothing *more* than possess it mitigates the severity of your crime. The Papilio School has worked out a deal for you with the Township of Dogwood. Taking your youth and clean background into account, the authorities have agreed that the most suitable punishment is a fine. The school will pay on your behalf, and the amount will be added to your student debt, to be paid back along with your tuition and other routine costs."

I look up, startled. "You're not expelling me?"

"Not at this time." Mistress Medina leans down toward me. "Make no mistake: You committed a serious offense. But the school has invested a great deal in your education, and given your recent success, it would be a shame to waste your potential. However, you are to be confined to your room, with the only exceptions being for rehearsals."

So that's it then. I get the same punishment as Eva D'Antonio, who cost Abigail Fleming her ability to dance. Meanwhile, Estelle, who cost me Dámiul and could have cost me my future, will get away with everything she did.

A hint of relief winds through me, but it's so entangled in a million other things that I find little gladness in it. I'm only getting a second chance because I'm highly ranked, and it bothers me that so much hinges on a number beneath my name.

Mistress Medina tells me to wait for the security bots that will escort me back to my dorm, then flickers out. I bury my face in my hands. I should be happy that I get to keep my place in the school, that one of my dreams, at least, has been returned to me.

Yet that only throws into relief how deep the crater left by the other one remains. My hard work and a stroke of luck saved my future career. But no amount of effort will bring Dámiul back to me, and that feeling of helplessness makes my eyes burn.

I glance up at the ceiling. Beyond it lies the sky, and beyond that, the infinite abyss of space. If I had wings, I'd do as Butterfly did, even if it meant sharing her ultimate fate. Around and around I'd fly, not caring how many pieces of myself I lost on the way.

The melody of Butterfly's Lament winds through my head. I spend half my life creating such tragedies. Through my instrument, I must have woven a thousand sorrowful tales—through the Opera's weeping arias, through the Ballet's despairing dances, through the Orchestra's wordless cries of profound desolation. I find beauty in sadness when it's happening to others in a world disconnected from my own. There's a strange fascination that comes with seeing an inescapable shade loom over the characters. Each time I lend my Art to another saga of anguish—or even when I'm just watching—I find myself adoring the suffering of fictional people. Perversely enough, I know I'd be disappointed if they escaped their dismal fates.

I've heard it said that tragedy brings out the true and the pure, and that's why people find it lovely. But it's not so beautiful when it's real, when I'm cast in the role of the mournful heroine, torn from the one my heart cries out for, feeling the shadows of fate close in around me. I want to fight my way free. I want to claw and kick and scream until I find my way out of this miserable story.

But I won't. There's no deus ex machina that will save me. And I can't help wondering whether, if someone were watching my life unfold on stage, they'd applaud at the tears spilling from my eyes.

I swipe my finger across the hologram projected from my watch, rereading the praise from the reviewers who saw me at the last Spectacle.

"An astounding performance by a gifted youngster."

"Brilliantly expressive and technically sound."

"Iris Lei is a force to be reckoned with."

I hoped seeing their praise would make me want to play again. Picking up my viola would be the best way to get my mind off Dámiul.

I flop over on my bed. This isn't helping. Only a few minutes have passed since Security brought me back to my room, but it feels like much longer.

A buzzing sound. I ignore it. I'm in no shape to talk to anyone.

The buzzing, again. I barely hear it through the dullness in my mind. For lack of anything better to do, I bring up my Linx profile. A green 12 sits under my name. At least my arrest didn't affect anyone's opinion of me as an Artist.

More buzzing, this time accompanied by banging against the door. There's only one person who would be that insistent. I don't want Milo to see me like this, but I don't want him to think I don't care about him either. Especially after the despair I saw during our last encounter.

I force myself to sit up. "Enter."

The door slides open. Milo walks in, and I go to greet him.

"What took you so long?" He gives me a forced smile, which quickly falls. "I saw them take you into the station, then heard about what happened. Don't worry—patrons don't give a shit about disciplinary records. They only care about your talents."

"I know." I quirk my lips. "I'm fine."

"Come on, I know that's not true. You looked like you were about to fall to pieces." Milo puts a hand on my arm. "Please, Iris, you can tell me anything."

I won't be able to keep lying. I'm having a hard enough time holding in my tears. The only reason I didn't tell Milo about

Dámiul before was because Dámiul was afraid the school would find out.

Well, that's not a problem anymore.

"I haven't been honest with you." I collapse in my chair. "I'm really sorry I couldn't tell you before. I wanted to, but… he made me promise not to."

"Who?" Milo leans against my desk.

"Dámiul." His name brings a slight smile to my lips. Speaking in a whisper in case the minders are watching, I recount how he contacted me and how we communicated through the Zexa device. I even confess that I met up with him at the Wintertime Masquerade, and that he's probably the reason I made it through my solo at the Spectacle.

When I finish, Milo lets out a low whistle. "I can't believe you had all that going on, and I had no idea. Breaking all those rules… that's pretty badass." He gives me a playful smirk. "Sounds like you really liked this Adryil."

I nod slowly.

"It never bothered you that he's one of them?"

I shake my head. Honestly, I never really thought about him that way. To me, Dámiul's just Dámiul, a person like me. That he's from a different star system made him intriguing, yet there was far more familiar about him than strange.

Milo's expression turns somber. "You miss him, don't you?"

The aching in my heart becomes acute, and I look away. "Do you know why I played 'Butterfly's Lament' so well? It's because I kind of meant it." I feel a hand on my shoulder and look over to see Milo standing beside me.

"Is there anything I can do?" he asks.

I shake my head. "Thanks for listening."

Milo crouches by my chair and peers into my face. "Hey." He lifts the corner of his mouth. "I'm no alien prince, but if it's any comfort, I'm still here. I guess you get me as a consolation prize."

I can't help returning his smile. "You're not a consolation prize."

A gust of air blasts toward me, and I whirl toward it. A security bot stands in the doorframe. I barely have time to

acknowledge its presence before it projects its yellow hologram around me. "Iris Lei, you are wanted in the office."

I blink in confusion. The school's authorities just sent me back here—why would they summon me again? Unless…

Coldness envelops me as I realize a minder must have heard me telling Milo about Dámiul. That means Papilio knows I lied to Officer Klassen—and that my crime is much greater than the one they just bailed me out of.

I should have known better. Perhaps the minders weren't paying attention to me before, but they certainly would have kept an eye on me after I was caught breaking the law. How could I have thought that whispering would keep them from hearing my words?

My breaths become short as the bot wheels forward. The holographic haze follows, but since my legs seem paralyzed, I don't.

The moment the hologram leaves me, a high-pitched beeping emits from the bot, which backs up and surrounds me with its cloud of light again. "Iris Lei, please follow me. Noncompliance will lead to forced removal."

Milo wraps his arm around me. "Don't panic," he says gently. "I'm sure it's nothing bad."

I look up at him, taking some comfort in the familiarity of his presence.

He smiles. "I'll come with you and wait outside. It'll be okay."

I'm still gasping as if someone wrapped a plastic bag over my face, but this time when the bot wheels forward, I manage to follow.

Chapter Eighteen

THE SECURITY BOT PAUSES BESIDE A STEEL DOOR WITH A violet stripe vertically bisecting it. I recognize the name stamped in thin black letters across the center. Master Sharma—the administrator in charge of placing us with patrons and negotiating contracts.

The anxiety releases my lungs, letting me breathe normally again. Master Sharma doesn't handle disciplinary issues, so I can't be here because I'm in trouble. Maybe he just wants to talk about my future employment prospects.

The door slides open, and the yellow cloud around me vanishes. Master Sharma, remoting in via hologram, sits behind a black desk, his hickory face placid and his dark eyes watching me with a look of calculated calm. I barely notice the rest of him as I find my eyes drawn to his left.

A slender woman in white with dark red hair stands beside him. I stare at her eyes. Bright yellow and glowing— she's Adryil. I blink, not quite believing what I see. I'm so used to the Adryil—other than Dámiul—being only distant audiences or recordings that seeing one up close and in the flesh is disconcerting.

"Hello, Iris. My name is Erayet." Her accent is smoother than Dámiul's, closer to the English spoken by Earthlings. "I am the liaison between the Papilio School and the nation of Adrye."

There's only one reason she'd be here. But it can't be… *No one* gets hired that fast. Even Inna Havener starred in two full-length operas before she landed a patron.

"Please take a seat." Master Sharma gestures at the chair across from him.

I obey, not daring to think anything until one of them tells me what's going on.

"Your unexpected solo caused much excitement among the pool of prospective patrons." Master Sharma folds his hands on the table. "I have the pleasure of informing you that Soraï and Gysát Ydaya, a prominent couple on Adrye, have offered you employment."

The meaning of his words slowly seep into my mind. I've been hired—I don't have to fear the future anymore. I should be ecstatic, but I'm too shocked to do more than stare at him. My gaze slides up to Erayet.

"They were very pleased with your performance." Erayet speaks slowly, as if I'm a small child who might not understand her. "They have requested your presence on Adrye as soon as possible. Fortunately, Master Sharma and I were able to agree on the terms of your contract, which means I can bring you, along with the other Artists who found patrons, with me when I return to Adrye. But we must leave for the spaceport immediately."

Immediately? Artists are usually given at least a day's notice before they have to depart. Everything is happening so quickly, my brain can't process it. Just an hour ago, I thought I was going to be expelled.

I recall the lenient manner in which Officer Klassen questioned me, and then Mistress Medina's appearance right after. The school must have already been in negotiations over my contract when the security bot discovered the Zexa device, so they quickly worked out a deal with the authorities because disappointing the patrons would have been terrible for their

reputation. I should be gladder, but my thoughts are churning too wildly.

"I know this must be very startling for you." Master Sharma's voice is almost robotic in its precision. "The urgency with which the Ydayas requested your presence is unusual. But circumstances required swiftness. The Ydayas employ a quartet; however, their violist retired abruptly, leaving them with a gap in their ensemble."

"You will, of course, be expected to perform solos as well," Erayet adds. "The Ydayas did not only hire you as a replacement. They saw your potential and wanted to be the first to sponsor you." Her burgundy lips stretch into a smile, but it doesn't reach her eyes. "You will be very comfortable on Adrye."

Adrye... I'm going to Adrye... It finally hits me: I have a *patron*. Everything I've been working for, everything I've wanted for as long as I can remember, is happening. What's more, I'll be on Dámiul's world in a matter of days. Perhaps I haven't lost him after all. If he hasn't left for his assignment yet, I still have a chance to see him.

And I'll find my mother. Together, we'll take care of my father—bring him to Adrye or at least keep in touch. My family will be reunited.

My mouth seems stuck on a smile. No more staring at a number that could decide my fate. The fear I've lived with all my life is gone.

"The... Ydayas?" I draw out the word, not sure if I'm saying it correctly.

"That's right. Soraï and Gysát Ydaya." Erayet enunciates each syllable carefully for my benefit.

Sor-AH-ee and Guy-SAHT Ee-DYE-ah. I sound out their names in my head, hoping that when the time comes to greet my patrons, I'll pronounce the words correctly.

"Let's review the terms of your contract." Master Sharma taps his watch, and a holographic document appears before me.

Black letters, as small as grace notes, march across the air. I lean closer to get a better look. Though I can make out words in English, I barely understand what they're telling me. I'd have a better time understanding if they were actual grace notes.

My confusion must show on my face, because Master Sharma says, "Would you like us to explain the terms to you?"

I nod, a little ashamed. "Yes, please."

"The payment is very generous, as stated here." He points at one sentence, which glows yellow at his touch.

The number looks high, but I have nothing to compare it to. Being born at Papilio, I've never had to handle money. What's more, this amount is measured in Adryil currency.

"It's twenty-six percent higher than the average payment for an Orchestra principal." He lifts his mouth into an almost-smile. "And yes, you are being contracted as a principal, even though you were billed as a section player. The Ydayas were hoping to hire you for less, but I made sure you were properly valued."

"Your school drives a hard bargain." Erayet's tone is dry. "You should be grateful that the Ydayas are so willing to accommodate you."

A thrill runs through me. I'm a *principal*. It should have been obvious from my ranking, but Master Raucci hadn't promoted me yet. I thought it was because the position belonged to Estelle. I suppose it still does, since I'll be gone before I can lead the section. I hardly care that I'll never actually sit in that coveted first chair. The whole point of being a principal is to get better terms from a patron.

It seems strange for something that was such a big part of my life to suddenly not matter.

"A percentage of the payment will go directly to Papilio to cover your debt." Master Sharma apparently takes my stunned silence for understanding. "This includes the standard fees— tuition, housing, dining, clothing, and such—plus interest. The cost of your instrument is included, since you will be taking that with you. Everything else will be provided to you by your new employer."

All I can do is nod, though a twinge of regret pierces me. I never cared much about belongings, but still, they felt like they were mine. At the very least, I wish I could have kept the gown I wore to the Wintertime Masquerade as a memento of my

dance with Dámiul. It's hard to accept that nothing here truly belonged to me.

"Of course, there is also the substantial fine you incurred earlier today." Master Sharma folds his hands. "Until your debts are paid off, the school will receive ninety percent of your payment."

"Ninety?" I give him an incredulous look. The standard terms—with three-quarters going to Papilio—seemed imbalanced enough. How is it fair that I'm to receive only ten percent of what my skills earn?

Master Sharma's eyes harden. "Might I remind you that, if the school had not negotiated with the Township of Dogwood on your behalf, you would be in prison?"

And they would never have received payment for my debts. It becomes even more obvious why Papilio bailed me out. But it's my own fault that I have all this extra debt. If I'd turned over the device, I would never have met Dámiul. At the end of the day, the price I have to pay for that is literally just a price. I wouldn't change what I did for anything.

"I understand," I say. "How long will it take to pay off what I owe?"

"Twenty years, assuming the Ydayas keep you in their employ." Master Sharma's voice is so clinical, it could have been spoken by a computer. Which seems glaringly incongruous compared to the enormity of his words.

Twenty years—it might as well be the rest of my life. I always knew that employment lasted decades, but it never seemed real before now.

"After your tenure, you and your employers can decide whether to extend the contract," he adds.

Erayet steps forward, fixing her golden gaze on me. "There are, of course, conditions you are expected to meet. As is standard, you will not be permitted to engage in any activities that could hinder your ability to perform. This includes marriage, pregnancy, and romantic trysts. You are to adhere to a schedule, and you are not to leave your employers' premises without permission. The terms of the agreement are confidential, and

you are not to discuss them with anyone. Violating any part of your contract is grounds for immediate termination."

She might as well have said, *You will not know freedom, happiness, or love.* Nothing about these terms is unfamiliar, but now that they're being imposed on me, I suddenly feel like a caged bird.

Yet there's another piece of the deal: *You also will not know want, misery, or fear.*

Erayet's smile looks painted on. "In exchange for your compliance, you will be provided with high-quality shelter, clothing, and food."

I sink back in my chair. "And if I don't accept, I'll lose everything."

Master Sharma leans toward me. "As stated in the school's policies, your enrollment ends once we've negotiated a contract for you. You are no longer a student, Iris, and what happens next depends on your decision."

Decision? What kind of decision do I have? Whether I go to Adrye or remain on Earth, the world I knew this morning is gone. I'll never be a Papilian again—I'll be a professional Artist or a struggling laborer.

Erayet glances at her watch. "If you delay, the Ydayas might change their minds and withdraw their sponsorship. I'm afraid you won't have time for goodbyes."

"Goodbyes?" It hits me that everything I know is about to be blown away by the gale whisking me toward a new life.

Master Sharma gestures at the contract. "If you are unwilling to meet these conditions, you can refuse. We will place you in another job, but know that the more coveted positions as school staff are reserved for retired Artists and those who age out."

I try again to read the document, but can't absorb its words. Even if I understood the convoluted language, I would probably hear the same ultimatum in my head: forfeit your freedom, or forfeit your future.

This is all happening so fast. It doesn't feel real, that these could be my last moments in the school where I've spent my entire life.

Erayet glances at her watch again "We need to leave soon. Iris, what is your decision?"

"I'll take it." I don't see any other choice.

"Very good." Master Sharma smiles. "You may indicate your agreement by pressing your hand against the document."

I comply, and when I withdraw my hand, the crisscrossing lines of my palm and narrow whorls of my fingertips glow white against the words.

Master Sharma swipes the screen on his watch, and the document dissolves. "It's been an honor having you as a student. I wish you the best with your new patrons."

"Thank you." I stare at the spot where the document hovered, and the ghost of my handprint lingers in my vision.

Erayet maneuvers around Master Sharma's desk. "The hovertram that will take you to the spaceport is waiting outside the East Gate. The other Artists are already on board. The security bot that escorted you here will lead you to them, and I've requested that a second bring your instrument from your dormitory." A floor panel opens before her. I nearly fall out of my chair when a translucent blue pod shoots out of the ground. It opens before Erayet, who lets out a slight laugh at my astonishment. "I shall travel by different means. I have a few errands to run before our departure." She steps inside.

The pod vanishes into the ground and whisks her away, leaving me to stare at a plain gray floor tile that apparently leads to some kind of underground transportation system. I turn to Master Sharma, only to glimpse him flickering out. The door slides open, and the security bot once again surrounds me with its holographic cloud.

I follow it out of the room. *What's happening to me?* Too much has occurred today, and it's not even dark yet. I almost expect to wake up and find that it was all a vivid dream, shifting inexplicably from tableau to tableau until reality returns.

The truth falls upon me like icy rain: I'm leaving. Really leaving. No more lessons with Vera, no more Spectacles, no more Semiannual Balls… And worst of all, no more Milo. The world I've known is gone. There's plenty I won't miss—the rankings, the pressure, the backstabbing—but all I can think about is what

I'm losing. My eyes well, and I hurriedly wipe them. I haven't even left the office building, and already, I'm homesick.

I'm not ready to leave. There's so much I haven't done yet—this part of my life can't be over so quickly. I've signed away so much… even the right to love.

Have I even been in love? Do I know what love is? I long for Dámiul with every breath I have, wishing and hoping against hope that reaching Adrye will mean getting another chance to see him. But if I succeed, what would I say? It was easy to tell Milo I loved him. He's the friend I've always known. Would I tell Dámiul the same? If I did, it would mean something so different, it deserves a new word.

I remind myself that twenty years isn't really so long. I'll be thirty-five when my debt is repaid—still young enough to have children if I want. I could retire and carry on with my life. My freedom isn't gone—just on hold. Though it seems like forever from here, there's a whole lifetime waiting on the other side of my tenure on Adrye, one that's safe and secure.

The bot exits the building. As soon as I step out behind it, Milo springs up from the bench he was waiting on.

"What happened?" He glances at the bot, which continues wheeling forward. "Where are they taking you?"

"I… I've been hired." The words sound strange coming out of my mouth. "I have to leave for the spaceport right now."

Since the bot won't let me stop, Milo walks beside me. "Wait… What?"

"My new patrons saw me at the Spectacle and want me on Adrye right away."

Milo stares at me, a look of dismayed shock plain in his eyes. It's clear from his expression that he can't believe I'm leaving so suddenly. I still can't believe it either. Or that I might never see him again. I wish I didn't have to leave him so lost. What will become of him when I'm gone?

"Milo…"

"Congratulations." He gives me a trembling smile. "This—This is wonderful news. I always knew you'd make it."

A spark of hope lights within me. "Maybe this isn't goodbye.

If you stay with the Ballet, I know you'll make it to Adrye too. I could see you there."

Milo looks down, his expression taut.

I bite my lip, wondering if I said the wrong thing. But I can't stand the thought of him surrendering to despair. Each time I've seen him truly happy, it was when he was doing what he was born to do: bring stories to life with movement in a way no one else could. "Remember how a few weeks ago, I thought I had no chance at all? You never know what'll happen, so please, don't stop trying. You're too good to give up."

Milo meets my gaze. "Don't worry about me."

Hearing the sounds of mechanical whirring, I face forward and realize we're just a few steps from the East Gate. The double doors open, and the scent of fallen leaves blows toward me on a faint breeze. Outside, a hovering transport with a rounded shape waits, its glimmering surface reflecting the backdrop of winter trees. The engines radiate green light and hum a pulsing minor third. "The Papilio School" glows in white letters across the hovertram's side. Through the windows, I glimpse the faces of half a dozen Papilians who seem more than eager to begin their new lives. I must be the only one who almost wishes she could stay.

Milo stops as the bot nears the gate.

I break away from the hologram and throw my arms around him. "I'll miss you. You're the best friend I could've asked for."

"Are you kidding?" He releases me and shakes his head. "I've been a terrible friend."

"That's not true."

The bot's shrieking alarm cuts me off before I can say anything else, and it wheels back toward me. "Iris Lei, please follow me. Noncompliance will lead to forced removal."

"Go on." A sad smile tints Milo's expression. "Don't forget me, Iris."

"I could never forget you." I reluctantly return to the holographic net, then turn back to give him one last wave.

He waves back as the gate slams shut, cutting me off from the world I knew.

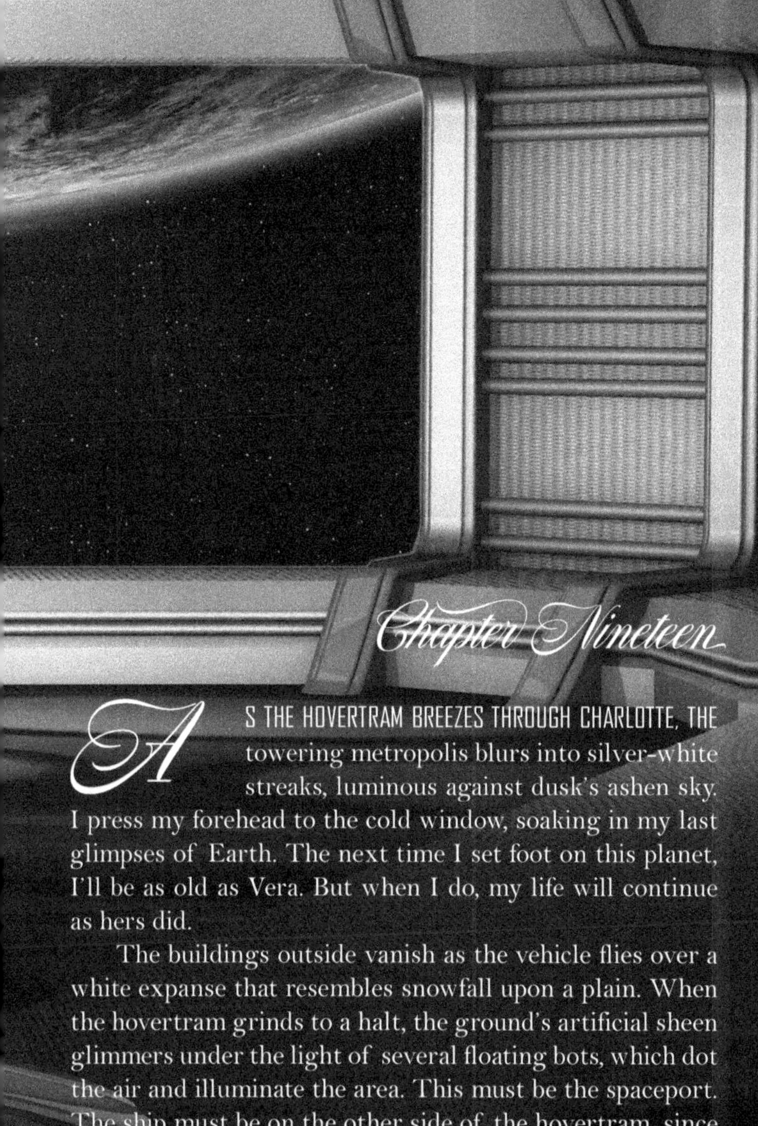

A S THE HOVERTRAM BREEZES THROUGH CHARLOTTE, THE towering metropolis blurs into silver-white streaks, luminous against dusk's ashen sky. I press my forehead to the cold window, soaking in my last glimpses of Earth. The next time I set foot on this planet, I'll be as old as Vera. But when I do, my life will continue as hers did.

The buildings outside vanish as the vehicle flies over a white expanse that resembles snowfall upon a plain. When the hovertram grinds to a halt, the ground's artificial sheen glimmers under the light of several floating bots, which dot the air and illuminate the area. This must be the spaceport. The ship must be on the other side of the hovertram, since all I see outside my window is an identical vehicle with the words "The Sinfonia School" across its side. Sinfonia is in Illinois—I wonder how long it took those Artists to reach here.

"Please exit the vehicle," the hovertram's automated voice says over the comm.

The others file out. The only one I know by name is

Eva D'Antonio. Though I shouldn't resent anyone's success, it disturbs me to see her here when she only became a soloist by sabotaging a fellow dancer.

I'm the last one out, and when I emerge, I find myself facing an enormous starship. Cyan lights glow from the multi-paneled surface. With its elongated contours and two large wings stretching toward the sky, it reminds me of a swan in flight. A long ramp extends down toward us. Erayet stands at the top with a security bot beside her.

"Single file, please." Her voice comes from all directions at once; the floating bots must be projecting it.

I follow several other Artists, most of whom are from the six other American schools, up the ramp and glance around nervously. Only strangers surround me; I've never felt more alone.

I wait my turn, shuffling slowly toward the ship. When I approach the security bot, it scans my face.

"Identity confirmed: Iris Lei. Sponsored by Soraï and Gysát Ydaya. Please proceed to Cabin Eleven."

Erayet waves me inside. A narrow corridor extends before me. Circular doors with black numbers stamped across their silver surfaces dot the steel-gray walls. While in transit, an automated message informed us that we'd be staying in the Artists' sector, which is separate from the main areas of the ship where the Adryil passengers will be.

I walk down the corridor until I find the door with the number 11 printed on it. It opens automatically when I approach.

The room I enter is not much wider than the door, which closes behind me. Three beds sit stacked against the left wall. A girl with a myriad of black braids sits cross-legged on the lowest bunk, chatting with a second girl, who stands before her with crossed arms.

To my dismay, the room has no windows. The only break in the featureless white walls is a large screen, which casts a silvery light onto the second girl's olive complexion. The words "Please remain in your cabin until after take-off" scroll across the top in letters so red, they seem to yell. In the center, a gray rectangle

displays my name. Identical rectangles display the names of the other two occupants—Ayana Washington and Sofia Cruz.

I give them a timid wave and say hi.

"You must be Iris." The girl with the braids grins at me. "I'm Ayana. Opera singer from the Coloratura School."

"Sofia." The second girl, who has cropped black hair and wide brown eyes, jerks her thumb at her chest. "Theater singer from the same, except apparently they teach you wrong on *that* side of campus." She gives Ayana a side-glance.

"Okay, listen up." Ayana launches into an in-depth explanation of how classical vocal technique harnesses the resonance capabilities of the human skull.

I nod along even though I have no idea what she's talking about. Sofia, however, seems to understand all too well, because she counters with an argument about why the belting she learned with the Theater allows a singer more freedom. By the time Ayana demonstrates her technique's superiority with a warbling high note, my mind is long gone.

Memories from Papilio parade through my head, and a wistful thread wraps around my heart, keeping it from beating too excitedly over going to Adrye. It occurs to me that no one's told me *where* on Adrye I'll be sent, and I make a mental note to ask the next time I get the chance. I also need to find out what it takes to send a transmission back to Earth. Surely, there must be a way for me to communicate with Milo, even if it's expensive. I'd happily give up the other ten percent of my earnings if it meant keeping in touch with my best friend. If I can't send him a message right away, maybe I can at least see how he's doing. Adryil patrons can view Linx profiles, so I should be able to as well—assuming Milo doesn't drop out. *Was it just this noon that I was begging him not to?*

This day has put my mind and heart through too much. Even my body is starting to feel the weight of exhaustion.

Wondering what the screen is for, I press my name. A schedule appears. According to this, the trip will take approximately fifty hours, and I have two three-hour practice sessions during transit. My viola is being stored in my assigned practice room. It'll be strange not having a coach to guide me—

just one more thing I'll have to get used to. My first session is in twenty minutes, and I'm glad. After all the madness of today, I'll finally be able to retreat into something familiar.

A tremor runs through the floor, and the message at the top of the screen switches to say: "Take-off in progress. Please remain in your cabins."

Exhilaration runs through me at the thought of blasting into the sky, and yet the actual circumstances are rather anticlimactic. Other than the faint rumbling, nothing has changed. I don't know what I was expecting—some kind of rush, perhaps.

A few minutes later, the cabin door opens. I take that to mean I can move around now. I wander down the corridor, wondering what else is in the Artists' sector. A door at the end retreats into the ground as I approach. I gasp at what it reveals.

I've entered some kind of recreational area—a large room with chairs, tables, and screens glowing against the lilac walls. But I hardly notice them as I stare at the wide window, through which a million stars shine.

I rush up to it. I'm actually *in space*, sailing through the boundless black universe. Yet I don't feel like I'm moving; the stars remain still outside. I search for the constellation Gemini, recalling what Dámiul told me about how his star lies on the other side.

The run from Butterfly's Lament flutters through my head, glittering with musical ornaments and every bit as luminous as the heavens before me. It no longer carries the weight of sorrow, but rather the fearlessness of hope. I imagine the moment before Butterfly took to the sky—the courage and blind determination she displayed. The strength that's forgotten after the tragedy's over. Yet without it, that final flight up the viola strings would not be so thrilling. With the starswept view before me and the starswept melody in my heart, I dare to dream too.

Finding my mother will probably be the easiest dream to achieve. The Kandar Family is famous—my new patrons might even know them. And then we'll find my father. I close my eyes and picture their faces—Theia Lei's powerful cheekbones and sharp chin, Ronan Lei's round eyes and broad smile.

I wonder if other families have succeeded in reuniting, but

the question fades from my mind as the answer becomes obvious. No, of course they haven't. Artists leave their Earthling lives behind when they go to Adrye. They are completely dedicated to serving their patrons, and their sole focus is on their performances. The people they knew while they lived on Earth are irrelevant.

Irrelevant? My own thought disturbs me, and I frown. How could I believe that? Without—

Most will never make it to Adrye, and those with patrons have already let go of their pasts. The thought hits me like a wall slamming into my head. I should not waste time dwelling on such matters.

What matters?

Weariness fogs my head. I try to recall what I was thinking about before, but all I remember is that it had something to do with the Kandar Family. But why should I care about them? My patrons are the Ydayas.

I blink slowly. The stars have lost their luster, and I wonder why I'm wasting my time staring at nothingness with my practice session so soon. The Artists' sector can be confusing. I should start heading to the practice rooms now to ensure that I am not late.

I turn toward the door and find Erayet standing under the frame.

"Hello, Iris." Her gold eyes fix on me. "I see you've found the recreation room. I am here to make your transition to Adrye as smooth as possible, so let me know if you have any questions."

"Thank you." I approach her. There was something I wanted to ask—I need to know where my assigned practice room is.

No, that's not it. A nagging feeling gnaws at me, telling me that there were more important things I wanted to ask. Something about Papilians... or Linx... I wanted to see someone's Linx profile...

I wanted to know if I could see how Milo's doing from Adrye. A bright patch appears in the clouds of my head, illuminating that one thought. "Is it possible for Artists on Adrye to view Linx profiles as our patrons do?"

Erayet lifts her shoulders. "Each household has different policies."

I can ask the Ydayas when I meet them, although I shouldn't dwell on my former schoolmates. My focus should be on my current priorities. Besides, it's rather petty to check the rankings of my former competitors, like Estelle.

No, it wasn't Estelle's ranking I wanted to see. And it certainly wasn't to gloat.

Milo. I wanted to see if Milo's okay. But I will never see him again, so I should forget him.

How can I forget him? Milo's face appears in my mind, and a surge of sorrow swells within me. He was devastated the last time I saw him, teetering on the edge of his sanity. Yet the moment he saw I was in trouble, he—

He's the past. I must forget him and move on with my own life on Adrye. The thought crashes into my mind. Nothing I knew before matters except what I learned as a member of the Orchestra.

The face in my mind fades. I don't remember why I was picturing it in the first place—or who it even was. I blink several times in confusion. What was I just thinking about?

Papilio—the answer appears like a spotlight in my mind. But there's nothing left at the school that I care about. The only people I knew were shallow acquaintances. I'll forget them all soon enough because none of them are important.

Erayet gazes at me, drawing me into the radiant golden pools of her eyes. "You are no longer a Papilian. You are a *Ka'risil*, a human Artist in the service of the Adryil who hired you. You are to fulfill your contractual obligations to the best of your abilities, keeping your skills sharp and performing as your patrons see fit. Do you understand?"

"Of course." Why would I do anything else? It makes so much sense, the most precise logic, and all I want is to go to the Ydayas and begin my duties as a *Ka'risil.*

Erayet's face warms. "Very good. Now, was there another question you had for me?"

For several seconds, only white noise fills my head. Then, I recall that my scheduled practice session is soon. I should start heading over. "Where are the practice rooms?"

Act Two

an advanced city
on an alien world

I WAKE TO WHITENESS. WHITENESS AND LIGHTS. STRANDS OF drowsiness stick to my mind like cobwebs. Soft humming buzzes in my ears, then abruptly ceases. The starship must have landed. I am to be taken to my new patrons shortly.

I sit up in my bunk. My two roommates are already waiting by the door. I climb out of my bunk and join them. The circular door opens, and a squat robot with three long arms stands outside. It is the same robot that delivered our supplies previously during the two-day journey. Multicolored outfits dangle from each of the metal appendages. I go to the one in the center—that is what has been assigned to me.

My roommates and I clothe ourselves in silence. I pull my dress, which is white and covered in patches of dark blue, over my head. The sleeves end at my elbow, and the flared hem brushes my knees. The material is so soft, it almost feels like a liquid. The bot then hands me a pair of pale pink shoes that resemble ballet slippers, and I obediently slide into them. Something about them causes an itch in the back of my mind… I once told someone I'd never wear ballet shoes…

But that's not important. I must not allow my mind to wander to useless places.

The bot's appendages retract, and it trundles away on stubby legs. I remain in the doorframe as I know I'm supposed to. Seconds later, a long, flat machine wheels toward me, carrying several items on its back. I recognize my viola case. It pauses briefly for me to pick up my instrument, then proceeds to the next room.

I wait. So do my roommates. None of us speaks a word.

A few minutes later, a tugging in my mind tells me that it's time to go. The transport that will take me to my patrons is waiting on the landing pad outside.

Along with the others, I march down the corridor. On the other side of the open doorway, winged silver transports, glimmering under Adrye's twin moons, wait in a semicircular formation at the bottom of the ramp.

Erayet stands by the starship's exit and directs each *Ka'risil* to his or her transport. When it's my turn, she points me to the one third from the right. I scarcely see the white landing pad or the hovering robots, which are virtually identical to the ones at the Charlotte spaceport, as I head over.

The transport's door opens to admit me. I slide my viola in first, then take a seat. A slight *thud* shakes the air as the door closes again. The engines whir, high-pitched and rhythmic, as the transport ascends into the sky.

City lights shine outside the window. I hardly notice them. I care about nothing but my destination—not the transport I'm in, not the Adryil pilot in front, and certainly not the hectic city we're flying through.

A white spherical structure comes into view. It's so familiar—where have I seen it before?

The Hall of Justice. Dámiul showed it to me once. For some reason, that feels important. I haven't thought of Dámiul since the starship took flight. I haven't needed to, since I was so focused on being a good Artist.

 *184* 

How can that be? I thought of Dámiul every day after I encountered him at Papilio…

The question clings to my mind. The feeling is odd after two days of simply knowing what to do. I half expect something to blow the thought away, and yet it lingers—longer than anything else has outside the practice room on the starship. I feel it digging its claws into my brain, and an uncomfortable shiver runs down my spine. My heart clamors, yelling, *Listen! Listen!*

Something's wrong, and my subconscious is trying to tell me what. It's like the feeling I get when I'm barreling through a fast song and accidentally skip a repeat. I never notice at first because I'm letting my fingers fly on their own, but something always nags at me until I realize what I've done. Whatever I've forgotten this time seems to be staring me in the face, and yet I can't see it.

We just passed the Hall of Justice…

A realization slams into my mind, so obvious that it knocks the cobwebs from my head.

I'm in Dámiul's city.

"Nathril!" The word tumbles out of my mouth. "Why didn't anyone tell me we were in the capital?"

"What did you say?" The pilot's accent carries a heavy lilt. He must not be as fluent in English as Dámiul or Erayet.

The city seems to brighten before me, as if a haze cleared from my mind. I press my forehead against the window. I recognize the buildings Dámiul showed me. The tall, spiral-like Museum of History, the clustered peaks of a science center whose proper name I've forgotten, the majestic columns of the senate building—we might fly by Dámiul's building any moment!

"Which sector of the city are we going to?" I ask.

The pilot doesn't respond. Thinking he didn't hear me, or that maybe his English isn't that good, I repeat the question, taking care to enunciate each syllable, but he still doesn't respond.

"Excuse me." I lean forward. "Sir? Can you hear me?"

"*Gorxit Karovyil!*" From the way the pilot spits the words, it

must be an insult. I recognize *Karovyil* as "Earthling," but I've never heard the first word before.

I must stop talking. I have no right to talk. I'm just a stupid Earthling. The surge of thoughts hits me so fast, it makes me dizzy. *I must be quiet for the rest of the journey.*

My head hurts so much, I feel nauseous. These thoughts aren't mine… they must be the pilot's. He's telepathically telling me to remain silent. But he's not allowed to do that—

Of course he is. I am on his world now.

The aching fades. I'm a mere *Karovyil*, and I have no right to speak with a superior being, let alone harangue him with questions. But now that I'm being cooperative, I should tell the pilot how I sensed his mental intrusion. As a *Ka'risil*, I shouldn't know how Adryil telepathy works.

He's still in my head. I suppress a gasp. "I once read an Earthling scientist's account of how Adryil telepathy affects the human mind."

I hope the lie is enough pacify his suspicions. In case it's not, I recall the training Dámiul gave me and focus on keeping my mind blank.

I think of nothing. Through the blankness, I sense the pilot's presence in my mind. I look within myself for that kernel of truth. I'm not inferior to the Adryil—just different. The pilot's opinion doesn't matter anyway. Dámiul never treated me as beneath him. And just because I'm on the pilot's world doesn't mean he has the right to violate the interstellar treaties.

The pilot's presence fades. My answer must have satisfied him. As long as I keep quiet, he should be content with ignoring me again.

I wonder if I should report what he did, but I don't know who I'd tell or whether anyone would believe me. The pilot certainly didn't seem worried about getting caught. *Is this what Dámiul meant when he said some thought themselves above the law?*

I look out the window, and the sight sweeps my worries away. A smile tugs at my lips. That exciting, far-off world across the stars is within my reach. And the boy who showed it to me might be nearby. How did I let the city pass me by for the first part of the journey? That seems so unlike me.

186

Because it wasn't me. A chill creeps down my spine. If the pilot could plant thoughts into my head, then Erayet could have as well. I never imagined she'd break the law, but then again, I never imagined *anything* while in her presence. She must have put my mind in a fog to keep me focused on my new duties. And everyone else too… I suddenly recall how animated my two roommates were when I first met them. Their silence earlier was more than unusual; it was unnatural.

Erayet must have been manipulating all of us, and none of us suspected a thing. We couldn't have—she would have erased the suspicion before it could land.

What else did she erase from my mind?

I try to bring up the memories of our conversations, but I keep drawing blanks. Frowning, I stare at the ground. My shoes—they made me think of something.

A shadow of a memory winds through my mind. I once told someone I'd never wear ballet slippers. And it was funny… part of some inside joke…

I squeeze my eyes shut, thinking as hard as I can about the first conversation with Erayet on the starship. That must have been when my thoughts first started slipping from me. Dámiul said that blocked memories could be recovered with enough focus. Whatever I was thinking of, it was important enough for Erayet to take it from me.

There was a face. A boy with gray eyes, blond curls, and a sad smile. Someone I was thinking of before Erayet put my mind in a haze…

I wrack my brain, but I can't remember whose face that was. No wonder Dámiul was so insistent on the mind training. If the Adryil can make me forget someone who must have meant a lot to me, what else can they do?

Dámiul must have known that his kind would use their abilities to manipulate me despite the laws. Unless… Could there be an exception to the telepathy ban, one that allows the Adryil to command Artists? There was so much in that contract that I didn't understand. Could I have signed away my own mind without realizing it? Why would they even need me to? The contract was already so restrictive. But I suppose rules and

incentives don't guarantee total obedience, which seems to be what the Adryil want from me.

An icy fist closes around my heart. This must have been why Dámiul was so afraid for me, why he said his people could erase me if they wished. They can take my memories and bend my will without me even realizing what's happening until it's too late. I want nothing more than to remember the boy with gray eyes, but since Erayet made me forget him, I must be careful. Dámiul warned me that the longer a person's under the influence of Adryil telepathy, the easier it becomes to control them, and the less likely they are to recover their minds. Next time, he could be the one they make me forget.

I can't let the Adryil take over my mind again. I don't know if I'd be strong enough to resist if they enter my thoughts once more. Already, Erayet has kept me in a fog for more than two days, and I didn't even notice until I was out of her presence.

As I gaze out the window, a light catches my attention—a bright sign that takes up the entire wall of a towering skyscraper. Only the left half is visible from my angle. Images of dancers and instrumentalists and acrobats flash in brilliant colors. They're Artists—or rather, *Ka'risil.* Why is that building blazing with their pictures? Are the Adryil really so fascinated by us?

The transport turns, and the right half of the sign comes into view. I suppress a gasp. An older version of Dámiul stares at me. Same black hair, same handsome features—same blue eyes, even. Yet there's something cold about the man's expression. Who is he? Dámiul mentioned that his father was important— could this be him? But why would he be on a sign alongside all those Artists?

Giant Adryil symbols splash across the enormous screen, and I wish I could read them. If that *is* Dámiul's father, then he must have something to do with the Artists. Maybe he arranges shows on Adrye. Or perhaps he's some kind of liaison like Erayet, only more important.

Dámiul seemed ashamed of what his father's company did. Is this why? Because his father profits from our labors while

we're left with debts so deep, we must sign away our freedom to repay them?

I have so many questions, but I can't answer them through wild speculations. I need to seek Dámiul out and make him explain. I cling to the hope that he's still in this city. Until I find proof that he left, I won't stop looking.

The transport slows. We must be getting close. If the pilot or anyone else hears my thoughts, they could invade my mind and obliterate them.

My only choice is to play along and hope they don't catch me—and wipe my memories completely.

Chapter Twenty-One

A BLACK CIRCULAR PLATFORM, LINED WITH BLINKING BLUE-and-white lights, hovers several stories above street level. The transport carrying me lands on it. A covered walkway extends from the platform to a gleaming black skyscraper. The door beside me opens. The pilot stands outside, and I'm overwhelmed by the need to go to his side.

Another telepathic order—I'd better obey. If he or anyone else finds out I know how to recognize and resist their telepathy, they could use more power to control me, and I might not be able to block them.

I pick up my viola, exit the vehicle, and approach the pilot, forcing my mind to remain as blank as possible. If he senses my fear, he'll wonder why, and the last thing I want is for him to probe my thoughts.

He leads me down the walkway. The square doors at the end open, and he stops. I, however, should keep going— that's what he's telling me with his mind. I recall how I knew exactly what was expected of me back on the starship and obeyed unquestioningly. Erayet must have been sending me similar commands.

I step through the doors and find myself in a room reminiscent of the Grand Hall: a wide, open area with walls of polished white stone. Above me, a three-dimensional metal star hovers, shooting dazzling white light out of its long, silver rays. A transparent elevator shaft stands in the corner. Arched doorways lead to rooms whose interiors I can only glimpse. Everything is so beautiful. One thought swirls though my mind, a light amidst the cloud of fears.

I'm on *Adrye*.

"Welcome, little *Ka'risil*." An Adryil woman with short, dark green hair and startlingly green eyes emerges from one of them. Her skin is almost as white as the wall behind her. Her high nose, sharp chin, and elegant black jacket-and-pants outfit give her an aristocratic appearance. She must be either Soraï or Gysát Ydaya—whichever of those names is a woman's.

I put my case on the floor and curtsey. "Pleased to meet you, Mistress Ydaya."

The woman lets out a chuckle. "Oh, I'm not your mistress. I'm your Keeper, Puna." She has a darker accent than Dámiul's, and the way she rolls her Rs makes me think of Master Raucci.

A *ding* chimes through the atrium, and I glance at the elevator. The transparent door slides open, and an Adryil man and woman step out. The man's eyes are blue, but not nearly as blue as Dámiul's. Closer to cobalt than Dámiul's brilliant azure. His cropped, dark red hair and smooth, ebony skin make him appear around thirty, but something about his stiff posture and harsh facial features tells me he's significantly older.

The woman, who is somewhat taller than him and has a slighter build than his barrel-chested figure, possesses a similarly odd combination of old and young on her face. Cream skin and long, thick waves of gold sharply contrast her large, tilted purple eyes. A thin, straight mouth and arched black brows accent her severe, almost frightening, beauty.

Both are dressed in floor-length outfits. The woman's purple-and-white one reminds me of a queen's gown, while the

 *192* 

man's red-and-black garment has a straight shape and a wide, circular collar that makes it look anything but dress-like.

Puna bows her head slightly as they approach. I follow suit—*those* must be the Ydayas.

"*Deh, tsot zaro Ka'rovyil dira.*" Mistress Ydaya's voice is low and rich. She puts her long, thin index finger under my chin and lifts it. I look up and meet her vivid purple gaze. "She is a pretty little one, isn't she, Gysát?" She retracts her hand and turns to her husband. "*Ganza stranone.*"

Puna glances at me. "She's saying you were well worth hiring."

"Indeed." Mistress Ydaya's eyes warm. "I look forward to seeing you perform."

Master Ydaya pulls his lips down and gives me an appraising look, then walks back to the elevator. Mistress Ydaya follows.

Wondering what Master Ydaya's expression meant, I glance at Puna in question.

Puna gives me a small smile. "Do not be afraid, little one. I assure you, both your master and mistress are pleased with you."

I nod, unsure of what to make of my new situation. All I know for certain is that I must keep my thoughts reined in until I have a moment to myself—away from these prying telepaths.

"Follow me." Puna walks across the wide floor. I pick up my case and rush to catch up. She takes me through one of the arched doorways, which leads to a small, empty room, then stops before a rectangular silver door on the other side. She presses a pad on the wall, and the door slides open, revealing a circular car with a round window at the back. I imagine it's another elevator.

I step in, and my guess is confirmed when we start descending.

Puna folds her hands neatly before her. "I am taking you to the *Ka'risil* quarters on the ground level, where you will be living with the rest of the quartet as well as the other Earthlings. There are about two hundred *Ka'risil* in this complex under the employ of various local patrons."

A faint thought glimmers—there was someone I was hoping to find among the *Ka'risil* on Adrye. The only idea that makes sense is that I was searching for an alum from Papilio.

Puna must have read my thought, because she gives me an amused look. "Of course there are a few here who also attended the Papilio School, although the majority are from other institutions. It's possible you'll recognize a former schoolmate, though doubtful. Adrye is a vast place."

It doesn't matter anyway. I need to focus on the present, and the past will only hold me back. Anyone I knew previously is irrelevant.

There it is again—irrelevant. Erayet told me the same thing once, possibly about the gray-eyed boy haunting my memory. But I can't think about that now. Puna's in my head; I can sense her.

I keep quiet, and her presence soon fades. Not wanting her to enter my mind again, I focus on the blur of the city outside and think about nothing.

The elevator doors open, and Puna leads me across a rectangular courtyard. Two smooth, black walls extend from the building we just left. On one of them, I make out the outlines of a rectangular door. A wide, one-story house with several rectangular windows and doors forms the fourth wall.

"Is this where the others live?" I ask.

"Yes." Puna stops and glances at a circular device on her wrist. "I've called the rest of the quartet. You must be excited to meet them."

"Of course, ma'am." A dark thought looms within me. What if I *do* recognize a former Papilian? If Erayet erased the gray-eyed boy from my memory, could someone have erased me from an alum's mind? I don't think I was close enough to any who were hired to merit that—after all, Erayet left my memories of Estelle, Beka, and several others intact—but the feeling that I meant to find someone here keeps clawing at me. What if I come face-to-face with that person, only to find that neither of us remembers the other?

I sense Puna's presence penetrating my mind. I must calm my thoughts before she realizes how suspicious I am.

"Find something that brings you peace," Dámiul told me once. "Something simple, boring even. Picture that and only that. The other thoughts will fall way."

In our training, I found that picturing my viola warm-ups worked best. I imagine myself, alone with my instrument, playing a four-octave scale. Each long, vibrating note rings in my head. Soon, it's all I hear.

Puna's presence retreats. She must be satisfied that I'm not asking questions I shouldn't be.

One of the doors to the house before me slides open. A tall man with dark skin, black hair, and a narrow build steps out, followed closely by a stockier man with brown hair and a tan complexion. They both appear to be in their mid-thirties and wear white shirts paired with navy blue pants.

A girl in a dress identical to mine emerges behind them. She's probably older than me, but next to the two men, she looks very young. I'm instantly jealous of her gorgeous chestnut hair, which cascades in large waves down her shoulders. Her thick bangs nearly reach her wide-set green eyes, which appear narrowed, as if she's permanently appraising whatever lies before her. Her strong cheekbones, athletic build, and proud posture give her an air of authority. Although she's several inches shorter than the men, she's by far the most powerful presence among the three. Something about her reminds me of Estelle.

"Sorry about the delay." Her dry tone tells me she's not sorry at all. "We wanted to finish the piece we were rehearsing."

Puna puts her hands on my shoulders. "Everyone, this is Iris Lei, your new violist."

The dark-skinned man, who is at least a foot taller than me, raises his eyebrow. "The Ydayas brought us a child?"

Puna lets out a slight laugh. "I know she's tiny compared to you, Temir, but she's fifteen."

Temir raises his eyebrows. "I would have guessed ten."

My jaw drops with indignation. "I don't look that young!"

"Of course you don't." The brown-haired man nudges Temir. "Only compared to this old man."

"Iris, this is the cellist, Temir Kader"—Puna gestures at the tall man—"and the first violinist, Andreas Konstantin." She gestures at the brown-haired man. "This is the second violinist,

Cara Vittoria." She nods at the girl. "That's *Carr*-a, not *Care*-a. Be sure not to mispronounce her name, or she'll become quite cross. She's seventeen." She gives Cara a small smile. "Cara, isn't it nice to have a companion your own age?"

"Yes." Cara speaks through gritted teeth, and I can tell she means, "No."

I make a mental note to be careful around Cara. I don't know what I've done to offend her already, but from the cold look she's giving me, I can tell she wants me gone. She and Estelle really do seem to be kindred spirits.

Temir extends his hand toward me. "Pleased to meet you, Iris. Where are you from?"

I try not to wince as his large hand squeezes mine. "The Papilio School."

He releases my hand. "I'm a Papilio alum as well! Though I left well before your time. Alan, your predecessor, was a Papilian too."

Puna turns to me. "I'm sure someone already informed you that our previous violist wished to retire early."

Cara lets out a disdainful noise. She catches Puna's eye and says, "Sorry." She sounds anything but sincere.

Puna narrows her eyes at Cara. Cara's expression goes blank, and I wonder if it's because Puna has entered her mind, keeping her from whatever scornful thoughts she was thinking before. The idea sends a shiver down my spine. That Puna's so freely commanding us reinforces the idea that, for whatever reason, the Adryil must be allowed to use telepathy on Artists. If I find Dámiul, I'll have to ask him why he didn't warn me explicitly about this danger.

Puna puts her hand on my shoulder, and I quickly push these notions out of my head. "Let me take you to your room so you can get settled. The rest of you may go back to your rehearsal."

The other three return to the room they came from while Puna leads me to a door at the end of the one-story house. She looks at a pad on its right, and the door slides open. "This is where you'll be living. Isn't it nice?"

"Yes, thank you." The small, cozy room reminds me of my dorm.

"To enter and exit, simply press your hand against the pad."

I find it both fascinating and frightening that the Adryil can control technology with their minds.

"Do not worry, little one. Your room is quite secure. Only certain Adryil—namely, myself and the Ydayas—can open your door telepathically. There are safeguards to prevent anyone else from doing so."

Puna must have read my unease. I nod with understanding and set my viola case down. A second door lies across the room from the first; I incline my chin toward it. "Where does that lead?"

"To the *Ka'risil* courtyard." Puna approaches the door, and it opens before her.

A wide, flat area lies outside. White tables and benches sit in a tidy row in the center, and a large screen, which displays a choral scene from an unfamiliar opera, towers over one corner. A handful of people sit at one of the tables, laughing as they chat in a language that sounds European.

Puna gestures at them. "During your free time, you are welcome to associate with the other *Ka'risil* here." She closes the door and points at the monitor on the desk. "I'm sure you're familiar with this from your time at the Papilio School?"

"Yes." I glance at the monitor, which displays a schedule just like the one I used to have.

"Good. It will tell you everything else you need to know." She heads to the door, turning her bright green gaze on me over her shoulder. "You have the rest of the day to adjust to your new home. Tomorrow, you will begin rehearsing with the others. Understand?"

"Yes." That seems to be the only acceptable answer to all Puna's questions.

She leaves, and the door shuts behind her.

I approach what looks like a closet door and open it. Inside lies a metal rack with a number of colorful outfits hanging off it. They all look my size—Puna must have prepared them in advance. A red light sits on each of the hangers except the empty one directly in front of me, which has a green light on it. Recalling how Cara and I have the same dress, which match the

outfits of the men, I realize that we must be expected to wear uniforms.

Your new home. Puna's words sound hollow in my head. I don't think it's quite hit me yet, that everything I knew is lightyears away. Further than I can even imagine.

Now that she's gone, I have a chance to collect my thoughts without her interfering. My mind whirls at the idea that even my homesickness was stolen from me aboard that starship. I recall being on the verge of tears when I followed that bot toward the East Gate. I must have been leaving behind something—or someone—that meant a lot to me. Yet every time my mind turns to the past, one of my Adryil watchers steers me back to the present and erases whatever I was thinking about. The same must have happened to the others, like Temir, Cara, and Andreas, and because they don't know it's possible, they simply accept their new lives.

But I can't accept mine. I don't know if I can recover what I've lost, but I have to try.

Who was the boy Erayet made me forget? I close my eyes and picture his face, determined to remember him. The effort makes my head hurt alarmingly, but if I let him stay forgotten any longer, I might never recall his name.

Don't forget me, Iris. Those words whisper through my mind—he must have spoken them to me. For several minutes, I just focus on his face and think, think, think.

The image in my mind changes. I see the boy's loose blond curls whipping through the air as he spins. He must have been a dancer. I see him taking my hand and leading me onto a ballroom floor…

Milo.

The memories flood back, and my eyes fly open in horror. How could I have forgotten him? My best friend, whom I laughed with, danced with, and even despaired with. Who I left behind. Last time I saw him, he seemed so broken, and I was going to find a way to help him. But how can I send him a message if I'm not even supposed to remember him?

I bite my lip. In coming to Adrye, I took one step closer to Dámiul, but now, Milo may be the one I've lost forever. And

I almost forgot him because of Erayet's mind tricks. I long to speak with him again and ask how he's doing.

But I know nothing about Adryil technology. If I bring the matter up with Puna, she'll purge Milo from my memories. Even if I manage to remember again, she'll keep erasing him over and over until there's nothing left.

What else have I lost? Who else have I lost? I close my eyes again, trying to recall why I thought there'd be a Papilio alum on Adrye that I'd want to see. I remembered Milo—surely I can remember more. But with him, I found a strand of a memory that I followed to the rest. Whoever this other person is, I can't even find something to grasp. A headache rages, and blood pounds in my temples.

Unable to stand the pain any longer, I open my eyes. Exhausted, I collapse backward onto the bed. I feel so defeated. I don't want to give up, but this battle is hopeless. Tears trickle hot down the sides of my face.

My future may be safe, but now, it's my mind that's in danger. And Dámiul knew. He must have feared that telling me what he knew would lead to his people finding out and wiping my memories. But it's the Earthlings who control Papilio... I don't understand. My mind buzzes with guesses and half-truths. Assuming the man in the sign was his father, he's more entangled in all this strangeness than I imagined.

I don't know how, but I'll find him. Or maybe he'll find me. Maybe, now that we're on a world without force fields to block Adryil telepathy, he can communicate with me through his mind. In case he can hear me somehow, I close my eyes and try to send him a message:

Dámiul, it's me, Iris. If you can hear me, I give you permission to enter my mind and tell me you're there. I need you, and if you can, please come find me. I'm with Soraï and Gysát Ydaya, if that means anything to you. Please, hear me, Dámiul...

 *199* 

Chapter Twenty-Two

TRAIL AFTER PUNA AND THE OTHER QUARTET MEMBERS into the Ydayas' grand apartment. I glance around surreptitiously, looking for something, anything, I can use to try to find Dámiul. A computer, maybe, or some kind of communicator. I haven't heard from him or sensed his presence in the four days since I arrived at the Ydayas' place. Sending out psychic signals must not be enough.

There was also nothing in the *Ka'risil* quarters I could use to contact him. Our computers can only be used to communicate with each other or Puna, and the only information I can access is a limited music library that Puna maintains. Despite her emphatic thought commands reminding me that I'm a willing employee, I'm beginning to feel like a captive or a slave. Though the Ydayas treat us well enough, we're kept in a locked area and forced to follow their commands. I don't know any other word for this but slavery. If that's what this is, I guess I unwittingly sold myself.

Puna leads us to a small, black stage that's been set up at the back of the Ydayas' main hall. "The rest of you already know this, but for the sake of our new member"—she gives me a slight smile—"I'll explain how this works. You will perform here, and your sound will carry throughout the apartment. The Ydayas may or may not watch you, but whichever room they're in, they will hear you, so play as though this were an auditorium, and they're sitting in the front row. Understand?"

"Yes, ma'am," I say.

"Good. This will be your regular routine, though there will be more public performances in the future. Not only are the Ydayas frequent hosts, but they also co-sponsor galas with other patrons or loan out the quartet for charity events. But for now, your only concern is to perform for them privately."

I walk up a short set of stairs onto the stage. Cara places her case on a black shelf at the back. Assuming I'm supposed to do the same, I place my case next to hers and open it. She glances at me slantwise but doesn't say anything.

I take out my instrument and make my way over to my stand. The screen before me displays the first song in the set we'll be playing. The other three players seem to be in lockstep when it comes to our pieces, and I hope I don't accidentally render my part jarring.

As I begin tuning my viola, Puna brings up a holographic document on her watch-like device. She knits her eyebrows as she reads it. Curious, I try to make out the myriad of symbols, clustered in what I imagine are words. I recognize one that Dámiul showed me once: the symbols for *Adryil*.

Knowing I'll need to understand more of the alien language than that if I'm to find him, I try to make out some of the other words. Except for the little Dámiul taught me, the only places I've seen Adryil writing has been on building signs on my way to the Ydayas and on Puna's device.

One cluster of symbols looks familiar. I think it's *Karovye*, which means Earth. I move my lips to the syllables, trying to figure out which symbol represents what.

"What did you say?" Puna gives me a sharp look.

"N-Nothing." Did I accidently mispronounce the word as something offensive?

Whatever I'm doing, I should stop. There's no need for me to learn to read Adryil…

That's Puna. Clearing my head is a familiar routine by now. I picture myself playing simple, ascending scales, mundane and peaceful. A few seconds later, she retreats.

The others start warming up, and I run through the scales I was just thinking of, fingers joining my mind.

But I can't concentrate on them any longer. Every time I start questioning, Puna invades my head. The other three seem perfectly content—that's what she's trying to make me. She wants me to accept the way things are, but I can't ignore the idea that people are having their memories erased.

One of my bow hairs snaps. I stop playing and go over to my case, aiming to yank the stray hair out and put it away, then throw it out later. Cara stops her warm-ups and walks with me. She catches my eye, and I wonder what she's up to. As I put my viola down, she grabs a cake of rosin from her case.

"Hey, Iris," she says. "I think we should meet one-on-one to go over that section in the new piece. You know, the part where the middle voices get the melody."

I don't understand. The passage she's referring to is incredibly basic. Maybe she wants to make sure our pacing is precise? "Sure."

"Why don't you come over to my room after we're done tonight, and we can at least go over it once or twice before curfew?"

"I'd be happy to." That's the most words she's spoken to me the entire time I've been here.

"Places, everyone!" Puna's voice reverberates through the large hall.

The warm-up noises die down, and Cara and I return to our spots. Andreas eyes each one of us to check that we're ready, then inhales and lifts his violin to cue the upbeat. I come in on the downbeat along with him and Cara. A measure later, Temir joins us with the bass line.

The song rolls along gracefully, rippling like a brook over stones. My placid tenor notes blend smoothly with the other strings, and I let the music wrap its soft harmonies around me. In this moment, it's the only thing that matters.

I press my hand against the pad by Cara's door, somewhat apprehensive. The door opens, and I walk in, viola case in hand.

Cara rummages in her closet. "You can put that down wherever." She doesn't look up as the door closes behind me.

I set my case on the floor. "So… How are you?"

"Marvelous." Her voice is deadpan. She turns, fixing her sharp green gaze on me. "We're not actually rehearsing, by the way. That was just an excuse to get you here."

"Oh?" My voice rises involuntarily, and my nervousness swells.

Cara tilts her head. "You scared of me or something?"

Figuring there's no sense in hiding what must be obvious, I shrug. "A little."

Cara pulls her lips in, turning her full mouth into a thin line. "Be straight with me. Were you trying to read Adryil earlier?"

I nod instinctively, too nervous to come up with a lie or excuse. *Why is she asking me?*

"You looked like you knew a word or two. Puna didn't seem too happy. Did she tell you to forget about it?"

I nod again. "She's told me to forget a lot of things."

"But you haven't." Cara narrows her eyes. "Your little innocent act may fool her, but I can tell you've got questions on your mind. Playing clueless works well for you, doesn't it? No one suspects the quiet girl."

The nervousness tightens its grip on me. "What's this all about?"

Cara goes back to the closet, then emerges, holding a black tablet. "You want to learn Adryil? Here's your chance." She hands me the machine. "Whatever you do, don't let Puna find it. If she does, I'll deny I knew anything about it."

I examine the flat device. A small button protrudes from

one end. I press it, and the screen lights up, displaying a list of English words with their Adryil equivalents. I tap one of the icons at the bottom to see what it does. It whisks me to a home screen, with options to read Adryil phrases or practice pronunciation. This tablet reminds me of the foreign language guides the Opera used to learn Italian, German, or whatever tongue their songs were in.

This is it—the answer I've been looking for. If I knew what their symbols meant, surely I could find some way to get a communicator and contact Dámiul.

I start to thank Cara, but the words freeze in my throat as I recall how Estelle feigned friendliness, then sabotaged me.

Cara crosses her arms. "What's the matter?"

"I…" I try to find some way to phrase my question without sounding like I'm accusing her of something. "Why are you giving this to me?"

She twists her mouth. "Look, I'm not trying to get you in trouble. I just don't like how the Adryil keep us ignorant. You're the only Earthling I've run into here that doesn't seem brainwashed yet, and I'd like to keep it that way. In case you haven't noticed, the Adryil are allowed to use their telepathy on the *Ka'risil.*" Sarcasm rings from her voice. "I hope I'm right about you. If I'm wrong, then I guess Puna will come knocking on my door soon enough."

"You can block them too?" I regard Cara in a new light. The blankness that seems to be her default expression must be an act, just like I pretend to be calm when I have a million questions demanding to be asked.

"I sure can." Cara smirks. "The hardest part is playing along, isn't it? I've been here for almost a year, and sometimes, I feel like I just can't keep it in. If that feeling ever comes over you, keep your mouth shut. We're not supposed to realize what's happening."

I shake my head. "Why would they do this to us? How is it allowed?"

"It's all part of the devil's bargain you make when you sign your contract. We're the only things from Earth the Adryil want, and they want absolute obedience from us, so our wonderful government gave them a loophole. Our patrons can do whatever they want to us, and do you know what they do to noncompliant *Ka'risil?* They erase your mind." She shifts her gaze. "I've seen it happen once, and that was more than enough. When they get serious, no amount of willpower can save your memories."

I bite my lip, knowing full well how true that last part is. I've tried several times to recall the Papilio alum I was hoping to locate. All I find is white noise in my head. If I'm not careful, Puna could send the rest of my memories sliding into that abyss. One mistake could cost me everything I know, everything I am. I knew it in my gut, but Cara's confirmation makes the danger more immediate. If they took my memories—what would I be? If I didn't know where I came from, or what I believed, or who mattered to me… I'd be a husk of my present self. A body with little more than breath, blood, and bones inside.

Cara brings her attention back to me. "Hey, I'm sorry I was kind of cold to you before. It was nothing personal. And neither is this." She nods at the tablet. "It's about something bigger than you and me." She looks me in the eye. "You can trust me."

I'm still not sure about that, but in any case, I need the tablet. "Thank you." I glance at the thin machine. "Where did you get this?"

"Someone passed it to me, like I'm passing it to you."

If she has forbidden technology, she must know more than she's letting on. My mind flashes to that sign—the one with a man who looked like he could be Dámiul's father. "Does the last name Verik mean anything to you?"

Cara's eyes widen. "What do you know about the Veriks?"

Her response tells me that Dámiul's family must be significant somehow. "I… saw a sign on my way here. It showed Master Verik alongside several *Ka'risil.* I was wondering what it meant." Until I know I can trust her, I'll keep the truth about Dámiul to myself.

Cara brings her hand to her chin, thinking. "Let's just say that Master Verik is pretty much in charge of Papilio, Sinfonia, and most of the other schools like them."

The man in the sign must have been Dámiul's father, then. Cara's lack of surprise or denial about what I saw means she

must know about it too—and know for certain that it's Master Verik who's pictured. But what did she mean when she said he was in charge of the schools? I was always told that they were Earthling institutions. I voice these thoughts, hoping Cara might reveal the truth, but she interrupts before I can finish.

"I'm going to stop you right there." Cara crosses her arms. "Those questions could get you erased, and for both our sakes, I won't be answering them tonight."

"Why not?"

"Because I don't feel like losing my memories for someone I barely know."

A mixture of disappointment and frustration churns in my gut. She has a point; she has as much reason to distrust me as I do her. But I'm getting closer. She *knows* what's going on—I'm sure of it. If Dámiul can't tell me, perhaps Cara will.

A buzz sounds from the monitor on Cara's desk, indicating that we have five minutes until curfew. Cara makes a face. "You'd better get back to your room. You know what to tell Puna if she asks what we were doing, right?"

"Of course." I blink innocently. "We were just rehearsing the second movement of 'Creator's Folly.'"

Cara barks out a laugh. "Oh, I wish looked as harmless as you. That's why Puna lets up so quickly with you, isn't it? I must have a villainous face, because she always thinks I'm up to something." She jerks her head at the tablet. "Hide that in your case."

I open my case and place the tablet over the fingerboard of my viola. Having the device scrape against the instrument makes me uncomfortable, but it's the only way to transport it unseen.

After saying goodbye to Cara, I head back to my room. Puna stands in the courtyard, eyeing the *Ka'risil* quarters. She watches me.

Just look innocent. In case she tries to read my mind, I mentally run through my part in "Creator's Folly."

"*Zeth onayil Iris.*" *My name is Iris.* "*Ona Papilioyil dira.*" *I am a Papilian.* "*Ona at'strat illátet fac.*" *I play viola.*

I move my lips to the Adryil syllables, barely whispering each. The courtyard lights went out hours ago, and the window above my desk is almost completely black. I only meant to peek at the Adryil language tablet before going to sleep, but couldn't resist reading more.

I yawn widely, stretching my arms over my head. Cramming dozens of alien words into my brain has taken its toll. I'll probably forget half of them by tomorrow. In any case, my alarm will wake me in less than six hours, so I should sleep while I can.

I get up from my chair, wondering where to hide the tablet, but a flash of blue light catches my eye. Puzzled, I look out the dark window. The light bobs toward the courtyard's wall, and I make out the vague outline of someone beside it. Long hair, medium height—*Is that Cara?*

The person presses something on the wall, and the light briefly flashes across her face. It *is* Cara. *What's she doing?*

A sliver of yellowish light appears in the courtyard—the door in the wall opened slightly. Cara slips out, and the door slides shut. But both the doors to our dorms and the doors leading out of the courtyard are locked. How did she get out? Where is she going?

First the illicit language tablet, then the mysterious hint, now sneaking off—she must be involved in something secret.

And until I find Dámiul, she's my key to finding the truth.

Chapter Twenty-Three

ONCE AGAIN, I'M THE FIRST ONE TO ARRIVE IN THE REHEARSAL room. The others are probably still socializing in the *Ka'risil* courtyard. I ventured out there a few times, but found the experience too unnerving to repeat today. Of the two hundred or so Earthlings around me, only Cara acts like an actual person. The rest seem like the chorus members of an opera: shallow outlines of people too content to be real. My spare time is better spent studying Adryil.

I whisper my actions in Adryil, just to see if I can. *"Ona talbat at'strat onayil bor etrin yarrek faro."* I place my viola case on the black shelf. *"Ona ata tortet ut at'strat gren."* I open it and take out the viola.

The phrases I've learned so far aren't very useful, but I think I've done reasonably well in three days' time. I might even know enough to figure out an Adryil communicator if I can find one.

The door opens, and Cara enters. She gives me a smirk and whispers, *"Tra'kel,"* which is Adryil for "hello."

I smile back. *"Ona larsal da."* I studied.

I yearn to know how and why she snuck out three nights ago, but I doubt asking for a seventh time will do anything other than annoy her.

"The other two are on their way." Cara places her case next to mine and takes out her violin. She flips her thick hair off her left shoulder. A flash of silver catches my eye in the split second before her hair falls onto her back.

"What's that?" I ask.

Cara ignores me and raises her violin.

I sigh. She's barely spoken to me since giving me the tablet, much less answered my questions. I glance at the closed door, then say softly, "What's it going to take for you to trust me?"

Cara tunes her violin without acknowledging me.

"Cara, *please.*" I try to catch her eye.

Cara plays an emphatic scale, like she's trying to drown me out. I start to say something else, but then the door opens to admit Andreas and Temir, chuckling over something mindless.

I turn back to my instrument in resignation.

I step off the elevator on the Ydayas' second floor and look around curiously as Puna leads us down a glimmering indigo corridor. We pass several archways rimmed with decorative white lights. Through one of them, I glimpse a computer monitor that looks similar to the one in my room.

I keep my gaze ahead so Puna won't suspect anything, but mentally note its location. *That computer's in the main house, so it won't be limited like mine. I could use it to contact Dámiul. But do I know enough Adryil to try? Do I dare, with Puna always watching?*

And if I succeeded, what would I say to him?

Dark thoughts loom over my mind. People's memories are being erased against their wills, and he knew all along. If my suspicions are right, then Dámiul's father is somehow behind this horror—maybe he even employed Erayet. Is Dámiul a part of his father's company?

My heart riots at the thought. No—he couldn't be complicit

in something so awful. Anger and sorrow clung to him each time he spoke of Papilio.

I need to talk to him. My mind keeps wandering back to the computer I saw. We'll get a short break after Temir's solo—maybe I can slip in then. *No, the door's wide open. Someone will see me.*

Puna glances at me, and I realize that I've let my guard down and allowed my mind to wander in her presence. I hurriedly turn my thoughts to mundane viola warmups, keeping my face as blank as possible.

She leads us to the end of the corridor, then glances down at her wrist device. Mechanical whirring hums behind the wall, and something clicks into place. A rectangular section of the wall slides up into the ceiling, revealing a small, circular balcony overlooking the apartment's main hall. In the center are four silver music stands, already adjusted for our heights. Our ensembles—black suits with green ties for the men and flowy emerald dresses for Cara and me—match the holographic backdrop, which features a lively forest reminiscent of the one surrounding Papilio.

"This is where you'll be performing from tonight." Puna looks up from her wrist device, and a table-sized slab extends from the wall beside her. "You may leave your cases here. The Ydayas' guests will be arriving in half an hour."

The others and I run through the familiar routine of tuning, warming up, and taking our places. I force myself to concentrate on the job at hand in case Puna reads my thoughts.

The Ydayas cross the hall below, and the double doors of the entryway open. In her sparkling scarlet gown, Mistress Ydaya seems to glow against the white walls. I can scarcely keep my eyes off her and the other glittering members of the Adryil elite, who enter with enthusiastic greetings.

Unlike on Earth, it seems that on Adrye, the men are every bit as ostentatious as the women when it comes to eveningwear. Master Ydaya's blue, robe-like ensemble with a high, stiff collar and bright yellow stripes streaking across it seems garish by the standards I'm used to, and his outfit is one of the more muted ones.

I recall the white, tunic-like jacket Dámiul wore to the Wintertime Masquerade and smile to myself. Either he knew enough about Earthling culture to tone down his kind's usual flair or he has more modest tastes. Remembering that night of wonder makes me miss him fiercely. In my search for answers, I haven't forgotten the person behind the mysteries. But it's been weeks since I last saw him. What if he's forgotten me?

That can't be. He's probably wondering what happened to me. Maybe he feels the same despair I did when Security took the Zexa device away. *I'll find you, Dámiul. Even if you've left for your secret assignment already, I'll find out where you are.*

I turn my focus back to the song I'm playing. After the first movement comes to an end, Andreas cues the upbeat, and we begin the second.

As I did so often from the Pit, I find myself relying on memory to play my part while my eyes wander toward the scene I'm accompanying. The Adryil laugh and chat as they sip colorful drinks. Some hold up their wrist devices and show each other holovids, many of which appear to feature performances by Earthlings. I wonder if they're comparing us, bragging about which of them has the most impressive Artists in their employ.

A woman with a mass of black hair arranged in high twist on top of her head shows Mistress Ydaya a holovid of two ballet dancers: a boy and a girl. Mistress Ydaya exclaims in delight and chatters excitedly. The woman looks down at her device, and a second holovid of the same dancers appears.

An idea sparks. From the interest Mistress Ydaya is showing, she could be considering adding dancers to her *Ka'risil* collection. Maybe I can convince her to sponsor Milo—assuming he's still with the Ballet. If only I could talk to him!

A familiar tension grips me. Worrying won't help, I tell myself. I try to focus on the piece I'm playing to keep the anxiety from rising.

An image catches my eye—a close-up holovid of a face. From where I am, I can barely make out the holovid's details, but it's so familiar, it calls to me. Tan complexion, handsome features, black hair—it must be Dámiul. I'd recognize him

anywhere, even from this distance. Or could it be his father, who looks so much like him?

"Iris!" Cara throws me a glare.

I realize that, in my distraction, I must have slowed the tempo. I turn to the music and concentrate, taking a moment to reorient myself in the notes. My fingers flicker along the viola strings automatically, and I can't stop myself from glancing down again.

The holovid is still playing, and I turn my attention to the Adryil woman whose wrist device projects it. She speaks to the woman beside her, and I try to pick out her voice from the music and the noise of chatter. Through the unfamiliar syllables, two familiar words jump out: "Dámiul Verik."

It *is* him. In the holovid, Dámiul appears to be speaking, but I can't hear his voice. The volume must be too low. My breath quickens, and I stare at the Adryil woman. Why is she watching him? Does she know him? She can't be related to him. With her snowy white skin, pale blond hair, and round face, she resembles Dámiul about as much as I resemble Temir.

Could she be a friend of his? She turns to the woman beside her, who was also watching the holovid, and wrinkles her nose. What does that mean?

"*Iris!*" A swift kick to the shin brings my attention back to the present. Cara looks ready to tear my head off, while Andreas and Temir glare at me with accusing expressions.

I glimpse Puna from the corner of my eye. She's approaching the balcony. I can't let her know why I was distracted. Fixing my eyes on the music, I clear my head of everything but my viola harmonies.

The archway to the room with the Ydayas' computer stares at me, beckoning. My heart thumps so loudly, I wonder how the others don't hear it. Now would be the ideal time to slip in and try to contact Dámiul. The Ydayas are distracted by their guests, and Puna's gone for the time being.

I yearn to ask that Adryil woman how she knows Dámiul, but if I tried, Puna would surely erase him from my memories. The computer is my best chance, and I should go now. If I don't, there's no knowing when I'll be this close to it again.

I glance around the corridor. It's empty. The other three players are in a nearby lounge. I take a breath, then tiptoe to the archway at a brisk pace.

The computer monitor stands alone on a semi-circular desk made of some kind of gold metal. A high-backed chair sits before the console, its orange color brilliant against the purple walls behind it. I dash to it and curl up on the seat, hoping I'm small enough that anyone who walks by won't spot me.

I do my best to control my breaths and hope the heat engulfing me won't make me sweat through my thin dress.

The monitor glows under my touch, and a second later, a list of symbols and icons appears.

"Ona pari fenst en clogamo?" I jump at the sound of the computer's voice and curl up tighter. *Please, please, please say no one heard that...*

I listen, certain that Puna will come rushing in any moment. After several seconds of silence, I release my knees. So far, it seems, I'm safe. *What did the computer say? "Ona" means "I"... "clogamo" means "help"...*

Some of the voice-activated computers at Papilio greeted users with, "How may I help you?" Maybe Adryil computers do the same.

If this computer is like the ones at Papilio, saying Dámiul's name should be enough to bring up his basic contact information. "Dámiul Verik," I whisper.

"Lorst mand?" *"Mand"* means *"again."* The computer probably couldn't hear me.

"Dámiul Verik." I repeat his name slightly louder.

"Ona balnásin luwell: Dámiul Verik."

A list appears before me. Large, black symbols with smaller ones beneath, like titles with subtitles. I recognize the symbols for Dámiul's name in each of the titles but can't make out much else other than *Karovye*—Earth—and *Ka'risil.* Beside each title

is a line of symbols representing numbers—I think they're dates. If I had to guess, I'd say this list looked more like news headlines than contact information.

Why would Dámiul be in the news? His father's important—is he as well? If so, that would explain why the Adryil woman was watching him. But what is he famous for?

Hoping to learn more, I press the title at the top of the list. A holovid appears before me. I gasp at the sight.

It's Dámiul—there's no mistaking him from this close. He's dressed all in white, like he was the first time I saw him at Papilio, when I thought he might be a ghost. His azure eyes gaze ahead with fury, his expression blacker than anything I've seen in him before. But that's not what's making me stare. It's his hands—they're bound together by metal cuffs, which are chained to a railing before him.

"*Ona dratuttin jatoi nur.*" His voice is soft but intense. I don't recognize the words, but as he continues, he speaks with such fervor, I can almost understand him. His tone is at once measured and aggressive, carrying the cadence of a warrior meeting his enemy before a battle.

Who is he speaking too? Why is he chained like a criminal? My gaze falls on the symbols behind his head, and I recognize them from the map he once showed me: "Hall of Justice."

This scene must have taken place after he broke into Papilio. It must be a record of the disciplinary hearing when he was banned from returning to Earth.

A woman's sharp voice cuts Dámiul off, and he flinches as if someone struck him hard across the face. He sags, suddenly looking exhausted, like he did before the Spectacle. Still, he keeps his head high as the woman spews venomous-sounding words at him.

Whatever she's saying, it must affect him profoundly, because his eyes glisten. Otherwise, his face remains a proud mask. The woman finishes her tirade with a question.

Dámiul repeats firmly, "*Ona dratuttin jatoi nur.*"

A man's stern voice starts speaking. A line of symbols scrolls along the bottom of the holovid. Once again, I only

recognize the symbols for "Earth" and "*Ka'risil.*" That seems to fit my theory that this holovid was taken at Dámiul's disciplinary hearing after he broke into Papilio.

But the severity of what I'm seeing doesn't line up with that idea. Why would they chain him? What did that woman say to him? Do they keep records of every disciplinary hearing on Adrye? Even if they did, why would there be so many records under his name?

Dámiul, who are you?

I always suspected that his refusal to answer my questions wasn't only to protect me, but to protect himself as well. Now I wonder just how powerful the danger to him was. What if revealing what's done to the Artists on Adrye and what lies behind his father's company would have led to a worse fate than being banned from Earth? Maybe my past theory about him being sent away as punishment wasn't so far-fetched after all. But where would they send him? Where is he now?

The unseen man finishes, and Dámiul speaks again. His eyes burn like blue-hot flames, and yet he otherwise appears calm. I do my best to catch his words. *Justice… not…*

A hand clasps my shoulder. I yelp, and my heart stops.

Master Ydaya glares down at me, his face twisted with rage.

Chapter Twenty-Four

ASTER YDAYA GRABS MY ARM AND DRAGS ME OUT OF the chair. "What are you doing?"

My insides clench with fear. I open my mouth to speak, but no words come out. He tightens his grip, and I feel a bruise forming on my arm.

"Answer me!" He gives me a shake so hard, my teeth clack together.

I try again to say something, but I can barely breathe.

Master Ydaya's glare seems to drill a hole through my head. He's going to use his telepathy on me—I know it. I try to focus on my usual defense of viola scales.

It's not working.

I have no right to enter his office. How dare I defy those who take care of me? I should be grateful and obedient. I have no business watching holovids about Dámiul Verik. Dámiul Verik is a troublemaking criminal, and he deserves his fate. I should forget him.

No...

I try to fill my head with mundane ascending notes, but

Master Ydaya's thoughts drown them out. *I must forget Dámiul Verik. In my mind, I see his face fading.*

No, no, no…

My eyes sting. The scales aren't working—I should try something else. Dámiul told me once that… What did he say?

I shouldn't remember. The name Dámiul Verik shouldn't mean anything to me.

I close my eyes, and tears fall down my face. I recall the melancholy notes of "Butterfly's Lament," which I'm supposed to play later this evening, and hope that focusing on a piece I care about will work better. The melody soars through my mind, but Master Ydaya's presence remains strong. I try to picture Dámiul's face, but see only a blur.

Butterfly watched, helpless, as they took her love away…

"*En swar fac?!*" Mistress Ydaya's shrill voice pierces the air.

I open my eyes in time to see Mistress Ydaya pull her husband away from me. Master Ydaya points at me accusingly and speaks in a low voice, then gestures at the still-playing holovid of Dámiul.

Mistress Ydaya narrows her eyes at the computer monitor. The holovid disappears, and the screen goes blank. She says something sharp to Master Ydaya, and I recognize the word for "art." She turns to me, and her eyes soften. "You did not mean to make trouble, did you, little one?"

I shake my head. Recalling what Cara said about my looking innocent, I make no effort to stop my tears. "I-I'm sorry, Mistress Ydaya."

"What were you doing with the computer?"

"I… was curious." I feel her probing my mind for the truth, and I bite my lip. I can't lie, but I don't have to tell her everything, either. "I was the one Dámiul Verik ran into when he broke into Papilio. I saw someone watching a holovid of him downstairs, and… I just wanted to know who he was."

Mistress Ydaya puts her hand under my chin. "And you thought maybe he could be your prince from the clouds, didn't you, my little butterfly?"

She must have heard me thinking about "Butterfly's Lament" and assumed it was connected to my searching for

Dámiul. If that's so, I'll gladly support her assumption. "I… I know it can't be, but… he was so handsome. I thought maybe, if I made myself part of the story and felt what Butterfly felt, I could perform better." I must sound like a complete idiot, but that's good right now.

"Always trying to improve your Art, aren't you?" Mistress Ydaya puts her light hand on my head and smiles fondly. "There's a good girl." She snaps her gaze toward Master Ydaya and narrows her eyes. "You could have destroyed her talent."

Master Ydaya scowls and says something in Adryil, keeping his voice a low growl.

Mistress Ydaya gives him a hard look, then turns back to me. "It was an accident, wasn't it? You didn't think there was any harm in venturing into one of the pretty rooms, did you?"

Unsure of whether to nod or shake my head, I say, "I only wanted to see what was inside. When I found the computer, I thought it could tell me who that Adryil boy was."

"Did you know that Dámiul Verik is a dangerous criminal?"

I shake my head, genuinely surprised. Knowing she can see my thoughts, I suppress the riot of questions in my head and focus on the simplest notion of who I thought Dámiul was: a mysterious young man from another world.

"To an innocent little thing like you, I suppose he would have seemed like a cloud prince." Mistress Ydaya strokes my hair. "You couldn't have known what he really is." She glares at Master Ydaya. "She is foolish, but her curiosity is part of what makes her unique. *On'en mut funihal mand fith dolare atiyil krináthnur.*"

Master Ydaya bristles, his lips pulled down in a deep frown. I repeat Mistress Ydaya's words in my head, trying to decipher them. *I something not you from changing—Or maybe adjusting? Or tampering?—with her something again.* Except the word for "not," when used as a suffix, makes a word its own antonym. My best guess is that she was forbidding her husband from tampering with my mind. Her stern expression and Master Ydaya's plain irritation support that theory.

Master Ydaya lets out a huff, then storms out of the room.

Mistress Ydaya looks me in the eye. "I forbid you from leaving your designated areas again."

I nod. "Yes, ma'am."

She grips my chin with cool fingers. "Here is all you need to know about Dámiul Verik: he's a delinquent who betrayed his family. Breaking into your school was just the last in a series of crimes he committed. He may look like a fairytale prince, but he is the lowest kind of lawbreaker there is. Do you understand?"

Her thoughts flood mine, and I nod again. I focus on the run at the end of "Butterfly's Lament," repeating it in my head to push back the questions clawing at my mind.

Mistress Ydaya releases my chin. "Good girl. Now, go back to the others."

"Yes, ma'am." I rush out of the room.

As soon as I enter the lounge, I stop and lean against the wall. I close my eyes, picturing Dámiul's face. His eyes, which say too much to express in words. That sometimes intense, sometimes melancholy azure gaze. The angles, the slopes, the symmetry of his face. I let out a shaking breath; he's still in my mind.

So are the questions. The Ydayas called him a criminal. Did he do more than just break into Papilio? I never believed him when he said he was ordinary, but now, I wonder just how much he left out. Reason tells me I should disregard everything he told me, but there were too many moments of truth between us. Despite everything, I want to believe in him. His anger over Papilio—is that what got him arrested? Was he as disturbed by the idea of Artists having their memories stolen as I am? He must have fought against his own father—that would explain why Mistress Ydaya said he betrayed his family.

And then there was the way he looked at me, the way he spoke. Maybe I didn't know everything about him, but I knew *him*… Didn't I?

"Back to your places!" From the loudness of Puna's voice, she must be right beside me.

I open my eyes and notice Cara watching me. She raises her eyebrows, as though telling me something.

Hope flits through me. Perhaps she'll finally decide I'm trustworthy enough to know the truth.

My entire body feels bruised. My legs from standing so long, my arm from where Master Ydaya grasped it, and my head from all the fond pats I received after I performed "Butterfly's Lament" for the Ydayas and their guests. I keep reminding myself as long as Mistress Ydaya sees me as her favorite pet, she'll excuse any mistake I'm caught making as due to my lowly Earthling stupidity. Accepting her condescension makes me feel powerless, but it's better than losing my memories.

I enter my room. Weary, I put my case down and flop back into my chair. The door starts to slide shut.

As it nears the wall, Cara slips in. The door closes behind her, trapping a lock of her hair. Cara yanks it out, apparently not caring that she's ripping out several strands.

I stand, surprised. "It's less than five minutes to curfew!"

Cara strides toward me. "Puna saw me enter my room, but she didn't see me leave. She'll assume I'm still in there unless given evidence otherwise, which I don't intend for her to find. So, you're stuck with me."

I tilt my head. "Why are you here?"

"You've been begging me for ages to let you in on my secrets." Cara crosses her arms. "Well, I'm about to grant your wish."

A rush of excitement floods me. "What made you change your mind?"

Cara leans against the wall and casually crosses her ankles. "Seemed like you were going to make trouble with or without me. The language tablet was something of a test to see if you'd crack under scrutiny. Well, you passed—and then some." She smirks. "I must say, Iris, you've got more guts than I gave you credit for. Illicitly accessing Adryil info?" She lets out a low whistle. "What were you looking for? Info about Master Verik?"

I consider how much to tell her, then decide that if I want

her to reveal her secrets to me, I should reveal mine. "Not exactly. I wanted to know about his son, Dámiul."

Cara drops her smile. "What do you want with Dámiul?"

I blink in surprise. "Do you know him?"

Cara picks up a strand of long, brown hair and examines the tips. "Maybe. Why does it matter to you?"

I hastily tell her about how I ran into Dámiul at Papilio and how he contacted me afterward, then conclude with a brief account of how Master Ydaya reacted to my watching a holovid of him.

Cara angles her mouth. "Shit. Dámiul must really care about you."

"What does that mean?" A barrage of questions rises up my throat, and I swallow them, waiting for Cara to respond.

She shifts her gaze toward the darkened window. "I think it'd be better if someone else told you. Someone outside the *Ka'risil* quarters." She looks at me, and I can't tell if her green gaze is sharp because she's examining me, or if that's just her natural aspect. "As far as Puna knows, I'm sleeping in my room, and you're sleeping in yours. In two hours, after the courtyard lights go dark, I'll take you to someone who can tell you everything you ever wanted to know about Dámiul—and what the Adryil are doing to us."

She's going to sneak out again, and she's taking me with her. I can scarcely believe it. I watch her, holding my breath, waiting for her to change her mind.

Instead, she reaches into her pocket, pulls out something silver, and unfolds it. "Put this on. It'll keep the Adryil from entering your mind." She pinches the ends of the silver arc between her fingers, and it glows green for a second before dimming again. She hands it to me.

I take the device and examine it. It doesn't look like much more than a metal headband. I recall the flash of silver I saw beneath Cara's hair. "Is this how you block them?"

Cara nods, then lifts the hair from her neck. A line of silver clings to her scalp by her nape, nearly invisible under her thick curtain of waves. "It's called a Grámed device. Keeps the Adryil out of our heads while making them think we're the compliant

drones they want us to be." She snorts. "Whenever Puna tries to read my mind, she just sees a bunch of inane thoughts, like 'it's warm today.' After a few months of constant telepathic brainwashing by their Keepers, most Earthlings lose the ability to think much deeper than that."

I close my hand around the machine. "Thank you." I glance at the door, and a thought occurs to me. "The Ydayas or Puna are probably watching me after what I did. Whatever you're planning, we should probably wait."

Cara tilts her head. "Put yourself in Puna's shoes. Your stupid little slave wandered someplace she wasn't supposed to go, got herself lectured until she cried, and ran scared back to where she belongs. She's not about to try again any time soon, is she?"

I can't help feeling apprehensive. "But what if—"

"Screw 'what if.' If I listened to all the 'what-ifs' in *my* head, I'd be no better off than Andreas, or Temir, or the other *Ka'risil* living in blissful ignorance." She pushes off the wall and steps toward me. "Don't you want to know what Dámiul was fighting for?"

I want that more than anything else. "Yes."

"Good." Cara flings a lock of hair over her shoulder. "We've got some time before it's safe to venture out. I suggest you either study that language tablet or get some rest while you can. It's going to be a long night." She goes over to my bed, falls back onto it, and closes her eyes.

Whatever she has planned, I'm not about to pass up a chance to learn what she's been keeping from me. I go over to my closet, retrieve the tablet, and start memorizing a list of Adryil nouns.

Chapter Twenty-Five

THE GRÁMED DEVICE PINCHES MY HEAD LIKE A VICE. ALL I CAN see is the faint blue light of Cara's watch as she aims it at the ground before us. I follow her toward the courtyard's gate and try to memorize her movements as she taps her fingers against the wall.

The gate silently slides open, revealing a dimly lit pathway. Cara presses her hand against the gate before it opens all the way, then slips out through the foot-wide crack. "Come on. Quickly."

I follow, hoping my mental resolution will calm my agitated body. If my deliberate breaths can't slow my heartbeat, I might pass out before we make it half a mile. We follow the pathway for a minute or so. I struggle to keep up with Cara's pace. My hair sticks to my face, and my dress clings to the sweat running down my back.

Cara draws to an abrupt stop at an intersection. The black streets, illuminated by the ice blue lights on the building walls, form an X before us. She checks around the corner, then turns. I run after her, wondering where she's taking me.

She grabs my shoulder. "Lie down." Her voice is a barely audible hiss. She flattens herself against the ground, and I follow suit, pressing my body against the cool, rough pavement.

A soft buzzing whirs above me. I glance up, but Cara grabs my head roughly and presses it down. Whatever the buzzing is, it must mean danger. I press my lips together, praying it will pass soon.

After a few minutes, the sound fades into the distance, and Cara pulls me up. "Let's go."

"What was that?" I pick up my pace to keep up with hers.

"Security drone. If one catches us, we're dead."

Apparently, the streets of Nathril have even more security than Papilio did. I follow Cara's example and look around in every direction, checking for other drones.

We round a corner and dart down another street. Almost every window in the buildings we pass is dark. Were we in a different situation, I'd take the time to appreciate the alien city surrounding me—their strange yet elegant architecture, their foreign decorations, their otherworldly civilization.

Cara stops suddenly, and I freeze in time to keep from crashing into her. "There's a fixed security camera ahead." She jumps up and grabs the edge of a windowsill jutting from the building to our left. "Follow me, and whatever you do, don't fall."

She pulls herself up onto the windowsill, then reaches down toward me. Hoping I won't need her assistance, I spring up with all my strength. Unfortunately, my barely more than five feet of height aren't enough to let me climb up as she did. I grab her hand, and she hauls me up until I can grab the ledge myself.

A thin lattice design protrudes from the pale wall to our right. Cara presses her back against the window and inches along the side. She grabs the edge of one of the diamond-shaped designs, then climbs it like a ladder.

I swallow hard, wondering how I'm supposed to do the same. She climbs all the way up to a window on the third level, then stands on the ledge. From where I am, she's so small and shadowed, I can barely see her motioning for me to follow.

The most I've climbed before tonight is a handful of

backstage ladders. I didn't think it was possible for my heart to beat any faster, but I guess I was wrong.

I approach the far side of the ledge I'm standing on and grab the edge of one of the protruding diamond shapes. Each diamond is only about three feet high, and I'm sure I could climb like Cara if I wanted to. If only my anxiety didn't leave me paralyzed.

I take a moment to recall why I'm doing this. For Dámiul: the faraway prince who remains a mystery to me. Cara promised I'd meet someone who'd tell me everything about him, and I won't let fear stop me. And for Milo: the best friend I left behind. Whoever I'm going to see, they might be able to help me get in touch with him.

If I could choose to send just one message, I don't know who I'd pick. Before my encounter with Master Ydaya, I would have said Milo. As much as I yearn for Dámiul's presence, at least he didn't seem broken. But after seeing that holovid and hearing what the Ydayas said about him, I'm no longer sure.

A delinquent, they called him. Someone who betrayed his family. He *must* have been working against his father's schemes. But what was he doing? And where is he being sent?

The memory of him bound in the Hall of Justice, his eyes glistening, hounds me. No matter how tall he stands, I can see the vulnerability beneath. I saw it at Papilio, when he confessed that I was his sanctuary, and I saw it in his eyes as he stood before the harsh, faceless judges.

He needs me too, wherever he is. Maybe even more than Milo does.

My only hope of finding either of them is by following Cara, so I grab the edge of the lattice and jump up.

The climb takes more strength than I expected. My arms ache under the strain as I pull myself up, and my legs protest as I use them in ways they're unaccustomed to. If I thought I was sweaty before, I must not have seen the worst yet. I'm glad the lattice is made out of something akin to concrete. It's the only thing letting me keep my grip.

I catch a glimpse of the street below me. It seems desperately

far. If I lose my grasp for just an instant, I'll end up a blood-splattered mess.

I squeeze my eyes shut and try to force myself to stop trembling. *I can do this.* I pull myself onto the next diamond, ignoring the objections in both my body and mind. By the time I reach Cara's level, I'm so exhausted, I almost want to fall forward onto the pavement below.

Cara raises her eyebrow at me. "What took you so long?"

"Haven't… done this before." My words rush between gasps. "Sorry… just need a moment."

She leans against the window behind her. "Fine." I can sense her rolling her eyes.

Irritated, I draw a new breath. "I'll be faster next time, okay?"

A pause. "Sorry, didn't mean to be a bitch." Even in the dim light, I can make out the slight smile angling Cara's mouth. "You're actually doing all right. I lost my grip my first time up. Would've fallen if it weren't for Alan."

My annoyance fades. "Alan?"

"Yeah. He's the one who showed me everything I know—how to break out of the dorms after curfew, how to escape the *Ka'risil* quarters, how to get to the underground hideout we're heading for."

My legs feel like jelly, and I sink down on the window ledge. "Is this the same Alan who was my predecessor?"

Cara sits beside me. "Yeah. He was part of the original quartet, along with Temir and Andreas. I was brought in because their previous second violinist died suddenly, and they needed a quick replacement. I never quite meshed with the *Ka'risil* culture, and Alan introduced me to the people we're going to meet."

"What happened to him?"

Cara's expression darkens. "The Ydayas attended a Papilian Spectacle. They were originally going to get a dancer, but then Mistress Ydaya saw this brilliant little violist she just had to have. She didn't want to wait in case someone else snapped you up. So she sent Alan into retirement to make room for you. I never got to say goodbye."

232

I bite my lip. "Is that why you hate me?"

"I don't hate you." Cara's voice emerges as a disgruntled grumble. "I just… well, you were the reason I lost someone who was like a father to me."

"I'm sorry."

"It's not your fault. How the hell could you have known? You thought you had no choice. So did I. So did all of us." She stands. "You ready to go?"

I rise. "Yes."

Cara climbs across the latticed wall to the next window, which looks so far away, it might as well be on a different building. I draw a breath and follow her.

Dámiul mentioned that forgotten underground buildings lay beneath Nathril—a dark, winding labyrinth of dusty corridors lined with doors that look old enough to crumble. Some are illuminated by lights, filled with glowing blue chemicals, that remained in place long after there was no one left who'd need to see by them. Others appear so black, you might as well be blind. I never imagined I'd be running through them someday.

By the time we reach a wide, brown door in the wall, my lungs feel ready to burst. Cara kicks the door three times, then knocks in a rhythmic pattern. A few seconds pass, and then the door starts sliding down into the ground, surprisingly soundless for something that looks so thick and bulky.

"Here we are," Cara says.

Though I still don't know where exactly we are, Cara's said enough for me to glean that it's a hideout of some kind whose location is only known by a few. A special knock doesn't exactly seem like top-notch security. "Couldn't anyone stumble upon this place?" I ask her.

"Probably, but all they'd find is a boring door they can't open. One that looks no different from the thousands of other doors in Nathril's vast, abandoned underground." Cara squints at the doorframe. "There's also a hidden camera that shows the people inside who's knocking, and someone's always keeping

watch. I know what you're thinking, though. You were expecting a hideout on a tech-filled planet to have more sophisticated security, weren't you?"

I nod in response.

"Well, so would the people these guys are hiding from." Cara gestures at the widening gap. "Machines can be traced and hacked, and if anyone spotted a security scanner or anything in a building that's supposed to be abandoned, they'd get suspicious. So these guys rely on the power of camouflage to keep from being discovered."

Before I can ask who "these guys" are, the door finishes its journey into the ground, and Cara spins away from me to enter the large, rectangular room, illuminated by flat sheets of yellow light that cover its low ceiling. The stained concrete walls and dirty floor remind me of Dogwood's tenements, and a musty smell drifts toward me.

Cara cups her hands by her mouth. "Atikéa? You here? I brought her this time!"

A high-pitched creaking sound grates on the air, and I cover my ears. A door on the far side of the room sinks into the floor.

A young woman strides out, her purple eyes glowing beneath ragged white bangs. Her smooth, sienna skin sharply contrasts her snowy locks. A second Adryil follows her. My eyes widen at the sight of him.

Slender, yet broad-shouldered. Thick, black hair. Glowing azure eyes. But his face is slightly older and somewhat on the long side, and he lacks the intensity that seems inherent in Dámiul. Yet he's definitely not the same man I saw in the sign— not only is he too young, but he looks altogether narrower. He appears somewhat nervous, but his mouth is pressed in the same firm line I'm so used to seeing on Dámiul's face.

The Adryil woman stops before me and puts her hands on her hips. "You're Iris Lei?" Her voice is a firm alto.

"Yes." I force my gaze toward her. "Who are you?"

"Atikéa Laksol." She offers me her hand.

"Atikéa. It's nice to meet you." I take her hand, but can't keep my gaze from wandering back to the Dámiul lookalike.

Atikéa releases her grip. "Is there something behind me?"

I try to focus on her purple gaze, but the man's face distracts me. "I'm sorry. It's just… he reminds me of someone I know."

The man steps forward. "Who?"

I glance at Cara, unsure of what to say. Cara gives me a nod. "Dámiul Verik," I say.

The man knits his thick eyebrows in an expression so similar to Dámiul's, it fills my heart with yearning. "How do you know Dámiul?" He even has Dámiul's accent.

"How do *you* know him?" The question escapes my lips. I realize too late how rude and confrontational it seems, but I have to know.

The man gives me an appraising look. "I'm his older brother, Jaerin."

My heart skips with excitement. Dámiul's brother—and Master Verik's other son. The answers I seek are at last within reach. "Where is he? Can I see him?"

"No." Jaerin's expression fills with sadness, and he looks down. "I know where he is, but by now, he's probably lost to us."

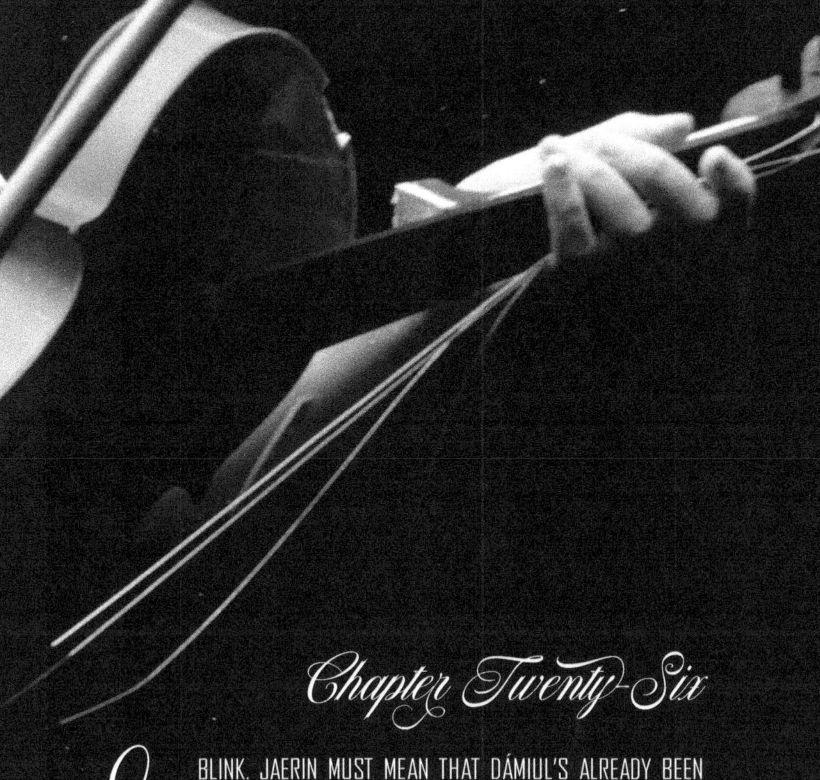

Chapter Twenty-Six

I BLINK. JAERIN MUST MEAN THAT DÁMIUL'S ALREADY BEEN sent on that secretive assignment, but why would that make him so sad? "What do you mean?"

Jaerin looks past me. "Cara, how much have you told her?"

"Nothing, really," Cara replies.

"Why not?"

Cara shifts her weight. "Because I'm blunt and unlikable. Do you really want *me* to be the one who crushes her past?"

Jaerin smiles. "You're blunt, but there's nothing wrong with that. I, for one, happen to like you quite a lot."

Cara's face brightens, but I hardly notice. *Crush my past?*

She tilts her head. "Well, I might have mentioned that your father runs the performing arts schools."

Jaerin gives me an apologetic look. "What you're about to learn will be shocking, and I confess, I was a part of it once. I ask you not to judge me for my past."

I stare at him, perplexed.

Atikéa gestures for me to follow her. "Come. There's something I need to show you."

I keep my gaze on Jaerin. "What are you talking about? And where's Dámiul?"

Any trace of his previous smile vanishes from Jaerin's face. "He was sent to a reeducation center. I've been doing my best to appeal the judgment, but I fear it may be too late."

"Too late for what?" A reeducation center—I don't understand what that means. It sounds like some kind of school… Is this where Dámiul was sent? But why would he think he might never come back?

Jaerin glances at the square device on his wrist, and his eyebrows gather with concern. "I'll be back soon."

He starts to walk off, but Atikéa steps in front of him. "Jaerin, I don't think—"

"I've tried everything else." Jaerin looks into Atikéa's eyes and says something soft in Adryil.

Atikéa shakes her head. She gives Jaerin a light kiss on the lips, then steps to the side. He strides away from me.

"Wait!" I start after him, but Atikéa blocks me.

"Don't worry, Iris," she says. "We'll tell you everything. It would just make more sense if you let me start from the beginning."

Jaerin disappears behind a door. I won't be getting any more answers from him for now, so I give Atikéa a reluctant nod.

Atikéa walks quickly toward the door on the far side, and Cara follows. I have to trot to keep up with them.

Cara pulls the Grámed device from under her hair, wincing as it slides off. She glances at me. "You can ditch yours too. No one here will mess with your head."

Glad to relieve the pinching, I pull my device off, fold it, and tuck it in my pocket. "Where are we?"

"The headquarters of the Abolitionists." Cara lifts her chin. "Atikéa's the founder and ringleader of an underground movement aiming to abolish what's being done to the *Ka'risil*. She and Jaerin are university classmates during the day." She makes a face. "In case you couldn't tell, they're also *together*."

Atikéa gives Cara an exasperated smile. "Oh Cara, how did you become a musician when you detest all things romantic?"

Cara wrinkles her nose. "I detest all things, *period.*"

Atikéa lets out a slight laugh. She enters the room and approaches a round, metal table in the center. "I used to just lead protests and petitions, but since Jaerin joined, we've gone underground. We're still protesting above ground, of course, but we're also working to spread the truth among the *Ka'risil.*" She sits down before the table.

I pull out the bronze chair beside Cara and take a seat, waiting for her to explain.

Atikéa looks down at a screen, which lies flat on the table before her. Her eyes flick from side to side—she must be telepathically commanding whatever computer the screen controls. A hologram of a school appears—it's Papilio.

"There it is: your old school." Atikéa looks up. "They tell you your one chance to escape a life of poverty is to find an Adryil patron, and that if you work hard enough, you can pay off your debts and become wealthy. But I suppose you know there's something wrong with that story." She glances at the touchscreen again. "This is an advertisement that recently aired in Nathril."

Elaborately drawn Adryil symbols stretch across the hologram, then morph into the word "Papilio."

A holovid of a stage replaces the image of the campus. A lithe aerialist twirls in red silks, and I recognize her immediately as Katarin Kaminski. A gentle female voice emits from the table, and English subtitles appear. "For over eighty years, TalentCorp has been dedicated to nurturing the skills of the finest Earthling Artists."

The holovid switches scenes, this time showing a close-up of Inna Havener, her face radiant with stage makeup and her voice ringing in a glorious melisma. "From the latest sensations to the one who started it all, each Artist is passionate, uniquely gifted, and highly trained to bring you the very best entertainment."

A montage of Artists flashes before me, accompanied by a rousing symphony. I recognize them as the greats from the Wall of Glory, and it reminds me of the sign I saw on my way to

the Ydayas. I wonder what this video means, and what Dámiul's father has to do with it.

The holovid returns to the image of Papilio, and a line of intricate Adryil symbols appears bit by bit, as though being drawn by an invisible hand. The subtitle spells the word: "TalentCorp."

The hologram disappears. I turned to Atikéa, puzzled. "Was that an ad for a Spectacle?"

Atikéa leans forward. "It was an ad for *you*, the Artists. TalentCorp is the oldest and largest trafficker on Adrye, and it's owned by Fyrin Verik—Jaerin and Dámiul's father."

Trafficker? That's a word used to talk about trading illegal items, such as drugs or weapons. Why would Atikéa use it to talk about my school? "What do you mean?"

"You weren't hired, Iris. TalentCorp—which owns Papilio and most of the other schools—sold you at auction."

Her words sit on the edge of my ears, refusing to enter my head. "I wasn't sold! I… I have an employment contract!"

Cara scowls. "So do I. But did you read it closely? Even if you tried, did you understand it?"

I shake my head. "One of the administrators and the Adryil liaison explained the terms to me." Erayet also erased Milo from my memories because I unknowingly gave her permission to. My stomach twists as I realize how little I understood about what I was signing.

"Well, they left out the part where you're agreeing to become property," Cara scoffs. "They trick their way into owning you. Twice. First when you enroll—your parents have to give the school custody. That means you belong to them until you come of age at fifteen. But by that point, almost no one thinks to leave. Then, as an independent adult, you forfeit your rights by signing that so-called employment contract. It's not hard to fool someone when you keep them from learning too much. I don't know how it is at Papilio, but back at Sinfonia, they don't teach *anything* other than what's relevant to the Arts. No math, no science, no history except the bare bones… Nothing that would take time or brain space away from honing our talents."

Looking back, I see everything in a new light. All that

nonsense the school told us about avoiding distractions was just that—nonsense. They kept us ignorant so we wouldn't question our circumstances and isolated us so no one else could inform us. Even if there were hints to be picked up, we were too obsessed with artistic glory to pay attention to anything else. It suddenly seems so clear, I wonder how I didn't see it before.

"I really did sell myself, then," I murmur.

"It's not your fault." Atikéa speaks gently. "The system of debts was put in place to control you, making you believe you're paying the school back when in reality, the salary you're told you'll receive is an annual payment from the buyer to the seller. The percentage you're told you can keep is a stipend you're supposed to save for after your patron retires you. When that happens, TalentCorp buys back your contract for a fraction of your price and places you in one of the secluded, school-adjacent towns they own, where the money flows back to them. By then, a *Ka'risil* has spent so much time under Adryil telepathy that his or her mind is altered permanently into accepting instruction without question. They behave autonomously, but they have little independent thought and lack personal memories from their own time as students."

My hand flies to my mouth. Vera was a retired *Ka'risil.* So were Master Raucci and Mistress Asif and every coach and director I ever encountered. The whole time I knew them, they were actually puppets. "What about the people they knew before they left? Surely they'd recognize retired *Ka'risil* who used to be their families or friends?"

"The company makes sure they don't," Atikéa says. "Retired *Ka'risil* are sent to live in towns far from the ones they grew up in. In the cases where coaches or staff members are needed at their former schools, they're made to remote in so they'll only be seen by students too young to have known them previously."

Which means Vera might have family in Dogwood she doesn't remember. *But Inna Havener moved her family to Charlotte—was that a lie?* I voice my question.

Atikéa twists her lip wryly. "No, her family is in Charlotte. Once in a while, TalentCorp chooses a *Ka'risil* to lavish rewards upon in order to motivate the rest of you. But those are the ones most tightly controlled. And they're the only ones permitted to remember their families."

"This is all so horrible," I murmur.

"Oh, and here's the worst part." Cara stabs the table with her finger. "This whole thing started out as an Earthling operation. The Earthling government and elites wanted fancy alien tech, but the Adryil weren't willing to sell at first. Our planet is worthless compared to Adrye, and the only thing we have that they want are our people."

"Katarin Kaminski was the first one traded." Atikéa sweeps her bangs out of her eyes. "She was a ward of the state attending the Papilio School, which at the time was a small performing arts center for underprivileged children called Dogwood Music and Dance. After her famed gala performance, a wealthy Adryil businessman told her he'd pay anything to hire her and bring her to Adrye. The age of majority used to be eighteen, meaning she was still legally a child, so the man negotiated with her public guardian. The matter was escalated into the highest reaches of the Earthling government until a deal was reached. Katarin believed she'd found a wonderful career opportunity, but the government declared her legally incompetent so they could control her earnings. They saw an opportunity and bought the school, renamed it Papilio, then sent their wards there in hopes of repeating their success. These were the children no one wanted, the ones who would do anything to escape a life of destitution and crime. The plan worked, but not everyone was willing to let go of their lives on Earth. So an exception to the telepathy ban was negotiated."

"Those in charge of our planet wanted to make their product more appealing." Cara's voice is almost a growl. "The first *Ka'risil* were problematic because they demanded ridiculous things like the right to visit their families and student debt forgiveness. That made the Adryil hesitant to 'hire' more. Our government put the telepathy exception in place so the Adryil could transform us into the single-minded objects they wanted, which encouraged them to keep buying. Eventually, the system was privatized and evolved into TalentCorp."

"Our government sold their own people?" I ask, incredulous.

"Yes." Cara's eyes flash. "The Adryil run TalentCorp now, but it was founded by fellow humans. And TalentCorp pays the Earthling government each year for the rights to control everything around us."

"Being an honorable and just society is a fundamental piece of Adryil culture," Atikéa says. "That is why they wanted to become allies and trade partners with Earth even though they could easily have conquered your world. But this doesn't mean they're immune to prejudice. Unfortunately, most view Earthlings as inferior beings and see nothing wrong with treating them as property, particularly because it was the Earthlings who first proposed the system."

I shake my head. One by one, I've watched my illusions about Papilio shatter. I used to think it was a haven where we could develop our talents for a chance no one else would grant us. Then, I saw how much madness and desperation simmered beneath the beauty. Now, I realize why Dámiul spoke so angrily about it.

It's not a sanctuary—it's a factory. And I'm a product.

When Cara said Mistress Ydaya "had to have" me, she meant that Mistress Ydaya wanted me the way a girl wants a new ballgown. All that time we were clamoring for the spotlight, thinking it would bring us opportunity and glory, we were helping TalentCorp turn a profit. No wonder only the poor attend schools like Papilio.

And Dámiul knew—his father as good as owned me. Why didn't he tell me?

"We're really slaves." I can't help a measure of disbelief. I never felt like I was being forced into labor. I still love music, and I'm sure the others still love their Arts. Maybe that's why so few of them question. "Do the other Earthlings know?"

"Like I said, it was their idea in the first place." Cara grimaces. "Most Earthlings are so poor, all they worry about is taking care of themselves. Some even envy us because we're the only ones with a shot at breaking into the elite class. They either don't realize or don't care what people like Inna Havener must give up. The rich few are just like the Adryil. They see us

as beneath them and think TalentCorp is doing us a favor by keeping us employed."

I'm reeling with disbelief. "And all the coaches and directors are brainwashed."

"Not just them," Cara says. "The minders, administrators, nurses—*everyone* you've ever encountered at school. Some are retired *Ka'risil*, and the rest are aged-out students who counted themselves lucky to get jobs on campus. They, too, sign employment contracts that turn them into property. Basically, they're 'recycled' into TalentCorp's labor force and never think to leave. Adryil telepathy is extremely powerful. It can make things that don't make sense seem like they do."

Everything seems so wrong. We work so hard, tantalized by false promises. How could they do this to us? I recall how the pressure nearly destroyed Milo—and how it could still be destroying him.

But Milo was on the verge of dropping out, and if he does, he won't receive a school job. "What about the factory workers?"

Atikéa puts her elbows on the table. "They, too, are part of the company's labor force, manufacturing everything from the costumes to the holoprojectors. However, their destitution prevents them from leaving, so TalentCorp rarely needs to brainwash them."

"They could if they wanted to." Cara's jaw is tight. "But telepathy takes effort, and they found an easier way: drugs. It lets people think they're rebelling in a way when really, it's another way to control them. Keeps them too fogged up to revolt or anything. It's genius, in an evil way."

I recall the way Phers suddenly lost his aggressive edge, how his eyes glazed over and his focus slipped away. The whole time he thought he was free, he was actually doing exactly what TalentCorp wanted.

"The world of TalentCorp is entirely separate from regular Earthling life," Atikéa says. "They created a kind of ecosystem, one that's renewable and genetically diverse. A lot of talent is innate—like facial bone structure for singers or body types for dancers. Therefore, the company monitors the children of their laborers, searching for potential *Ka'risil*. That's why they instituted the beginner education system."

"That's also why they hold social events for us." Cara rests her elbows on her knees. "Not just to train us for similar events on Adrye, but also to encourage us to pair up and pass our talents down to the next generation. The pill they give girls doesn't actually prevent pregnancies. The ninety-five percent stat is bullshit—they made it up so people wouldn't get suspicious when the odd 'accidental' pregnancy happens. The pill contains nanobots that play watchdog over a girl's uterus. The moment she conceives, they scan the embryo and project how a child will develop before she even knows she has one inside her. If the kid doesn't have the physical traits TalentCorp wants… bye, bye, baby."

I glimpse my hands, with their freakish flexibility and long fingers, and realize they're probably the only reason I was born. This is all too much. Even the Semiannual Balls, which I thought were wonderful gifts from Papilio, were designed to serve a purpose. And everyone in Dogwood belongs to TalentCorp.

"They keep people poor so they can't try to contact those on Adrye," I muse. "Parents of *Ka'risil* won't find it strange that they never hear from their children."

"That's right," Cara says. "Same goes for spouses who age out."

Like Alfred Winters. The memory of the day he left pierces my heart. Caroline can't keep her promise to take care of him. If she's hired, she won't remember he exists. Everything we were told about alums supporting families on Earth must have been a lie.

Something about the recollection nudges my heart, telling me I had a personal reason to find their story so tragic. Was it tied to the Papilio alum I can't remember? I replay the scene in my head, searching for a clue. Caroline was crying… Alfred put his hand on her stomach… she was pregnant…

My parents. My family. This could have been us.

I look up with a start. My parents—where are my parents? Who are they? *Erayet must have erased them.* She must have erased my ability to wonder about them as well because until now, it didn't even strike me as strange that I don't know my own parents' names.

Cara knits her brows. "Something wrong?"

"I can't remember my parents." I dig my fingers into my hair. "They could be here too, and I wouldn't recognize them if I saw them."

"Yeah, it's awful." Cara twists her mouth. "At least you came to that revelation yourself. Until Alan told me about all this, the very idea of *having* parents never occurred to me. Like I said, Adryil telepathy is a powerful thing. I was born at Sinfonia, so I probably wouldn't have remembered them anyway, but it's still weird not knowing who they are."

Tears prick my eyes, and I squeeze them shut. I have parents out there somewhere. I used to love them. The Papilian I was hoping to find—that must have been one of them. And the other must have aged out like Alfred did—but which one?

"I used to know." I glance at Cara. "I think I was hoping to reunite with them. Maybe if I'd thought of this earlier, I could have recovered the memories, but now… there's nothing."

"Well, even if you remembered them, finding them would be impossible." Though Cara maintains her matter-of-fact tone, a strange look clouds her eyes—maybe regret, or maybe guilt. "It's not like there's a central database of *Ka'risil* we can search. And they wouldn't remember us either."

My parents were taken from me, and I from them. And TalentCorp tried to take Milo from me too.

I bite my lip. I asked Milo to stay with the Ballet because I thought a bleak future awaited him otherwise. Now, I'm not sure staying would be any better. I remembered him because Dámiul showed me what telepathy feels like. The same won't be true for Milo. If I find him on Adrye someday, he won't know who I am. If only I could warn him! If only I could warn them all—Caroline, Sabina, Estelle… She's not someone I care for, but she's still *someone*. Nobody has the right to take her very self away from her.

Knowing that stirs my anger. "No one should have to go through this."

"I agree." Atikéa's voice is low.

"Is there some way to contact the Papilians from here?"

"I'm afraid not. If there were, our mission would be considerably easier. I've opposed *Ka'risil* slavery for years, but no one listened to my petitions. They claimed it wasn't even slavery, since you willingly sign the contracts. So I started something else." Atikéa straightens. "The Abolition movement seeks to inform the *Ka'risil* of the truth. We're targeting the younger ones, since they haven't been mind-controlled as long as the others, so their memories have a better chance at being recovered."

"And you're going to free them?"

"Believe me, I want to. But if I did, where would they go? Here?" She gestures at the stained wall. "Technically, you and Cara are both free right now. You don't have to go back to the Ydayas, and if you want to stay, you're more than welcome. But you would be branded a fugitive, and if you were ever caught, your mind would be wiped."

"I see." I slump in my chair.

Cara puts her chin in her hand. "We've considered sending people back to Earth. The problem is, not only would that involve hijacking a starship, but we'd be in the same bind. Where do you send a bunch of people who only know how to sing or dance or something? Especially since Earth's government is in on all this. They'd send us right back to TalentCorp." She twists her mouth. "We're kind of stuck on the freedom front."

Atikéa leans back with a contemplative expression. "Also, most of the *Ka'risil* we've talked to don't want to leave. They enjoy their present lives, where they're taken care of and spend their days doing something they love. They don't remember anything worth going back to. So all I can do for the time being is quietly inform them of what their lives really are." Her gaze turns distant. "Dámiul thought I was being too cautious. Maybe he's right."

"Caution's a luxury I can't afford anymore." Jaerin's voice comes from the door, and I turn to face him. He stands by the doorframe with a stormy expression.

Atikéa gets up. "*En ganza ato sui clogamo navar?*"

All I understand from that question are the words "help him."

"I have no choice." Jaerin holds up a gleaming disc. "I know you don't believe me, but you'll change your mind once you see this." He turns to me. "You're the Earthling Dámiul ran into at Papilio."

"Yes, that's me." I stand, eager for more information. "What was he doing on Earth? Is he an Abolitionist like you?"

"In a way." Jaerin approaches the table. "I tried to keep him out of it. 'You're too young for this,' I told him, but he said justice couldn't wait for him to grow up. I hoped if I fought on his behalf, he could stay away. But he wouldn't listen." He glances at Atikéa. "Did you tell her about Ximena?"

"I thought it'd be better coming from you," Atikéa says.

I cock my head. "Who's Ximena?"

"I apologize, Iris." Atikéa tilts her brows. "There is one *Ka'risil* who was freed. Just not by us."

"She's a *Ka'risil* Dámiul encountered." Jaerin's eyes grow distant. "She managed to recover the memory of her older sister, who had aged out and was working in a TalentCorp factory back on Earth. She wanted nothing more than to return. Dámiul brought her here hoping the Abolition could help, but I told him sending her back would be too dangerous for everybody. I thought we'd never succeed, and we'd expose the entire movement in our failed attempt. He said if he could free even one of the wrongfully enslaved, then his life would have been worth living."

I smile to myself. That definitely sounds like Dámiul.

"I agreed with Jaerin." Atikéa sighs. "All starships are closely inspected before takeoff and monitored during flight. I didn't think we could get Ximena on board one. Or get her sister out of the TalentCorp-controlled town she lived in."

"Yet my brother found a way." Jaerin's tone conveys fondness and disbelief. "He convinced our father to send him to Charlotte to attend a business meeting on his behalf. *Vabeth* was so excited about Dámiul finally taking an interest in the company that he agreed. I don't know how my brother smuggled Ximena over

with him, how he got in contact with her sister, or where he sent them. But somehow, he succeeded."

I *knew* Dámiul had a purpose beyond what he told me. The thought of him risking himself to free one of my kind—to take one step, however small, toward righting the world—makes my heart swell. This must have been what he meant when he said he was defying his father—*not* the part about breaking into Papilio. I wish he'd told me.

"He wasn't finished, though," Jaerin continues. "I don't think this was part of his original plan, but he broke into the Papilio School to alert the students to what the employment contracts actually say."

So why didn't he? Confused, I sink back into my chair. "He never told me anything, no matter how I asked." A question flutters through my head, and I hesitate, wondering how to phrase it. "Jaerin... If your father owns TalentCorp, why are you and Dámiul fighting it?"

Jaerin's expression darkens. "*Vabeth* told me that TalentCorp is ultimately good for the Earthlings, and for most of my life, I was foolish enough to believe him. But Dámiul was never as blind. The first time he tried to free a *Ka'risil*, I thought he'd gone mad. Still, I began to question, and I came to realize that the *Ka'risil* are people like us. Dámiul made his views known, and our parents nearly disowned him for it. But I kept mine a secret. *Vabeth* still expects me to take over the company someday. If that happens, I could change *everything*. But in the decades in between now and then, thousands of *Ka'risil* will remain enslaved and lose their selves to Adryil memory wipes. And so I live a double life, pretending to be the good son while doing what I can for the Abolition." He knits his black eyebrows. "*Joth'en, Dámiul!*" He slams the table. "He already had four strikes—he knew what a fifth would do, and still, he went so far beyond that!"

Strikes? "What does that mean?"

"Because of his fight for the *Ka'risil*, he's been in and out of disciplinary centers since he was thirteen. No matter what I said, he wouldn't stop, and now..." Jaerin trails off. "Smuggling Ximena back to Earth killed any chance he had for clemency.

He's been locked up ever since they caught him at Papilio, and I don't know how much of him is left."

"What?" I think back to all the times I met with Dámiul. He was in prison the entire time—is that why he was so vague about himself? And when he appeared worn out at the Spectacle—was that because of what they did to him?

I stare at the ground. *No matter how dangerous the truth was, I would rather have known.*

Atikéa leans over Jaerin's shoulder and says something in a quiet voice. I can't make out her words, but her tone is harsh.

Jaerin grabs her hand. "Please, Kéa, I need your help." His tone speaks of desperation. He turns to me. "They say the reeducation centers are meant to rehabilitate criminals. In truth, they wipe the minds of the prisoners and attempt to mold them into someone else."

Atikéa takes a seat beside Jaerin. "I understand that you're worried about your brother, but committing the kinds of crimes you proposed can't be the solution."

Jaerin presses the disc into the edge of the table; there must be a slot there. "I knew you'd say that. That's why I brought this. It's a record of what they're doing to him. They say his crime was so severe, it warrants extreme methods."

A horrible feeling grips my gut. Soft humming emits from the table. Seconds later, a hologram of Dámiul appears. He's sitting at a narrow metal table across from a white-haired man in gray whose back is to me. His hands are bound to the table before him, and he glares defiantly ahead.

I bite my lip as I recognize the black outfit he always wore, the one I thought meant he was in the military.

It's a uniform, yes. A prison uniform.

Chapter Twenty-Seven

*D*ÁMIUL, WHY DIDN'T YOU TELL ME? I THOUGHT I KNEW HIM, but he let me believe so many things that turned out to be deceptions. Why would he lie when his mission was to spread the truth? Wouldn't telling me and letting me help in his cause have been worth the risk?

In the holovid, Dámiul remains motionless. The white-haired man speaks sharply in Adryil. His words run together, and I can't make out a single one.

"What's he saying?" I ask.

Jaerin reaches under the table and presses something. Subtitles appear along the bottom of the holovid: "…and I've had enough. I told you yesterday was your last chance, and now, you leave me no choice."

The man gets up and marches over to Dámiul. I notice a metal crown ringing the man's head, gold lights glowing along its edges. With his clinical white outfit, his gleaming yellow eyes are the only sign of color on him other than the crown's luminosity spilling onto his locks.

Dámiul stares ahead, ignoring the man. The man holds

up a metal crown, identical to his own except with blue lights, and wedges it onto Dámiul's head. He pulls a small, rectangular device out of his pocket and presses it. The device whirs. Dámiul flinches slightly, but otherwise remains still.

I start to ask what that thing is, but Cara beats me to the question.

"It amplifies the telepathic effects of one person on another." Jaerin answers through clenched teeth. "The brighter the lights glow, the more power he's using."

The man sits down across from Dámiul and speaks in a precise, formal manner. According to the subtitles, he says, "Stage One. I am going to remove the criminal's memories of his most recent crime: illegally entering a TalentCorp facility. In addition, I will excise any memories of what followed in order to set him back to the state of mind he was in prior to that particular crime. Following that, I shall work backward to erase all recollections of any illicit activities he has been involved in."

I gasp. This recording is from the past. If he succeeded, that means he forced Dámiul to forget me. Is that why Dámiul vanished? Is that what he meant when he said he wouldn't be here by the time I arrived?

The lights on the man's crown glow so bright, they make his white hair appear bright yellow. The blue lights on Dámiul's crown blaze. Dámiul doesn't say a word, but in his eyes, I see the same vulnerability as when he stood in the Hall of Justice. A fear he refuses to show, but that is nevertheless present.

Seconds stretch into minutes. I can't take my eyes off Dámiul. Whatever the man's doing, it's hurting him, and I wish I could reach through the hologram and snatch the device away.

The lights on both crowns dim.

"*Gorxit sthanga!*" The white-haired man collapses forward, leaning on his hands. The subtitles say: "Worthless criminal!" From the way his back rises and falls, he must be panting.

Dámiul lifts the corner of his mouth in a triumphant half-smile. Despite his cool façade, his deliberate breaths and the sweat on his forehead betray the effort he must have exerted. "*Ona sui botsel nur,*" he whispers. The subtitles say: "I won't forget."

The man looks up and spews venomous words. "Yes, you will."

He gets up, reaches behind him, and leans over the table. He grabs Dámiul's hair and yanks his head to the side. I gasp, clenching my fist over my mouth. The man plunges a thick metal syringe into Dámiul's neck.

Dámiul's expression contorts with pain for a split second, then returns to his composed mask. The man yanks the syringe out, and he curls his mouth into a sneer.

Dámiul's head droops, and his eyes glaze over. Whatever drug the man injected him with must be taking effect.

My eyes tingle. The whole time I knew him—is this where he went when he disappeared? Looking back, I remember anger, fierceness, and a touch of melancholy, but never anything that made me suspect he was in so much distress.

The gold lights on the white-haired man's crown glow again. So do the blue lights around Dámiul's head. Dámiul lifts his chin, but I can see the pain behind his eyes, and his breathing grows increasingly labored.

Dámiul's hands shake. He clenches his fists, but the spasms move up his arms. The white-haired man's face contorts. Even though his back is mostly to me, I can make out the sliver of a smile.

I grip the edge of the table, reminding myself that I'm watching a recording.

Dámiul blinks rapidly, and a horrible shudder runs through his body. The lights glow brighter, and red blood trickles down the side of his face from under the crown.

His eyes close, and he slumps forward.

"*Dámiul!*" I clap my hands over my mouth.

In the holovid, Dámiul convulses against the table, breathing in audible gasps. More blood seeps from beneath the crown, and a line of red escapes the side of his mouth.

The lights on both crowns dim again. The white-haired man watches unsympathetically as Dámiul continues shaking. I want to reach through the holovid and scream at him.

The convulsions stop, and Dámiul lies limp against the table, gasping for air. The white-haired man leans toward him

and speaks with a satisfied lilt. "Tell me, Dámiul, have you met any Earthlings other than the *Ka'risil* on Adrye?"

Dámiul's breath steadies. His eyes remain shut, and I wonder if the white-haired man really expects him to answer when he's unconscious. The man grabs Dámiul's shoulder and shakes him. He lets out a harsh exclamation. "Answer me!"

Dámiul's eyelids flutter, and he whispers, as though too weak to voice his words. "What did you say?"

The man repeats his question.

Dámiul slowly lifts his head and meets the man's gaze. His eyes blaze with determination, and a defiant smile lifts his lips. "*Zeth atiyil Iris Lei.*"

My heart skips a beat. I don't need the subtitles to understand: *Her name is Iris Lei.* Unexpected joy rushes through me—he hasn't forgotten me.

"*Contuk en!*" The man's curse is almost a scream.

"*Ona sui botsel nur.*" *I won't forget.* Dámiul's eyelids fall shut, and he collapses onto the table.

The holovid flickers out. Jaerin's gaze is fixed on the ground beside him.

Atikéa shakes her head, her mouth open in horror. She whispers something to Jaerin, and I only make out the last words: "*On'en sui clogamo.*" *I will help you.*

I turn to Cara, wondering if she knows more about what's going on between them.

Cara leans toward me. "Jaerin wants to break Dámiul out of the reeducation center, and he needs Atikéa's underground connections to pull it off. She kept refusing because she didn't want him to do anything rash while Dámiul's case was still in appeals. I guess she's changed her mind now that she's seen what they're putting Dámiul through."

"This record is from weeks ago." Jaerin voice sounds strained. I turn to see his eyes fixed on me. "The holovid was taken shortly after he was sentenced. I don't know how much they've put him through since then, but I can't let it go on any longer."

Weeks. That means I probably spoke with him after he went through the hell I witnessed. Is that what he was escaping from

when he said I was his sanctuary? "When we communicated through the Zexa device, he seemed… fine."

Jaerin gets up and walks around the table toward me. "What did he say to you?"

I summarize my interactions with Dámiul—well, the parts about mind training and his disgruntlement toward Papilio. I finish by telling him how I last saw Dámiul three days before the Zexa device was taken from me.

Jaerin looks down at me with a contemplative expression. "He would have mapped the Zexa device to his brain to use it telepathically, though…" He presses his lips together.

"Though what?" I ask.

"The reeducation centers sometimes use brain implants when a prisoner is especially stubborn. Judging from what we've just seen, Dámiul would qualify. Those implants would have broken his connection with the Zexa device. Even if I get him out, they might have already erased who he is."

Atikéa approaches him. "Memories can be recovered."

"Only if he remembers in time!" Jaerin whirls toward her. "What if I'm already too late? What if whatever blank slate they replaced his mind with has already overridden the brother I know? *Contuk fuzettin!*"

Atikéa puts her hand on his arm and speaks soothingly.

I rub my eyes furiously, trying to make the tears stop. I can't believe it. Dámiul is so close, in the same city as I am, and yet, I might have lost him anyway. If only he'd told me! Did he think I would shun him for being a prisoner?

I look up at Jaerin. "Can I help?"

Jaerin tries to smile, but it falters. "Just be here when I get Dámiul out. I'm sure he'll be glad to see you."

Atikéa turns to Cara. "I'm afraid our other plans for the *Ka'risil* will have to wait."

Cara cocks her eyebrow. "Put our entire mission on hold for one person? What kind of strategy is that?"

"It's not a strategy," Atikéa murmurs.

"Then why—"

"Because that's my little brother they're torturing." Jaerin interrupts Cara's question. "I have to get him out."

Cara puts her hands on her hips. "Oh, so he matters more than all of us?"

"I didn't say that." Jaerin sighs. "You've never had a family, so I don't expect you to understand. But please, try."

Cara's irritated expression remains, but she doesn't argue. Jaerin and Atikéa leave the room. My mind feels like a hurricane blew through it. First, I learned that my entire life was a lie, and now, I find out that the boy who captured my imagination, then captured my heart, might have had his mind erased.

"How can they do this?" I say. "I thought the Adryil were supposed to be… peaceful."

Cara lets out a humorless laugh. "Oh, they're perfectly nice, as long as you listen to them. The Ydayas are nice enough to us, aren't they? You can't say they're abusing us or anything. Speaking of which…" She glances at her watch. "We should probably start heading back. Normally, I'd stay another hour or two, but I figure it's your first time out, and I don't want you to be too sleepy on the return trip, with all the climbing and everything."

Sleep is the last thing I'm capable of right now, but I suppose with Atikéa and Jaerin gone and no other Abolitionists in sight, there's no sense in us lingering here. "What do you usually do out here?"

"Strategize, mostly." Cara stands and walks to the door. "Decide which *Ka'risil* we can trust with the truth. Pass around Adryil language tablets so the Earthlings won't be so lost. Cook up ways to convince *Ka'risil* owners that what they're doing is wrong. Nothing dramatic—well, until Jaerin decided to try busting his darling brother out of jail." She rolls her eyes. "Not the usual kind of mission."

I walk beside her, and we cross the wide room leading to the exit. "What can I do to help?"

"For now? Just learn Adryil. I've already scouted the other *Ka'risil* in our quarters. They're all too ingrained in their ways to join us." Cara presses a pad by the door, which slides down into the ground. "There aren't that many of us Abolitionists. Atikéa has a plan to infiltrate more *Ka'risil* quarters, but I guess that has to wait until Dámiul's out. Someday, we'll shut down

TalentCorp and all the other slavers. I don't know how, but it's going to happen."

I look back at the dingy underground complex that serves as the Abolitionists' headquarters. It's such a contrast to the high-tech school TalentCorp built. From the looks of things, we don't stand a chance.

But we have to win. We can't let the Adryil keep controlling people. Dámiul said that individuals aren't valued on Adrye as they are on Earth, but I never imagined his kind would go so far as to erase people.

Cara tucks her Grámed device under her hair. "Put yours on."

I pull my device out of my pocket and place it over my head, protecting the one thing I used to believe would always be mine: my thoughts.

Chapter Twenty-Eight

I'M GLAD THE YDAYAS HAVE SCHEDULED MORE FREQUENT performances for us. Surrounding myself with beautiful string harmonies is the only way I can keep calm. The tension of the past few days since I returned from meeting Atikéa and Jaerin is driving me insane. There's so much I want to do, and yet I'm stuck here, uselessly scratching at a wooden instrument.

I finish the phrase and lift my bow, then start counting out a ten-measure rest. An orange glimmer catches my eye, and I glance up to see the Ydayas. Mistress Ydaya, in a rich coral dress, hooks her arm around Master Ydaya's and surveys us. I move my hair over my right shoulder, hoping it looks like I'm just clearing it away from my instrument. I wish my locks were as thick as Cara's. She doesn't need to put any effort into hiding her Grámed device.

Mistress Ydaya says something to her husband. I catch the words "*Ka'risil*," "Papilio," and "*zaro*," which means "new." I force my eyes back to the music so I won't forget to come in and do my best not to jitter. *New Ka'risil… Cara said the Ydayas went to the last Spectacle to get a dancer.* A far-fetched but irresistible hope lights within me. *Milo…*

I don't know whether him coming to Adrye would be a good thing, but it seems no matter which path his life takes, he will always belong to TalentCorp. At least if he's here with me, I'll have a chance to undo the damage Erayet or another liaison does. I've spent ages mulling over his fate, but though him aging out on Earth is his best chance at keeping his memories, the sense of failure would tear him apart. I don't think he'd make it that far anyway. He'd drop out first—and be trapped in a life of hollow misery like Phers. *Please, Milo, give yourself another chance with the Ballet…*

Hearing my cue to rejoin the quartet, I force myself to concentrate on what I'm doing. I strike the last few chords in time with the others, then lower my instrument.

Mistress Ydaya eyes me from below the stage. "Well done, Quartet. You may take a five-minute break." She lifts a finger and beckons me.

What's going on? I get up and nervously walk to the stairs. Cara gives me a questioning look, then flicks her hair. I recognize the gesture as her telling me to make sure my Grámed device is covered up and fan out the hair falling down my back.

I approach Mistress Ydaya, nervously clutching my viola. "Yes, ma'am?"

Mistress Ydaya narrows her eyes. "Why were you watching me?"

"I heard you say 'Papilio,' and I was curious." I widen my eyes, trying to look as innocent as possible.

"Oh, sweet girl. You're curious about your old school, aren't you?"

I nod mutely.

"You used to accompany dancers in the orchestra pit." Mistress Ydaya gives me an appraising look. "Is it different from performing in an ensemble?"

"Not really. You just have to pay attention to their tempo during rehearsals." Hoping to plant a suggestion without sounding too forward, I say, "I miss the Pit. It was such fun collaborating with other Artists, especially ballet dancers.

They're so beautiful, and seeing their movements helped me interpret the music better." My heartbeat speeds up. *Could this work?*

Mistress Ydaya unhooks her arm from her husband's and raises her eyebrows at him. "Even the little one knows that *Ka'risil* perform better when exposed to other Arts. We've kept a quartet for so long, I think you've forgotten that most patrons employ a variety of *Ka'risil.* We were the only household in Nathril that had only a quartet to contribute to last month's gala! It was downright embarrassing. I told all our friends I would have more for the next event, and I intend to keep my word."

Master Ydaya grumbles, and I recognize the word for "value." If they're discussing what I think they are, then this is my chance to bring Milo here, where I can look after him. Mistress Ydaya seems to like me as a special favorite—maybe I can use that.

I consider my next words. Mistress Ydaya said my curiosity made me unique. She probably won't mind a few harmless-sounding questions. "Are we going to be accompanying dancers?"

Mistress Ydaya smiles slightly. "We are considering hiring more *Ka'risil.* You could have more Earthlings your age to play with. Wouldn't that be nice?"

Her condescension makes me want to grimace, but I keep my expression innocent. "That would be wonderful. Will they be from Papilio?"

Mistress Ydaya narrows her eyes. She's probably probing my mind for my intentions. I'm glad I have the Grámed device to block her. Apparently satisfied that I'm not thinking any conspiratorial thoughts, she relaxes her expression. "That depends on if any Papilians are worthy of our patronage."

"Of course." I lower my gaze, figuring I shouldn't say anything else unless prompted.

Mistress Ydaya holds up her wrist device, and a holographic portrait of Nikolai appears. She speaks coolly to Master Ydaya, and I recognize the word for "best."

I press my lips together, hoping my face doesn't betray my

nervousness. If it's the best she wants, would she even consider Milo after the lukewarm Spectacle reviews?

Master Ydaya grumbles, and the word for "value" is mentioned again. His eyes flick down a line of holographic icons to the left of the portrait projected from Mistress Ydaya's device. A hologram of another boy dancer, whom I recognize from the corps de ballet, appears. Mistress Ydaya shakes her head and speaks in an exasperated voice. Master Ydaya points at a string of numbers below the dancer's portrait—I'm guessing it's either his ranking or his price.

Price. The idea makes me uncomfortable, and I try not to cringe. The Ydayas must be arguing over how much to bid on the new dancer Mistress Ydaya wants, with Mistress Ydaya desiring the best and Master Ydaya aiming for the cheapest. They might as well be discussing the purchase of a new piece of furniture.

Mistress Ydaya waves her hand at me in a dismissive gesture. "Go back to the others."

I turn to leave, but then a hologram of Milo replaces Nikolai. I stop, and a sense of relief courses through me. If he's on the list of *Ka'risil*, at least I know he didn't drop out. And it means he wants to come to Adrye.

Mistress Ydaya catches my eye. "Still there, little one? What are you looking at?"

Despite the tension gripping me, I have to take a chance for Milo's sake. I brighten my expression. "I knew those dancers. Nikolai had the highest ranking among the boys, but everyone knew Milo was better. The only reason Milo's ranking was lower was because he got nervous before the last Spectacle." That's not entirely true, but if Master Ydaya is grumbling about value, maybe I can convince him and Mistress Ydaya that Milo is a bargain.

Bargain… How could I call him that? I stifle the thought. Outrage won't help my cause. "I've seen Milo dance much better than Nikolai in rehearsals."

Master Ydaya shifts his gaze toward me. "Indeed?"

"Oh, yes." I keep my tone as casual as I can. *Just sound clueless.* "Even Mistress Duval thought so. She often asked Nikolai why he couldn't be more like Milo. But Milo was worried about his

first Spectacle with Sabina as his partner, and he didn't do his best. We were all disappointed when his ranking dropped. I'm sure it will climb again after the next show."

Mistress Ydaya regards the portrait of Milo. She pats me on the head, and I pray that she won't stroke my hair and realize there's something beneath it. "Run along."

I return to the stage, wondering if there's something else I could have said to convince her to bring Milo here.

Although my mandatory practice time ended a few minutes ago, I keep playing. Working on "Archangel Ascendant" is the only way to quiet my mind. I repeat a particularly tricky phrase in the song, focusing on the notes only.

The door slides open, and Cara slips in. She waits for the door to close, then turns toward me. "If Puna comes in and asks what we're doing, we're just chatting about dresses and shoes. You know, girl talk."

I put my viola down and approach her. "Right. As usual."

Cara leans against the wall. "What was all that with the Ydayas this afternoon?"

I tell Cara how Mistress Ydaya's interest in dancers might mean she'll buy Milo, who I miss more than I care to think about.

Cara raises one eyebrow. "So you're pimping out your friend? Nice."

I open my mouth in indignation. "That's not how it is! I just… I don't know what else to do! I can't send him a message, I can't return to Papilio—if it were up to them, I would forget him, but I won't do that. At least if the Ydayas bring him here, I can look out for him. Maybe even keep him from forgetting his family."

Cara pulls her lips in. "You've actually got a decent shot of seeing your bright-eyed fantasy come true. Mistress Ydaya has been talking about expanding her collection of *Ka'risil* for months. From what I've overheard, she and Master Ydaya recently made a killing off some business deal, and they're pretty much rolling in riches. That's why Mistress Ydaya was

willing to splurge on the must-have Artist of the last Spectacle. You were freaking expensive."

A hint of pride at my skills being worth so much rises within me, but almost immediately, a sense of disgust at myself deflates it. I'm not a knickknack to be valued with money. Yet being so prized, even in this twisted way, feels like the recognition I always yearned for.

"Do the Adryil… um… buy *Ka'risil* from the same schools often?" I ask.

"Yeah, it's easier for them to just pick up a collection from their favorite vendors. The original quartet—Temir, Andreas, Alan, and the guy I replaced—all came from Papilio at the same time." Cara shifts her weight. "In fact, they were friends and pretty thrilled that they were all sponsored by the same patrons."

Seeing a troubled look in her eyes, I ask, "Is something wrong?"

"Nah." Cara picks up a lock of hair and fiddles with it. "You're lucky you remember someone you left behind enough to still care about him. I remember names and faces, but not much else. By the time Alan gave me a Grámed device, I'd already lost most of my personal memories, and it was too late to get any back."

Not knowing how else to respond, I say softly, "I'm sorry."

"About what?" Cara scoffs. "I don't remember anyone, so it's not like I miss them. Sometimes I think it's better that way. This whole slavery thing bothers me enough as it is. I'm glad I don't have to live with knowing people I care about are stuck in the system." She splits her lips into a wry grin. "Come to think of it, I don't care about anyone except Alan, and he's gone. Sometimes, I think it would have been better if he'd let Puna brainwash me like the others. Then, at least I would fit in here, and I'd have something akin to friends."

I never thought to wonder what Cara's life must have been like before I got here, or how hard it must have been for her to watch the one person she cared about be taken away. No wonder she hated me when I first arrived. "What about Atikéa and Jaerin?"

Cara shrugs. "I guess they count. But I don't see them very often, so most of the time, it's just me and my violin."

"What about me?" I smile sheepishly. "Do I count?"

She gives me a funny look. "Let's face it. We only spend time together because we've got a shared place and a shared cause. If I'd encountered you at Sinfonia, I wouldn't have spoken two words to you."

Back when I first met her, such talk from Cara would have bothered me. But now that I've gotten to know her, I can tell she's not nearly as callous as she pretends to be. I give her an annoyed look. "Do you have to be so negative all the time?"

Cara crosses her arms. "Hey, if I were a cute guy, you'd find my bad attitude hot."

Despite myself, I smile. I know what she's talking about—plenty of girls back at Papilio seemed intent on chasing boys who were jerks to them. "I don't think so."

"Then you're smarter than the giggling ditzes back at school." Cara tilts her head, as though seeing me in a new light. "Okay, sure, I guess you count as a friend." She tosses a lock of hair over her shoulder. "Well, I hope if this Milo of yours comes here, he'll have enough of his memories left to remember who you are."

He will. I have to believe that. TalentCorp can't wipe *all* his memories without destroying the years of training they've invested in him. Our individual passions are what make us Artists, rather than compuplayers. You can program a synthetic instrument to play the notes, but you can't imbue it with the joys or sorrow it takes to pull off a stirring performance. That's why Mistress Ydaya wouldn't let her husband tamper with my mind, and that's why, whatever they end up doing to Milo's memories, some piece of me will remain, at least for a little while. As long as I reach him before the effects of their manipulations become permanent, I'll find a way to make him remember me. Half a lifetime of friendship can't disappear so easily.

Cara glances at her watch, then straightens with a start. She presses it, and a small hologram written in Adryil appears.

"What's that?" I ask.

Cara's eyes dart over the hologram, and she furrows her

brow. "It's a message from Atikéa. Jaerin and the strike team just returned from their rescue mission."

"They got Dámiul out?" My words rush with eagerness. "Is he okay? When can I see him?"

"Why so excited?" Cara smirks. "You *like* him, don't you?"

Heat rushes into my face. "I… I just…"

"Holy shit, you do! I knew it!"

Embarrassed, I look away.

Cara elbows me. "Ah, don't be such a wilting flower about it. You wouldn't be the first Earthling to be dazzled by a pair of shiny Adryil eyes. I swear, every Adryil I've ever seen is attractive by Earthling standards, even old assholes like Master Ydaya. It's not fair." She goes over to my chair and plops down. "Anyway, I'm planning on making another HQ run tonight. I assume you want to come?"

I brighten. "Of course!"

She makes a face. "Try not to be too lovey-dovey in public, will you?"

Her sarcasm slides right off me. Tonight, I'll see Dámiul again. I don't know what I'll say to him, or how he'll react when he sees me. It doesn't matter—for now, all I care about is that, at long last, I'll be reunited with my alien prince.

 268 

Chapter Twenty-Nine

THE DOOR TO THE ABOLITIONISTS' HIDDEN HEADQUARTERS sinks into the floor, and I rush inside. "Dámiul?"

"He's not here." Atikéa emerges from one of the rooms.

"Where is he?" I glimpse Jaerin through the open door behind her, sitting at a table with his head in his hands. The room suddenly feels dark with gloom, and I wonder what I'm missing.

Jaerin lifts his head, revealing a wide gash across his forehead. "I failed."

Cara speeds toward him. "What happened to you?" She examines his wound. "I'll get a med kit."

"Don't bother." Jaerin's voice is dull. "I'll wear it as my mark of shame." He slams the table. "We were *so close!*"

"Don't be stupid. Getting yourself infected won't help your brother." Cara starts walking away.

Jaerin grabs her wrist. "I'm *fine*. It's not me you should be worrying about."

She yanks her arm free. "What the hell does—"

"Cara." Atikéa shakes her head. "I've been trying to get

him to accept a bandage for hours. He won't listen—just let him be."

Cara glowers fiercely, but stays quiet.

Atikéa glances at me. "Dámiul was scheduled to be transferred from one reeducation center to another today. Jaerin and the strike team ambushed the transport, hoping to break him out. But there were more guards than we anticipated." She approaches Jaerin and puts her hand on his shoulder. "I'm just glad no one saw you."

Jaerin shakes his head. "I should have fought harder. Dámiul was right there—I *saw* him. Even called his name." His mouth tightens. "He looked at me like I was a stranger."

I bite my lip, refusing to fear the worst.

Atikéa takes the seat beside Jaerin. "I'm sure when you have a chance to speak with him, whatever barriers they put in his mind will crumble."

Jaerin stares ahead. "Only if I get to him before it's too late. The brother I knew could already be gone."

I feel a swelling behind my heart and lean back against the doorframe. I can't believe what's happening. I thought I'd be seeing Dámiul again, and instead, I learn that I might have lost him for good.

A loud *clunk* startles me. Cara stands beside Jaerin, her hand on the metal box she apparently just slammed onto the table. She opens it and pulls out a silver tube.

Jaerin glares at her. "I said—"

"Shut up." Cara coolly adjusts the nozzle. "I don't know what kind of misguided badge you're holding onto, but I'm sick of looking at that mess on your forehead."

Jaerin starts to stand, but Cara grabs his shoulder and pushes him back down. "*Joth'en, Cara!*" He throws her hand off.

Cara grabs his shoulder again. "You want to fight me over it? Screw you! Stop wallowing in self-pity and let me clean you up!"

"Jaerin, please." Atikéa leans toward him. "This way of punishing yourself won't do anyone any good."

Jaerin glares at Cara, but doesn't move as she brings up the tube. She aims the nozzle at his forehead, then presses the end.

A line of clear gel flows out of the device, and she slowly covers his wound. She then takes a white cloth and wipes his forehead, removing the gel and the blood. She keeps her mouth hard, but the gentleness of her movements and the soft look in her eyes betray her caring.

My mind feels as though it's floating through a haze, unwilling to accept the facts before me. I should be coming up with other escape plans, but I don't know where to begin. A sense of helplessness envelops me, and no matter how I try to shake it, it clings to me. What can I do? What can *I*, a mere musician who barely understands what's going on, possibly do to save Dámiul when rebels with underground connections have failed?

Cara grabs a second tube from the box and squeezes its opaque white contents onto Jaerin's injury. Jaerin looks stormy, but doesn't resist as she spreads the liquid bandage across his forehead. She finishes and tosses the tube back into the box. "There. Now, if you'd just listen to me, I have a plan for freeing your brother."

I stare at her, startled.

Jaerin, who appears equally surprised, looks up at her. "I thought you were against this."

"Strategically, yes." Cara meets his gaze. "But contrary to common belief, I *do* have a heart."

Hope ignites in me. Eager to hear what she has to say, I approach her. "What's your plan?"

Cara pulls out a chair and sits down at the table. "Well, the Adryil, as you know, like to think of themselves as the good guys. So that means they want to take care of the criminals they're rehabilitating. After all, the whole point is to *fix* them, not punish them. To boost morale behind prison walls, they do things like take them on trips and put on shows. It's mostly an excuse for the rich to show off their generous spirits, but hey, if it makes the prisoners happy, I'm not objecting." She puts her elbows on her knees and leans forward. "One of the things these rich people like to do is lend their *Ka'risil* to the prison for a night of art therapy. The Ydayas did it once about six months

ago, and I'm sure they'd be happy to do it again. Mistress Ydaya loves showing off her little collection."

I sink into a chair. My mind remains in a fog, refusing to let the hope shine too brightly after the disappointment of learning that Jaerin's mission failed. But I hear what she's saying. "If they loan us to the prison, we can get inside."

"Exactly." Cara straightens. "Breaking open a door won't be a problem for the likes of Atikéa. It's getting Dámiul to that door that's the trick. Once I'm inside, I'll wander off and get him."

"No." Atikéa gives Cara a firm look. "It's too dangerous. I won't put you in harm's way."

Cara throws up her hand. "If I don't care, why should you?" She prods Jaerin. "Back me up here. I know you'd go to the prison yourself, but since you're banned from going near the place, I'll have to be your proxy."

"Cara." Jaerin's voice is soft. "If they catch you, they'll erase your mind and send you to work as a laborer."

"I know." Cara shrugs.

Jaerin meets her gaze. "Why would you take this risk?"

"Because I know how much your brother means to you, and I hate seeing you like this." Her tone takes a gentle turn. "I, on the other hand, don't have anyone who'll miss me."

Jaerin shakes his head. "That's not true."

The fog clears from my mind, and a realization hits me. Everything that Cara's proposing could be done by me instead of her. "I'll go." My own words startle me. Everyone stares at me, and I straighten, ready to stand by them. "I'll be the one who finds Dámiul and leads him out."

Cara raises her eyebrow. "You trying to steal my heroics?"

Annoyed, I give her a sharp glance. "Dámiul knows me. We communicated pretty frequently at Papilio. He'll recognize me, and that might break down the mental barriers you were talking about earlier."

Cara's other eyebrow lifts, joining the first. "Communicated?"

I feel a blush rise into my cheeks and try to ignore the teasing glint in her eyes.

Atikéa opens her mouth, as though about to object again.

"Listen." I meet her gaze. "Dámiul means a lot to me, and I can't stand by and do nothing when he's in trouble. If I never see him again, I'll…"

I trail off, unable to find the right words. For the first time since coming to Adrye, that possibility really hits me. I held onto the hope that he was nearby, and that I'd find him. Even when I learned he was a prisoner, I hoped that Jaerin would rescue him for me. But if Dámiul didn't recognize his own brother, is there any sense in hoping at all?

The swelling behind my heart grows stronger. The need to see him again rushes into my thoughts, and I clench my jaw, trying to stave off tears.

"Please, let me do this." I speak slowly, trying to keep my voice from shaking.

"I can't." Atikéa's jaw is set. "Whatever we do, I'm keeping both you and Cara out of it."

"Why?" Cara protests. "We're not helpless!"

"Because my mission is to *protect* you, not send you into danger!" Atikéa's voice rises. "I won't do this!" She seems unusually upset about Cara and my volunteering for a mission, and I wonder if something else is bothering her.

Jaerin turns to her. "It could be Dámiul's only chance. I don't think there's any other choice." He whispers something to her in Adryil.

Atikéa shakes her head again. As she speaks, her eyes seem to plead. For several minutes, I watch them go back and forth, unable to understand anything.

I look to Cara, who regards them with a puzzled expression. Apparently, she doesn't know what they're saying either.

Jaerin appears to grow insistent, and Atikéa's lip quivers. She looks down and nods.

Cara gives Jaerin a quick poke. "What's going on?"

Atikéa gets up and rushes out of the room without a word.

Jaerin watches her with an expression of sorrow. "Atikéa agreed to the plan." He turns to me. "I think you're right. You should be the one to find Dámiul. You won't be alone, though." He glances at Cara. "Your task will be to ensure that no one

notices that she's missing. And I… I'll be around in case of trouble. I'll make sure neither of you are caught."

Cara frowns. "You're *banned*, remember? Going within a hundred yards of that prison counts as a strike for you. And if they decide to probe your mind, that's bad for all of us. Unlike Dámiul, who was acting on his own, you're actually *part* of the Abolition. Our hideouts, our plans, which *Ka'risil* know the truth—you could reveal it all. What'll become of the rest of us if you do?"

Jaerin's eyes tilt with sadness. "You're right, of course." He presses something on the edge of the table. A rectangular panel slides open in front of him, revealing a brightly lit screen. "In case you were wondering, Iris, tonight's mission was my second attempt to free my brother. I broke in right after Dámiul was sent to a reeducation center. I was caught before I found him, but thanks to my father's influence, they didn't press charges. However, I'm forbidden from nearing *any* reeducation center, and they've been watching me, which is why I had to wait for them to transfer Dámiul someplace before trying again." His expression tightens. "I didn't know they were moving him because they'd already finished their task of erasing him. Until I saw him tonight." He inhales, then glances at the screen. "But while I was in the facility during my first attempt, I managed to talk to a guard—one of the mid-ranking officers. For the right price, he can be quite helpful." A hologram of a wide building appears. "This is a map of the facility Dámiul is being held in now. I obtained it a few days ago in case the second attempt failed."

Cara points at him. "So you were considering something just like *my* plan this whole time!"

Jaerin nods. "I even started making preparations, but until you suggested it just now, I didn't know how I'd get someone into the facility to lead Dámiul out." He turns to me. "I wish I didn't have to resort to asking for your help, but Dámiul's time is running out, and I have no other options. Are you sure you're willing to do this?"

"Yes." I don't hesitate to answer.

"All right." Jaerin looks down at the screen again, and the

hologram switches to an interior view. A no-nonsense attitude replaces his previous distress. "My family runs in the same circles as the Ydayas. I'll make a social call and suggest that they lend their quartet to the next charity show at the prison. They shouldn't be hard to persuade. I'll also get you an access card for the facility from my officer 'friend.'"

"Don't the Adryil control doors with their telepathy?"

"In most cases, yes. But detention centers are full of those considered dangerous, and so they're equipped with telepathy-blocking devices to prevent the prisoners from using their abilities against the authorities."

"By the way," Cara quips, "Earth uses the same devices in their telepathy-blocking satellites. You can imagine how many *Ka'risil* they had to sell to pay for *those*."

Jaerin gestures at the hologram. "Security cameras are employed in every corner of the facility to keep watch over the prisoners, but my contact has access to them. He'll shut them down so no one will see you."

I nod, glad that Jaerin's so prepared.

Cara gives Jaerin an incredulous look. "You thought of *everything*, didn't you? Did you *know* you'd fail Attempt Number Two?"

Jaerin glances at her. "I knew there was a chance we would. And if that happened, I wanted the next attempt to happen as quickly as possible, before Dámiul's memories are lost forever." A wry smile curls his lips. "If there's one thing my father taught me, it's how to be ready for every possibility." He turns back to me. "Now, I'm going to show you how the prison is laid out so you won't get lost. Pay attention."

I watch keenly, ready to memorize every detail of the place.

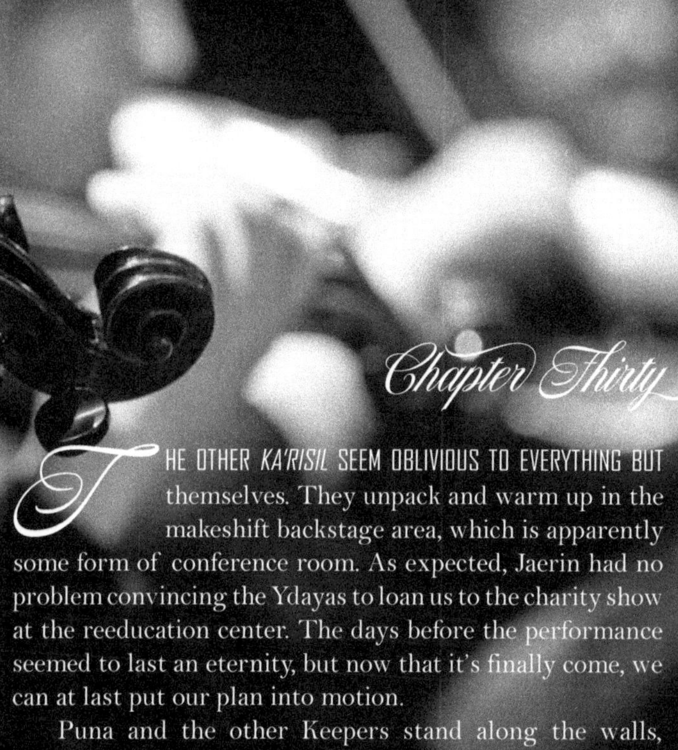

HE OTHER *KA'RISIL* SEEM OBLIVIOUS TO EVERYTHING BUT themselves. They unpack and warm up in the makeshift backstage area, which is apparently some form of conference room. As expected, Jaerin had no problem convincing the Ydayas to loan us to the charity show at the reeducation center. The days before the performance seemed to last an eternity, but now that it's finally come, we can at last put our plan into motion.

Puna and the other Keepers stand along the walls, watching us. Puna glances at me, and I keep my expression blank so she won't suspect anything. I didn't dare wear my Grámed device today, since she made a point of inspecting our outfits before we came.

I find a sliver of space by the edge of the table and gently nudge someone else's case a few inches to make room for mine. The moment Puna looks away, I open one of the compartments in my case and fish out the access card Jaerin gave me. Good thing it's so small, because I don't have much space to hide it on my person. The red-and-black concert dress I was assigned doesn't have any pockets.

I purposely drop my shoulder rest. I duck under the table, pretending to hunt for it, and slip the card into my shoe.

I retrieve the shoulder rest and straighten. Why was I so clumsy? I've been nervous all evening—something must be the matter…

It's Puna. She's in my head again; she must have sensed my unease. I focus on the melody of "Butterfly's Lament," but all the music in the world doesn't seem capable of calming my mind.

"What are you trying to do?" Cara's voice cuts through the noise of warm-ups around me. I turn and see her glaring at a small woman with blond hair. She glances at me briefly and raises her eyebrows, then starts talking over the woman, who yells in what sounds like Spanish.

Puna strides over to the bickering pair, and I silently thank Cara for distracting her.

"Puna won't even look for you," Cara said earlier today. "I'm the one with the villainous face and bad attitude, remember? You just do your whole innocent thing while I make a fuss. She'll be so busy dealing with me, she won't notice you're gone."

I put my viola down in the case and take out my bow. Cara and the small woman's quibbling voices, along with Puna's stern commands, somersault through the room. The anxiety in my heart makes breathing take far more effort than it should, and, hoping to calm myself, I go over what Jaerin and Atikéa told me.

During our last "HQ run," as Cara calls them, Atikéa put together an animated hologram depicting just what we would be doing.

She pointed to a door at the back of the prison. "I'll make sure the door's open and wait right outside with the getaway vehicle. Jaerin's contact on the inside will disable all the security cameras for fifteen minutes after your quartet's performance. That's your window to find Dámiul."

Jaerin then told me again he wouldn't let me get caught. I stopped myself from asking how he could promise that when he can't even come near the reeducation center. So many fears and doubts crowded my mind then, and despite my efforts, I feel them taking over again.

What kind of person volunteers to risk *everything* for

someone she's only met through holograms? Someone who never told me a thing about himself? Everything I am could be stripped from me, and I'm nothing short of crazy for stepping up as I did. I'm not the hero of an epic fairytale. I'm barely a member of the Abolition. Even if I succeed, only more trouble lies ahead.

What kind of person rejects a safe, worry-free life? I could have happily spent my days doing what I was born to do: playing an instrument that seems connected to my very soul. The life of a *Ka'risil* isn't a terrible one. The safer thing to do would have been to quietly accept orders. If I were smarter, I would have let them take my memories of both Dámiul and Milo so I could settle comfortably into my new life. There's nothing wrong with being sheltered and taken care of, and if I hadn't resisted Erayet and Puna's telepathic commands, I could have been content like Andreas, like Temir, like all these other Artists around me.

But if I had, what kind of person would that have made me?

I draw a breath. I may not have much experience in the realm of underground missions, but Atikéa and Jaerin do. They took care of the complicated aspects—all I have to do is go into one of the so-called classrooms. The guard will command Dámiul to go there, and I'll convince him to come with me. After that, it's just a matter of crossing a few hallways and leading him to freedom.

I'm coming for you, Dámiul. I finish applying rosin to my bow and pick up my viola. As I start playing a scale, I close my eyes and picture his face. I recall his smile and the wondrous way he looked at me. I can't imagine how much pain he must have been hiding. I understand now what that strange combination of rage and sorrow meant, why he said he wouldn't be here by the time I got to Adrye. He must have known that no matter how hard he fought, he wouldn't be able to resist the mind-wipe forever.

I finish my scale. Instead of running through another warm-up, I choose to play a melody—the melody carried on a solo clarinet the night we danced. Keeping my eyes closed, I let it take me back to that enchanted evening, when I chose to forget the galaxies lying between us.

Now, it's only a few walls and my own fears, and I won't let either stop me.

I wait in the wings, awed by the current performance. A group of barefoot women, garbed in loose, colorful silk and towering gold headdresses, glides across the stage to the strange music of a woodwind instrument. The dancers all appear to be of East Asian descent, like me. Actually, since they all spoke an unfamiliar language backstage, I guess they're actually *from* East Asia.

Is this the kind of world my ancestors came from? Their dance is so different from anything I've seen before. Each movement is performed with deliberate tranquility. Yet, there is seldom a still moment on the stage. A soft tension simmers behind each turning of a hand or flexing of a foot.

There was a time when Papilio contained my entire world. I let them take me whole; it never occurred to me to want more. Seeing the other Artists today has shown me how big Earth really is, and how little I actually know.

The performers conclude their dance, and the audience applauds. A light at the top of the stage tells me it's our turn to perform.

Andreas leads us onto the stage. I follow Cara toward the semi-circle of music stands that rises from the floor. As I take my place, I survey the audience below. The black-clad prisoners sit clustered in a rectangular formation of seats to my left. Seeing Dámiul's crisp jacket worn by hundreds of blank-faced captives sends a chill frosting down my spine.

On the other side of a wide aisle, to my right, the Ydayas sit with other members of the Adryil elite who lent their *Ka'risil* for the event. Guards in indigo uniforms stand between the prisoners and the wealthy, and I wonder if one of them is the man Jaerin bribed into helping us. A bright bolt runs through the air to their left. There must be a force field keeping the prisoners confined.

The contrast between the left and right sides of the

audience is chilling. The flamboyantly dressed elites watch us with curiosity, their eyes bright with interest. They appear as an audience should: engaged and attentive. Some have little smiles on their faces, and others wear critical expressions.

The prisoners, on the other hand, hardly look alive. None of them show any trace of interest in their eyes; they might as well be statues. They sit with straight, stiff postures, and they don't move except to blink. They're… empty. Robbed of their minds and hearts. This show is really just for the elite—perhaps an excuse to show off their *Ka'risil* collections for each other. The prisoners certainly don't seem to care.

Andreas cues the opening of our piece. Although I try to concentrate on the song, my gaze wanders back toward the crowd of prisoners.

Where are you, Dámiul? Dozens of gleaming Adryil eyes color the darkness with shades of gold, green, purple, and orange. I see blues of every variety from cobalt to ice.

Then, I spot them: azure. Toward the back of the prisoners' section, on the left. My heart jumps, and I quickly turn my gaze back to the music, not wanting to raise suspicions.

I conclude the song with a series of double stops, then step forward for my solo. The Ydayas wanted to show off their expensive new pet. I never thought I'd grow weary of "Butterfly's Lament," but after playing it every other day for weeks, it's getting tiresome.

As I wait for the other quartet members to leave, I spot those azure eyes again. Even in the darkness, I can tell it's Dámiul. A rush of emotions floods me—joy, relief, and the ever-present anxiety. The first time I played "Butterfly's Lament" on stage, I was playing for him. Now, here I am again.

I inhale, then draw my bow across the string, letting the mournful opening notes ring out. Maybe, once he hears them, Dámiul will recall that night at the Spectacle. He's so near, I could run up to him if it weren't for the guards. *Can you hear me, Dámiul?*

As the song progresses, I feel Butterfly's plight. Mine's the same, except my prince isn't just trapped by guards in an

unreachable kingdom—he's also bound by telepathic weapons and mind implants.

A surge of despair floods through me, and I move into the final run. I let it rage. This is my last chance to panic, my last chance to doubt. If he refuses to come with me, there's nothing I can do. Atikéa waited until Jaerin left before telling me that if that happens, I should go back to my designated area and carry on as though nothing out of the ordinary occurred. But I don't know if I could leave Dámiul behind like that.

I conclude the Lament, and enthusiastic applause rises from the right side of the audience, interspersed with calls of *"Toká!"* Apparently, even in my distraction, I haven't lost my affinity for the piece. The prisoners clap politely, but give no indication of having any opinion about my performance.

I look to the back, hoping to catch a sign that the song impacted Dámiul in some way, but I don't see him. Jaerin's officer contact probably already summoned him to the room I'm supposed to meet him in.

I take a bow, resisting the urge to run off stage to find him.

Chapter Thirty-One

DUNA'S ATTENTION FIXES ON CARA, WHO SOMEHOW managed to provoke another argument with a performer who doesn't speak English. Cara's apparently so talented at conflict, even linguistic barriers can't hinder her. I clutch the access card and inch toward the door.

Fifteen minutes. That's how long I have to find Dámiul and convince him to come with me. There's no time to be afraid.

I tap the card against the pad by the door, and it slides open. As Jaerin instructed, I tap it again before it opens all the way, then slip out through the crack as it starts closing again.

The door shuts, and I find myself alone in a long, white corridor. There's something menacing about its pristine appearance. I feel exposed, like a million eyes are watching me. In a way, they are, since tiny cameras line the walls. But they can't see me. Jaerin's contact blinded them—for now.

According to Jaerin, all the guards are either out in the auditorium with the prisoners or standing by the doors to the outside. I shouldn't run into any. If I do, I'm to pretend I got lost like the *Ka'risil* simpleton I'm meant to be. Since devices preventing the Adryil from using their telepathy are embedded within the walls of the facility, anyone I run into won't be able to read my mind. At least not without either shutting down the devices, as they did in the backstage area so the Keepers could keep an eye on the *Ka'risil*, or using machines like the crown-like device the white-haired man used on Dámiul.

I speed down the corridor, passing several doors. Each has a large, rectangular window in it, through which I glimpse the classrooms the prisoners are reeducated in. Adryil letters splash across the fronts of many of these group rooms. I don't recognize enough to read them, but Jaerin told me what kind of messages they display. Here, cooperation, conformity, and compliance are rewarded, and individuality is seen as a disease. On Adrye, uniqueness is a trait only valued in products and property—like the *Ka'risil.*

I turn a corner, recalling the layout I spent all week memorizing. I was afraid I'd panic again, but I seem to have passed the point of fear.

After winding through a few more corridors and using the access card to bypass a handful of gates, I reach the hallway at the end of which my destination lies. I see it ahead: the door at the end, to my right. Dámiul's probably there already.

My steps speed up, and the next thing I know, I'm running. Through the window in the door, I glimpse the back of a boy with black hair. It's him; I know it. I tap the card against the security pad and rush inside.

"Dámiul!" I run to him. He turns to face me, and I freeze.

I'm looking at a stranger. Dámiul's eyes are as blue as ever, but the intensity that once took my breath away is gone. He blinks, as though waiting for me to continue.

"Dámiul, it's me, Iris." I walk cautiously around the metal table, approaching him.

He watches me blankly, but otherwise doesn't react. Even if he doesn't recognize me, I expected to see some measure of confusion. Shouldn't he at least ask me who I am, or what I, a *Ka'risil,* am doing here?

They've even taken his ability to question away from him, leaving me with a tantalizing shell. At Papilio, I had all of him except his physical presence. He kept secrets, but his fundamental being was with me. I sensed so much when I was with him, even though he was just a trick of light, a creation of technology.

Now, I sense nothing. If I wanted to, I could finally feel the warmth of his touch, but it would be no different than laying my hand on a handsome statue.

I can help him remember who he is. I just have to get him out of here first. "Come with me." I motion for him to approach. "I'll explain everything later."

Dámiul doesn't move. "*Zeth ut inyana enyil lorst.*" I understand the statement: *State your name and number.*

Did the mind-wipe take his memory of English? "*Zeth onayil Iris. En bektát fith ona razan.*" *My name is Iris. You must come with me.*

Dámiul blinks, but otherwise remains still. "*Ona fenst nur. Zeth ut inyana enyil taen dira nur.*" *I cannot. Your name and number are not correct.*

He speaks like a machine, needing an access card to activate. There's nothing—*nothing*—in his voice or his expressions.

I clench my jaw, willing my tears to stay behind my eyes. Is this what they've reduced him to? Dámiul, whose eyes once burned with energy, whose voice could carry both the power of conviction and the softness of compassion, who smiled defiantly in the face of torment. Have they destroyed him for good?

No, I won't believe it. Maybe I can coax him into following me. Once we're someplace safe, I can spend all the time I need helping him remember. My Adryil vocabulary is too limited to express much, so I repeat the words for, "You must come with me."

His eyes remain fixed on me, but convey no reaction. I reach out and take his hand in mine. I don't feel like I'm touching another person; I might as well be holding a language tablet. I give him a gentle tug. "*Dámiul, ona en shraïn, fith ona razan.*" *Dámiul, I beg you, come with me.* My eyes brim, and I wipe the tears away before they fall.

Dámiul blinks, and for the first time, a hint of emotion flickers through his gaze. "*Zeth ut inyana enyil taen dira nur.*" *Your name and number are not correct.* His eyebrows come together, as if he's confused. "*Ona fathrad idur yaerid.*" *I should sound the alarm.* His tone wavers with uncertainty.

I tug his hand again and keep my pleading gaze on his. "*Ona en shraïn.*" *I beg you.*

Dámiul looks down at my hand, which still holds his, and the confusion on his face deepens. "You're the *Ka'risil* who performed the viola solo."

He remembers English! Hope ignites within me. In my own language, I can say so much more than my stilted knowledge of Adryil could express. "Yes, that's me."

"What are you doing here?"

"I don't have time to explain, but you have to come with me."

"The law says I should alert the guards. Noncompliance is immoral." He sounds as if he's quoting words he doesn't believe.

I wish I could destroy the devices blocking his telepathy so I could tell him to look inside my mind and see my memories of who he is. If I knew where they were, I would try. "Please, trust me. I know you."

"But I don't know you."

"Yes, you do." I squeeze his hand and take a step closer. "You know you do."

"I have never met any *Ka'risil* before." Dámiul draws back, but his hand remains in mine.

"They've taken the memories from you. But please, believe me…" I trail off. If he sees me as a stranger, then he has no reason to listen to a word I say. Yet he hasn't yanked his hand away—some part of him must remember me. Maybe a prompt will help bring him back. "Do you remember the song I played?"

Dámiul looks at the ground. "That melody… I've heard it before."

"That's right." I manage a smile, hope quavering in my heart. "I played it for you at Papilio. Ever since we met, each time I've played it, it's been for you."

"Papilio…" Dámiul brings up his hand, and mine with it. For several seconds, he stares at our interlocking fingers.

My mind flashes back to the Wintertime Masquerade and how much I longed to hold his hand like I am now. My eyes sting, and a tear escapes.

Dámiul's eyebrows tilt with sympathy. "Why are you so sad?" He reaches toward me.

I let him brush my tears away, keeping my eyes on his. The Dámiul I know is in there—I can sense him returning to me. They took his memories, but they can't erase who he is inside. Even in this brainwashed state, he's choosing to speak to me instead of sounding the alarm. He's defying them.

"Because I remember you," I say. "But they've taken me from your mind."

He knits his eyebrows. "We were friends, weren't we?"

I nod. "You danced with me once." Hoping a hint will help bring back the memories, I place my hand on his shoulder. "We stood like this, except I would have been a telepathic vision to you." I feel Dámiul's hand on my waist, and my breath catches in my throat, both from his touch and the idea that the memory might be stirring in his mind.

Dámiul presses his lips together, and I know he must be struggling to remember more.

"There were stars and snowflakes," I say. "You created them with the holoprojectors."

"There was a song." Dámiul's voice is a whisper. "Played by a solo clarinet."

Hope ignites in my heart. "Yes, that's right." I hesitate, then softly hum the melody.

Dámiul brightens, and I can tell he recognizes it. "You wore a silver mask. I remember wondering why you would cover such a beautiful face. You told me…" He trails off.

I take a step closer. "'Just dance with me.'"

The life has returned to him, and I can scarcely contain the deluge of joy and longing racing through me. I want to babble on and on about everything we shared, to quote our conversations and describe our interactions, but Atikéa warned me that doing something like that would overwhelm and confuse him. Only

he can recover the memories in his head, and no amount of insisting can force them to return. So I hold my tongue, waiting.

Dámiul's eyes widen, as though a window has opened before him, and he's seeing light for the first time after being trapped in a dark room for weeks. His hand tightens around mine, and his mouth falls open. "*Iris!*"

A flurry of emotions crosses his face—confusion, joy, anxiety, shock. I can almost hear his thoughts whirling. His gaze locks onto mine, blazing like the blue-hot fires I know so well.

My tears of sorrow turn to tears of happiness, and I smile through them. In that one exclamation, he's told me everything I need to know. "Hello, Dámiul."

Dámiul puts his hand on my cheek, and he stares into my eyes in disbelief. "Am I hallucinating again?"

"No." I put my hand over his. "I'm really here." My heart threatens to burst from the overwhelming excitement. At last, after everything, he's really here with me. Unable to help myself, I throw my arms around him. "I knew you'd remember me."

His arms encircle my waist, drawing me closer. Suddenly, I don't know where I am or what I'm doing. There's only him and me, sharing the warmth we were once denied. I feel as if the sun has split open the ceiling above us, and in my mind, I hear the swelling of a thousand-piece orchestra—the soaring string melodies, the brass accents, the great choir shimmering above it all. If this were an opera, now would be the moment the prince and princess were finally reunited, holding each other's hands on the stage and singing a devastatingly beautiful duet.

Dámiul grabs my shoulders and pushes back with alarm. "How are you here?"

"I came for you." I use both hands to wipe my cheeks. A sense of urgency hits me, and I recall that time is short. "We have to go. Jaerin's waiting outside."

"Jaerin?" Dámiul furrows his brow.

"Your brother." There must still be gaps in his memories. Maybe my presence only recovered the ones of me.

"My brother... He's the one who attacked the transport, isn't he?" Fury clouds his expression, and I can almost hear him say, *How could I have forgotten my own brother?*

"Yes. We're going to get you out of here. Now, let's go!" I grab his hand and run to the door, then tap the access card against the security pad.

The door slides open. I freeze in terror, unable to believe what stands before me.

Two security bots tower in the doorway, massive and threatening, seeming to stare down at me with the angry red lights flashing across their domed heads.

Chapter Thirty-Two

THE SCREAM BARELY ESCAPES MY LIPS BEFORE A PAIR of metal ropes shoots out from one of the security bots. They wrap around my wrists, forcing my hands together. The access card falls from my grasp.

"*Lidar'ati!*" Dámiul rushes forward, but the second security bot launches a metal arm at him and knocks him back. His head slams against the wall, and he crumples to the ground.

"*Dámiul!*" I cry.

The bot shoots metal ropes at him and binds his hands. It yanks him up, forcing him to stand.

Paralyzing fear rushes through me, and I gasp for air. How did they find us? It hasn't been fifteen minutes yet, has it?

"*Ona tunka en.*" A low, menacing voice comes from the corridor.

An Adryil man in a stiff gray jacket steps into view between the two bots; his differently colored uniform must mean he outranks most guards. I recognize him immediately as the white-haired man who tortured Dámiul in the recording.

The man's gold eyes fall on me. "I knew Jaerin was reckless, but I never thought he'd resort to using an *Earthling*." From the way he spits the word "Earthling," he might as well have called me garbage. His lip curls. "Even Fyrin Verik can't save him now."

A realization dawns on me. "Are you the officer Jaerin bribed?"

The man lifts his chin with disdain. "Well, it looks like the Earthling isn't completely stupid." He leans toward me with a smug expression. "I saw how desperate Jaerin was and decided I might as well reap the profits. He was so eager, he trusted me even though I never told him my name or even showed him what I looked like. I knew it was only a matter of time before I caught him as well."

Dámiul glowers at the man. "Your dispute is with me, Martoke. Let Iris go."

Martoke sneers. "She's an Earthling who violated Adryil laws. There is only one solution for such noncompliance."

From the menace in his voice, I can tell he's only speaking English to stir my fear. My face and fingers turn to ice, and my stomach twists. I try to harden my expression and look brave, but even my lip is trembling.

I glance at Dámiul. If rage could kill, Martoke would be reduced to a pile of ashes by the heat of Dámiul's gaze.

Martoke holds up his wrist and presses something on the black device strapped to it. The rope between the security bot and me stiffens. It wheels forward, and I nearly fall as it forces me back.

"*Lidar'ati!*" Dámiul shouts, more venomously this time. He, too, is forced back by the security bot holding him.

Martoke glances up with a malicious smile, then strides away. The door slams shut, leaving me alone with Dámiul and the machines.

The pressure on my wrists is too much to resist. I nearly trip as the bot pushes me back into a corner. It shoves me against the wall, knocking the breath out of my chest.

The other bot yanks Dámiul toward the table. It pulls down, and he collapses into the chair. It drags his hands onto the table. A set of restraints rises from the metal surface and wraps around his wrists.

Dámiul keeps his expression firm, defiant as in the recording Jaerin showed me. In fact, everything I'm seeing is as it was in that recording. The room. The table. The restraints. What have I done? Because of me, he'll go through that torment again.

He glances at me. "I won't let them hurt you, Iris."

I nod, even though there's no way he can keep his promise. I can't let him see the despair creeping into my thoughts, and I chastise myself for being so terrified. I knew this could happen, and I volunteered to take the risk. I meet Dámiul's gaze and try to smile to tell him I'm okay.

The anger in his eyes fades, transforming into something my feeble command of words can't describe. A look of admiration. An unspoken respect, telling me he understands the chance I took for him, and he wants nothing more than to prove that it was worthwhile. And something else—something that tells me that in this moment, I'm all that matters to him.

I recognize that look as one I've seen between others—the way Milo used to look at Sabina, the way Kiki looked at Brent. I always dreamed of finding someone who would inspire that look to cross my face, but never imagined I'd be worthy of receiving it.

"How much do you remember?" I ask.

Dámiul breaks his gaze. "I remember you. I remember trying to speak to you, and accidentally frightening you because you thought I was a hallucination. I remember frightening you again when you realized I could read your mind, then wanting to trade anything for the chance to fix things." He stares at the table. "I remember telling you we both wished for the impossible."

I release a breath. Jaerin and Atikéa worried that it would take days, even weeks, to bring him back, but it seems just a few minutes were enough to return the Dámiul I know. His mind must be stronger than they imagined.

Dámiul closes his eyes. "The barriers they erected are crumbling. Your performance at the Spectacle, teaching you to block your mind, showing you images of Adrye… I remember everything since running into you. And I can feel more memories returning." He opens his eyes, and his expression darkens. "I remember Martoke trying to wipe my mind. I fought him, but I must not have been strong enough."

"You were fighting him the whole time I knew you." The questions hammering on my mind demand to be asked. Even if the answers will be stolen from me as soon as Martoke returns, I need to know. "Why didn't you tell me?"

"It wasn't your burden. Also, when I was with you, I could forget where I really was." Dámiul's voice grows soft. "You're the reason I was able to hold on for so long. Knowing you were out there, waiting for me, made me fight harder, no matter what Martoke did to me."

A warm blush creeps into my cheeks. I wish I knew how to respond, but my capacity for words fails me. Meanwhile, the questions pound relentlessly against my head. "If you came to spread the truth about Papilio, why didn't you?"

Dámiul hesitates. After a pause, he says, "I take it someone told you about TalentCorp?"

"Yes." My wrists ache from the security bot's grip, but I ignore them.

"I meant to tell you." Dámiul looks at me apologetically. "It wasn't part of my original plan, but when I realized how close your school was to Charlotte, I couldn't leave without trying. When I ran into you, you were just a Papilian. I meant to use you as my proxy and have you spread the word for me." He drops his gaze. "Then, I found you were so much more than I expected. I tried to make myself tell you the truth about the Papilio School, but each time, I realized doing so would only bring you danger."

"I would have taken the risk."

Dámiul meets my gaze. "I must have contemplated what to do a thousand times. Do I warn you not to sign the contract, as I first intended? Or do I spare you the immediate danger and let you wander into their trap? Either way, I couldn't save you." A pained look fills his eyes. "I realized that warning you would do you no good. TalentCorp has ways of guaranteeing that you forfeit your rights. If you refused your contract, they would

have assigned you to a job that nevertheless required you to sign away your freedom, then manipulated you into agreeing to come to Adrye to serve your patrons."

"And if I accepted the contract but knew what would happen, the liaison would have found out while brainwashing me in transit and made me forget anyway." I lean my head back against the wall. "There was no way out for me."

"Exactly. Also, if you'd agreed to tell the other Papilians about TalentCorp, the people watching you would have realized you were the source of the trouble. They would have taken your mind and those of everyone you'd told. They would have wiped you out if they had to—every student, every staff member, every resident of Dogwood."

I try to wrap my head around how expansive TalentCorp's reach is. If Dámiul had told me the truth, and I'd told Milo, then Brent or Estelle or anyone else who would have listened… TalentCorp would have destroyed us all. Everyone I knew— gone. Transformed into mindless shells. "But… What about the treaties?"

"TalentCorp would have found a loophole that permitted their actions. Or else paid a fine and called it justice. They'd rather lose some money and one branch of their operation than endanger their entire business." Dámiul looks away. "At first, I told myself it would all be worth it if I could incite some kind of uprising that would force TalentCorp and everyone else to recognize that the deception is wrong. When I broke into Papilio, I only cared about my cause. But after knowing you, I realized… I care about you too. So I chose to sacrifice my mission rather than risk your life—or those of your peers."

"Maybe you shouldn't have." Though the thought of TalentCorp mind-wiping everyone at Papilio horrifies me, I wonder how different the world might be for all the other Artists if we *had* revolted. "The Abolitionists' cause is more important than any of us."

Dámiul's eyes turn stormy. "That's how Martoke and the other so-called teachers here want people to think. But the moment we stop caring about individuals in the name of the group, we start losing the element that separates us from

299

animals." Glancing at me, he softens his expression. "That's something I learned from the literature of your kind, and it's something I choose to believe in. If I'd used you to make a statement... I would have been no better than my father."

He said if he could free even one of the wrongfully enslaved, then his life would have been worth living. Recalling Jaerin's words and listening to Dámiul now, the intentions behind Dámiul's actions finally make sense. I'm not sure if I agree with him, but I understand. "That's why you chose Ximena over the Abolition."

"Ximena?" He furrows his brow, and I can almost see him hacking through the barriers in his mind. After a few seconds, he lifts the corner of his mouth. "Yes, Ximena. Freeing her proved that TalentCorp is not all-powerful. They'll never find her. I made sure of that." His expression falls. "Yet I couldn't free you. And now, you're here because of me." He bows his head. "I'm sorry I brought all this upon you."

"I'm not. I'm glad I met you, no matter what happens next." If it weren't for the bot restraining me, I would take his hands to let him know I mean every word.

"You wouldn't say that if you knew who I really am."

"You mean that you're the son of the man who runs TalentCorp? Or that you're a repeat offender in the Adryil courts?" My hands are starting to go numb, but I manage to smile anyway. "The Abolitionists told me all about your past. I don't care about any of that."

Dámiul raises his eyes to meet mine. "I couldn't tell you about my family because it would have meant revealing Papilio's true nature, and... I thought you'd turn away from me if you knew I was a criminal. But other than that, I was always honest with you." He gives me a sad smile. "I guess, if I were you, I'd say that doesn't leave much."

"No, it's enough." A tension I didn't know was still holding me releases my senses. Yes, I know him. I knew who he was in those moments at Papilio, and I know who he is now.

I gaze at him, letting my heart take in all it wants to. I choose to ignore the doubts and believe in the boy I see. A rebel who refused to stand by while injustices were committed. A fighter willing to lose his very self in hopes of achieving one

300

more victory. A compassionate heart who threw all that away for one person: me.

I never imagined I'd be worth so much to anyone—enough to turn someone's world around, the way Dámiul says I turned his. In him, I found something rare and beautiful, and I'm glad I fought to save him, even if my efforts were ultimately in vain.

He's worth the price I'm going to pay.

"Dámiul—"

I break off as the door slides open.

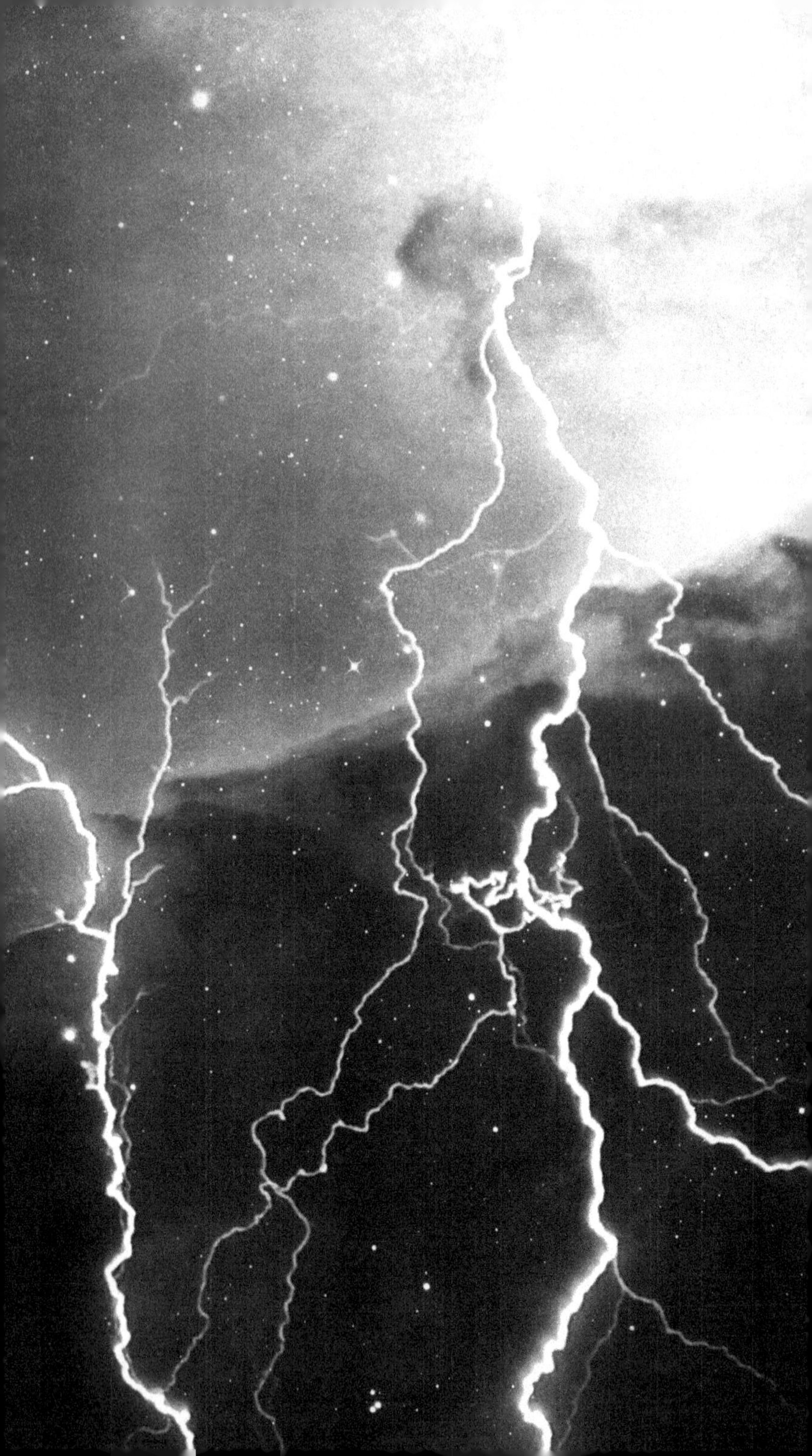

Chapter Thirty-Three

MARTOKE'S PRESENCE INVADES MY MIND, STRONGER than anything I've felt before. He must have disabled the telepathy-blocking devices in this room. All my defenses fail, and I can hardly form a thought of my own.

My name is Iris Lei. I am a *Ka'risil* belonging to Soraï and Gysát Ydaya. I am also the Earthling that Dámiul Verik ran into at the Papilio School, the one he communicated with while in captivity. I volunteered to help Jaerin Verik with his plan to free Dámiul even though I knew what the consequences of failure would be. I was willing to take the risk for Dámiul because I love him.

My own thought, pulled to the surface of my mind by Martoke, startles me. Martoke's presence retreats, and he lets out a disgusted noise.

Because I love him. Why should that thought surprise me? It's been obvious for a while. The longing, the despair, the willingness to risk it all—all that foolishness could only be explained by love. Yet, it's different thinking those words so bluntly. It's a confession I've been afraid to make to myself, but now, it's been forced out of me.

I love him.

I turn my gaze to Dámiul, whose eyes are fixed on Martoke. A metal line runs around the back of Martoke's head—he's wearing a Grámed device. He sets the case he's carrying down on the table with a *thunk*.

A tall robot wheels into the room. Martoke pulls out the chair across the table from Dámiul and glances at it. The machine whirs as it draws closer to the table, and the door shuts behind it.

Martoke sits down and sneers at Dámiul. "Shall we do this in English for the sake of your little Earthling friend? It would be educational for her."

Dámiul glares at Martoke in silence.

"So, we must play this game again." He pulls the case toward him and opens it. "Shame. All those weeks of work, undone. However, this situation is not without its advantages. You have been a particularly difficult case, Dámiul Verik, and I've been petitioning the Board to let me try experimental methods for a while now. They gave permission if you relapsed again." He twists to face me. "For that, I should thank you."

The sadistic glee in his eyes makes me sick, and I grit my teeth. "You're a monster."

Martoke lets out a mocking laugh, then turns back to Dámiul. "As long as you're starting to remember things, maybe you can resolve some questions that went unanswered before your last mind wipe."

Dámiul gives Martoke a wry smirk. "You'll fail as you did before."

Martoke's face twists into a hideous scowl. He turns to the bot. "*Adbis.*"

A panel in the bot's center slides up, and a tentacle-like appendage unfurls from within. A long, thin needle is attached to the end. A second metal tentacle reaches toward Dámiul's arm with a sharp blade.

I gasp, but when Dámiul turns to me, I feel a sense of calmness descend. *Don't be afraid for me*, he seems to say. *I'll be all*

right. I let his telepathic message ease my dread. I shouldn't be the one he's worried about right now.

The bot inserts the blade under Dámiul's cuff and slices up the sleeve, exposing his arm. It moves its other tentacle toward his wrist and presses the needle into his skin.

Dámiul doesn't react. He turns his gaze to Martoke, expression blank. Martoke reaches into the case and pulls out two familiar metal crowns. He walks around the table and shoves one onto Dámiul's head, then removes the Grámed device from the back of his own head and replaces it with the second crown. The rims of both devices glow—Martoke's yellow, Dámiul's bright blue.

For several seconds, Martoke stares down at Dámiul, contorting his expression with effort. He must be trying to probe Dámiul's mind. Dámiul stares ahead, keeping his face placid. Despite his efforts, I see the pain in his eyes.

Unable to stand the sight, I look away. My wrist bones grind together under the grip of the bot binding me, and I know any attempt to escape would be useless. Why must I be so helpless? If I were strong enough, I would break through these restraints and tear those machines away from Dámiul.

"*Mand!*" Martoke's harsh voice grates on my ears. Mechanical humming crescendos ominously as the tall robot reacts to Martoke's command.

A movement calls my attention back to the table. Martoke leans over Dámiul, adjusting something on Dámiul's metal crown. The lights on both crowns have dimmed. A spasm shakes Dámiul's body, and he clenches his fists. His breathing grows labored, and blood trickles down the side of his face.

I bite my lip. Even though I know it's useless, I tug at the restraints binding me. What wouldn't I give to break through them? The bot tightens its grasp on me, sending a jolt of pain up my arms. I stifle a cry.

Martoke goes to his case and withdraws a long metal tube. A sharp needle protrudes from the tube's end. He holds the device up to the light, examining it, then plunges the needle into Dámiul's crown at the center of his forehead.

A scream escapes my throat. Martoke twists the device,

burrowing it deeper into Dámiul's head. Dámiul's breathing grows heavier, and he clenches his jaw. His eyes glisten. He must be holding back agonized cries. I want to tell him that it's all right to let them out, that he doesn't have to put on a brave front. I can't imagine how much pain Martoke must be causing him.

I want to scream and fight and demand that Martoke let him go. I only hold back because I know yelling won't do any good, and because I don't want Dámiul to see my anguish.

Martoke presses the end of the device, then lets go, leaving it embedded in its place. He places his hands on the table and leans down toward Dámiul. The lights on his crown brighten. Those on Dámiul's glow so glaringly, they give him a blue halo.

Although neither says a word, I can almost hear the combat between them: Martoke struggling to learn Dámiul's secrets, perhaps get him to betray Jaerin and Atikéa or say where he hid Ximena; Dámiul using every ounce of strength he has to push back, despite the machines and drugs.

And I'm trapped in the corner, unable to stop this nightmare. I close my eyes, and tears stream down my face at the cruelty— both of Martoke and of a universe that would bring me to my love, only to have me watch him suffer, powerless to save him.

"*Contuk en!*" Martoke's shout is accompanied by a loud *slam*.

I open my eyes in time to see him collapse into his chair. Sweat runs down his face, and his eyes are bloodshot. The lights on his crown are dark. He pants, as though catching his breath after running a long race.

Blood streaks Dámiul's face, but he holds his head high. His blue eyes blaze with triumph, and he lifts the corners of his mouth. "Give up, Martoke. You'll have an easier time erasing my mind again, and we both remember how difficult that was."

Martoke warps his face into a look of pure hatred. For several seconds, he just stares, and I fear what horrors he'll try next.

He straightens, and his eyes glint with abrupt energy. "It occurs to me that someone else has the knowledge I seek." He twists toward me. "I take it this little Earthling means a lot to you."

"*At'aest!*" Dámiul yanks at his restraints.

Martoke stands. What will he do to me? Terror overwhelms me, and I feel myself trembling.

Martoke's presence invades my mind, and I can feel him probing. I'm a member of the Abolitionists. I joined when—

No. I won't betray them. I repeat that thought in my head, hoping it'll be enough to keep Martoke from finding what he's looking for.

Dámiul continues shouting in Adryil, but I can't see him past Martoke's glowing gold eyes.

I am here because Jaerin Verik sent me. He and I plotted with—

No, I won't. My head aches from the effort. I feel like someone is hammering on the inside of my skull, and again, I repeat that one thought, letting it take over my entire mind. *I won't tell you anything.*

Martoke's presence retreats. He narrows his eyes. "I can see why she interests you, Dámiul. She's more stubborn than the Earthlings I've encountered in the past." He walks toward the case. "I've never used a Velslote device on an Earthling before. I wonder how she'll react."

"*Nur scren'ati!*" Rage consumes Dámiul's expression.

I wish I could stop shaking and reassure him, but although I open my mouth to try, no words come out.

"You have been a relentless nuisance to me, Dámiul." Martoke's voice is cold. "When I get all the information I want from her, I'll let you watch as I take her mind away."

My chest is so tight with terror, I can hardly breathe. My eyes follow Martoke's movements as he removes the metal crown meant for me.

Martoke approaches me. I shrink against the corner. *I can't be afraid,* I tell myself, but it's useless.

He raises the crown over my head, and my breath freezes in my lungs.

He stops abruptly, paralyzed in place. His expression goes blank. The luminosity in his eyes fades, and his hands become slack. The crown drops onto the floor. *What's happening?*

"Get away from her." Dámiul's voice is quiet but firm.

To my surprise, Martoke retreats. I turn my gaze to Dámiul. His azure eyes glow brighter than I've ever seen before. His breath quivers, and I can't tell if he's shaking from rage or effort.

Dámiul's gaze follows as Martoke walks across the room. His eyes are blank, as Dámiul's were when I first found him. He's become a shell of himself—how did that happen?

Martoke stops walking and turns stiffly to face Dámiul.

"Shut down your machines." Dámiul's voice is soft, and yet the air seems to shake from the intensity of his words. "Tell your bot to release Iris."

"*Lidara poatil.*" Martoke's voice is a dull monotone. "*Ibdis fuzettin.*"

The mechanical humming goes silent. The metal ropes around my wrists uncoil, and the security bot backs away from me. I rush to Dámiul.

The restraints binding his wrists to the table open. His eyes meet mine, and his blue gaze is almost blinding in its brightness. "Everything's all right, Iris. Martoke is under my command now." The tall bot retracts the needle from his wrist. Dámiul closes his eyes and pulls at the device embedded in his forehead. He winces. The long needle he removes drips with blood. He sets the device down, and his hands shake as removes the crown. A trail of blood runs across his forehead.

A gale of questions blows through my mind, but helping Dámiul is more important than any of them. But what can I do? I put my hand on his face and do my best to wipe away the blood. It doesn't count for much, but it's better than nothing.

Dámiul clasps my hand and gives me a reassuring smile. "I'm all right." He turns to Martoke. "Take off your Velslote device and disable the force fields in the corridor."

Martoke obediently removes the crown from his head and sets it down on the table. As he looks down at his wrist device, I ask, "How is this possible?"

"Telepathy works both ways." Dámiul keeps his eyes on Martoke. "Even with the Velslote device, Martoke's mind was never safe from me. I couldn't let him hurt you."

I feel his hand shaking in mine. Blood dribbles from Dámiul's nose, and he hastily wipes it away.

Apparently seeing my alarm, he says, "It's not easy controlling Martoke, but I'll be all right." He releases my hand and holds the table as he stands. "Let's go."

Chapter Thirty-Four

THE ACCESS CARD LIES ON THE FLOOR WHERE I DROPPED IT. I pick it up, open the door, and walk out. "This way."

The exit where Atikéa waits with an escape vehicle shouldn't take too long to reach. I don't know how much time has passed, and I hope she'll still be there by the time we reach the meeting place. She wouldn't leave me behind, but what if she gets caught?

Then, I'll find another way out. I square my shoulders and march down the corridor, leading Dámiul and the blank-faced Martoke. Whatever Dámiul's doing to keep his hold over Martoke, it's taking its toll. Red rims his eyes, and his nose keeps bleeding. Crimson stains his hands from all the times he's had to wipe the blood away, and his breath trembles. Yet his eyes are as bright as ever, in sharp contrast to Martoke's dull, empty gaze.

I wish we could run and get out of here as quickly as possible, but I don't think Dámiul has it in him to go any faster. Though he keeps his posture upright and holds his head high, I can tell how much effort his movements are taking.

A pair of metal gates lies ahead. I approach the security pad and tap the access card against it. The pad glows red, and the doors remain shut. I try again, but it makes no difference.

Martoke steps forward and pulls an access card from his pocket, his movements mechanical in their stiffness. The security pad turns green after Martoke taps his card against it, and the doors open, revealing an indigo-clad guard. The guard stops and turns to us.

I freeze, unsure of what to do.

The guard approaches with a questioning look, and Martoke steps forward. I glance at Dámiul, who keeps his brightly glowing eyes fixed on him.

"*En swar fac?*" The guard knits his eyebrows with confusion.

Martoke puts his hands behind his back. His response comes out stiff and stilted. I pray the guard won't notice there's something wrong with him. I can't understand his words, but I imagine Dámiul is trying to make the guard believe that Martoke is the one in charge, and we're his prisoners.

The guard eyes Martoke uneasily, then glances at me. "*Glan fith en Ka'risil dosketh?*"

Martoke answers, his tone is firmer than before. He says something that sounds like a command, and I recognize the word for "leave."

The guard's gaze shifts to Dámiul, and his eyes widen. He speaks rapidly and gestures at Dámiul, clearly concerned.

Martoke opens his mouth to speak, then freezes. Behind him, Dámiul doubles over and starts coughing violently.

I rush toward him, but Dámiul holds up a hand, halting me. He covers his mouth with his arm and tries to straighten, then doubles over again.

The guard shouts at Martoke, his voice rising with alarm. Then, the luminosity returns to Martoke's eyes, and he looks around with an expression of bewilderment, which soon turns to rage.

Dámiul must have lost his hold over him. I try not to let the fear threatening to overwhelm me enter my mind.

Martoke opens his mouth to speak. Before any words can emerge, Dámiul lunges at the guard and grabs the weapon attached to his belt. He fires twice, and flashes of white fill the air. Martoke falls toward me, and I jump out of the way. Beside him, the guard's eyes flutter shut, and he crumples to the ground.

Dámiul's hand shakes, and blood crawls down the side of his mouth. He wipes it away, then crouches over the unconscious Martoke and takes the access card still clasped in his fist.

He straightens and hands me the card. "Lead the way." His eyes have returned to their usual glow, no longer blinding.

A part of me is glad that we ran into the guard, since it means Dámiul no longer needs to control Martoke. He looks so tired, and I wonder how he's still standing. I wish I had some way to help him, but the only thing I can do is lead him out.

"Faster, before someone realizes something's wrong." Dámiul quickens his pace to a run, passing me.

I speed up as well, marveling at his energy.

A dead end lies ahead, with metal gates on either side. Knowing the left one leads to another corridor, I tap Martoke's access card against the security pad. To my relief, it opens.

Something clatters behind me, and I whirl. The weapon lies on the floor, and Dámiul collapses beside it. He falls on his back, convulsing violently.

"*Dámiul!*" I drop down next to him. *What do I do?* I slide my hand beneath the back of his head to keep it from striking the hard floor.

"*Clogamo!*" Even though it means capture, I scream for help as loudly as I can.

Dámiul meets my gaze, teeth clenched. "Go!"

Does he really expect me to abandon him? I continue yelling. "*Shraïn! Ona clogamo torna!*" The Adryil think of themselves as good people, don't they? It's a matter of pride with them. They have to help him; they wouldn't leave him like this. I take his hand. "It's going to be okay."

He tries to speak, but uncontrollable spasms wrack his body.

I know what he's trying to tell me and shake my head. "I came for you, and I won't leave you." I look up, hoping to see

someone rushing our way, but only empty hallways lie ahead. I open my mouth to yell again.

"Don't!" Dámiul grabs my hand.

I look at him. His eyelids droop with weakness, but, to my relief, he's no longer shaking.

"It passed. I'm all right." His voice is firm, but I'm not sure I believe him. "We can make it." He lets go of my hand and starts pushing himself off the floor. He manages to sit up, then lists to the side.

I catch his shoulders. "Dámiul…"

"I just need a moment." His eyelids droop.

If we still have a chance at escaping, I'll take it. He can't stay here, with the people who did this to him. "Is there anything I can do?"

He shakes his head. "I think it's the drugs Martoke injected me with. Or maybe it's because of what I did to him." He looks up, and, in spite of everything, lifts his bloodstained mouth in a half-smile. "I made my brain do something it wasn't meant to do, and I think it's revolting." He gives me a firm look. "If I collapse again, go on without me."

"No! Dámiul—"

"It won't make a difference if you stay. The same thing will happen to me whether you're here or not. You might as well escape."

"I'm either leaving with you or not at all." I don't care what consequences my stubbornness brings, or how idiotic my actions may be. I could never live with myself if I left him behind. I look him in the eye to make sure he knows I mean what I say.

He stares at me incredulously. "There's no way I can persuade you to save yourself, is there?"

"Not a chance."

"Then, we'd better make it out." Dámiul pushes himself up. I hold his arm and help him.

An ominous whirring sounds from the corridor ahead. I turn toward it to find a security bot wheeling toward me.

Alarmed, I grab the card I dropped and tap it against the security pad. The doors slide toward each other, but freeze

halfway. The red lights on the security bot flash, and it raises one of its metal arms.

Dámiul grabs the weapon on the floor. Crouching behind the door, he fires down the corridor. Sparks spew from the bot, but it keeps approaching. I duck beside him, hoping the door is thick enough to shield us. Dámiul fires again and again, until the bot topples onto its side. Bright lines of electric blue run down its metal body, and its lights darken.

"We should go." Dámiul stands. His head falls forward, and he grabs the wall for support.

I get up as well, but I barely make it two steps before a second bot rounds the corner, followed by a third. Behind them, four guards run toward us, each holding a weapon like the one in Dámiul's hand.

"Get down!" Dámiul steps in front of me and fires at the oncoming attackers.

Terrified, I duck by the door. Dámiul's white blasts take down one of the security bots. I look up at him. His face is a strange combination of exhaustion and strength, as though his body's telling him to give up, and he's refusing by sheer force of will. He leans his shoulder against the door and fires out at the attackers. How is he still fighting? I think the door is the only thing keeping him upright.

A spasm shakes his body. I gasp and spring up. He grabs the edge of the door and coughs violently. Though he covers his mouth, blood escapes. I hold his arm, trying to keep him from falling.

He collapses against me, unconscious.

"*Dámiul!*" I lower him to the ground.

A blast rings through the air. I whirl. One bot remains, and the four guards slow to a walk. Behind them, another bot rounds the corner.

That's it—we're finished. Dámiul's fallen, and I…

My gaze lands on Dámiul's weapon, which lies in his limp grasp. I can pull a trigger, can't I?

I grab the weapon and aim it at the security bot. I stay crouched and fire over and over. The security bot turns its

weapon toward me, and I scramble to get out of the way. I keep pulling the trigger, encouraged by the sight of spewing sparks.

It's not over until I fall, too. My shots are erratic, and only a fraction of them hit their targets. The guards' blasts fly toward me, and I press myself against the door, keeping as little of myself exposed as possible.

Again and again—I just keep firing. The security bot finally falls, but the guards are drawing close. My heart pounds, and a surge of heat swallows me. *Don't stop*, I tell myself.

Another group of guards rounds the corner. I don't stand a chance. What will happen when they catch me? I can fight as bravely as I want, but I can't fight forever. Soon, the guards will reach the doors, and I'll have no way to hide.

We're as good as gone.

I recall Dámiul's steadfast strength and fire anyway. I fire and fire, even though I know I'm waiting for my doom.

A white flash fills the air. I squeeze my eyes against its blinding brilliance. When I open them, I see three guards lying unconscious on the ground. The others shout at each other, and they seem confused. One shoots at me, but the others turn and fire in the direction the blast came from.

What's happening? My finger keeps pulling the trigger.

Another burst of white. I briefly turn away from the glaring light, then look out again. A figure rounds the corner, wielding a pair of weapons.

Chapter Thirty-Five

"**I**RIS! GET BACK!" THAT VOICE—IT'S JAERIN'S. I ONLY saw him for a split-second, but there's no mistaking Dámiul's brother.

I duck by the door. *What's he doing here?* I should help him—I think it's just him out there. But with my clumsy shots, I could end up hitting him by accident.

At least I'm not alone anymore. Jaerin seemed as if he knew what he was doing, and he's clearly much better with a weapon than I am.

Dámiul lies beside me, his face slack. I put my hand on his shoulder and shake him. "Dámiul!"

Dámiul doesn't respond, and I shake him again.

The commotion on the other side of the door ceases. Footsteps approach. I chance a look out and, to my relief, it's Jaerin who's walking toward me. Broken robots and unconscious guards litter the corridor ahead.

Jaerin tucks his weapons into a pair of holsters on his belt. "Are you all right?"

I nod. "What—What's going on?"

"When I heard Martoke's voice in the recording, I

realized the man torturing Dámiul was the same one I bribed. Of course he'd cross me." Disgust coats each word Jaerin speaks. "But he was our only way into the prison. Most government workers aren't so corruptible, but Martoke was willing to give me what I needed in hopes of both reaping a profit and trapping me. I had to work with him—or at least pretend to while preparing for the worst. I only wish I could have gotten here sooner."

The words sink in, and I'm both glad that Jaerin was prepared and furious that he let me think all would be lost if I were caught. "Why didn't you tell me?"

"If I had and Martoke read your mind, then even this contingency plan would have failed." He kneels beside Dámiul. "What happened? Was he hit?"

"No, he… collapsed. Martoke…" I trail off, and my eyes sting as I recall what Martoke did while I stood there watching, helpless to intervene.

"I see." Jaerin reaches toward Dámiul, his expression filled with a combination of anger and sorrow. He puts his hand on Dámiul's shoulder and stares into his face. His blue eyes glow brighter, and I wonder if he's trying to use his telepathy to wake Dámiul.

Dámiul stirs, and his eyes flutter open.

"*Ona esi dira, dáven teris.*" Jaerin smiles.

Dámiul stares at Jaerin, brow furrowed. He must be trying to remember his brother, like he tried to remember me. "I've seen you before—on the transport. I know you're my brother, but there's so much I can't remember."

"You will." Jaerin helps Dámiul stand. "Come, we don't have much time." He enters the corridor ahead.

Dámiul follows, then grabs the edge of the door. His head falls forward, and both Jaerin and I rush to him. Dámiul holds up his hand and starts to speak, but doesn't seem to have the strength to form words. Jaerin takes Dámiul's arm and puts it over his shoulder. "Let me help you. I'll get you out of here."

I step forward, aiming to take Dámiul's other arm. Even if he falls again, Jaerin and I can carry him out.

"Iris." Jaerin pulls a weapon out of his holster. "Take this.

I need you to run ahead and see if there's any trouble coming our way."

I accept the weapon. I glance at Martoke's access card on the ground, then realize I won't need it. The next door I encounter will be the one Atikéa opened from the outside. Holding the weapon in front of me, I make my way around the unconscious guards.

I glance back. Dámiul leans against Jaerin, and the two slowly make their way forward. From the way Dámiul's head keeps drooping, I can tell he's struggling to stay conscious.

As much as I want to rush over and comfort him, Jaerin gave me a job to do, and we're not out of trouble yet. I carefully make my way forward, listening for any movement. To my relief, I see no one when I reach the end of the corridor. "It's safe."

"Good." Jaerin approaches me. "I disabled the alarms, so as long as no one comes this way, we should be all right."

"How did you get in?"

"Through the door we're about to leave from, but opening it turned out to be more complicated than we thought it would be." Jaerin rounds the corner with Dámiul, and I notice an unexpected sorrow in his expression. "We don't have much further before we reach Kéa."

The corridor is eerily silent. Except for my own footsteps and the noise of my breath, I don't hear anything. I reach the end. A rectangular door lies to my right with the Adryil word for "exit" glowing above it in orange lights. Recalling Atikéa's instructions, I press my hands against its cold surface and push to the left, relying on the friction of my palms to move it. The door slides open, revealing a dark alley. The wide gate before a neighboring building opens, and a hovering black vehicle emerges. Atikéa's purple gaze glows through the windshield.

She stops the vehicle and steps out. The door to the vehicle's back opens. I move out of the way so Jaerin can help Dámiul inside.

Dámiul scarcely seems aware of his surroundings. He crumples onto the seat.

Jaerin puts his hands on Dámiul's shoulders and looks into his eyes. *"Ona en eládor, dáven teris."* He kisses Dámiul's forehead,

then straightens and turns to Atikéa. "He needs medical attention immediately."

Atikéa nods. "Yandria is waiting at our headquarters."

"Good." Jaerin turns to me. "Make sure Dámiul stays conscious. He's fading."

"What do you mean?" I ask.

Before Jaerin can answer, the white corridor behind him turns red from flashing lights. Cacophonous buzzing sounds from the building, and I tense.

Jaerin turns back to the door. "Go!"

Atikéa grabs his shoulder. "Jaerin!" She pulls him close and kisses him, wrapping her arms around him tightly.

A second later, Jaerin pushes her back. "I'm sorry, Kéa." He runs back inside, and the door shuts behind him.

"Get in the vehicle." Atikéa wipes her eyes and returns to the pilot's seat.

I automatically respond to the authority in her voice and climb into the back beside Dámiul. The vehicle's doors slam shut.

Dámiul sits up with a start, as if startled out of a reverie. "Where's my brother?"

Atikéa steers the vehicle up toward the dark sky. "He went to lead them away, giving us the chance to escape."

Dámiul turns toward the window with alarm. "We can't—"

"Dámiul!" Atikéa's voice is sharp. "This was always part of the plan. If they saw us, they'd be upon us within minutes. Jaerin's going to draw them off."

"How will he escape?"

"He won't." Atikéa veers the vehicle around a skyscraper. "He knew he wouldn't be able to. When they capture him, he'll use his last resort." Her voice quivers. "He had his own head implanted with memory erasers, except they haven't been activated yet. He has the trigger with him. When he presses it, they'll wipe all his memories from the past four years. No matter how they probe him, they won't get any answers."

"How could you let him do that?" Dámiul's voice is labored, and I can tell he's growing weak again.

"It was the only way we could get you out." Atikéa twists to

face Dámiul. "Do you think I want to be forgotten? I love him, but tomorrow, he won't even remember my name." She turns back. "You matter too much to him, and if I'd tried to stop him, I would have lost him anyway."

"We have to go back. I—"

"This is what Jaerin wants. If you love him, you'll accept his choice, as I did."

Dámiul leans back and closes his eyes. "I'm sorry."

I recall how a part of me wanted to die when Dámiul didn't remember me. I can't imagine how Atikéa must feel, knowing Jaerin chose to forget her. But if Dámiul could recover his memories, surely Jaerin could as well. "Maybe we can get Jaerin out later, and his memories will come back."

"No." Atikéa's voice is soft. "He told me not to come for him. It would be too dangerous, and he made me swear I wouldn't let Dámiul try anything either. But he'll still be who he is, and I hope that someday, when we meet again, he'll know in his heart that we're meant to be."

I can believe that. Even before he remembered me, I saw the core of who Dámiul was behind the shell they tried to turn him into. Surely, the same will be true for Jaerin.

Dámiul falls toward me, and his head drops over his chest. "Dámiul?" His eyes are closed, and he doesn't respond. Jaerin told me not to let him lose consciousness. I shake him hard. "*Dámiul!*"

Dámiul's eyelids flutter. He tries to speak, but no words come out.

"Stay with me." I put my arm around his. "Please, Jaerin said you have to stay awake."

"What happened to him?" Atikéa sounds worried.

I tell her what happened when Martoke tried to interrogate him, then how Dámiul took control of Martoke and what that did to him.

"Keep him awake." Atikéa sounds tense. "I'm going as fast as I can."

"Why? What's happening to him?"

"What Dámiul did could have killed him. If he loses consciousness again, he might not wake up."

He could die—because of me. Tears stream down my cheeks. *Please, don't take him away from me. Not now. Not when we're so close to safety.* I don't know who I'm calling to anymore, but I want to believe that someone will hear me.

Dámiul's head sinks against my shoulder. He blinks slowly, as if his eyes want to fall shut again, and he's fighting to keep them open. Once brilliant in their luminance, they hardly glow anymore. "I'm trying, Iris." His voice is barely a whisper.

I hold him close, wishing I could transfer my strength to him. Maybe if I can keep him talking, he won't slip away again. "What was it like, the first time you used the Zexa device to talk to me?"

For a moment, Dámiul doesn't reply. "I barely knew how to use it. I stole it from TalentCorp's office in Charlotte the same day I broke into Papilio. Before that, it never occurred to me that I'd need one, since using one to keep in touch with Ximena would have put her in danger if she were ever caught with it. All I knew about you then was that your curiosity was stronger than your fear, and that was why I entrusted the device to you. Then I came to know you, and you were such a surprise to me."

I feel an involuntary smile spread across my lips.

"I've spent my entire life surrounded by *Ka'risil*, but other than Ximena, I never really knew them." Dámiul continues before I can respond. Weary as he appears, an undying brightness burns on in his expression. "I thought she was the rare exception, and that most Artists would be subservient drones, like the *Ka'risil* here. Instead, I found you—someone devoted to an unshakable belief in something sublime, who found light in everything she encountered and would rather believe foolishly in the good than try to outsmart the world by believing in evil. You're so beautiful, and yet you don't seem to realize it. I remember how you tried to tell me you were considered plain and wondering how that could be when, each time I saw you, everything around you seemed to disappear."

My face grows warm. I've never had someone admire me like that before. "I think our standards at Papilio are different from yours."

Dámiul gives me a weak smile. "I see nothing's changed." His smile falls, and his eyes close.

I give him a shake. "Dámiul!"

He opens his eyes.

I need him to start talking again, so I quickly say, "How did you become an Abolitionist?"

"If you're referring to the actual organization, the answer is 'by being rescued by them.'" He pauses, then shakes his head slowly. "It's a blur… I remember arguing with Jaerin—him telling me to stay out of the fight and me refusing. I remember coming to the meetings anyway, but walking out because I thought they weren't moving fast enough. Then trying to enlist them to help Ximena and walking out again when they refused." He knits his eyebrows. "My father showed me TalentCorp's operations when I was a child. He wanted me to understand his business, but something terrible happened…" He trails off.

The strain is visible in his expression, and I realize the folly in asking him about memories still buried beneath the prison's telepathic manipulations. I open my mouth to give him a different topic to talk about.

"He took me to see them," Dámiul continues before I can speak. "The ones who had just boarded a starship from Earth. He wanted me to see how the Artists were molded into obedient *Ka'risil.* There was a girl… She had a family. Instead of forgetting them, she realized that someone was taking her memories, and she fought back. She was screaming."

"That's horrible." I shudder. If I'd realized what Erayet was doing, that could have been me.

"My father ordered her mind erased and assured everyone that such incidents were extremely rare. His only concerns were how he would refund the customer and protect TalentCorp's reputation." Dámiul glances away. "He was so cold."

The pain in his voice makes my heart ache for him. I squeeze his hand, yearning to take the hurt away.

"I wish I could have trained every Artist to guard their minds, but TalentCorp was always watching." His voice is so soft, I can barely hear him. "So I only trained the one who

mattered most to me. Perhaps it was selfish, but if they'd found out what we were doing, all would have been lost."

I lean back, wrapping my mind around his words. It's still hard to believe how all-powerful TalentCorp really is to those living under their control. I wonder what choices I would have made, had I been in Dámiul's position. I wish I could whisper the truth to everyone at Papilio, as he once intended, but with TalentCorp's omnipresence, it wouldn't have taken long for the secret to come out. A revolt would have damaged the company, yes, but the cost would have been the lives of those involved.

I wouldn't have done it either. For Papilio, salvation can only come from outside.

A light catches my attention, and I look out the window. Atikéa steers the vehicle down a long, brown passageway illuminated by dim yellow lights. She stops before a wide door, which I recognize as the one leading to the Abolitionists' hideout.

I exhale. *We made it.*

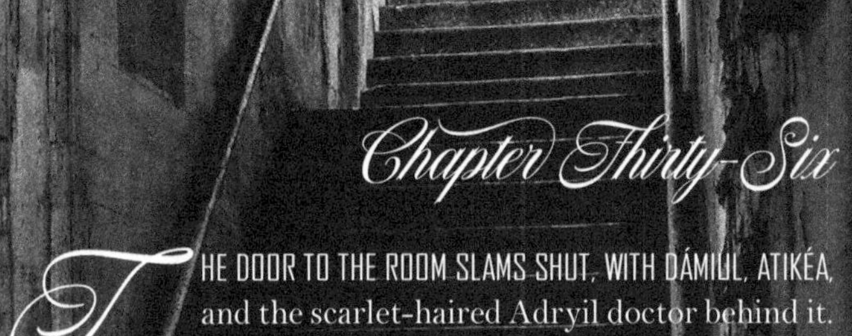

Chapter Thirty-Six

HE DOOR TO THE ROOM SLAMS SHUT, WITH DÁMIUL, ATIKÉA, and the scarlet-haired Adryil doctor behind it.

I couldn't make out any of the hurried Adryil words Atikéa exchanged with the woman. I wish the room had a window so I could see what they're doing.

My mind seems incapable of forming even the usual self-reassurances. Tension grips me so tightly, I wonder how I haven't shattered into a million pieces yet. The horrific images of blood streaming down his face, of him convulsing on the floor, of him fighting just to keep his eyes open, run wild through my mind. What if the doctor can't save him? What if we've come all this way, only to lose him now?

I never told him I love him. The realization hits me like a cold fist, and the sobs that have been threatening to emerge shake my chest. I cover my face and let them out. Maybe it doesn't matter, but I can't stand the thought of losing my chance forever.

The door slides open, and an acrid, chemical smell floats toward me. I look up in time to catch a glimpse of Dámiul lying in the white med pod with the doctor standing over him. Atikéa steps out, and the door shuts again.

I have so many questions, but the tension seems to have stifled my words.

Atikéa approaches me with a look of sympathy. "Dámiul will be all right, Iris. Yandria is a skilled doctor, as well as a trusted member of the Abolition. She's going to remove the implants the reeducation center put in Dámiul, and he should be able to regain all his memories."

I try to find comfort in Atikéa's words, but the tension keeps its hold over me. "What about everything Martoke did to him? Can she fix that too?"

"Yes." Atikéa gives me a reassuring smile. "Believe me, any worries you have, Jaerin already thought of them. He knew there was a good chance Dámiul would be hurt during the escape, so he had as much medical equipment smuggled here as he could. He wanted to be prepared for everything from blast wounds to drug withdrawal. Fortunately, much of that won't be needed."

I manage to nod mutely. My eyes remain fixed on the door behind Atikéa.

Atikéa puts her hand on my back. "Come. It won't do you any good to stand here like this."

Knowing she's right, I let her guide me away. "When can I see him?"

"You may visit after Yandria finishes the surgery, although Dámiul will be asleep by then." Atikéa leads me toward one of the doors on the other side of the room. "In the meantime, I think you should get some rest as well." She opens the door, which leads to a dimly lit corridor. "I'm afraid our hideout won't be as comfortable as your *Ka'risil* quarters were, but I hope you'll find your room decent enough."

My room? I never thought about what would happen to me. If everything had gone according to the original plan, I would have returned to the backstage area before anyone noticed I was missing. But I realize now that since Martoke and a number of other guards saw me helping Dámiul escape, there's no way I can go back.

"What's going to happen to me?" I ask.

Atikéa stops before a door with the Adryil symbol for the number seven painted on it. "You'll have to stay here, in hiding, until I can figure out how to get you to safety. We may be able to return you to the Ydayas if we can convince the authorities that you were a clueless Earthling manipulated by Adryil telepathy. Don't worry, Iris. I'll take care of you."

"Thank you." I hope I can find a way to go back. In the *Ka'risil* quarters, I can do for others as Cara did for me: spread the truth and recruit supporters for the Abolition. There's not much—if anything—I can do here in the hideout.

The door opens, revealing a small, square room lit by a white, circular light on the left wall. A cot sits in the corner, and there's a narrow door across from it.

Atikéa motions for me to enter. "That door leads to a bathroom shared with the room beside you, which is currently unoccupied. Our supporters come from all parts of Adrye, and sometimes they stay here." She gives me a fond smile. "I must say, I never imagined you'd take part in an Abolitionist mission. When Cara first told me she had a new recruit, I thought the most you'd be doing was whispering the truth to the other *Ka'risil* you came across."

"I never thought I'd do anything like this either." I approach the bed, and it hits me how far I've come since I first met Dámiul. I used to be invisible, known only as "viola girl" by most of the Orchestra. The most I dared hope for was a job as a performer. My destiny was so set, I could see it: I would find a patron or accept whichever job my school placed me in. Either way, I would have been a cog in a system, never worrying about what came next because it was all decided for me.

Now, the future is clouded, and I can't see the way forward. But at least I helped save the boy I love. Perhaps, together, we can change the fates of thousands of Artists like me. And then, if we fight hard enough, maybe we can change the way the Adryil treat the noncompliant. What Martoke did to Dámiul was nothing short of evil, and I can't stand the thought of it happening to anyone else.

Atikéa reaches into her pocket. "Here." She hands me a watch similar to the one I used to always wear at Papilio. "If you need

anything, my contact information is in here. It's also connected to the Adryil Planetary Network. I had it programmed with a function that translates everything into English."

"Thank you." I examine the watch.

"I must return to the university. I'll see you soon." Atikéa leaves, and the door shuts behind her.

Weariness descends. I approach the cot and lie down, but sleep won't come. I think about Dámiul in that room, fighting for his life, and send a prayer to whichever forces of fate might be listening.

Dámiul looks so peaceful in his sleep. I would never have guessed that, less than a day ago, he was killing himself trying to protect me. He lies in a white med pod, which takes up half the room, but he occupies only a very small part of it. Yandria left it open, since Dámiul doesn't have an illness. Several small, round pads adhere to his face, attached to wires snaking into the pod's sides. An opaque tube protrudes from each of his wrists, and they, too, are attached to the pod. It's the most complex-looking machine I've ever encountered, and seeing him connected like that disturbs me a little even though I know it's saving him.

Yandria departed before I could ask any questions, but she left a note on a tablet telling me she would be back in the evening and that, if Dámiul wakes up, I must make sure he stays in the pod. Actually, the note was addressed to another Abolitionist, but I wanted to be the one to watch over Dámiul. Tadrien was more than happy to let me take over.

A white bandage covers Dámiul's forehead. Dried blood still stains his face and hands. I spot a sink in the corner and approach. A white towel sits beside it, along with a number of shining instruments that I assume are medical equipment. I pick up the towel and put it under the faucet. Cool water streams down automatically.

I return to Dámiul's side and gently dab his face, careful not to disturb the round pads. Other than the humming of the pod, the hideout is silent. Almost everyone has gone back

to their daily lives, and the few people here are meeting in a room on the other side of the complex. From the snippets of conversation I caught before they closed the door, it seems like they're discussing ways to get more people to come out with their support for the Abolition movement.

I'll worry about the cause later. Even if I wanted to join the conversation, I don't know enough to add anything helpful. There are so many things I wish I could do, but can't.

Watching over Dámiul is the only thing I can do right now. I rinse off the towel, then return to his side.

The days blur into a quiet haze of anxiety and boredom. Either six or seven have passed since we broke Dámiul out of the reeducation center—I've lost track. It's hard to have a sense of time when my surroundings don't change, and my only glimpses of the outside world are through the Adryil Planetary Network, which I've spent hours browsing.

This is the longest I've gone without my viola, and its absence makes my fingers itch with discontent. Sometimes, I close my eyes and shadow play, letting the notes take me back to a simpler time. If I only had my instrument, these underground days wouldn't seem so dull. Without it, a piece of my soul is missing. But each time I find myself longing to go back to my old life, I think about Dámiul, and all that goes away.

The other Abolitionists come and go, but I haven't seen Atikéa since she gave me the watch. According to Yandria, Dámiul's escape caused quite a stir, and she's keeping a low profile for the time being so no one will suspect she's anything more than an outspoken university student.

Having used up the hour break I allotted myself, I deactivate my watch and pick up the language tablet on my lap. I adjust my position in my chair. The collar of my ill-fitting shirt, which I found in a closet Tadrien directed me to, slides down my shoulder. I pull it back up, wishing I wasn't so ridiculously small.

I glance at Dámiul, who remains unconscious in the med pod. The wounds on his forehead are gone, but he hasn't shown

any sign of waking up. Yandria told me that it's normal for people with his kinds of injuries to remain unconscious for a week or more while they recover.

Worry invades my thoughts nonetheless. I can't help wondering: is this my fault? If Cara had been the one to find him at the reeducation center, she wouldn't have wasted time reconnecting with him, as I did. Even if he refused to listen to her, she would have dragged him out the door and shoved him into the escape vehicle before Martoke had a chance to catch up.

Martoke was in control of the whole situation. She would have been caught, too. My repeated self-reassurances do little to comfort me. If I hadn't been such a whimpering coward, we might have been all right until Jaerin found us, and Dámiul wouldn't have hurt himself so badly to protect me. If there's ever a next time, I'll be braver—like Cara. Knowing her, she would have put up a fight from the start instead of letting the security bot get her. Maybe if I'd at least tried to escape, I could have—could have what? I was unarmed and faced with a powerful, towering machine. What could I possibly have done?

The maybes won't do me any good, and I stare at the language tablet, hoping it'll keep my mind off of them. What happened is over. Dámiul is here now, safe in the care of the Abolitionists and an expert doctor. And me—I just want to be here when he wakes up.

I read through a simple passage in Adryil, sounding out the syllables and trying to make sense of them. Considering how little time I've spent learning the language, I'm doing all right with the speaking and listening. My good memory for music apparently also applies to spoken languages. Reading and writing, however, is a different story. The Adryil alphabet isn't too long, but the symbols always get mixed up in my head.

A soft, rustling sound rises from the med pod, and I look up with a start. Dámiul stirs. He hasn't moved except to breathe since he got here. Enough time has passed—he must be waking up at last.

My heart pounding, I leave the tablet on my chair and approach him. "Dámiul?"

Dámiul blinks. He looks around in confusion for a few

seconds, and then his gaze meets mine. His eyes, which had faded so much right after his escape, have regained their usual glow.

Just the sight of him, awake and with me, takes my breath away. The fretfulness that's been gripping my heart releases me, and I exhale. "Welcome back."

"Where am I?" Dámiul starts to sit up.

I put my hand on his shoulder to stop him. "You have to stay still. You're in a med pod, connected to equipment that's healing you. We brought you to the Abolitionists' underground headquarters, and Yandria—the doctor—has been taking care of you. She took out the implants they used to wipe your memory."

Dámiul lies back, expression confused. He blinks a few times, then widens his eyes. "I remember everything. My school, Jaerin, my parents…" His face falls with dismay. "I suppose they're not my parents anymore. And Jaerin won't recall fighting with me—he'll probably listen when they tell him I'm a delinquent not worth remembering." He stares at the ceiling. "They're all gone."

"You still have Atikéa and the Abolitionists." I take his hand and squeeze it. "And you have me."

"I never thanked you for saving me." Dámiul's eyes fill with admiration. "I don't know how I ever could."

My mind balks at the notion that I'm the one who should get credit for his escape. "I didn't save you. Jaerin and Atikéa did, acting on an idea Cara came up with."

"You're fugitive now, aren't you? You're trapped underground because of what you did for me."

"I don't mind." It's true—I really don't. Even though there's much about living with the Ydayas I miss, I don't regret trading the world I knew for someone I love.

Dámiul closes his hand around mine. "Why would you give up so much for me?"

My heart beats faster. *Because I love you.* How can I just tell him that? Would it be too bold of me to utter those words? Would it scare him away? But he must feel the same about me— I've seen it in his eyes, heard it in his voice. Maybe he's as afraid

of those words as I am, and I should just lay my heart out before him to erase any questions he might have.

I've pictured this moment so many times—telling my first love how I feel. I used to daydream about saying those three magic words to a faceless fantasy before I met Dámiul. The closer that daydream drew to reality, the further I pushed it from my mind. It was frightening once I realized I'd actually have to confess to another. For the longest time, I wouldn't even confess it to myself.

I need to tell him and let whatever happens happen. But before I can work up the courage, the door opens. Surprised, I whirl toward it, releasing Dámiul's hand.

Cara stands in the doorway with her arms crossed. "They said I'd find you here. Hey, he's awake!" She looks past me. "I'm Cara, by the way. If it weren't for this one"—she jerks her head at me—"I would've been the one running through the reeducation center saving your hide. But *someone* stole my spotlight." She gives me a playful smirk and steps out of the doorway.

Yandria enters. She purses her lips, approaches Dámiul's med pod, and asks him a few questions in Adryil. Though I can't catch every word in their exchange, I get the idea that she's asking how he's doing, and he's insisting that he's well.

Cara nudges me. "Hey, can we get out of here?"

I don't want to leave Dámiul, but he glances at me and says, "Go on. Yandria needs to conduct her examination, and it won't be pleasant."

"I'll be back as soon as she's finished." Reluctantly, I turn away from him and follow Cara out of the room.

Cara sweeps her bangs out of her eyes. "So, what the hell happened with the escape? I overheard some things from the Ydayas, but I've basically been in the dark. Would've made an HQ run sooner, but they were watching us all too closely after your little stunt. I didn't even dare wear the Grámed device."

I give her a brief summary of that night's events. I hope I don't sound too pathetic as I describe how I had to stand by and watch Dámiul suffer, then get rescued by Jaerin. "If it hadn't been for Jaerin, we both would have been caught."

Cara gives me a grudgingly impressed smile. "Hey, you

336

held your own. So, what happened to Jaerin? Everyone's been mysterious about him."

I tell her about how he led the guards away and then wiped his own memory. Her smile falls, and a desolate expression darkens her eyes. I never expected to see a look like that on her usually hard façade.

"So Jaerin's gone." Cara firms her mouth. "I should've known the idiot would do something like that. He should've told me… Screw him! I was going to put it all on the line to save his precious brother, and he couldn't even be bothered with saying goodbye when he knew he'd never see me again?"

Her outburst surprises me. There's something familiar about her pained look—it's reminiscent of the one that crossed Atikéa's face.

Even though I don't say anything, Cara throws me a glare, as if she knows what I was thinking. "Yeah, like I said before, you're not the only one to be dazzled by a pair of shiny Adryil eyes. Not that it mattered." She tosses her head and throws on a carefree expression. "So, what's it like being underground?"

"Boring," I confess, choosing to let her change the subject.

"Heh, I've been kind of bored too. Quartet's a lot less fun without you. But luckily, the Ydayas brought in someone else to entertain me." She glances at the closed doors along the walls. "In fact, Tadrien should finish crushing his past any time now."

Hope kindles in my mind, and I try to keep it from sparking too brightly in case I'm wrong. "Who is it?"

Cara makes a face. "Aw, look at you, all jumpy and excited."

She makes another snide comment, but I don't take in the words as a door behind her opens. Glimpsing a familiar head of loose blond curls, I dash past her. "*Milo!*"

I ZOOM INTO THE ROOM, NEARLY CRASHING INTO TADRIEN on his way out. I didn't dare believe that my scheme with Mistress Ydaya would work, especially after I was caught at the reeducation center. I thought she'd disregard everything I once said to her, and for the past several days, I've been worrying about how I might never see Milo again.

Milo stands and faces me. "Iris?"

I run up to him, flooded with relief and happiness. "You remember me!" I throw my arms around him. "I was so worried you wouldn't."

"What can I say?" He releases me, and a grin lights his face. "You're unforgettable."

Someone makes a disgusted noise. I turn to find Cara standing beside me. She wrinkles her nose. "You know, I had something to do with that too." She glances at me. "Your pretty pal here arrived this morning. Normally, I would've watched him for a few days, like I did with you, to make sure he was trustworthy before letting him in on all this." She points up and twirls her finger to indicate the hideout. "But the longer things stay forgotten, the harder it is to remember them, right? So I hounded him with your name and picture until he remembered you." She crosses her arms. "You're welcome."

I give her a grateful smile. She's the reason I've now found both Dámiul and Milo again, and I've never even told her how much I appreciate everything she's done. "I don't know how to thank you. If it weren't for you—"

"Yeah, yeah." Cara rolls her eyes. "I only did it because reuniting you guys is another little triumph over the system, and I happen to like winning. You know what my name means in Italian? 'Sweet victory.'"

She smirks and glances at Milo, but he doesn't seem to have heard anything she said.

He stares at me with a look of disbelief. "Of all the patrons who could have chosen me... I can't believe we ended up in the same place."

Cara raises her eyebrow. "It's not a coincidence, you know. I mean, it's pretty freaking convenient, but it wasn't all fate or destiny or whatever the hell other magical forces you think it is. Nah, it was good old bargain hunting. Mistress Ydaya wanted to claim you before the next Spectacle, in case you ended up doing something amazing and your price spiked like Iris's did."

Despite what she said, I take a moment to appreciate all my good fortune. If Mistress Ydaya hadn't already been thinking of getting ballet dancers, if Master Ydaya hadn't been concerned about costs, if they hadn't bought me in the first place and I hadn't met Cara... It hits me how lucky I've been, and how easily my story—and Milo's, and Dámiul's, and maybe even Cara's, if she'd gone through with her mission—could have ended tragically.

"I missed you." Those words seem too small to convey all the longing I felt in Milo's absence. I need to find something else to talk about, or I might break down and sob about all the anxiety I went through when I thought I might have lost him. My gaze falls on the hologram of Papilio projecting from the table. "It looks like you were right about Papilio's injustice."

Cara pulls out a chair and plops down. "Holy shit, you should have seen him when he first arrived at the Ydayas'. He

kept going on about how wrong everything seemed, and even when he wasn't talking, he had this shifty look about him. If I hadn't slipped him a Grámed device within five minutes of meeting him, Puna would have wiped his entire mind by now." She spreads her arms. "Again, you're welcome."

Milo shoots Cara an exasperated look. "Thank you, okay? How many times are you going to make me say it before you'll leave me alone?"

Cara shrugs. "Hey, if it weren't for me, you'd be a complacent little slave with no memory of darling Iris. Just saying."

"Thank you, Cara," I say, wishing I had some way of repaying her.

She leans back in her chair. "Whatever."

I put my hand on Milo's arm. "I can't tell you how glad I am to see you again."

Milo's eyes warm. "Likewise. You're the only reason I made it. I was so ready to drop out, but after you left, I realized the only way I might see you again was if I found a patron too. So I stayed. Rankings and employers weren't worth killing myself over, but you were." He takes my hand.

For a moment, I just look into his familiar, friendly gray eyes, wondering what—if anything—he's trying to tell me.

Cara stands so quickly her chair rattles, and the sound draws my attention back to my surroundings. She grimaces at Milo. "You could at least find a private corner or something before confessing your feelings."

Milo releases my hand and throws Cara a look of irritation. A scornful attitude radiates from her as she marches out the door.

"How did you ever live with her?" Milo stares after her. "I've known her for one day, and I want to wring her neck already!"

"If it weren't for her, I'd be a stranger to you." I think back to my first moments on Adrye, when my best friend was only a nameless face to me.

Milo's expression sobers. "You're right. You know, she also harangued me about my family. Pushed me so hard, I almost wanted to hit her. But it worked. I remember my parents and

Alice, though my head felt ready to split in half by the time Cara was done with me."

I can only imagine how much yelling must have been involved in that scene. It does seem odd that Cara would work so hard to help someone she doesn't even know. Then again, she hates injustice more than anything, and I told her previously that Milo has a family on Earth. "I guess that's her way of fighting what's being done to us."

"A noble cause." Milo speaks with exaggerated grandeur. "But does she have to be so annoying about it?"

Footsteps approach from the direction of the door, and I turn to find Dámiul striding into the room.

Relieved that he's no longer confined to the pod, which must mean he's recovering well, I smile. "You're up!"

Milo elbows me lightly. "Is this your alien friend?"

I nod, then look at Dámiul. "Dámiul, this is Milo."

Dámiul glances at Milo. "I remember you telling me about him."

I approach. "How are you doing?"

"Yandria says I shouldn't use my telepathy for at least two months, but otherwise, I'm all right, as long as I don't do anything extreme." He gives a slight smile, but there's something sad in his eyes.

Before I can ask what's wrong, Atikéa walks into the room. "I'm glad you're awake, Dámiul." She approaches the table and motions for him to follow. "I have something you need to see. Actually, I have two things. Iris, you might want to see them too." She glances at Milo. "You're new, aren't you?"

"Yup." Cara reenters, responding before Milo can. "Just brought him here."

"I see. You don't have to stay for this," Atikéa says to Milo. "You can if you want, but you probably won't find it interesting."

Milo shrugs and grabs a chair. "I'll stay."

I take the chair next to him, but keep my gaze on Dámiul. I'm glad to see that his eyes have regained their energy, but I wonder what the troubled look on his face means.

Atikéa glances at the screen, and Cara takes a seat next to her. A hologram of Jaerin appears in the center of the table.

Dámiul stares at it. The furrows between his brows deepen, and I realize what's upsetting him. *Of course, he's worried about his brother.*

"Jaerin recorded this right before the prison break." Atikéa glances at the screen again, and the hologram animates.

"*Tra'kel, dáven teris.*" In the recording, Jaerin smiles sadly. I don't need the subtitles to understand the words: "Hello, little brother."

Jaerin speaks in a measured voice. I can make out most of the words, but I read the subtitles anyway to make sure I don't misunderstand him.

"I know you're upset with me, and I'm sorry I had to do things this way." Jaerin sighs. "Please understand, this plan was the closest I could come to guaranteeing your safety. If I don't remember anything from the past four years, there's no way they can use me to find and arrest the underground members of the Abolition—or recapture you. You're probably wondering why I would rescue you from a place that stole memories, only to suffer the same fate myself. The answer is simple: Because I love you, little brother."

The look on Jaerin's face turns stern. "Whatever happens, do *not* try to make contact with me. It would be too much of a risk. Erasing four years of memories won't change who I am. I'll be confused for a period of time, but I'm sure I'll eventually rediscover the cause and find the Abolition again on my own. Until then, I'm afraid I can't help you anymore. Good luck, and when we meet again, I hope you can forgive me."

The hologram flickers out. Dámiul's expression doesn't change.

Atikéa turns to him. "Jaerin left me a similar message. He's not gone, Dámiul. Just absent."

Dámiul nods slowly. "Do you know where he is now?"

"Yes. That's the second thing I want to show you." Atikéa narrows her eyes at the screen, and another hologram appears.

Master Verik stands behind Jaerin and speaks firmly in Adryil. Beside him, Jaerin looks from side to side, as though puzzled by everything around him. I read the captions to see what Master Verik is saying.

"I am appalled by what happened at the reeducation center a few nights ago." He places his hand on Jaerin's shoulder. "However, my son is not to be blamed for the actions of others. As evidenced by the implants discovered in his head after he was found wandering the facility in a dazed state, he was never a part of the criminal group that broke Dámiul out. They used technology meant to reeducate the criminally minded to control him, and then wiped his memory so he wouldn't be able to name his attackers. I'm sure the courts will come to the same conclusion. As for Dámiul—I'm ashamed that I ever called him my son."

The hologram switches to that of a female reporter. I don't pay attention to her summary of the events that happened at the reeducation center. Instead, I turn to Dámiul. "Jaerin's all right, at least. Master Verik seems very protective of him."

"I'm glad." Dámiul's tone is flat, and he doesn't look at me.

I run through the possible things I can say, but none of them seem adequate. How do you comfort someone whose father told the world that he doesn't want you anymore?

My own face appears on the holovid, and I look up with a start. The captions say that I'm an unfortunate *Ka'risil* who must have been brainwashed by the Abolitionists.

Mistress Ydaya's distressed face fills the holovid. "Iris was a curious little *Ka'risil*, and the criminals must have used that against her. I wish I'd watched her more closely. I know the policy for rogue *Ka'risil*, but I hope the courts will be more lenient in her case and let her return to me. I miss my charming little violist."

She speaks of me like I'm a lost pet, but there's genuine concern in her voice. I feel a slight twinge of guilt. The Ydayas did take good care of me. I may not have had freedom, but I can't complain about how I was treated. My room there was certainly more comfortable than the one I'm living in now, and I enjoyed the pleasure of performing so often. If she were a true patron, an employer who allowed me freedom, I would gladly play for her.

Atikéa stops the holovid. "That's the world's reaction to what happened. The Abolitionists are a criminal underground

organization who brainwashed and used an upstanding young man to break a delinquent out of jail. And Iris is an innocent little *Ka'risil*, also brainwashed and used. That's good for them, I guess, since it means Jaerin's not in trouble with the law, and getting Iris back to the Ydayas won't be much of a problem once I find a device that can block telepathy without being detected. But not so good for the Abolitionists. According to them, we're monsters." She stands. "Before, we were just outspoken activists. Now, we've committed an actual crime."

"This is my fault." Dámiul's voice is low.

"Don't you dare talk like that," Atikéa snaps. "Guilt won't do you any good. This is a setback, but it won't deter us. Jaerin and I had two goals for the Abolition: inform as many *Ka'risil* of the truth as possible, and persuade those who sympathize with us to speak up. Remember, just because people aren't willing to join an underground movement doesn't mean they don't believe as we do. If we can get one of the more influential silent sympathizers to go public, more will follow."

She walks around the table. Dámiul follows her out of the room. I get up, aiming to talk to him, but stop when he calls Atikéa's name.

I feel a light smack on my arm and turn to see Cara.

"Hey, want to help me explain this crazy planet to Clueless here?" Cara points her thumb at Milo, who looks like he's trying very hard not to make a face at her.

I turn to look at Dámiul, who asks Atikéa in Adryil to tell him more about the Abolition. I suppose that's more important than anything I have to say. "Sure."

Atikéa leads Dámiul into a room, and the door closes behind them. He needs to know more about everything that's going on, and I shouldn't interrupt. Meanwhile, Milo just arrived on Adrye, and he needs to know more about what it's like here. And Cara needs my help explaining everything, if for no other reason than to act as a buffer between her and Milo. I don't understand how two people who just met can irritate each other so much.

What about what I need? If Cara had opened the door to

the med room a minute later, I would have told Dámiul that I love him, and all this miserable uncertainty would be over.

Come on, Iris, I chastise myself. *There'll be another moment.*

I turn to the table. Cara presses something on the screen, and a hologram of Nathril appears. I point to the buildings and start describing them for Milo, as Dámiul once did for me.

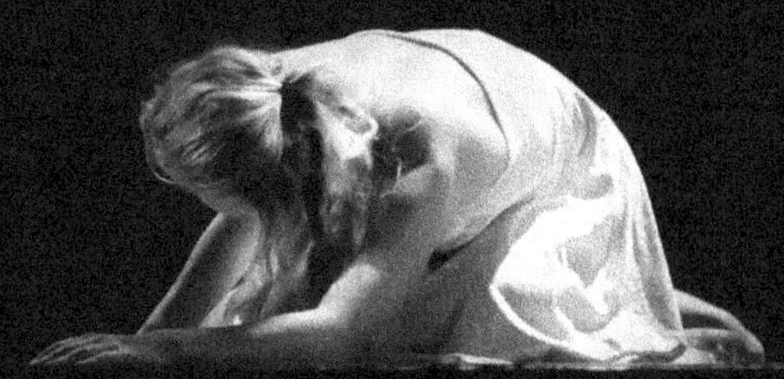

Chapter Thirty-Eight

NEVER THOUGHT I'D FIND MYSELF WONDERING AGAIN WHERE Dámiul disappeared to. But hours have passed since I spotted him leaving the hideout, and I haven't seen him since. I can't help wondering if he's avoiding me.

Maybe he senses there's something amiss with me. Maybe I misread all the signs, and he doesn't love me after all. Maybe he looked in my head and saw how I feel, and he doesn't know how to let me down. But he swore he wouldn't use his powers on me—he wouldn't break his promise, would he? Especially since Yandria told him not to use his telepathy.

Maybe! Maybe! Maybe! Now I know why so many love songs are terribly depressing. It's the worst feeling in the world, all this not knowing.

"Hey, are you okay?" Milo peers at me with concern—when did he get here?

I shrug. "Of course. Why?"

"You've been gone a long time for a language tablet."

I realize that I've spent the past several minutes staring

blankly at the hideout's door, wondering where Dámiul went. I turn my attention to Milo, annoyed at myself. He and Cara were talking about how they're going to change the world for the *Ka'risil* in their quarters, and here I am, pining over a boy.

"Sorry." I walk quickly back to the room, clutching the language tablet I'd left it for. "Just got lost in thought."

"Oh?" Milo gives me a questioning look.

I can't tell him where my mind was, but I don't want to lie to him either. So I keep my mouth shut and reenter the room, where Cara greets me with a cocked eyebrow.

"What happened to you?" she asks. "Did you have to dig that thing out of the ground or something?"

I hand her the tablet. "Just got distracted."

Milo's face still carries questions, but he doesn't ask them. His jaw tightens, and I can tell he's not happy with me. I wish I didn't have to keep things from him, but my love is one thing I can't talk to him about—not before I've told Dámiul.

Cara glances at him, then back at me. She makes a derisive noise. "While you were distracted, Ballerina Boy realized that the Papilian Spectacle is today."

Milo shoots her a cross look. "Don't call me that."

She twists her mouth into a disdainful smirk. "Can't take a joke?"

"Cara, please," I say, before Milo can unleash a rude retort and escalate this into the third shouting match tonight. I've become accustomed to Cara's attitude, but I swear, she's been worse tonight than she ever was previously. Something about Milo's presence seems to bother her to no end. "Do you have to snipe at him all the time?"

Cara narrows her eyes. "Well, we can't all be sweet little butterflies." She turns to the screen on the table and swipes something on it. "Anyway, as I was saying before Master Sensitive interrupted, the time difference between here and Papilio means the Spectacle's actually happening right now. Want to see what you look like to the Adryil?"

Intrigued, I nod. Cara presses something on the touchscreen. She doesn't seem to notice Milo staring daggers at her.

A holovid featuring a stage appears in the center of the round table. I regard it with fascination.

Cara gestures at it. "This is what your Spectacle looks like from here. Most people in Nathril won't watch it until tomorrow, when it's not the middle of the night, so you guys are getting an advance peek."

In the holovid, the stage's gold curtain goes up. Holographic trees and flowers decorate the stage in a forest scene. A lone ballerina in an elegant white costume stands in the center of the stage with her back to the audience and her arms posed gracefully above her golden head. Above the upper left corner of the stage, a portrait of Sabina appears. "Sabina Laclair, Ballet Dancer" is spelled out underneath in bright blue Adryil symbols, along with two numbers: her Linx ranking and her starting price. The sight makes me recoil.

The music starts, and I recognize the fervent violin solo as Brent's playing. There was always something about the way he lifts his notes that made him stand out from the others. I'd almost forgotten about him. And to think, I once swooned in his presence, like all the other girls in the Orchestra. My life then seems so far from the one I know now, it might have happened to someone else.

Brent's image appears beside Sabina's, along with his name, ranking, and price. In his picture, he poses with his instrument, and it occurs to me that it's the same one that will show up on the Wall when someone buys him. All those portraits I used to gaze at—they weren't to honor the alumni. They were to display a product for sale. The thought infuriates me. We're people, not items. I'll do whatever I must to make everyone see that.

Sabina glides across the stage, as graceful as ever. Brent's violin notes speed into broken chords, and she performs a set of spins, whipping one long, elegant leg out and drawing it back in perfect time with the music.

"Nice fouettés, Sabina." Milo sounds impressed.

Loud applause rises over the music. A movement above the stage catches my eye: Sabina's price turning green. It goes up by a hundred.

Milo furrows his brow. "What does that mean?"

"Someone bid on her." Cara tilts her head. "People usually don't live bid during a performance because it distracts from the show. I guess someone in the audience decided they must have her, like Mistress Ydaya did with Iris."

A line of ballerinas leaps onto the stage. Six portraits—one for each of them—appear. Their starting prices are each about one tenth of Sabina's, which goes up again as someone else bids.

"So… she's going to sign that contract?" Milo says. "They're going to make her forget everyone who matters to her?"

"Of course." Cara gives him a look that says he should have known better than to ask. "The auction will stay open for a few days in case anyone who didn't watch the Spectacle live wants to catch up on the bidding."

A distressed look descends on his face, and he covers his mouth with his fist.

"What's wrong?" I ask.

Milo lowers his hand. "It's just that… she was hoping to get married before she left. When I was with her, she gave us a real shot, but we just didn't work. She seemed pretty smitten by this one Troupe dancer—Aiden something-or-other. I guess if they ever meet again, they'll be strangers. I wish there were a way they could stay together."

Cara raises her eyebrow. "You're rooting for your ex and some other guy?"

"I care about her, okay?" Milo glares at Cara. "Do you have to be such a bitch?"

The harshness of his words startles me. Equally surprising is the hurt look that crosses Cara's face. But it vanishes as quickly as it appeared, and she scowls. "Do me a favor and keep your drama to yourself. I don't care about your or anyone else's past. It's the future that matters." She turns her gaze to the performance.

Milo's eyes take on an apologetic expression. "Hey, Cara, I didn't mean—"

"Save it." Her countenance remains frosty.

For a moment, he looks like he's about to say something more. But then he shakes his head and turns back to the holovid.

 352 

On the stage, Nikolai enters, accompanied by a soaring flute solo. Two portraits appear: his and Kiki's.

A hot fury rises from the pit of my stomach. These are my people being auctioned off. Maybe I didn't know them well enough to call them friends, but still, I understand their dreams. Those were once my dreams too. And it's all a lie, designed to wring the most out of us.

Cara glances at her watch and frowns. "Milo, we have to go. Sun'll be up soon, and if we don't get back before daybreak… things could get bad."

Milo continues staring at the scene on the holovid. "This is so wrong."

"I know." Cara's voice is unexpectedly gentle. "We'll stop it." She holds up the language tablet. "Starting with communication. One *Ka'risil* at a time."

Milo nods, then turns to me. "I'll see you soon, I hope."

I give him a smile. "I'll be here. Or who knows, maybe Atikéa's plan to get me back to the Ydayas will work."

He brightens. "I hope so."

Cara smacks his arm. "No time for gooey goodbyes. Let's *go!*"

Milo lets out an exasperated sigh and leaves the room with her. Even though I know it'll be a dangerous journey back to the Ydayas' building, I'm not worried about him. If anyone can look out for him, it's Cara. As long as they don't kill each other.

"Iris!" Atikéa calls me from the doorway.

"Yes?" I approach her.

She gives me an apologetic smile. "I'm sorry you've been stuck here for so long. But I might have found a way to transport you back to Earth. My original plan was, of course, to get you back to the Ydayas' as soon as I can. Not only because your life would be better there than down here, but also because I'm forming a new plan, and I need as many active *Ka'risil* as are willing. But if it's freedom you desire, I have a contact in the United States who can help you start a new life as an ordinary citizen. It will be a challenge, but if you want to go, I can figure something out."

"No, thank you." I don't even have to think about the answer.

"Everyone I care about is here. I'd rather live underground than among strangers."

Atikéa smiles. "I'm glad. We could use a brave one like you. And I know Dámiul will be happy you're staying."

"Atikéa!" Tadrien approaches from the hideout's door, and Atikéa turns her attention to him.

Turmoil churns through my head. What did Atikéa mean when she said Dámiul would be happy I'm staying? Did he say something about me?

A lush orchestral melody sweeps toward me, and I turn back to the still-playing holovid of the Spectacle. Despite my consternation at seeing the people I knew put up for auction, I soon find myself drawn into Sabina and Nikolai's performance. He stretches his arms toward her, and she spins into his embrace. The two lock gazes, then dance with their hands in each others'. I suddenly feel like I'm back at Papilio, watching them rehearse from the empty orchestra pit. My entire world has changed, but I'm still the same hopeless idiot, caught up in a beautiful fantasy. There's so much romance here, and I want nothing more than to be a part of something like the ideal portrayed on stage.

Dámiul, could that be us? So much longing fills my heart, I can't even watch the dancers anymore without feeling a sharp pang. I press the icon to shut down the holoprojector.

I need to find him. Even if he turns away from me, at least I'll know I gave us a chance. I won't sleep tonight anyway until I let my heart tell its truth, so I leave the room and walk toward the hideout's exit.

Chapter Thirty-Nine

"Dámiul?" I WALK DOWN THE UNDERGROUND passageway, hoping I don't get lost. This is the furthest I've ventured from the hideout. The corridor directly before me and the ones branching to the left are dark—he wouldn't have gone down one of those, would he? "Dámiul, are you there?"

"Iris?" Dámiul emerges from the blackness ahead, holding a small light before him. "What are you doing out here?"

"Looking for you." I approach him, and my heart speeds up.

"You have good timing." Dámiul approaches me with a smile. "I have something to show you. I was going to wait until tomorrow, but since you're here, why not now?" He takes my hand, and I hope he doesn't notice how slippery my palm has become.

I let him lead me down the corridor. Whatever troubled him before seems gone, and eagerness shines in his eyes.

"What were you doing out here?" I ask.

Dámiul's eyes glint teasingly. "Looking for something

You'll see it soon." He turns into a staircase and walks down. "Hold on to the railing. These steps are hundreds of years old, so they're a bit uneven."

Curiosity displaces my nervousness. I don't think I've ever seen him like this before, so bright and enthusiastic. The sight makes me smile. I don't want to say anything to ruin the moment, so I bite down the questions—and the confession I still plan to make.

"Where are we going?" I follow him around a bend in the staircase, my hand still in his.

"A place I discovered while exploring the underground as a child." Dámiul leads me into another corridor. "I wasn't sure if I'd be able to find it again."

I look around. "How do you know your way around? These corridors all look the same to me."

"I could ask you the same about Papilio." Dámiul sweeps his light, then turns into another staircase. "Those streets all looked the same to me. That's how I got lost the night I broke in, even though I made sure to memorize a map beforehand."

I see what he means. There wasn't much to distinguish one concrete-lined slab of pavement from another. "Papilio was my home. I knew every corner of it."

Dámiul looks back at me. His azure eyes are startling in the darkness. "Do you miss it?"

I take a moment to consider my answer. A wave of nostalgia washes over me. Despite everything, I still believe in what we, the Papilians, stood for. The Arts are older than TalentCorp's manipulations, and they'll remain long after we're gone. They're the masters and mistresses that would have enslaved me with or without Papilio, and I never want them to break their hold over me.

"I miss what I thought Papilio was, before I realized what lay beneath the Arts I love so much." I sigh. "I knew people were desperate for glory, but it wasn't until the last Spectacle that I realized how the pressure could break a person. If we weren't being tricked and sold, I think I would like living there still." I imagine what Papilio might look like if we succeed, and the thought of all those empty stages fills me with sorrow. "I want

the Abolition to win, but at the same time, it'll be a pity to see Papilio shut down."

"There must be some way we can abolish *Ka'risil* slavery without destroying the school." Dámiul sounds contemplative. "Perhaps if the mechanisms used to control the students were destroyed, it could become what it was meant to be before Katarin Kaminski changed everything."

I brighten at the thought. "Maybe."

"But before we can worry about things like that, we need others to see everything that's wrong with their system, even though they believe it's worked well for decades. I've tried for three years, but they won't listen."

"We'll make them hear us." I follow him through a doorway on the stairs' landing. "The spread of ideas can't be stopped, but you can't force them on people either. If there's anything the history of the Arts taught me, it's that change takes time."

"That's what Atikéa said, too. I think she worries that I'll do something violent." He lifts his mouth into a wry smile. "I promised her I wouldn't. Our battle can't be fought with weapons, or we'll only succeed in confirming the world's worst fears about us. I know what I have to do, though it won't be easy."

"I'll be with you every step of the way." I cross the corridor with him, biting my lip. *Was that too much?*

If Dámiul read anything in my tone, he doesn't acknowledge it. He stops before a pair of doors, releases my hand, and presses a button beside them. They slide open, revealing an elevator lit by a flickering sheet of yellowish light. "Trust me, it's safe."

Trying not to let my uneasiness show, I step in after him and bite down the urge to ask him again where we're going.

The elevator jolts, and I yelp in surprise.

Dámiul tilts his eyebrows in a sheepish expression. "Unfortunately, this is the only way to get to our destination."

I feel his hand on my back and realize I'm clinging to his arm. Embarrassed, I let go. "How old is this elevator?"

"Older than you'd care to know."

The elevator stops with a lurch, and I suppress another yelp. Dámiul takes my hand again and leads me out into another

corridor. It must be shorter than the rest, since I can see the end of it.

"We're almost there." He leads me up a staircase.

I've lost all sense of direction and can only guess that we're still somewhere underground. We reach the top of the steps, and I gasp. All of Nathril sparkles below, and the glittering night sky stretches above us.

Dámiul smiles. "You once took me to a roof to show me your home. Now, I'd like to return the favor." Still holding my hand, he leads me toward the metal railing at the edge.

I've never been so high above anything in my life. Colored lights shine through the nightscape, and Adrye's two moons adorn the sky. In the distance, the dark night fades to a pale shade of blue. The sun must be about to rise. "It's beautiful."

Dámiul points to a silver building, which I've only seen before in miniature holographic form. "That's where my parents and Jaerin live." He points at a tall black structure. "And that's where you lived when you were with the Ydayas."

I stare at the onyx tower. Except for a brief glance when I first arrived, I've never really had a chance to look at it from the outside. Each time I ventured out with Cara, I was too busy worrying about not getting caught to take in the sights around me. I walk along the railing, and I catch a glimpse of the *Ka'risil* quarters on the ground level. Milo and Cara might be returning there this very moment.

I feel Dámiul's hand on my shoulder and look up at him. "I hope Milo and Cara made it back all right."

"I'm sure they did." Dámiul takes his hand off my shoulder, and a look I can't interpret crosses his face. "If it weren't for me, you'd be with them right now, safe with your friends instead of stuck underground." His lips quirk into a half-smile. "And with only me for company, since Atikéa and the others come and go infrequently."

"That's not so bad." I smile back. "Dámiul, I chose to be here."

His eyes become distant. "You gave up everything."

"It's no less than you did when you were fighting for my kind. Some things are worth more than 'everything.' Like family

for Jaerin. Or the Abolition for Cara." I hesitate. "And for me…
It's you." I hesitate again, more afraid than I've ever been before
in my life. *Just say it.* "I love you, Dámiul."

The drumming of my racing heart and the hum of my
rushing blood fill me as I watch him, wondering how he'll react.

For a moment, Dámiul just stares back. Then, he reaches
toward me and puts his hand on my face. That breathtaking
intensity returns to his gaze, but there's none of the torment
I've seen in the past. Now, there's only light.

"I love you, too." So much truth clings to his words, spoken
in a voice that's soft, yet powerful.

An overwhelming feeling of joy and relief rushes through
me. I can scarcely breathe.

A smile brightens his face. I've seen him smile before, but a
hint of sorrow always clung to him. Not anymore. This is the
first time I've seen him truly happy, and the sight warms me to
the core.

My heartbeat quickens as he draws closer. I put my arm
around his neck, and my lips tingle with anticipation, longing
for his.

In the corner of my eye, I catch a glimpse of gold light.
Across the city, the sun breaks over the horizon, brightening the
night with its flames.

I feel Dámiul's breath on my face, and I lean in to meet his
lips. My eyelids fall shut as he kisses me. I melt into his presence,
and his heart beats against mine.

For so long, I've wondered what this moment would be
like. Now that it's here, I can say without hesitation: the Arts
were right. Every soaring viola melody, every brilliant operatic
aria, every intertwining dance. Imagine all the sweetness of a
rare fruit on one eager mouth, all the warmth and comfort of
sunlight in one strong body. This is my love.

I know it's madness. He's from another world, and there's
so much I still don't know about him. That's part of what
fascinates me: the mysteries waiting to be unveiled. At the same
time, I know who he is in the moment, no matter what his past.
I've seen his how great his mind is, how fierce his heart, how

pure his soul. Behind all the fight is someone willing to throw everything he worked for away to protect someone he loves.

Imagine all the stars in the galaxy in one pair of eyes, all the sureness of home in one pair of arms, all the heroics of a thousand epic tales in one noble heart.

This is my love.

Brief Glossary of Adryil Terms

Note: The Adryil language does not use plurals or conjugations

Adbis [ad-bis] to begin or engage

Adrye [*ah*-drahy] the homeworld of the Adryil people and the fourth planet in order from the star Irinn

Adryil [ah-*drahy*-il] of or from Adrye, also used to refer to the people of Adrye

Aest [eyst] to leave

At'strat [*aht*-straht] an abbreviation of *atka strat*, or "string instrument" (e.g. violins, violas, cellos, guitars, etc.). Violas are referred to as *at'strat illátet*, or "medium string instrument."

Ata [*ah*-tah] it

Ataroyil [ah-tah-*roh*-yil] them/belonging to them

Atayil [ah-*tah*-yil] its/belonging to it

Ati [*ah*-tee] she/her

Atiyil [ah-*tee*-yil] hers/belonging to her

Atka [*aht*-kah] string, rope, or cord

Ato [*ah*-toh] he/him

Atoyil [ah-*toh*-yil] his/belonging to him

Balnásin [bahl-*nah*-sin] information, facts, evidence

Bektát [bek-*taht*] must

Bor [bohr] on or in

Botsel [boht-sel] to forget

Cambr'endra Adryil [cahm-*bren*-drah ah-*drahy*-il] an abbreviation of *Cambraïn Endra Adryil*, or "Common Language of Adrye," used to refer to the universal language spoken by all Adryil

Cambraïn [cahm-brah-*een*] language

Clogamo [cloh-*gah*-moh] to help, assist, or aide, also used to call for assistance

Contuk [kon-took] to copulate with, used as a vulgar swear word

Da [dah] added after verbs to indicate the action occurred in the past (e.g. *ona larsal* means "I study" while *ona larsal da* means "I studied")

Dáven [*dah*-ven] brother

Deh [deyh] an interjection used as an exclamation of joy or satisfaction

Dira [*dee*-rah] to be and all its conjugations (am, are, etc.)

Dolare [doh-*lahr*-ey] mind, thoughts, brain

Dosketh [*doh*-sketh] to have, possess, or hold

Dratuttin [drah-*too*-tin] anything

Eládor [eh-*lah*-dohr] to love

En [en] you (singular)

Endra [en-drah] common

Enroyil [en-*roh*-yil] your (plural)/belonging to you (plural)

Enyil [*en*-yil] your (singular)/belonging to you (singular)

Esi [*eh*-see] here

Etrin [eh-*trin*] shelf, ledge, or mantle

Fac [fahk] to do or perform

Faro [*fah*-roh] to put or place

Fathrad [fahth-rahd] alarm, signal, or warning

Fenst [fenst] can, may, or has the ability to

Fith [fith] alongside, accompanying, with

Funihal [foo-*nee*-hal] to tamper, adjust, or change

Fuzettin [foo-*tseh*-tin] everything

Ganza [*gahn*-zah] in a high degree, very

Glan [glahn] why

Gorxit [*gohrk*-sit] worthless

Grámed [*grah*-med] to block, shield, or defend

Gren [gren] to remove, take out, or extract

Ibdis [ib-dis] to stop or cease

Idur [ih-*door*] to call, sound, or warn

-il [il] a suffix added to nouns to indicate belonging (usually meaning of, from, or belonging to the noun)

Illátet [ih-*lah*-tet] medium, midsized

Inyana [in-yah-nah] number or numeral

Irinn [ih-*rin*] the star around which Adrye orbits, a yellow dwarf similar to Earth's sun

Jánen [*jah*-nen] sister

Jatoi [jah-*toi*] to regret, repent, or apologize, also used to mean "sorry"

Jotha [*jawth*-uh] to curse or wish misfortune upon someone, commonly used as profanity

Ka'ris [kah-*rees*] an abbreviation of *Karovyil rees*, or "Earthling arts," used to refer to human music, dance, and other performing arts

Ka'risil [kahr-*rees*-il] an abbreviation of *Karovyil reesil*, or "of or from the Earthling arts," used to refer to human performing artists

Kaenjel [*keyn*-jel] older

Kal [kahl] man/male

Kal meda [kahl meh-dah] male child, boy, son

Karovye [*kahr*-oh-vahy] the Adryil name for the planet Earth

Karovyil [kahr-*oh*-vahy-il] of or from Earth, also used to refer to the people of Earth

Kel [kel] day

Kinas [*kee*-nahs] to complete or finish

Krináth [krih-*nahth*] to allow

Lan [lahn] woman/female

Lan meda [lahn meh-dah] female child, girl, daughter

Larsal [lahr-suhl] to study, learn, or review

Lidara [*lee*-dah-rah] to release, free, or liberate

Lorst [lohrst] to talk, say, or verbalize

Luwell [loo-well] to search, explore, or seek

Mand [mahnd] again, more, or repeat

Meda [meh-dah] child

Mut [moot] from

Nateth [*nah*-teth] mother

Nathril [nah-*thril*] capital, seat of government

Navar [nuh-*vahr*] to run, escape, or flee

Nur [noor] used after words to negate them (e.g. *navar nur*
    means "does not escape") or as a suffix to make a word its
    opposite (e.g. *krináthnur* means "will not allow" or "forbid"),
    also used to mean "do not"

Ona [oh-nah] I/me

Onaroyil [oh-nah-*roh*-yil] our/belonging to us

Onayil [oh-*nah*-yil] my/mine/belonging to me

Otás [oh-*tahs*] to wake, awaken, or rouse

Pari [pah-*ree*] how

Poate [poh-*aht*-ey] prison, detention center

Poatyil [poh-*aht*-yil] prisoner, detainee

Razan [*rah*-zahn] to walk, go, move, or come

Ris [rees] representations of objects or ideas, most often used
    to refer to art

Ro [roh] added to pronouns to make them plural (e.g. *ona ro*
    means "we/us")

Screna [skreh-nuh] to make physical contact with, to touch

Selár [sel-*ahr*] beautiful

Shraïn [shrah-*een*] to beg or plead, also used to mean "please"

Sthanga [*sthahn*-gah] aberrant, deviant, or abnormal, always
    used in a negative manner

Stranone [strah-*noh*-ney] worthwhile, valuable, or satisfying

Strat [straht] instrument, device, or machine

Sui [soo-ee] used before verbs indicate future action (e.g. *sui
    clogamo* means "will help")

Swar [swahr] what

Taen [teyn] correct, right, or appropriate

Talbat [tahl-baht] case, box, or container

Teris [*tair*-is] younger

Toká [toh-*kah*] an interjection used in praise, often meaning
    "well done"

Torna [tohr-nah] to need or require

Tortet [*tohr*-tet] to open, uncover, or expose

Tra'kel [trah-*kel*] an abbreviation of "traktan kel," or "good day,"
    used as an expression of greeting

Traktan [trahk-tahn] good

Tsot [tsoht] this

Tsuvot [*tsoo*-voht] still

Tunka [*toon*-kuh] to apprehend, capture, or trap

Ut [oot] and

Vabeth [*vah*-beth] father

Velslote [vel-*sloht*-ey] to amplify or increase

Yaerid [yey-*reed*] should, ought to

Yarrek [yah-*rek*] black

Zaro [*zah*-roh] new

Zeth [zeth] name/named

Zexa [*zehk*-suh] connection, link, or communication

Acknowledgements

Special thanks to Elizabeth Corrigan, Stephen Kozeniewski, and Nikki Thean for reading through early drafts of this book and helping me hammer it into shape. And an extra special thanks to Lana Popovic, whose insights sharpened the story and brought it all together. Thanks as well to Joanna Schnurman for letting me bounce ideas off her. And thanks to Lyssa Chiavari and Karissa Laurel for their encouragement, which really helped me cross the finish line.

Thanks to all the music teachers, directors, advisors, and conductors who've shown me the sublime—Dorothy Kitchen, Mia Wu, Robert Loughran, Fernando Raucci, Sarah Pelletier, Sarah Khatcherian, Martha Elliott, Penna Rose, Dan Trueman, Barbara White, and Susan Gaylord. For all you've taught me, I'm forever grateful.

Thanks to my sister, Angel Fan, for spending a whole day posing underwater in a ball gown to get that cover shot. And of course, thanks to my parents, Yonghua Wang and Jianqing Fan, for being my champions.

Other Books by Mary Fan

The Jane Colt Trilogy

  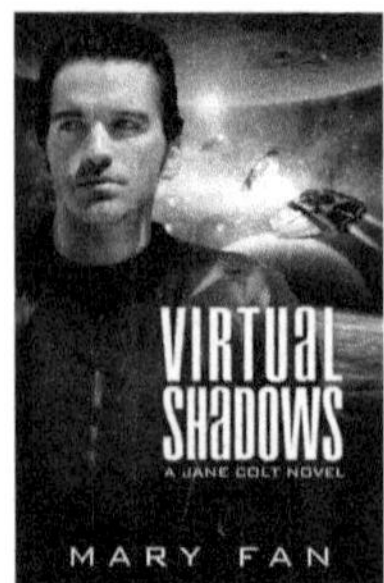

A friend's kidnapping and a plot to frame her brother for murder throw Jane Colt's world into a tailspin. Her quest for the truth takes her on galaxy-spanning adventures that unearth more than she bargained for… conspiracies surrounding artificial intelligence, secrets from the past, and dangers her once-ordinary life could never have prepared her for.

"The fast-paced action is balanced by thoughtful meditations on what it means to be human. Readers will zip through this exciting story."
—PUBLISHERS WEEKLY (starred review)

IN THE SERIES:
Artificial Absolutes (Red Adept Publishing, 2013)
Synthetic Illusions (Red Adept Publishing, 2014)
Virtual Shadows (2015)

The Firedragon Novellas

 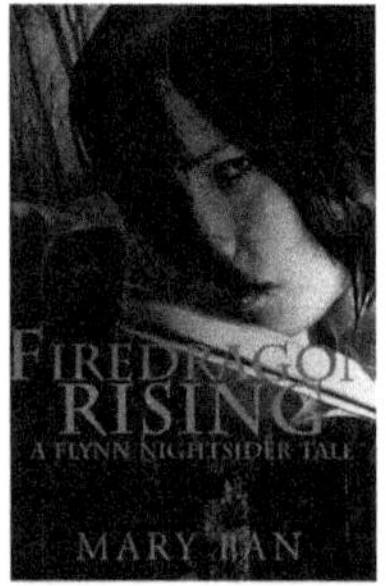

Teen monster fighter Aurelia "the Firedragon" Sun made a name for herself as one of the best combatants in the war against the supernatural. But she soon comes to realize that the powerful, Enchanter-run government is not what it seems…

IN THE SERIES:
The Firedragon (Glass House Press, 2014)
Firedragon Rising (Glass House Press, 2015)

The Brave New Girls Anthologies

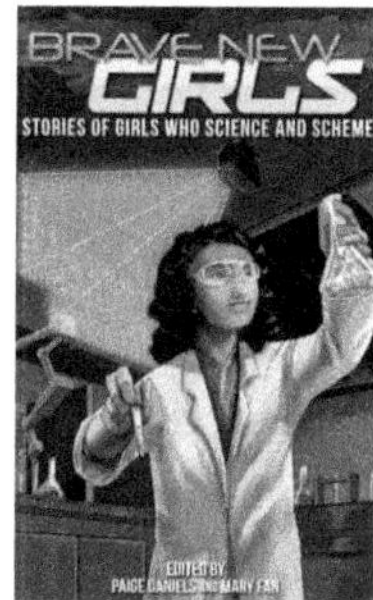

Edited by sci-fi authors Paige Daniels and Mary Fan, these collections of sci-fi stories feature brainy young heroines who use their smarts to save the day. Girls who defy expectations and tap into their know-how—in the depths of space, or the bounds of dystopia, or the steampunk past, or the not-to-distant future—to solve despicable crimes, engineer solutions, and take down powerful villains.

Proceeds from sales of the anthologies are donated to the Society of Women Engineers scholarship fund.

IN THE SERIES:
Brave New Girls: Tales of Girls and Gadgets (2015)
featuring "Takes a Hacker" by Mary Fan

Brave New Girls: Stories of Girls Who Science and Scheme (2017)
featuring "The Case of the Missing Sherlock" by Mary Fan

The Fated Stars Novellas

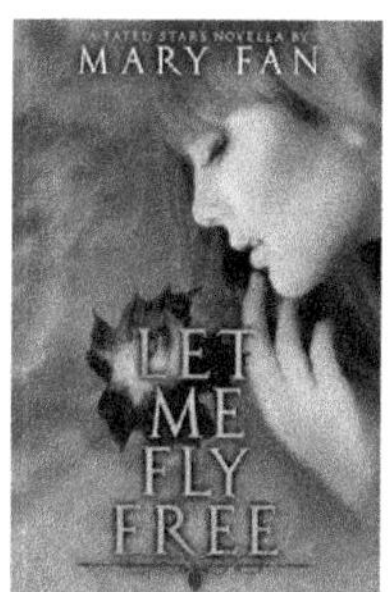

In a fanastical land of enchanted creatures and dark magic, two teen girls, each of whom is more than what she seems, face unthinkable dangers as an ancient evil emerges, threatening everything they've ever known.

IN THE SERIES:
Tell Me My Name (Glass House Press, 2014)
Let Me Fly Free (Glass House Press, 2016)

About the Author

Mary Fan is a sci-fi/fantasy writer hailing from New Jersey. Her books include the JANE COLT novels (space opera/cyberpunk), the FLYNN NIGHTSIDER series (young adult dystopia/fantasy), and the FATED STARS series (young adult high fantasy). She is also the co-editor of the BRAVE NEW GIRLS young adult sci-fi anthologies about tech-savvy girls, which aim to inspire more young women to enter science and technology careers and raise money for the Society of Women Engineers scholarship fund.

Mary has a B.A. in Music (specializing in composition) from Princeton University. When she doesn't have her nose buried in either a book or a laptop, she can usually be found at the opera house, the beer garden, or on an airplane heading anywhere.

Find her online at www.MaryFan.com.